PRAISE FOR THE *PANTHEON* SERIES

"A love poem to both comic books and the Hindu faith.
As always, Lovegrove's style is easy going and draws
you in quickly... One of the best series in
urban fantasy available today."
– *Starburst Magazine* on *Age of Shiva*

"Lovegrove is the as-yet-undisputed King of the Godpunk
Throne... Action-packed, engaging, well-paced and with
a great concept, it's probably the best introduction to
Lovegrove's works to date."
– *Strange Currencies* on *Age of Shiva*

"Lovegrove has very much made 'godpunk' his own thing...
Another great example of Lovegrove's skills as a writer of
intelligent, fast-paced action adventure stories. The fact that
he is equally adept at writing novellas as full-length novels is a
very pleasant surprise; I hope he returns to the form soon."
– *SF Crow's Nest* on *Age of Godpunk*

"This is smooth, addictive and an amazing ride.
If you scratch the surface of the writing, there is plenty of
depth and subtext, but it's the fun of having spies fighting
monsters that will keep you enthralled throughout."
– *Starburst Magazine* on *Age of Voodoo*

"A fast-paced, thrill-filled ride... There's dry humour,
extreme gore, tension and large amounts of testosterone
flooding off the page – and a final confrontation
that leaves you with a wry smile."
– *Sci-Fi Bulletin* on *Age of Voodoo*

"5 out of 5. I finished it in less than three hours,
yet have pondered the revelations found within for days
afterwards and plan to reread it soon."
– *Geek Syndicate* on *Age of Aztec*

AGE OF LEGENDS

ALSO BY JAMES LOVEGROVE

Novels
The Hope
Days
The Foreigners
Untied Kingdom
Worldstorm
Provender Gleed

Co-writing with Peter Crowther
Escardy Gap

The Pantheon series
The Age of Ra
The Age of Zeus
The Age of Odin
Age of Aztec
Age of Voodoo
Age of Godpunk
Age of Shiva
Age of Heroes

The Redlaw series
Redlaw
Redlaw: Red Eye

The Dev Harmer Missions
World of Fire
World of Water

Novellas
How the Other Half Lives
Gig
Age of Anansi
Age of Satan
Age of Gaia

Sherlock Holmes
The Stuff of Nightmares
Gods of War
The Thinking Engine

Collections of Short Fiction
Imagined Slights
Diversifications

For Younger Readers
The Web: Computopia
Warsuit 1.0
The Black Phone

For Reluctant Readers
Wings
The House of Lazarus
Ant God
Cold Keep
Dead Brigade
Kill Swap
Free Runner

The 5 Lords of Pain series
The Lord of the Mountain
The Lord of the Void
The Lord of Tears
The Lord of the Typhoon
The Lord of Fire

Writing as Jay Amory
The Clouded World series
The Fledging of Az Gabrielson
Pirates of the Relentless Desert
Darkening For a Fall
Empire of Chaos

AGE OF LEGENDS

JAMES LOVEGROVE

SOLARIS

Huge thanks to Eric Brown, without whose assistance and expertise this novel would not have been possible.

First published 2019 by Solaris
an imprint of Rebellion Publishing Ltd,
Riverside House, Osney Mead,
Oxford, OX2 0ES, UK

www.solarisbooks.com

ISBN: 978 1 78108 577 6

10 9 8 7 6 5 4 3 2 1

A CIP catalogue record for this book is available from the
British Library.

Designed & typeset by Rebellion Publishing.

Printed in Denmark

ONE

THE SOLDIERS MOVED in a line through Hyde Park, sweeping east to west. Each was separated from the next by a gap of five yards, strictly maintained. When one of them spied a target, the soldier shot without hesitating. The sound of rifle discharges rippled across the park, sometimes single reports, sometimes clusters, like a mad drummer struggling to keep the beat.

Every time a 5.56mm round found its mark, a parakeet toppled out of a tree or plummeted from the sky in an explosion of feathers. The lawns were soon littered with mangled bird bodies and drifts of jade green plumage.

A few of the parakeets had fled at the first sign of gunfire, seeking sanctuary in roosts at the top of neighbouring buildings. The majority, however, stayed put, frightened by the noise but failing to recognise what it signified. For several generations the flocks of parakeets had lived in the park unmolested, their only enemy the occasional peregrine falcon. They were tame by the standards of wild birds. Their forebears had all been caged creatures which had either escaped from captivity or been released by their owners when the cost of upkeep became too high, and this domestication remained somehow inbred, a hereditary conditioning. The parakeets simply weren't prepared for a slaughter.

The media outlets were not calling it a slaughter, of course. The preferred word was "cull", usually prefaced by "necessary". The government's own press statement referred to it as that, and lauded the exercise as "a robust disposal of interlopers from overseas who have no place on British soil". None other than the prime minister himself had sanctioned the action. Interviewed on a breakfast radio show that morning, Derek Drake had cheerily opined that the elimination of the parakeets would pave the way for "our own proper pigeons" to return to their rightful homes in Hyde Park's trees.

In all, the killing lasted three hours. By the end, over a thousand parakeets lay dead. The cordon that had been set up around the park was lifted, and pest control vans filed in along West Carriage Drive. A small army of men and women in head-to-toe coveralls disembarked to collect up the corpses in thick polythene bags.

Major Dominic Wynne, who had overseen the operation, took questions from a pack of TV reporters assembled at the Albert Memorial. Since he was head of the Paladins, the prime minister's personal protection squad, Wynne's presence carried weight. It didn't hurt that, with his forthright nose, piercing blue eyes and shovel-sharp jaw, he was marvellously telegenic.

"We came, we saw, we culled," he said, flashing the grin that had earned him an army of devoted admirers on social media. It wasn't a pleasant grin but it was perfectly rectangular and revealed white, even teeth, so it was admired for its geometrical regularity as much as anything. Some said it made him look dumb. Others swooned.

"And let what we have done today stand as a warning to all immigrants," Wynne added, his brow furrowing sternly. "Avian, Asian, whatever. You will not be tolerated here. This is not the place for you. Thanks to Prime Minister Drake, our nation has been brought back to its senses. Mr Drake has truly made Great Britain again."

AJIA SNELL, WATCHING a live feed of the broadcast on her phone, grimaced.

"Made Britain grate again, more like," she muttered. "Tosser."

She swiped the image of Major Wynne's face off the screen, wishing every annoyance could be erased at the touch of a finger. How could a man so handsome spout such bullshit? It was almost as though some law of nature was being defiled. The same genes which gave Wynne his movie-star good looks also gave him the IQ of a drooling moron, and that just should not be.

Ajia slowly finished the cup of tea in front of her. Across the road from the café where she sat was the site of a former Starbucks. She would much rather have been over there enjoying a vente skinny latte than here at a formica-topped table, sipping weak milky tea from chipped chinaware, surrounded by the smell of frying bacon. But there wasn't a Starbucks left in London, let alone the entire UK, not since the election. The company had upped stakes and abandoned the country, citing "an atmosphere uncongenial to business" as the reason. All that remained were hundreds of empty premises with adhesive mermaid logos peeling away from the windows.

She missed Starbucks. She missed a lot of things. At the age of eighteen, Ajia pined for a lost past as keenly as an eighty-year-old might pine for the simplicities of a long-gone youth. It had been scarcely half a decade since Derek Drake came to power, and in that time the country she had grown up in had changed beyond all recognition. And not for the better.

Stoically she stood, paid, and went outside to unlock her road bike. Within moments she was veering through the midday Shoreditch traffic, her legs pumping, her head low. Astride the saddle, in her skintight compression wear and streamlined helmet, her courier pouch slung over her back, Ajia was a demon, a thing of pure velocity and trajectory. Her world became narrowed down to the essentials: the spin of the pedals, the click of the gear shifters, the thrum of tubeless tyres on tarmac. Everything around her was either a conduit or an obstacle. Her brain was performing calculations at lightning speed, on the alert for every variable, every potential hazard. Was that pedestrian with the pram about to step off the kerb without looking? Was that number 26 bus going to pull out in front of her? Was the boy racer in the twin-exhaust hatchback really going to change lanes without indicating, like a complete dickhead?

Could she avoid the drain grating sunk into the roadway ahead of her or would she just have to steer straight over it and ride out the disruption with her knees bent like shock absorbers?

When she pulled up in front of Benny-Boy's Independent Couriers, off Bethnal Green Road, she was barely out of breath, in spite of having covered a mile and a quarter in under four minutes. She padlocked the bike to the rack outside and went in. Behind the counter, Benny-Boy glanced round at her and one look at his face told her she'd had a wasted journey.

"How was your lunch break?" he asked. His fingers were greasy from the sausage roll he was eating, bought from the bakery on the corner—previously a Chinese takeaway.

"Fine. Nothing for me, then?"

"Nothing for anyone," said Benny-Boy with a half-apologetic shrug. "Not a single booking."

"Shit. And only one run this morning. What the hell's going on?"

"Nobody seems to want biking stuff today. Must be the parrot killing or something."

"Parakeet."

"Whatever. It's got people keeping their heads down. Soldiers firing rifles in a public place will do that."

"It's a ridiculous PR stunt," Ajia said. "That's all it is. Derek Draconian making a big song and dance about some bloody birds nobody even cares about, all so he can show us what a tough guy he is."

Benny-Boy chuckled. "Derek Draconian. That's never not funny. Did you come up with it?"

"No. *Private Eye*. They called him it back when the Resurrection Party were first starting up and Drake was a political joke, and they kept calling him it all through the election and beyond, right up until he shut them down and put the editor in jail. Because, hey, taking the piss out of the rich and powerful, that's just not on."

"You know, Ajia, you need to be a bit careful with this sort of talk." Benny-Boy's expression turned serious. It looked incongruous on him. He had babyish features—round head, pudgy cheeks, button eyes—which was why his school nickname had stuck well into middle age. His face didn't naturally lend itself to solemnity. "I mean, when it's just you and me, no one else around, fine. Mock our beloved leader as much as you like. I don't mind. But say the wrong thing when the wrong ears are listening…"

"I know."

"We live in dodgy times. People disappear, you know that. Poof! Gone in the night. Especially people with a touch of the tar brush, like you."

She didn't kill him for using that expression, although she ought to have. Benny-Boy wasn't a racist. At least, not by current standards.

"All right, you old fart," she said. "I appreciate the lecture."

"Hey. Less of the 'old'," said Benny-Boy. "I'm just looking out for you, that's all, girl. Got your best interests at heart. And mine, 'cause you're the fastest fucking thing on a bike I've ever seen."

Ajia nodded noncommittally. "Not much use when I'm not being paid to ride it."

"Want to hang around, in case any work comes in? I've sent the other guys home, so if maybe a job comes up, it's yours."

A couple of hard plastic chairs. Some ancient newspapers. A coffee-pod machine producing beverages that tasted like burnt cork. Daytime television wittering away on a wall-mounted set. The office was not exactly paradise.

"Nah," she said. "Tempted, but I'm going to cut my losses and call it a day. See you in the morning."

"Mmmph," said Benny-Boy agreeably through a mouthful of sausage roll.

Ajia rode back to her bedsit, collected her stencils and spray cans, and headed off on an art spree.

Biking was her hobby, one which brought in a trickle of income. Street art was her passion.

She rode to one of her favourite spots, the back of a row of garages just west of Brick Lane. A dozen street artists shared it, using the brick walls as their canvas. The styles ranged from glorified graffiti tagging to sticker art to fully-rendered murals that had all the sophistication of an Old Master.

There was perpetual competition for space at this outdoor gallery, and no image survived longer than a month. An artwork was allowed a reasonable amount of time to be seen and appreciated, before someone would ruthlessly paint over it.

Her own most recent contribution was already gone, subsumed beneath a large composition consisting of crude, multi-coloured figures dancing. She recognised this as the work of someone who went by the pseudonym Blue Cat. She quite liked Blue Cat's stuff, even if it was derivative of Keith Haring. He or she had a striking primitivist aesthetic. There was something compelling about those cavorting figures. There was glee on their crude faces, but also pain, as though to be this ecstatic was an effort. You could almost hear the music they were moving to, some piece of pounding, rhythmic plainchant underscored by thunderous percussion, *Carmina Burana* to a taiko beat.

Ajia found a patch of wall adorned with a shoal of tissue-paper fish. The delicate little cut-outs had been battered by rain and were barely clinging on. She removed them with a scraper, showing what she hoped was due reverence even as she destroyed them. Then she took out a set of A3-sized stencils and got busy.

She sprayed six shades of paint through six separate stencils, pausing for a couple of minutes to let each layer dry before applying the next. During these intervals she checked to see if anyone was watching. The site was overlooked by several houses and a tower block, but it wasn't civilians she was worried about so much as the authorities. Police routinely patrolled here, hoping to catch people like Ajia in the act. Any kind of street art, for all that it brought brightness and vivacity to a drab environment, was considered vandalism. Especially the kind of street art she did.

The picture, when complete, portrayed Derek Drake. The image was derived from one of his publicity headshots, which she had altered and stylised, creating a cartoonish version of the prime minister. Drake had froglike features to start with, but she had made him look downright batrachian—eyes protruding, cheeks bulging, double chin a great fleshy hammock like a membranous vocal sac—

while still being recognisably him. He had his mouth open as though to speak, and Ajia had added a long, projecting tongue. The tongue was lashing out greedily towards a passing insect, a butterfly with patterning on its wings that spelled out the word OTHER.

She took a step back to admire her handiwork. It was always a thrill to see a fresh piece in position. "AmphiBias", as she titled it, wasn't the most scathing image she had ever created. That honour went to "True Love Never Dies", which depicted Drake French-kissing the mummified corpse of Adolf Hitler. It was, though, up there with her more savage commentaries, and was by far the most overtly political artwork out of all those present. The other artists either avoided anti-establishment messages altogether or disguised them well. Blue Cat's dancers, for instance, seemed uncontroversial enough. There was a subtext about liberty and self-expression if you looked for it, but to most they would be just a bunch of blobby, brightly-hued figures throwing shapes.

Ajia didn't go in for subtlety. If you had something to say, why not just come out and say it? The clearer the message, the greater the impact. If just one person came across a picture of hers and laughed, or smiled sardonically, or was moved to think, then she had done a good thing. If it increased someone's dislike of Drake, or sowed doubt in the mind of one the prime minister's fans, so much the better. Perhaps there would be some passer-by who truly felt the depth of her loathing for the man, etched into every jagged line of the image. In that case, it would all be worthwhile.

Ajia proceeded to another three sites, reproducing "AmphiBias" at each. The afternoon light was starting to wane as she commenced on a fifth piece. This time she was in an alley behind a row of shops, among overstuffed wheelie bins. She was beginning to apply the third layer of spray paint when movement at the mouth of the alley caught her eye. She looked round.

Her stomach knotted. Her mouth went bone dry.

A three-strong police patrol.

Armed.

Oh shit, oh shit, oh shit...

Hurriedly Ajia began stashing her art materials into her rucksack.

None of the police officers was looking her way. They were sauntering along the street, semiautomatic carbines held loosely at waist level. But all it would take was for one of them to turn, glance in her direction...

"Hey!"

Ajia slung her rucksack onto her back and lunged for her bike.

"Hey! What the hell do you think you're doing?"

She jumped onto the saddle.

"Yeah, you, young lady. I'm talking to you. Off that bike. Now."

She didn't even look over her shoulder. She slotted the recessed cleats on her shoes onto the pedals and pushed down with her right foot while pulling up with her left. The bike sprang to life under her like a spurred horse.

Go go go go go go go!

She poured on speed, using all the strength in her legs. The bike hit a pothole and slewed, but she maintained control. The other end of the alley was a hundred yards away. She arrowed towards it, shifting frantically up through the gears.

The police officers gave chase. Ajia could hear their feet pounding behind her. One of them was still shouting, but she was no longer listening to what he said. She was concentrating on getting to the end of the alley and turning the corner. Once she was on the main road and zooming along at top speed, they would never be able to catch up. She'd be away and free.

As she reached the exit, a man stepped out in front of her. He was just some guy ambling along, eyes on his phone, earbuds stuffed in his ears. Ajia swerved to avoid a collision. The bike seemed to buckle under her. Next thing she knew, she was on the ground, rolling into the road. A taxi screeched to a halt, stopping just inches away. The cabbie laid on the horn and swore at her out of his window.

Ajia scrambled to her feet. The bike lay on its side a few yards away, front wheel spinning. She limped over and picked it up by the handlebars. Nothing seemed bent or broken, thank fuck. She jumped on and got going again. This time the process was laborious, because she had left the bike in high gear. She bore down hard on the pedals, but it was as though the wheels were rolling through hot tar.

The three police officers were almost on her. She glimpsed "gotcha!" looks on their faces. The frontmost of them had his phone out and appeared to be taking a picture of her. Another of them said, "Last warning, missy. Stop where you are."

Stop, be arrested, get carted off to some shithole police-station cell, face charges of vandalism, subversion and who knows what else?

Yeah, right.

Ajia dropped several cogs in one go. The pedals clunked loosely, but suddenly she was in low gear, the bike more responsive to her efforts.

She flipped the cops the finger and scooted away.

She didn't hear the gunshot. She saw the wing mirror of a car parked just in front of her shatter. She felt the bike shimmy, as though she had tapped the brakes, which she hadn't. She kept pedalling.

Shooting at me. The fuckers are shooting at me!

She nipped round the front of a slow-moving van, putting the vehicle between her and the police officers. On she went, zigzagging through the rush-hour traffic, sometimes pulling out into the opposite lane if there was a gap, then tucking back in.

She rode like this for half a mile, heading through Whitechapel down to Aldgate. Her heart was pounding, her whole system electrified by adrenalin. She had left the police officers far behind her but she wasn't going to stop. The one with the phone hadn't simply been getting a snapshot. There was every chance he had tagged her. An image of her—clothing, helmet, bike and all—was now in the Met central computer. So were the GPS coordinates where the picture was taken. Algorithms were processing the data for network-wide distribution, ready to parcel it out to every security camera in the immediate area. She had to go far. She had to get lost. Otherwise...

She arrived at the junction of Fenchurch Street and Leadenhall Street, just inside the western perimeter of the City of London. A twice-lifesize bronze statue of Drake had been erected here, in recognition of the fact that before taking up politics he had been a hedge fund manager. The effigy had one arm raised as though in welcome, and its eyes and mouth gaped with manic delight.

Just above the statue's head, a drone hovered. Ostensibly it was there just to monitor traffic flow, but if you believed that, you weren't paying attention. Ajia hunched low, praying its electronic gaze was elsewhere. She veered south onto Lloyd's Avenue, a narrow thoroughfare with five-storey buildings looming on both sides like canyon walls. The drone had not spotted her. Surely the drone had not spotted her.

She heard a wasp-like buzzing. She darted a glance back.

The drone was following her.

Fuck!

All she could do was pedal faster. But her breathing was becoming laboured, and she was developing a stitch in her side. This was odd, because she didn't normally get stitches. In fact, she couldn't remember the last time she'd had one, and she had ridden harder than this in the past. Nor did she get out of breath easily. Her aerobic fitness had never been subjected to formal testing but she was pretty sure it was professional-athlete league.

A second drone swooped into sight ahead. It and its companion kept pace with Ajia as she wove her way past Fenchurch Street Station down onto Lower Thames Street, where she took the westbound route. This stretch of road was dual carriageway and dangerous for cyclists because drivers thought they were on a motorway and ignored the speed limit. But there was method in her madness. Lower Thames Street became Upper Thames Street, and Upper Thames Street had tunnels. The drones would not follow her into a tunnel because they would lose signal, and that meant there was a chance she could outwit their pilots.

She raced into the last and longest of the tunnels, which passed beneath a set of office buildings and terminated just before Blackfriars Bridge. She had to assume that the drone pilots would guide their craft overground to the other end and wait for her to come out. They would be waiting a while.

Vehicles rumbled alongside her along both lanes. In the confined space, the roar of motors was deafening, and the stench of exhaust fumes burned Ajia's nostrils.

There were in fact two tunnels here, one for traffic travelling in either direction, a solid concrete wall dividing them. Doubling back would therefore involve going against the flow of two solid lanes of traffic. It was pretty much suicide, but Ajia had little choice.

She hit the rear brake and skidded round through 180°. The manoeuvre was greeted with a barrage of protest—flashing headlights, honking horns. She sped along the dotted white line between the two lanes, cars, buses, vans and lorries hurtling by on either side of her, mere inches away. She emerged from the tunnel the way she'd come in, and veered off immediately onto the pavement. She drew up beside a bollard and leant against it. Her lungs were heaving now. Her stitch was worse than ever. Her Lycra shorts were soaked with sweat. There was even sweat dribbling down her right knee onto her shin.

Except, it wasn't sweat.

It was blood.

Ajia looked down at the blood with a strange, detached dismay. It occurred to her that she must have cut herself. She had grazed her leg when she'd fallen off the bike.

But there was too much blood for a graze. Far too much. The whole of her shin was coated in it, glossy with it.

That was when she noticed the hole in her side, just above the hip. It was about the thickness of her forefinger. She felt gingerly at her back. Her fingers found a matching hole. She could just make it out, by twisting her head round to look. It was slightly larger than the hole at the front.

The bullet which had struck the parked car's wing mirror hadn't missed her. It had gone through her.

She was overcome by a sudden nausea. The world seemed to be trembling. Her head swam. She stumbled off the bike.

Shot. Shot. Fuck me, I've been fucking shot.

Her legs felt as weak as a newborn foal's. She sagged to her knees. Then she slumped onto her side.

All at once the bullet wound was sheer agony. She could scarcely catch her breath.

There were people gathering around her. Peering down.

Concerned citizens. One of them was making a call. She heard the words "emergency services".

She wanted to tell these people to help her up, get her indoors, take her somewhere safe.

Distantly above her, black asterisks in the blue sky, the two drones hovered. They had found her again. They circled around each other like vultures, their beady gaze fixed on her.

The drones blurred.

So did the faces of the people.

Ajia said something, but she had no idea what it was.

Then she passed out.

TWO

"AJIA SNELL?"

Groggily Ajia looked up. She had awoken moments earlier to find the policewoman sitting beside her. The policewoman had a tablet in her hand. Ajia glimpsed a photo of herself on the screen, along with information—date of birth, education history, home address, and so on. Her file from the national ID database. The policewoman was consulting this, her expression distinctly unimpressed.

Ajia was lying on a bed of some sort, but it was not a hospital bed. More like a bunk. Nor was the room she was in a hospital room. It smelled of disinfectant and urine, as a hospital room might, but it was too bare, too functional. Single neon striplight embedded in the ceiling. Brickwork painted pale ochre, the colour of lost hope. No windows.

"That is your name, isn't it?" the policewoman said. She had the kind of face that you could not imagine ever having known a smile.

Ajia nodded. Her head ached. Her throat was parched. Her midriff felt on fire.

"And did I get the pronunciation right? Ah-jee-yah?"

Ajia nodded again.

The policewoman sniffed. "Foreign names, you know. Never easy."

"Water," she croaked.

"Yes," the policewoman said, but she said it in a way that sounded very much like no.

"Please."

"We'll see. Just need to get a few facts straight first. Your name is Ajia Miranda Snell. You're eighteen. Father: Tony Snell, deceased. Mother: Padma Snell, maiden name Bakshi, repatriated. Employment: bike courier. No priors. You were, however, observed by three officers of the law at five thirty-five PM on the afternoon of April the ninth engaged in an act of sedition."

"Art."

"Sorry?" The policewoman cupped a hand behind her ear. "Didn't catch that."

"Art. I was doing art."

"Oh yes. Art. Of course. Art which just so happened to make fun of our prime minister. Art, as well, in an unsanctioned location. All of which makes it not so much art as an offence against public order."

"Still art," Ajia said. "Satire."

"Nice. Satire. Yes. Well, your satire, young lady, has landed you in a ruddy great heap of trouble, I hope you realise that. Not so funny now, is it? You're looking at a hefty prison sentence, and that's no laughing matter."

Ajia tried another tack. "Where's my phone?"

"We've got it."

"I want it."

"You can't have it. You don't get a call, you know. That's not how this works. You're here for as long as we say you're here, and nothing's going to change that. What happens from now on is out of your hands."

Ajia asked for water again, but the policewoman just stood and walked to the door, a bolt-studded slab of steel.

"We've patched up your wound," she said. "Not perfect but it'll do. That's a concession. Maybe you could think about cooperating in return. I'll leave you a while to think about it."

The door creaked open. The door slammed.

* * *

THEY CAME FOR her an hour later.

Two of them, both male, both large.

They plucked her from the bed. They bellowed at her, threw her around, slapped her a few times.

They left her shrieking at them on the floor, calling them every foul name she knew.

THEY CAME FOR her again, this time after a shorter interval.

She fought back, but it was futile. She bit, punched, kicked, scratched, but the policemen only laughed. Together they overpowered her, then one held her down while the other pounded her ribcage with a baton.

She crawled onto the bed, broken, bleeding. She felt like a bag of loose, ragged flesh held together by pain.

A prison sentence. That was what the policewoman had said. *You're looking at a hefty prison sentence.* Ajia clung to the thought like a lifejacket. She would be going to jail but they weren't going to kill her. She wasn't going to die here. She was going to survive this.

It didn't feel like it, though. It felt very much like the cell, liberally spattered with her blood, was the last place she was ever going to see. It was where she was going to take her final breath. It was her tomb.

THE POLICEWOMAN RETURNED, took a look at Ajia, and was not an ounce more sympathetic than before.

"Right, so you know what to expect now," she said. She brandished the tablet. "I have here a written statement, prepared for you. All you have to do is sign it. It'll make things easier. Smooth the judicial process. You won't have to bother with a trial and all that nuisance. You'll get processed through the system and whisked off to a young offender institution. Do not pass Go, do not collect two hundred pounds. I can read it out to you if you like, but you can pretty much guess what it says. Here's the dotted line. Let's wipe your finger first, get all that blood off. Otherwise the touchscreen won't work. No?"

The policewoman was offering her a sheet of paper towel, but

Ajia would not hold up her finger.

"Be like that. I'll give you some time to rethink. Constables Yelland and Yates might come back in the interim, to offer you a bit more encouragement."

Her face softened just a fraction.

"You seem like a nice girl, Ajia," she said. "Can't be easy for you. Mixed-race, in today's Britain. Nobody's exactly championing your sort. Deportation orders left, right and centre. Pray to the wrong god, have the wrong complexion, fall in love with the wrong person— bang, that's it, you're out. But you, your skin's so pale brown, you could almost pass for white. If you'd kept your head down, kept your nose clean, you could've been okay. Instead you had to be stupid and cause trouble. And this is how people who cause trouble end up."

"Doctor," Ajia mumbled.

"You'll get seen by a doctor, to get that bullet wound properly attended to and also all the other injuries you incurred while resisting arrest. But only if you sign the statement. Are you going to sign the statement?"

Ajia's silence was her answer.

"Stubborn little shit, aren't you?" The policewoman glanced at her wristwatch. "I'll give it another three hours. I reckon you'll have changed your tune by then."

THE THIRD BEATING was almost apologetic. Constables Yates and Yelland seemed to be going through the motions, their hearts not really in it. They just wanted her to give in. They wanted her crawling and abject and defeated. Was that too much to ask?

Ajia refused to give them the satisfaction. She held out, even though she knew that all she had to do was tell them she would sign their bullshit document and the suffering would end. And as the blows rained down, withstanding the punishment seemed to become easier. She found herself retreating inward, moving further and further away from the pain. She was losing touch with her physical self. Somebody else was taking all those punches, not her. She experienced a weird pang of sympathy for that person, that other Ajia Snell. So small and scrawny compared to the two hulking great brutes who were battering her. So helpless.

She told the other Ajia just to close her eyes and go to sleep. Then it would all be over.

The other Ajia listened and complied. Sleep brought peace. There was nothing any more, no knowledge, no sensation. Just pure, sweet oblivion.

CONSTABLE YATES LOOKED at Constable Yelland. Something was wrong. They both sensed it. The girl had gone limp, but there was limp and there was limp. The body of an unconscious person was floppy but still had muscular tension, a kind of cohesion. The level of floppiness shown by Ajia Snell, the absolute absence of rigidity, meant something else.

"You don't think…?" Constable Yates began.

Constable Yelland squatted beside Ajia. He tapped her cheek a few times, put his ear to her mouth, then felt her wrist.

He fixed his accomplice with a solemn gaze. "Bugger," he said.

"She's…?"

Constable Yelland nodded.

"Shitting hell," said Constable Yates. "It was an accident, right? I mean, we didn't mean to. How were we supposed to know?"

"Don't panic." Yelland was the senior of the pair. He'd been on the force six years longer. This wasn't his first death in custody. He knew the drill. "It's going to be fine. You lose one every so often. It happens. The suspect isn't strong enough. Maybe there's some underlying medical condition we weren't informed about. Not our fault. No one's going to have our head for this. There are protocols. We just have to get rid of the body."

"We can do that?"

"We're the London Metropolitan Police," said Yelland, straightening up. "We have the special powers vested in us by the Extraordinary Regulations Act. We can do as we bloody well please."

THREE

THE TENDRIL COULD not be seen. It could not be heard. It could not be touched, tasted or smelled.

The tendril could still be sensed, but only subconsciously, instinctively, and only by some, not all.

As it snaked across the night-time rooftops of London, the tendril's proximity caused a sleeper in a house below to stir uneasily, plagued by dreams of a missed doctor's appointment which would have dire health ramifications. In a back garden a prowling cat raised its head and hissed, hackles rising. Dogs barked at the intangible, pseudopod-like presence passing sinuously overhead, without knowing quite why they were so agitated by it. A baby awoke in her crib, wailing for no good reason.

The tendril was seeking a suitable home, but with no more sentience than a column of ants marching out from the nest, seeking food. It quested this way and that, attuned to certain emanations, currents it alone could detect. It was designed to register the complex ebb and flow of life and death in this city of millions. Invariably it was drawn to sickbeds, hospital wards, care homes, hospices, anywhere where mortality loomed large. Drunk drivers and would-be suicides were attractive to it. And if it detected someone carrying a grudge and a lethal weapon—a loaded gun, say, or a knife, or a bottle of acid—the tendril hovered over that person speculatively, gauging the likelihood of them acting on their murderous impulse and, more importantly, the fittingness of the victim.

For there were criteria the tendril had to follow, conditions it had to meet, in order to be successful. It could not recruit simply anyone. Everything had to be just right, otherwise the tendril's purpose was forfeit and within a few hours it would shrivel and dissipate like fruit withering on the vine, its potential squandered.

A sudden flurry below, a particular disturbance which caught the tendril's attention. A recent death. It snagged the tendril like a spike catching a breeze-blown ribbon.

The tendril circled. In as much as it could feel anything, it felt excitement. As though running through a mental checklist, it noted the name of the deceased, the youthfulness, characteristics such as impudence and a love of speed...

Perfect.

Oh yes, this one was absolutely perfect.

Downward the tendril spiralled towards its target, its mission at an end. Within moments it was sinking into cool flesh, immersing itself, suffusing, merging, like liquid into liquid. What the tendril had been, and what it had entered, became one.

There was darkness.

Then, amid the darkness, a spark.

CONSTABLES YELLAND AND Yates were careful. They informed just one other person about the death of Ajia Snell, and that person was Sergeant Hayley Egan, who'd had responsibility for processing the girl's arrest. Egan gave them a five-minute bollocking, which both men took with good grace, then told them to dispose of the body where it wouldn't be found.

"I don't want to know where," she said, "I don't want to know how, I just want it done. Meanwhile I'll clean up the cell and fix the paperwork, and if anyone asks, which they won't, we say we interrogated Ms Snell and released her under caution. That's our story and we're sticking to it. Have you two geniuses got that?"

Zipping the corpse into a bodybag, Yelland and Yates carried it to the boot of an unmarked patrol car and drove to a patch of industrial wasteland. Yelland knew of a drain cover there which led to the sewers. Drop the corpse in and it would be swept away by the torrent of sewage. By the time it saw the light of day again, if it ever did, it would be so waterlogged and rat-gnawed that an identity would be hard to establish and the cause of death harder still. He had used the method before, so far without repercussions.

Yelland unzipped the bodybag while Yates kept lookout. The area was deserted, but Yates couldn't escape the feeling that something wasn't quite right. A breeze tickled the hairs on the nape of his neck, yet the weeds which sprouted here and there in the cracks between the concrete paving slabs were absolutely motionless. In addition, he could almost have sworn someone was watching, even though there was nobody in sight. It was fucking creepy.

"Give us a hand here."

Yates helped Yelland slide the girl out of the bodybag. She was clammy to the touch. One of her eyes was swollen shut. The other stared blankly, reflecting the tawny light of the overcast sky, itself a reflection of London's ambient illumination.

Yelland got to work with a crowbar, prying open the iron drain cover. Yates stuck his hands in his pockets and studiously avoided the girl's one-eyed stare. His gaze kept being drawn back to it, however, and her half-pulped face. She looked defiant, even in death. He almost felt bad for working her over so hard. She'd been good-looking, in an elfin, tomboyish way. If circumstances had been different, he'd have quite fancied her.

She blinked.

Yates almost screamed.

"What the actual—?" exclaimed Yelland. "Gav, why'd you jump like that? You startled the life out of me."

"She... She moved. Her eye. She blinked it. Or winked it. Whichever."

"She did not."

"Swear to God, Dave, she did. I saw her."

"No, you didn't. Even if you did, it was probably one of them involuntary thingies. Like, a spasm. A death twitch. Last little bit of electricity in the nerve endings." Yelland bent back to the task of dislodging the drain cover.

Disconcerted, Yates brushed a hand back and forth over his close-cropped head of hair. The sooner they got the body down into the sewers and out of sight, the better. The whole situation was starting to freak him out. He wondered if he was developing a guilty conscience. The great bonus about being a cop was you could get away with pretty much anything. Your warrant card was a licence to indulge your every whim. That suited Yates, who'd always resented how, back in school, his life had been one long round of detentions and suspensions. He'd thought of it as high spirits; the teachers had called it "repeated and sustained bullying". As a policeman, he wasn't answerable to the wimps and the finger-waggers any more—especially nowadays, in the Drake era. These were strong times for strong people.

Ajia Snell sat bolt upright.

Yates pissed himself.

Even as his bladder let go in sheer fright, he backpedalled away from the corpse, a weird, mewling noise coming from the back of his throat. He lost his footing and fell to the ground, and still he kept putting distance between himself and the dead-but-somehow-now-alive girl, crabbing backwards on all fours while she, for her part, peered around her as though in a daze.

Gavin Yates was a big fan of zombie movies, the gorier the better, and all he could think was that Ajia Snell must have joined the walking dead. It was the only possible explanation. She had been infected by a zombie virus and any second now she would stagger to her feet and start munching on him or Yelland, whoever was closest. Yates didn't much care which of them got eaten, as long as it wasn't himself.

Dave Yelland, it must be said, was no less alarmed than his colleague by the girl's sudden return to the ranks of the living. The difference between them was that Yelland's thoughts did not immediately stray to zombies. His assumption was that he had misidentified Ajia Snell as deceased. She must have been breathing so shallowly, he'd been unable to detect it. Same for her pulse—too feeble to register. It seemed he had made a serious, but perhaps forgivable, blunder.

The only solution he could see was to finish what he and Yates had started. Yelland firmed his grip on the crowbar. Two or three purposeful blows to the skull, and the girl would be as defunct as she was supposed to be. Then the crowbar would join her down in the sewers, taking with it any DNA evidence that might be clinging to it.

Yelland took a step forward and swung, but Ajia wasn't there. The crowbar whisked through empty air. He'd missed. How the hell could he have missed?

"Gav? Have you seen her? Where the fuck has she gone?"

Yates was a gibbering wreck, mumbling something about "the undead", no help whatsoever. Yelland pivoted on his heel, looking for the girl.

There she was, a dozen paces away, bent double, hands on knees, swaying somewhat. How she had got so swiftly from right in front of him to that spot over there, Yelland had no idea. Maybe he'd hesitated before trying to hit her, closed his eyes for a second, and she had scurried off. He didn't think this was the case, but it was possible.

She wasn't going to get away from him again, though. She seemed disorientated and dizzy. Yelland strode towards her with the crowbar raised, determined to make the best of the opportunity.

The girl glanced round, saw him, and was off, running so fast she reached the edge of the wasteland—at least fifty yards away—in just a couple of heartbeats. Next thing Yelland knew, she was climbing the chainlink perimeter fence, still extraordinarily fast, like a spider scuttling up a wall.

Yelland lumbered after her, but by the time he had covered half the distance between them, Ajia Snell was over the fence and dashing down the road on the other side. He'd never seen anything like it. She was inhumanly quick, like an Olympic sprinter on crack. Within seconds she was lost from view.

"You saw that, Gav, right?" Yelland said, halting in his tracks and scowling. "Wasn't just me. You saw how she moved?"

Gavin Yates nodded blearily. He was now less certain that Ajia Snell had been brought back as a zombie. Even the zombies that didn't shamble with arthritic slowness, the ones in movies where the story said they could run, couldn't run the way she had run. He hadn't known a human being was capable of running that fast.

"Should we go after her?" he said. "In the car?"

The unmarked patrol car sat nearby, but Yelland thought that by the time they got in, started the engine and pulled off, there would be little hope of finding the girl. The streets around the wasteland were a warren of side roads, back alleys and underpasses, and if she kept up the pace she'd set off at, she could already be half a mile away by now or more, and getting further with every passing second. Yelland had no idea how long she could run at such a speed without exhausting herself, but then it was pointless speculating, since no one could run at such a speed. Maybe she could sprint like that indefinitely.

Dave Yelland came to a decision. "This never happened," he said. "She didn't wake up. She didn't give us the slip."

"If Egan asks…"

"If Egan asks, we dumped the body down the drain, just like we said we would. End of."

"We can track her, can't we? The girl? Using CCTV footage and what-have-you. We can hunt her down wherever she goes."

"What would be the use?"

"So we can finish this," said Yates. "What if she wants payback? If we don't do something about her, she could, I don't know, file a formal complaint, get a lawyer onto us, something like that."

"You think she's going to?" Yelland scoffed. "Me, I think she's going to hole up somewhere nice and dark and far away from here, and never come out again. She will if she's got any sense. And even if she did try legal action of some sort, how far do you think she'd get?"

"What about the papers?"

"Journalists? Pah! No, Gav, there's no way this is going to come back and bite us on the arse. You can count on it. Now, why are your boots wet? And by the looks of it your trousers too?" Yelland's nose wrinkled. "Fuck's sake, mate! You didn't. Tell me you didn't. Oh Gav!"

FOUR

LONDON WAS MOVING in slow motion. Vehicles traipsed along the neon-glossed streets as though the national speed limit had been set at "dawdle". The few small-hours pedestrians Ajia passed trudged like sleepwalkers. As she ran, she was conscious of everything around her drifting, idling. Sometimes she felt like this when she was on her bike. She knew the secret of speed and no one else did. A hare in a world of tortoises.

But this wasn't the same. This was different.

For instance, she noticed that lights in shop windows were flickering oddly, as though emitting a visual version of Morse code. A startled pigeon, awake and scavenging during the perpetual twilight of the nocturnal city, rose into the air not with panic but with leisurely nonchalance, almost as if floating upward. The traffic signal at a junction ahead took an age to change from amber to green. And sounds had taken on a strange, echoey quality. Car engines droned like the bass pipes of a church organ. Voices were unintelligible.

There seemed to be a thickness in the air, an unseen resistance which only Ajia was unaffected by. London lay at the bottom of the ocean, where the pressures were enormous, and she alone, shark-sleek, had evolved to cope.

On she ran. She wondered if she might be dreaming—hallucinating, even—but she knew deep down she wasn't. The solidity of the ground beneath her feet, for one thing. The feel of the breath filtering in and out of her mouth, for another. Her hair flapping against her neck in time to the alternating piston action of her legs. These were real sensations. Tangible.

As for a destination, she didn't have one. There was her bedsit, but she didn't think it was safe. The police must know where she lived, and it would be the first place they looked for her. Aside from that, nothing came to mind. Ajia did not have close friends. Nor did she have any immediate family in the country, apart from a couple of cousins she had met perhaps three times. And even if there had been someone she thought might give her shelter at their home, she couldn't go there. She couldn't bring the trouble she was in to someone else's door.

All she could think of to do was keep running. The two cops would surely be chasing her. She was surprised they weren't right behind her in that car of theirs. At the very least they'd have called in reinforcements, wouldn't they? They weren't just going to let her slip through their fingers.

Eventually there came a point when she had to rest. She'd been running flat-out for ten minutes, she estimated. Which meant she had put a couple of miles between her and the place the policemen had taken her, that abandoned industrial zone or whatever it was. She needed a breather, time to gather her thoughts and regroup.

She decelerated, on the alert for any sign of law enforcement—a siren, a flashing blue light, a drone. She didn't recognise where she was. It was the suburbs, that much she could tell. A leafy street of large, detached houses. The air quiet, with the constant background rumble you got in central London reduced to just a whisper. The loudest sound she could hear was her own panting.

Once she had got her breath back and her tired legs had stopped trembling, Ajia tried to get her bearings. She found a street sign. The name of the road was unfamiliar—not that she'd expected she would know it—but the sign carried a district code, NW10, and the name of the borough, Brent. Okay, so she was in... Willesden?

Harlesden? Somewhere like that. She had done courier runs up this way a few times.

Odd, though, because she could have sworn that she had been running through Hackney and Dalston earlier. She had recognised a couple of landmarks, including the Empire theatre and the Museum of Childhood. She must have been mistaken. She couldn't have run from the East End all the way to Brent—nine miles, more or less—in such a short span of time.

It was then that Ajia realised she was very hungry. She couldn't remember when she had last eaten. Nor did she know how long she had been held in the police station cell, but it must have been several hours. Everything that had happened since the two cops started beating her up had become fragmentary in her memory, a broken jigsaw of images. Even the events leading up to her incarceration were blurred. Vaguely she recalled being caught stencilling on a wall, getting on her bike, pedalling off... Shot. Hadn't she been shot?

With a start, Ajia looked down at her belly. How could you forget being shot?

There were still holes in her cycling top, front and back. The garment was encrusted with dried blood. She rolled it up and examined the bandaging beneath, which was blood-sodden. Gingerly she peeled away the dressing over her stomach. The bullet wound...

Was not there. She couldn't even see any scarring.

She checked her back with her fingers, looking for the exit wound. That, too, was absent, gone without a trace.

Bruises. Surely she had some bruises from the punishment the policemen had dished out?

There were none of those either. Her torso, her arms, her legs—no evidence whatsoever of the abuse.

She was healed all over.

How is that even possible?

What should have taken weeks, even months, to recover from had mended in just a matter of hours.

A sense of unreality washed over her, until her hunger reasserted itself, grounding her again. She was famished. If she didn't eat soon, she was afraid she might pass out.

Pushing thoughts of her near-miraculous recuperation to the back of her mind, she went in search of a high street. She knew this was a risky move. Surveillance cameras everywhere and facial recognition systems in operation. Her cycling top had a hood, however, which she pulled tight over her head.

It took her half an hour of wandering, but eventually she found a late-night mini mart nestled amid a parade of charity shops and national chain stores, many of the latter now closed down. The mini mart was the kind that at one time would more than likely have been run by an Asian family, but its present proprietor was an overweight white man who looked peeved, as though being a mini mart owner was beneath his dignity. He sat at the checkout, peering through thick spectacles at a copy of *The Sun*, "The Paper That Supports the New Britain".

Only when she was through the doors of the mini mart did Ajia realise she had no money on her. The police had confiscated all her personal effects, including not just her phone but her wallet too.

Shit.

Ajia had shoplifted only once before, a tube of mascara from Boots when she was twelve, and she had felt awful about it for days afterward. But that had been a spur-of-the-moment thing and she'd been just a kid. The circumstances were different now. This was necessity.

Aside from the proprietor there were two other people on the premises, both customers. One was a bleary-eyed stoner looking for something to satisfy his munchies, the other a heavily pregnant woman who was in the grip of a food craving, to judge by the jar of pickled beetroot and the tub of ice cream in her shopping basket. Ajia didn't think either of them was going to give her much trouble. The main thing was not to draw attention to herself, which was hard because she knew she looked a mess.

The shelves were half empty, and what stock there was, was overpriced even by independent-retailer standards. A glass-fronted refrigerator offered a selection of prepacked foods, including sandwiches and samosas. Ajia grabbed a couple of each and a bottle of water. She ambled towards the checkout, casual as anything, like someone who had every intention of paying for her purchases. The door lay just four yards away. She reckoned she could be outside and halfway down the street before the proprietor roused himself to go after her. That was assuming the man could even be bothered. He looked as though he didn't engage in any activity more energetic than using the stairs, and even that would leave him short of breath.

"Excuse me," said a voice behind her.

It was the pregnant woman.

Ajia pretended not to have heard, but the woman was persistent.

"Not my business," she said, "but I couldn't help noticing." She indicated Ajia's torn, bloodied clothing. "Did a boyfriend do this? Because if he did, I hope you've reported him. Can't let the bastards get away with it, can we?"

"I tripped and fell," Ajia said.

"That's a lot of blood for someone who 'tripped and fell'. Listen, love, I'm an A&E nurse. I've seen it all. Girls in the state you're in and worse. We're trained to look for signs of physical abuse. If you haven't gone to the police yet, you should."

Ajia almost laughed.

"At least think about it, would you?" said the pregnant woman.

Having overheard the conversation, the mini mart proprietor and the stoner were now staring at Ajia, intrigued. The pregnant woman had managed to blow whatever chance she had had of doing this subtly. Her only tactic left was just to go for it.

She said, "Thanks for the advice," and pelted for the door with her armful of food.

None of the three people even attempted to stop her. They just stood stock still, seemingly too astonished to react. As she burst through the door, Ajia glanced back, and they were as statue-like as before. They weren't even looking towards her. They were staring at the spot where she had been standing a moment ago, frowns forming on their faces.

Ajia raced off along the street, clutching her ill-gotten gains to her chest.

*   *   *

LATER, ON A park bench, she wolfed down the food. The sandwiches were tasteless, the samosas more so. A hint of spiciness was somehow worse than no spiciness at all. Maybe there was a cap on how hot an Indian foodstuff could be these days. There were rumours that, in the wake of Drake's election, the chefs at certain curry houses had started toning down the intensity of their vindaloos for fear of seeming unpatriotic. Or maybe the samosa was just a piece of flavour-free mass-produced crap, that was all.

Either way, it was nothing like the ones Ajia's mother used to make. Those samosas were gorgeous, crispy treats with just the right mix of vegetables and enough green chillies to make the lips burn deliciously. As a kid, every morning when Ajia went to school, her mother used to pack a fresh samosa in her bag, wrapped in kitchen foil. "In case you need it," her mother would say, and even if she wasn't peckish, Ajia would eat it regardless at some point during the day.

Thoughts of her mother brought an extra layer of misery to the miseries Ajia was suffering. Padma Snell had been among the first wave of deportees when the Drake government came to power. Being born in the UK and a resident for forty years did not, it seemed, guarantee UK nationality any more. Padma and her parents, Ajia's grandparents, were put on a plane and flown to Mumbai, arriving in a country Padma had never visited and her parents remembered only faintly. This, of course, was in contravention of international law and had provoked an outcry from the UN and various charities and NGOs, which had not troubled Derek Drake one bit. He had simply accused "bureaucratic busybodies" of interfering in his country's inalienable right to do as it pleased with its population.

What had become of her family members after their deportation, Ajia had no clear idea. The last she'd heard, they were in an internment camp and being treated as displaced persons—glorified refugees. That was four years ago, and every attempt she had made since then to communicate with them or trace their whereabouts online had come to nothing. There were no official records of them having been transferred out of the camp, but the camp itself had been dismantled. Their social media accounts stood idle. Their phone numbers had been disconnected. It was as though they had vanished into limbo.

India was not to blame for this, at least not wholly. The subcontinent was struggling to cope with the influx of arrivals from Great Britain. Tens of thousands of individuals per year were being added to its already vast population, some coming because they were forced to, others to escape a Britain where tolerance of difference was at an all-time low. India's infrastructure was cracking under the strain.

Ajia herself had been allowed to remain behind solely because of her Caucasian father. If he too had been of Indian ethnicity, they would all have been deported. Sometimes, in the light of how her life had turned out after her mother was taken away, she wished they had. At least then they would all be together. And her father would not be dead.

Grief welled within her. Old grief, deep grief, not yet healed. Ajia fought it down. Now was not the time. What was important now was survival. She was in serious shit. On the run from the police. Nobody to turn to. Nowhere she could go. The fact that her injuries, not least the bullet wound, had somehow magically vanished was some consolation. It was also extremely weird, and she supposed it should have bothered her more than it did, but just then it felt like simply an added layer of complication for her to deal with. It was almost surreal how screwed she was, and how quickly it had happened. One moment, she was merrily going along, business as usual. The next, this clusterfuck.

Yet somehow it seemed inevitable, too. You couldn't do what she'd been doing—putting up images in public places lampooning Derek Drake—without at least acknowledging the possibility you might someday get into trouble for it. For months she had been making her art ever more inflammatory, ever more provocative, practically courting disaster. In today's atmosphere, you played it safe or faced the consequences, and Ajia had made a conscious decision not to play it safe. She was angry and she wanted people to know how angry she was.

The state, however, did not like anger. Anger posed a threat to order. The state wanted the masses complacent and docile, and it visited its own anger on anyone who did not conform to its will.

As she cast her mind back over recent events, a thought occurred to Ajia. Why had the two policemen taken her from the station and brought her to that piece of waste ground? What had they been planning to do? She had no memory of getting there, but then presumably she had been unconscious during the journey. What she did remember, vaguely, was one of the policemen attacking her with a crowbar. She remembered, too, a sack made of black, rubberised fabric, gaping like an open cocoon.

The sack—had that been a bodybag? Had the two cops been going to kill her and stash her in it?

If so, then the situation was even more dire than she'd supposed. *They want me dead.*

Her only viable option, then, was to disappear. Vanish, the way her mother and grandparents had done in India, only by choice, not through bureaucratic chaos. Somehow she had to slip between the cracks and never be seen again.

Right this moment, however, Ajia wanted only to sleep. The food sat heavy in her stomach. She was wrung out, physically and emotionally. Every part of her ached, except for the bits that were plain agony. Just a couple of hours' kip, that was all. It would be dawn soon. A new day. She could figure out what to do with herself then.

She curled up on the bench, making herself as comfortable as she could, one arm for a pillow. The night air was chilly, but she soon fell asleep.

SHE AWOKE AS hands grabbed her roughly. She smelled the stink of unwashed body, unlaundered clothing, and stale alcohol. She herself did not smell great, but it was the intensity of the odours, and above all the stale alcohol, that told her the reek was someone else's rather than her own.

A man was growling at her. "My bench! My fucking bench! You get off!"

Next thing Ajia knew, she was being rolled off the bench. She landed hard.

As she lay sprawled on her side, stunned, a tremendous blow struck her from above. A stamp from a booted foot, delivered viciously. She felt something—a rib—snap. The pain was so excruciating, she couldn't even scream; she could only gasp and whimper.

Then she was rolled over onto her back. The same hands that had ousted her from the bench now encircled her wrists. Hot breath, reeking of booze and rotten teeth, gusted in her face.

"Little bitch. The nerve of you. My bench. Nobody sleeps on my bench."

Still crippled by pain, Ajia writhed, but the man's grip was too powerful.

"Fucking teach you a lesson. That's what I'm going to do. I served, you know. Army. Ten years. They taught me how to hurt people good and proper. Never forgotten it."

A knee pressed down on her sternum, doubling the agony from her fractured rib. The man transferred control of her wrists to just one of his hands, freeing up the other. Coarse, iron-hard fingers clutched Ajia's face.

"Break your jaw. I can do it. Snap it right off its hinges."

A cry built in the back of her throat, a guttural yell of defiance. Desperately, without really thinking about it, Ajia brought her knee up between the man's legs.

But the angle was wrong. The blow struck the inside of the man's thigh, not the tenderer parts it was aimed at.

"Missed! Nice try. Won't let you have a second shot at that."

The man used his other leg to weigh down both of Ajia's legs. He was so much heavier than her, so much stronger.

"Now, where was I? Oh yes. The jaw."

The fingers dug harder into her face and began twisting. Ajia felt the joints connecting her jawbone to the rest of her skull creak. Could he really do it? Could he break her jaw just like that?

From a few yards away, a deep, clear, cultivated voice said, "I would advise you to leave her alone, Rich."

The pressure on Ajia's face eased just a fraction.

"Smith?" the man said. "Is that you?"

"It's me," said the man called Smith. His accent carried a faint West Indian lilt. "And I won't ask again. Get off her. Now. Or you'll have me to answer to."

"Oh yes?" The man whom Smith had addressed as Rich let go of Ajia and reared up. "You're big, Smith, but you're not so tough. Not as tough as me."

"How about my hammer and I decide that, Rich?"

"You and your ruddy hammer. I'm not scared. I've got this."

Rich rummaged in a pocket. Ajia glimpsed him drawing something out. There was a click. A knife blade glinted in the dark.

As for Smith, he did indeed have a hammer, as advertised. A carpenter's tool, long-handled, the head square at one end and tapered at the other, and he was holding it out at the end of a lanky arm. He loomed over Rich, tall and imposing, the hammer raised. If Rich's knife intimidated him, he didn't show it.

The two of them held each other's gaze for several seconds, their weapons poised. Ajia braced herself for them to start fighting. She anticipated a short-lived flurry of violence, a decisive, perhaps fatal blow struck sooner rather than later—a stab to the gut, a clout around the head with that hammer. She was in too much pain to do anything but lie there and watch.

Then Rich backed down. Like a dog capitulating to a larger, fiercer dog, he bobbed his head low and grinned servilely.

"Yeah, well, not worth it, is it?" he said. "I mean, sun comes up in an hour. It's just a bench."

"Quite," said Smith. "I'm not sure one can even claim a park bench as one's own. Aren't they public property?"

"Yeah. Yeah, yeah." Rich put away the knife. He gathered up a heap of bulging plastic carrier bags which sat beside the bench, his worldly possessions. Grumbling under his breath, he began shuffling away.

Smith presented himself to Ajia. At first glance, he and Rich had much in common. Both had straggling, unkempt beards and both were in need of a good bath and a change of clothing. In that respect, they were more or less your typical homeless rough-sleepers.

Smith, however, had a straight-backed bearing, compared with Rich's hunched posture, and he didn't smell like a brewery. His outfit, too, was somehow more dignified—a military-surplus greatcoat and a trilby hat, where Rich favoured castoff sportswear—and his dreadlocks were the genuine article, properly palm-rolled, while Rich's were just the result of matted, filthy hair. Rich looked shabby, and Smith also looked shabby but in a somehow classy way.

Smiling, Smith extended a hand to Ajia.

"Permit me," he said.

Ajia did not accept the proffered assistance. "I can get up on my own, thanks."

She proceeded to try, and, with a lot of wincing and hissing, just about managed it. She got as far as slumping onto the bench, at least. She was breathing hard, and every inhalation and exhalation hurt.

"You made that look easy," Smith said.

Ajia grimaced. "Listen, thanks for helping me out with that guy. Don't get me wrong, I appreciate it."

"You're welcome, good fellow."

Good fellow? Who did Smith think he was? Fucking Aslan the lion?

"But," she said, "I'm okay now. You don't have to hang around. I've got this."

Smith's expression could not have been any more sceptical. "Have you now? Because to me it looks as though you haven't got anything except what seems to be a broken rib, along with bloodstains on your clothing suggestive of an older injury. In short, you aren't in great shape."

"So what if I'm not?"

"All I'm saying is you seem as though you could do with a friend," said Smith, "and I could be that friend."

"'Friend' as in you want me to give you a gratitude blowjob or something? Because, I can tell you this, Mr Smith, that is not going to happen. Not in a million years."

"Just Smith."

"What?"

"No 'Mr'. Just Smith. And no fellatio is called for, or any other sexual favour. I'm willing to do you a kindness, that's all. You're like me, I can tell. We are cut from the same cloth. You may not realise that yet, but we are. I have found you, and I can take you to a place where there are more of us. Others who share the secret."

"Secret?"

"We have become as new," Smith said. "We have died and been reborn, and now we are transformed. Improved. Exalted."

This, to Ajia, sounded like Jesus talk. With an ultra-right-wing, devoutly religious prime minister in charge, it was hardly surprising that there had been a significant uptick in Christianity all across the land. Not only was church attendance on the rise, faith outreach centres were flourishing as well, and a number of homeless shelters were now offering food and beds solely to those prepared to endure an hour or two of hardcore evangelist preaching beforehand. Smith, Ajia reckoned, was a convert and had adopted the role of shepherd, rescuing lost lambs and bringing them into the fold.

This particular lamb, however, would rather end up on the dinner table than join the flock.

"Yeah, no," she said, eyeing Smith's hammer, which he had tucked into a loop of his belt. Godly or not, anyone who walked around open-carrying a hammer was not to be trusted. "Whatever it is you're selling, I'm not in the market. Thanks again. I'm off now."

She rose to her feet, and immediately was overcome by pain, and accompanying that, a wave of light-headedness. She staggered and keeled over.

Smith caught her as she fell. "Good fellow," he said pityingly, supporting her. "Like it or not, your fate and mine are bound together. We are kin, and nothing can change that."

These were the last words Ajia heard before she plunged down a deep, dark hole into unconsciousness.

FIVE

AJIA DREAMED OF that day.

It was one of the worst days of her life, the other being the day the officials from the Resettlement Council came to take her mother away.

The day when she came home from sixth-form college to find the flat strangely silent. Normally at this hour her father would have been getting ready to teach his after-school lessons. He'd be running through scales or practising his blues fingering, or else trying out some flashy flamenco piece or a Keith Richards riff. Over the next three hours the front room would be occupied by a succession of pupils, some better than others, all learning to play guitar under Tony Snell's calm, measured tutelage.

Today there wasn't a sound coming from the front room. Ajia, though, wasn't worried. She assumed her dad had just popped down the road, maybe to buy some new strings at the music shop or get something in for tea. She went straight to her room. Her plan was to take her bike out for a spin later, but first she wanted to get some drawing done in her sketchbook. Her likenesses of Derek Drake were coming along nicely. The image she was working on at the moment, and was particularly proud of, showed the prime minister and his chief Paladin Dominic Wynne from the waist up, side by side, shirtless. Each was reaching out of frame in such a way that it was clear his hand was at the other's crotch. From this and the smiles on their faces, the viewer had to infer that mutual jerking-off was happening.

Of course, she was careful to keep the sketchbook hidden at the back of a drawer. If her father found it, he'd flip his lid. And if someone in authority ever saw it…

When the door buzzer rang, Ajia went down the hallway to open it. Obviously her father had forgotten his keys. Again. Duh, Dad. He'd been doing that a lot lately. In fact, lately he hadn't been just absentminded—he'd been absent, in the sense that he could be there with you in the room, even talking to you, but his mind would be elsewhere. Two years since his wife was deported, and he'd been putting up a brave front but it was starting to wear him down. Ajia could see it. The effort of carrying on as normal, hoping that things would get better, that somehow, miraculously, his Padma would come back. The agony of not knowing where she was. If she was even still alive. It was etched around his eyes. His eyes looked so tired.

Ajia was feeling the strain too, but she had been able to cry about it, and scream, and mope. And she had her drawings through which to vent her bitterness and frustration. Her father, in his oh-so-English, masculine way, just internalised it all. He seemed to think that by remaining stoical, not showing his pain, not giving it any outlet, he was somehow protecting Ajia. Do his teaching, perform the odd pub gig, make sure there was food on the table, everything as it was meant to be. He was a sensitive man but it was all on the inside, not on the surface.

At the door stood Nathan, her father's first pupil of the day. Earnest twelve-year-old Nathan, fresh off the bus, with his guitar case slung over his back.

"Not late, am I?" Nathan said, seeing her look of mild surprise.

"No," Ajia said. "Bang on time. I just thought you were my dad."

"He not in?"

"If he isn't, he'll be back in a mo. Wait here."

A thought had occurred to her. Maybe her father was taking a nap. That was something else he'd started doing these past few weeks, sleeping at odd times and not sleeping at night.

"Dad!" she called out. No response. "Dad!"

She knocked on the door to his bedroom.

"Dad, you dopey twit, you'd better get up. Nathan's here. Dad?"

Still nothing.

"Right, well, I'm coming in. You'd best not be naked. I'm closing my eyes just in case."

She opened the door.

"Dad?"

Even with her eyes shut, she could tell he was there. She could smell his aftershave. That and another odour, mustier, less pleasant. Sinister.

She knew then that she did not want to look, and that she must look.

She knew exactly what he had done.

He lay propped up on the pillows, staring straight ahead, sightlessly.

There was an empty glass on his bedside table, and next to it an empty packet of paracetamol.

Ajia stood in the doorway, trembling. The enormity of what she was seeing drove the breath out of her, like a gigantic tonnage pushing down on her from above.

The loll of his head. The grey pallor of his face. The sheer stillness of him.

"Is your dad all right, Ajia?" Behind her, Nathan was peeking round the door jamb. She hadn't even heard him approach. "He doesn't look all right. Is he ill? Should we call the ambulance?"

Ajia dreamed of these events exactly as they had happened, with as much clarity as if they were happening now. It was a loop of memory she chose not to replay if she could help it, but in her dreams she had no say in the matter. She could do nothing but relive the moment as though it was all brand new, the first time every time. It was her private hell.

She struggled out of the dream, clawing her way back up to reality.

"Whoa, whoa, whoa. It's okay. Be calm, good fellow. Nothing's the matter."

She blinked around her. It was Smith who was speaking. She was on a bare mattress on the floor. Smith sat nearby, cross-legged. He was heating up a frying pan over a camping stove.

"Bad dream?"

"You could say that," Ajia said.

The waking world brought with it pain. Ajia's body felt stiff and brittle, as though she were made of broken glass. But at least it was just physical pain. It wasn't the mental torment of walking in on her dead father and knowing that she had been sitting in the adjacent room for half an hour with no idea that he was there. Knowing, too, that this was something he had been hiding from her for weeks if not months—this loneliness, this despair, this anguish that had gradually sapped his will to live.

Smith cracked eggs one-handed into the pan. As they started to sizzle, Ajia took stock of her surroundings. A flat in a high-rise. Tenth or eleventh storey, must be, judging by what she could see out of the grimy, curtainless windows—a vista of rooftops beneath a broad noonday sky. Aside from the mattress and a wooden chair, there was no furniture to speak of. The wallpaper was peeling, as was the linoleum, exposing jagged patches of bare concrete. A smell of blocked drains permeated the air. It might have been quite a nice flat, once upon a time, but nobody had lived here, not properly, for some while.

"Not the dezzest of rezzes," Smith said, following her gaze. "But the rent is cheap, by which I mean free, which is the best price of all. Strictly speaking, the building is condemned and unfit for human occupation, but as far as I'm concerned it remains habitable until someone actually gets round to knocking it down. The views are excellent. On a good day you can see all the way to the Shard, or on a bad day, depending whether monuments to unbridled capitalist greed are your thing or not. From other flats you can see Wembley Stadium, if you'd rather, but I was never into football."

"A squat."

"Such an ugly word. I prefer to think of it as 'repurposed domicile'. Not all of us can afford a roof over our head, and if there's a perfectly acceptable dwelling lying vacant..."

"Look, Mr Smith…" Ajia began.

"Ah-ah!" Smith held up a hand. "Remember? No 'Mr'. Just Smith."

"Smith, then. Look, I owe you again, obviously. I guess I must have passed out back there in the park and you carried me here."

"You are a slender little thing. It was no great labour."

"But…"

"You're uncomfortable being here, alone in a flat with a strange man you don't know."

Emphasis on strange, Ajia thought.

"That's putting it mildly," she said.

"I understand. Rest assured, I harbour no sinister intentions towards you. I am no torturer or rapist. You are free to go, should you wish, any time."

Ajia debated how easy it would be to take him up on the invitation. The way she felt right now, if Smith wanted to prevent her leaving, there wouldn't be much she could do about it. She was a wreck. He was in much better condition, not to mention bigger and bulkier. Plus, there was that hammer of his, still tucked into his belt.

"I would just ask," he continued, "that you stay to have a fried-egg sandwich with me and listen to what I have to say. After that, what you do is entirely up to you."

It sounded reasonable, Ajia supposed. And those frying eggs did smell good.

THEY TASTED GOOD, too, slapped between two slices of butter-lathered white bread. Ajia ate and almost felt contented.

"First of all," Smith said, licking grease off his fingers, "I think I should know your name. The name you used to have. It's only polite to ask."

"Used to have?"

"Humour me."

"Ajia," she said. "Ajia Snell is the name I used to have, and as a matter of fact still do."

"Pleased to meet you, Ajia Snell. I used to be Auric Wright."

"I see. So, do, er... people like you, do you have before-and-after names? Is that a thing? Before you became homeless and after? Like, a change of identity. A street alias. I didn't know that."

"Oh, my name change has nothing to do with my social status, or lack of same," Smith replied. "It's somewhat more complicated. Tell me, Ajia, do you remember dying?"

"What?"

"I said, do you remember dying?"

"I heard what you said. I just didn't think you'd said what I heard. No, I don't remember dying, because I haven't died."

"Haven't you? Cast your mind back. At some point, very recently, you will have lost all sensation. You will have entered a state of complete and utter extinction."

"You mean when I blacked out when I got up from the bench? But that was just, like, fainting."

"No, not then. Earlier. Try and think. I know it can be hard. The mind has a tendency to draw a veil over uncongenial experiences, and experiences don't come much more uncongenial than dying. It's a kind of self-protection mechanism. You may dimly recall becoming detached from your body, being able to observe yourself with dispassion and, perhaps, a certain compassion too. Does that sound familiar?"

"No," Ajia said, but it did. Back in the police cell, during her third beating. The feeling of watching herself getting pummelled. Telling herself to close her eyes and go to sleep.

"Are you sure?"

"Yes. Well... Okay, I might have gone through something a bit like that." Briefly she outlined the sorry tale of how Met officers had shot, arrested and abused her. "But I didn't die."

"How do you know that?"

"Because I wouldn't be sitting here now chatting with you," she said, as if it could not be more obvious. "I'd be in heaven, or the spirit plane, or hanging around in the bardo waiting to be reincarnated, or none of the above, delete where applicable."

"Is death so easy to verify?" said Smith. "One's own death? After all, no one has come back and definitively described how it feels to die. At least, no one has gone on record about it. Some have darkened death's threshold and been revived at the last instant. They have come close but, self-evidently, they have not actually died. A few of us, however, have indeed passed through death's portal and returned. We are the ones who can say with some accuracy what it is like. I include not just myself in this category, good fellow, but you as well."

"Why do you keep calling me that?"

"What? Good fellow?"

"Yeah. Is it just some affectation?"

"No. No affectation."

"I notice you didn't call that other guy, Rich, it."

"Rich?" Smith chortled. "Rich is just Rich, as in short for Richard. That's his name, ironic as it is. 'Good fellow' is yours."

Ajia was not greatly enlightened.

"But back to my point," Smith went on. "Death came for you. Now that I tell you that, you must see it's true. But life was not done with you. Life had other plans. That is why you are still breathing, still extant. And why, also, you are not quite you any more. You are different."

"Different? I don't feel different."

"Tell me, has anything unusual occurred since you came back from the dead?"

"Don't think so."

"What is the first thing you remember after your brief spell of nothingness?"

Ajia pondered. "The cops. The two rozzers who did me over. They were going to put me in a bodybag, I think."

"Were they? Or had you perhaps just been in that bodybag? Had they thought you dead, until you soundly disabused them of that notion?"

"Don't know. It's all a bit of a haze, on account of the whole getting-shot-and-then-having-the-crap-beaten-out-of-me-several-times thing."

"But you got away from the policemen."

"Now that I do remember," said Ajia. "I ran like fuck, and they were too old and slow, or just too bloody lazy, to run after me."

"Or," said Smith, "you were just too fast for them."

"Same difference."

"No. Not the same at all. Didn't it seem peculiar to you, how fast you were going?"

Ajia shrugged. "I'm a bike courier. I'm pretty fit."

"When you ran, did it feel as though nobody on earth could ever keep up with you? As though you were faster than anyone has ever been? I'm only guessing about this. I can't know what it's like. I'm just projecting from my own experience of developing a new-found ability."

The conversation had taken a bizarre turn.

No, Ajia corrected herself. *It hasn't taken a bizarre turn. It was bizarre to begin with, and it's getting bizarrer.*

"I was scared," she said. "I was running for my life, or so I thought. I didn't really have time to analyse it while it was happening. Didn't conduct a scientific study. Too busy just doing it."

"You don't, in hindsight, consider that there was any unnatural about your speed? Preternatural, even?"

"Nope."

The traffic signal that took so long to change. The way sounds became attenuated, long and slow, like whalesong. The three people at the mini mart, not looking at where she was but at where she had been, as if their gazes were lagging behind.

"Let's try another tack," said Smith, and he picked up the frying pan and flung it at her.

Ajia heard the hollow *spanggg* of the pan hitting the wall and bouncing off. She herself was in the opposite corner of the room at that point.

Smith turned to look for her. "Ah, there you are."

"What the hell did you do that for?" Ajia demanded.

"I think your question ought to be 'How the hell I get from one side of the room to the other in less time than it took for a hurled frying pan to travel a few feet?' And from a standing start, what's more. Don't you see, good fellow, that what you just did was impossible. I gave you no warning. I threw the pan as hard as I could. I was aiming for your head. If you hadn't moved like you did, it would be you who now had a dent in you instead of the wall. Your reaction time was incalculably swift, and the distance you covered in a split-second—remarkable. You were human lightning."

"No," said Ajia, shaking her head. "No, I just... just got out of the way, that's all. So I have good reflexes. So what?"

Smith stooped to retrieve the frying pan.

"Don't even think about trying that stunt again," she said menacingly.

"Wouldn't dream of it," Smith said, dusting the pan off and setting it back down beside the camping stove. "Even if I did, I know I couldn't touch you. You would dodge the pan every time. But perhaps some other sort of demonstration is in order. You seem unconvinced of your own talent. How about I show off mine? That might clinch it."

He drew his hammer from his belt.

"You are definitely not going to chuck that at me," Ajia said.

"My hammer is not for violence."

"Could have fooled me. You were ready to hit Rich with it last night."

"Again, wouldn't have dreamed of it. I was bluffing. Not that Rich realised. I needed a prop in order to out-bully the bully. No, this hammer, good fellow, is a construction tool. It does not cause damage. It creates."

Smith grabbed the wooden chair with his free hand, raised it up and smashed it onto the floor. The first time, a leg broke off. The second time, one of the spindles in the back came free. The third time, the entire chair collapsed, disintegrating into so much tinder.

"I am Wayland the Smith," Smith intoned, brandishing the hammer. "I am the Forger. The Maker. The Crafter of Things."

He began to tap the ruined chair with the tapered end of the hammer head.

And the chair began to reassemble itself.

With every tap, the sundered parts came together. Legs reattached to seat, seat to back. The spindles were restored into place one after another. Splintered ends knitted, like fractured bones healing.

Within half a minute the chair was complete again, as if it had never been destroyed.

"There," Smith said. "Good as new. How about that?"

Ajia gaped.

"IKEA," she said at last. "New type of IKEA chair. Comes apart, springs back whole, if you press it in the right spots. Haven't seen that one in the catalogue but I bet it's there."

"You know that's not the case. You saw with your own eyes. This was no trick. What I unmade, the hammer remade. And that is just a fraction of my abilities. Consider your broken rib. I imagine it still hurts, but does it hurt as badly as it did? No. In fact, what you are feeling is just a mild residual ache. Does that describe the pain?"

Hesitantly Ajia nodded.

"Your range of movement is not inhibited, as it would be were the rib still broken," Smith continued. "We've seen that."

"I had a bullet hole in me," Ajia said. "That's gone too. Maybe I heal super fast, like Wolverine from the *X-Men* movies." It sounded crazy even as she said it, but given all the other strangeness she was experiencing, it didn't seem beyond the realms of possibility.

"Or," said Smith, "you healed once, and fully, from the various traumas that contributed to your death, but I healed you from the later injury you received at Rich's hands. I did the major part of the work, at any rate. The rest is up to your body's natural ability. I've given you a helping hand, accelerating the process. Much as I mended that chair, I mended you."

"With your hammer?"

He nodded.

"You fixed my broken rib with your hammer?"

He nodded again.

Ajia felt the need to sit down on the floor. "This is nuts."

"It's a lot to take in," Smith said. "I understand. If it's any consolation, I myself struggled. To undergo a metamorphosis such as you and I have—there is no frame of reference for it, no ready comparison, not even 'caterpillar to butterfly'. The mind rebels. We think we have a grasp of how reality works, and then something like this comes along and sweeps the rug out from under our feet.

You need time. I can let you have time. Not a lot, but some. A day, maybe. Twenty-four hours. And then, I feel, we should move on."

"Move on? Where?"

"There are others like us, good fellow. A whole host of others. I can take you to meet them, if you wish."

SIX

DEREK DRAKE WAS not a vain man. He did not think he was, at any rate. But appearances mattered. When your face was one of the most recognisable on the planet, you had to look your best. For some, that meant an exercise routine, a strict diet, regular visits to the tanning salon, perhaps Botox or fillers if wrinkles were starting to creep up on you. But Drake did not have time for any of that.

For Derek Drake, looking his best meant makeup. He never went anywhere without it. A touch of foundation on the cheeks and forehead to add colour, a little concealer under the eyes to disguise the bags, so discreetly applied as to be all but imperceptible. He had a cosmetician come to Charrington Grange—his private residence, a rambling former monastery nestled in the heart of the Cotswolds—first thing every morning to spruce him up for the day ahead. Her official job designation was simply "presentational assistant", and she had signed a stiffly-worded non-disclosure agreement which prevented her from revealing the true nature of her work.

Today Drake had a major television interview scheduled, so his presentational assistant spent that little bit longer getting him ready. He surrendered to her ministrations with an almost blissful contentment. The feathery strokes of her makeup brush, the delicate little dabs with cotton-wool pads. He thought of it as a smattering of fairy dust.

Then came breakfast with Harriet in the conservatory. They ate in silence, Drake perusing the morning papers, Harriet tapping at her phone. Outside the French windows a long lawn stretched away, mown into meticulous stripes of dark and light green. At the end lay a pair of towering cedars which had been cultivated over the decades so that their trunks and boughs formed a kind of arch with the ground, a frame for the panorama of rolling Gloucestershire farmland beyond.

To look at, the breakfasting couple seemed companionable. Every now and then Drake might glance across the table at his wife, smile, and she would look back and return the smile. In her mid-fifties, the same age as him, Harriet was still ravishingly beautiful, and she made sure to keep herself that way through the methods—exercise, diet, tanning bed, dermal lifts and the like—which Drake himself spurned. She was not the sort of woman to let her looks go. It was one of the traits her husband appreciated the most about her.

As a servant cleared away the breakfast things, Major Dominic Wynne knocked and entered. He was wearing his Paladin's tactical uniform, a form-fitting one-piece in royal blue ripstop fabric with integral padding on the torso, elbows and knees and embroidered name badge on the sleeve. His helmet, with its chevron visor and knightly crest, was tucked under his arm.

"Morning, sir."

"Morning, Wynne."

"Ma'am."

"Dominic."

"Anything to report?" Drake asked his head of security.

"Quiet night, I'm told," said Wynne. "Patrols didn't rustle up anything in the grounds more dangerous than a stray fox. Guards on the gate had to turn back a car. Driver was lost. Looking for a country-house hotel, I believe. I have a team all set to take you into London. Ready whenever you are."

"Thank you, Wynne. I shan't be long."

The Paladin turned to Harriet Drake. "Any trips planned today, ma'am?"

"I'm heading into Cheltenham later. Pilates class, followed by a lunch date with a girlfriend."

"I shall arrange a close protection detail to accompany you."

"That would be lovely. Might you be able to oversee it yourself?"

"If the Prime Minister is amenable to the idea..."

Drake waved a hand airily. "Fine, fine."

"You can manage without me?"

"I'll muddle through somehow."

"Then, Mrs Wynne, I am at your service."

"What a relief. I always prefer it when your hand is on the tiller, Dominic. I feel so much safer."

"I aim to please."

After Wynne had left the conservatory, Drake refilled his coffee cup from the cafetière, gave Harriet a peck on the cheek, and went outside. Briskly he crossed the lawn, passing by the tennis court and the swimming pool and disappearing through a gap in a yew hedge. Moments later he arrived at an outbuilding, a stable block which had been converted into a spacious private museum.

Just as he was about to enter, a pair of Paladins ambled by on their rounds. Drake acknowledged their salutes with a lift of his coffee cup, and waited until they were out of sight before tapping in the door code and going in.

THE TWO PALADINS knew, as did all their comrades, that the prime minister spent approximately half an hour in the museum each day. What exactly he got up to while in there, they could only speculate. The Venetian blinds in the windows were permanently closed, and nobody else went in or out of the place except Drake himself. Domestic staff didn't clean there, and Drake alone knew the entry code.

Because the museum housed Drake's collection of Christian relics, the assumption was that he must be admiring these artefacts, which he had gathered assiduously over the course of several years. Perhaps he prayed to them, too. His devoutness was legendary, after all.

The museum, in other words, was a private place of worship and contemplation. It was Drake's sanctum sanctorum, his holy of holies, and trespassers were forbidden.

WHEN DRAKE RETURNED to the house, an armoured limousine was waiting out front to collect him. The limo was flanked by a pair of black Range Rovers, also armoured. The three cars set off down the Grange's long gravelled driveway, the Range Rovers at front and back.

Within an hour the motorcade was approaching the outskirts of London along the M4. Through tinted ballistic glass, Drake watched Windsor Castle glide by and thought of the royal family, now living in exile in Monaco. Hard to feel sorry for them. They had got out with most of their money and had set themselves up in a series of lavish apartments and villas. They weren't exactly suffering down there on the Riviera, with beaches, nightclubs and casinos on their doorstep and a horde of their fellow idle rich to hobnob with. Other expats had it far worse. But there had simply been no question of the royals continuing their lives in Britain as before. They were far too outspoken, especially the heir to the throne. They were also too high-profile to be hushed by the usual means. Drake had given them the option of staying, as long as they behaved, or else he would confiscate their assets. They had elected to leave. They were principled, he supposed. You had to grant them that. But they were pragmatic too. Ruling was all very well, but wealth was as, if not more, important.

The city began amassing around him, its soft halo of suburb giving way to the densely-packed unruliness of urban buildup. The television interview was scheduled for twelve noon, and it was nearing that hour when the motorcade pulled up at the gates of Downing Street.

There had been a time, early in his term of office, when protestors would routinely block the entrance as Drake arrived, waving placards and shaking their fists. They would spit at his car, throw eggs, and yell slogans about freedom, fascism and human rights.

On one occasion, somebody even fired a starting pistol at him, a mock assassination attempt. Alas, the culprit suffered asphyxiation while antiterrorism officers were attempting to restrain him in the back of a police van, a death which had all the hallmarks of a tragic accident.

The protests had been a disgraceful state of affairs, but had been dealt with. Nowadays, there was always a joyful crowd to greet Drake, cheering him and throwing flowers. Really, out-of-work actors would do anything for a fee.

Nor, for that matter, was every person in the crowd being paid to be there. Among a certain sector of the populace Derek Drake was much-loved, and with the activists—those professional malcontents—gone, his admirers felt emboldened to show it.

The sight of all those happy faces never failed to cheer Drake. Altogether it was the kind of image he wished could be shown around the world, to prove to the doubters and the naysayers that Britain under the Resurrection Party was a positive place, a thriving place and most of all a contented place.

THE INTERVIEW TEAM were setting up in the White State Drawing Room at Number 10. Two plush wingback armchairs, upholstered in cream damask, sat facing each other at an angle. Back lights masked with diffusion cloths were angled over them, while key lights glared baldly from tripods in front.

Drake made sure to shake the hand of every member of the team. Ingratiating yourself with the technical staff was just as essential as getting along with the on-camera talent. An interviewer could be handled, manipulated, controlled. It was the people in charge of the visuals who could really make or break you.

This lot were Russian, from one of the state-owned channels. They had been lobbying for an exclusive audience with him for months. Drake had finally relented after seeing a picture of the journalist he would be talking to.

And here she came, sashaying into the room in waisted jacket and pencil skirt.

A right humdinger of a girl. That had been Drake's opinion of the woman in the photograph, and the actual woman, in the flesh, was every bit as appetising. Her hair was long, glossy and blonde. Her lips were fulsome. Her figure—va-va-voom!

"Miss Bazanova," he said, beaming his broadest smile, and the two of them kissed cheeks like old friends. "Did I pronounce it correctly?"

"Close enough, Prime Minister."

"Or may I call you Tatjana? That would be simpler."

"You may. How are you this morning, sir?"

"Oh please. None of this 'Prime Minister' and 'sir' stuff. Call me Derek."

"Of course. Derek."

"And I'm well. All the better for seeing you. Care for a drink? Some mineral water, perhaps? I'm sure somebody can sort that for you." He clicked his fingers, and one of the Downing Street flunkies scurried out of the room. "I'm looking forward to this," he added confidentially. "I think you and I, Tatjana, will find we have much in common."

HARRIET DRAKE GOT her workout that morning, but Pilates had nothing to do with it.

She rolled off Dominic Wynne with a deep sigh, tingling all over. He, disciplined chap that he was, clambered off the bed and went to the en suite bathroom to dispose of the condom and clean himself up. When he returned to the bedroom, Harriet had wrapped a sheet around herself. It was a demure gesture, but she had left enough cleavage exposed to indicate that she might not be averse to a second go-round, once he had had time to recover.

Wynne lay down beside her, hands folded behind his head. Harriet nestled against his chest and toyed with the tuft of hair between his pectorals. For a while, neither spoke.

Then Wynne said, "I trust madam is pleased with her close protection detail."

"I am," Harriet said. "You took into account all the angles and you made sure I arrived at my destination."

"Don't forget how I scoped out the secure locations first, checking the entrances and exits."

"You were very thorough in that respect. You also definitely have a knack for manhandling your subject."

"What can I say? It's been known to get rough when the bullets start flying."

"I didn't feel threatened at all. I found it exhilarating. I only hope that, in all the excitement, I didn't cling on to my brave defender too tight."

Wynne examined the fingernail scratches down his front. "Wounds sustained in the line of duty are the best kind."

"I'll see to it you get a medal. I'll drape it on you myself."

He frowned at her. "Are we still talking in double entendres?"

"I'm not sure," Harriet replied. "I'm a bit lost, myself."

They laughed.

"You really are a life saver, Dominic," she said, her tone softening. Sincere now. "You have no idea what it was like for me before we started doing, you know, this."

"You've said. You told me he wasn't paying you any attention."

"It wasn't just that. Derek hadn't simply lost interest in me, sexually. He couldn't even get it up."

"Yes, you said that too. It's his age, I suppose."

"No. It started a few years back, while he was still relatively young."

"Was it the crash that caused it?" Wynne asked.

"The helicopter crash?" said Harriet. "Why?"

"I just thought, that kind of trauma, it might done a number on him. Messed with his head. Made him lose confidence."

"Have you met my husband? Confidence is hardly something he lacks. No, the problem pre-dates the crash by some while. Things were fine for the first decade of our marriage. I mean, the fucking was starting to become sporadic by then, but that's only to be expected. But we were still getting round to it every now and then, and even if it wasn't epic, it did the trick. Wham bam, over and done in a couple of minutes, but we both got something out of it. Then there were a few failures, a few misfires on Derek's side of things, not rising to the occasion, or rising and then falling—and after that it just became a pattern. The failures soon outnumbered the successes, and then it was one failure after another in a constant succession."

"You've been married how long now?"

"Coming up on twenty-five years. Our silver anniversary."

"So for almost ten years...?"

"Nothing." Harriet waggled a limp forefinger downwards. "No matter how hard I tried. No matter what I did. Closed for business."

"Jesus. Nightmare." Wynne shuddered, imagining himself in that predicament. "Did he try magic blue pills?"

"And counselling too. Nothing helped. You cannot imagine how frustrating it was. We were still sleeping together, but we weren't sleeping together. Derek just shied away from it. I didn't even dare raise the topic. Then came the famous helicopter crash. That seemed to put paid to any hope we had of getting the problem fixed. First, Derek had to recover from the shock. He wasn't hurt physically, but there were psychological repercussions, not least having to adjust to the death of his best friend. And then he started setting up the Resurrection Party and he was busier than ever. Up and down the country, canvassing, rallying support, getting financial backing. Hardly ever home."

"A Resurrection Party, but still no resurrection for Derek's erection."

"Ha! Yes. That's where all his energy was going, his bid for power. I hardly mattered any more."

"You didn't think about divorcing him?" said Wynne. "On grounds of, I don't know, not meeting his marital obligations."

"Oh, I thought about it. But I still love him, and we have a nice life together. He looks after me well. And then there's the 'optics', as they say. How would it look, me walking out on him? The prime minister? I couldn't be that disloyal. I knew I had to do something, though. The itch had to be scratched somehow. So a fling here, a fling there, with whoever I fancied. The man who cleans the pool. My Pilates instructor. The boy who interned for Derek for a summer, son of a friend of ours—I'm not proud about him. Some soap opera hunk I met at a fundraiser. Him I'm not proud about either, but totally worth it."

"And I'm the latest notch on the bedpost."

"You know you're not that," Harriet said, rapping him with her knuckles. "Stop fishing for compliments."

"I suppose after three years, this hardly qualifies as a fling any more. Haven't you ever worried about getting caught? Your husband finding out about your affairs?"

"I'm always discreet. Besides, I think Derek knows. He might not admit it, even to himself, but he knows, and he doesn't mind because it's his fault, pretty much."

"He doesn't know about us, though." Wynne sounded confident, but there was a question implicit in the remark.

"God, no. It's one thing to boff the pool boy, but his chief Paladin? His right-hand man? He'd go ballistic."

"But still you take the risk."

"How can I not? You're pretty damn special, Dominic. Christ, there are hundreds, no, thousands of women who'd give their left tit to be where I am right now. I've seen how they talk about you online. The Dominic Wynne forum on Mumsnet—it's pure filth."

"I must take a look at that sometime."

"You must know how sexy you are. And here I am, old enough to be your mother, and I'm the one who gets to have your cock inside her. Speaking of which…"

Her hand roved down the ridge of his abdominals.

"Is it too soon?" she said.

"Have a look. I think you'll find the answer's no."

"Oh good," said Harriet. "Because, now that I think about it, I reckon you have been neglectful in your work. You haven't been covering my rear."

"And what kind of bodyguard would I be if I didn't guard your entire body?" said Wynne, turning her over.

MEANWHILE, RECORDING OF the interview was under way.

"Derek," said Tatjana Bazanova, "you have described yourself as 'a pretty ordinary bloke'. Did I say that right? My English is not so good, and my accent…"

"Tatjana, your English is perfect, and your accent exquisite. And to answer your question, I think I am a pretty ordinary bloke. I may be the prime minister of Great Britain, with all the baggage that comes with that, but at heart I'm still just good old Derek, the type of chap, if you met me in the street, you'd think, 'He's okay. He looks like someone I could have a natter and get along with.'"

"You went to a private school. Not everybody in the UK does. That is not 'ordinary'."

"True, true, but a very minor private school, and my parents scrimped and saved to send me there. You understand that expression? Scrimped and saved?"

"I know this phrase, yes."

"And after school, I went straight into a job. Didn't go to university, get a degree, any of that. Started working in the City, and pulled myself up through the sweat of my brow. By twenty-five I was running my own hedge fund. By thirty I was a millionaire several times over. All my own work. Nobody helped me. That's the kind of can-do attitude I have. My net worth is a lot higher than that now, by the way."

"You are a Christian."

"Very much so. Regular churchgoer and proud of it."

"Can you make so much money and have Christian values?"

"Don't see why not," said Drake. "I have been as ethical in my business dealings as is humanly possible."

"But Jesus and the bankers in the temple…"

"The money lenders. And put it this way: if God hadn't wanted me to prosper the way I have, He'd have made me a pauper."

"Let us turn to your rise to power, then. Our viewers at home in Russia will be very interested in this. You had a moment of, how do you say? Clarity?"

"Well put," said Drake. "One might even call it a Damascene conversion. I was in a helicopter crash, as you probably are aware."

"I know. I have seen the footage of the wreck. You were lucky to survive."

"I was. Oh so lucky. My Bell 407 came down as we were flying back from Spain. We were over the Channel, literally just in sight of the English coast, when there was an engine malfunction. Sudden, catastrophic. The pilot, Captain John Unsworth, did his best. Brave man, he fought to keep us airborne as long as he could. Got us over land, so we didn't come down in the sea. We'd probably have drowned otherwise. Got us past Portsmouth, so we didn't hit any buildings. Brought us down in a cornfield. Hell of a landing, it was. I don't honestly remember much about it. I remember the rotors screaming. I remember warning lights flashing and a computer voice saying, 'Warning: excessive rate of descent', over and over. I remember the chopper being shaken around like a baby's rattle. I remember an almighty, thunderous thump as we hit the ground. After that, it's all a blank."

Drake shrugged, as though the accident was in the past, no big deal, he had moved on; but he allowed himself a tiny wince of distress, so that anyone watching would know it was not the sort of thing a man ever quite got over. It was never a bad idea to show a hint of vulnerability, to let people think they were peeking through a chink in the armour to the person beneath.

"You survived," Tatjana said.

"I did. Captain Unsworth, God rest his soul, did not. Neither did my long-time friend and adviser Emrys Sage, who was a passenger with me. Somehow, by some miracle, I was the only one of the three of us who wasn't killed instantly, and even then it was touch-and-go for a while. I was in a coma, near dead for several hours, and the doctors weren't sure I would pull through. But I did, I did, and that's wonderful because, if I hadn't, I wouldn't have had the honour and the pleasure of being interviewed by you right now, Tatjana."

She blushed fetchingly, tossing her hair. Drake liked a woman who could take a compliment.

"You say the crash helped you come to the decision to go into politics," she said. "Is that so?"

"It was a wake-up call," Drake said. "In the aftermath I kept asking myself, 'Derek, what do you want to do with the rest of your life? Do you want to carry on making vast sums of money? Is that all there is? Or would you like to channel that drive of yours, that ambition, that enormous reserve of get-up-and-go, into helping others?' Our country was in a right old state just then. An absolute shambles. I could see it all around me. People so unhappy, so disgruntled and resentful. Nothing functioning as it should. Public transport, healthcare, welfare, schools, the criminal justice system, all overburdened and on the brink of collapse. Too many workers, not enough jobs. And foreigners—so many foreigners over here who had no right to be here, causing trouble, putting a strain on the fabric of society, not to mention committing acts of violence. Terrible, terrible violence. You have no idea. Or perhaps you do. Your homeland has had its dark times in the past."

"It has," Tatjana agreed.

"In fact, it was seeing the Russian economy fall apart in the wake of the Soviet Union collapsing, and what it took to pull it back together, which inspired me. Strong leadership. That was the answer."

"That has always been Russia's answer to its problems."

"Yes! And we didn't have strong leaders in Britain at the time. We had pathetic, snivelling brats who were completely incapable of making a decision, not a statesman among them. Someone had to take the bull by the horns. That's another of our British sayings, 'take the bull by the horns'. It means—"

"Yes, to do a difficult thing, even though it is a risk to yourself."

"Exactly. And I said to myself, 'I like how the people in charge of Russia do business. I like how they're focused and don't let sentiment or finer feelings stand in the way of getting the job done. I want a leader like that for this country. I want to be that leader.' Then, of course, we had the atrocities."

"The Summer of Terror," said Tatjana.

"So they call it. We'd had attacks in public spaces before. People running rampant with knives. People driving vans into crowds. People blowing themselves up in busy streets. And always there'd been this sense of, 'Well, that was bad, but it's a rarity, an isolated incident, it won't happen again, it won't happen to me.' But this time it was constant. One horror after another, on a seemingly daily basis. The death toll inexorably rising. And all these politicians wringing their hands and saying something should be done, but no one doing anything! It was our country's hour of need, and our leaders were failing us!"

Drake gritted his teeth and pumped his fist. His voice had dropped to a growl. Here was righteous Derek Drake. Forceful Derek Drake. Man of power.

"Enough is enough," Drake said. "That's what I thought. That's what I said while campaigning. We couldn't have these outsiders taking diabolical liberties. We all knew who they were, and it seemed to me the easiest way of dealing with them was simply to get rid of them. Them and anyone like them. Send them packing. And if the human rights lawyers should object, and the carpers should carp, and the liberals should whinge, so be it. Let them. That was my policy, and I'm glad to say it's what got me appointed as an independent constituency MP in a local by-election and what swept my Resurrection Party into power a year later in a landslide victory, with me at the forefront."

"A landslide of populism."

"You say populism, Tatjana, I say popularity."

"Derek, is the country better for having you in charge?"

"Of course it is." Drake snorted as though he had never heard anything so preposterous. "We are a leaner, fitter Britain now. We have carved away the dead wood. We have shed the undesirable elements who were weighing us down. We have cast off the shackles of excessive, overprotective external legislation that were holding us back. Things work the way they used to, and that's good."

"Do they? Some would say Britain is no longer a player. Your economy is suffering due to lack of external investment. Multinationals have pulled out, taking their business elsewhere. Your GDP is down, so is your trade surplus, while inflation is rising and the pound is at an all-time low. Shops do not stock enough food. Doctors and teachers struggle with antiquated equipment and too little funding. The trains do not even run on time."

Ah, thought Drake. The old butter-them-up-then-stick-the-boot-in tactic. Inevitable.

The best response was always to go on the offensive.

"Where are your figures?" he said, leaning a little closer to her.

"Where are you getting these facts from? It's all very well you sitting there and spouting this sort of stuff, but without hard data, it's just so much hot air. I, on the other hand, have reliable statistics that prove Britain is a happier, wealthier, healthier place than ever it was. I could recite them all, but instead I'll ask this simple question. If it wasn't, would I be here, in Number Ten, talking to you? No. This being still a democracy, I would have been hounded out of office by now. Whereas I was recently re-elected with, once again, a substantial parliamentary majority."

"It has been suggested by some international observers that the election was not free and fair. Some citizens were turned away at the voting places. The—what is the name for them?—the ballot boxes, they were filled with false votes."

"Tatjana, Tatjana, it shames you to repeat these lies. Would you do that in Russia? No, you would not. As a great man once said, 'The people who cast the votes decide nothing. The people who count the votes decide everything.' The votes were counted, and counted accurately. The voting was a fair reflection of the electorate's will. That is the truth."

LATER, WHEN IT was over, Tatjana asked Drake if he would give her a private tour of the premises. Drake was only too happy to oblige.

"You do not stay here, do you?" she said as he escorted her upstairs.

"Not if I can help it. I prefer my own house out in the country."

"Not Chequers? Or your castle in Somerset?"

"No. Charrington Grange is larger and much nicer. Fairleigh Castle is a little too far from London, and I find Chequers a fairly grim place. And there's too much history there. All those previous prime ministers who've passed through those halls. No sense of permanence. Look, Tatjana, I feel I should apologise."

"What for?"

"I got a little testy towards the end of the interview, and I shouldn't have. I'm a passionate man, that's all. Passionate about this country, and I get cross with people when they try to talk it down. I realise you have a job to do—and you do it, if I may say, very well—but some of your questions rather pushed my buttons. I hope you aren't offended."

"Not at all," said Tatjana. "To quote from Stalin, though… How bold."

"Thought it might play well with the viewers at home."

"It very well might. Where is the bedroom?"

He showed her to the master suite, where she immediately set down her Louis Vuitton handbag on a side-table and began disrobing. Drake had anticipated this outcome but hadn't thought it would occur quite so quickly and easily. He'd been expecting at least a little more flirtation beforehand. Perhaps even dinner at a restaurant. But she seemed keen to get down to business.

"A gift," Tatjana said, stretching out on the bed in her black, lacy lingerie. "From our leader to you. In admiration."

"The feeling is mutual," Drake said, undoing his tie.

Within moments he was hilt-deep inside her and thrusting. She was eager, or at any rate good at feigning it. The distinction didn't matter to him.

He rammed like a sword into a scabbard, over and over.

The hard man of British politics.

Hardest of the hard.

SEVEN

AJIA AND SMITH headed west, leaving London. Smith had scrounged up some fresh clothing for her out of a recycling bin. None of it fitted, and the Justin Bieber T-shirt was mortifying, not least because she used to be a fan, back when she was too young to know better. The trainers were pretty decent, however, and she wasn't going around in bloodstained biking gear any more, meaning she looked a whole lot more anonymous. So, overall, a win.

They avoided main roads. Ajia had proposed the idea, and Smith agreed it was a good one. He himself was often harassed by the police, he said, and occasionally abused by civilians who would call him a layabout, a sponging bastard and, on account of his skin colour, a lot worse. There were other hazards as well, he added, although he did not specify what.

"As a general rule, the fewer people we encounter," he said, "the better."

Ajia had questions. Some of them were for Smith, but some of them were questions for herself. Such as: Why am I doing this? Why am I with this man I hardly know? Why am I accompanying him to God-knows-where when, if I had any sense, I should be running like fuck in the opposite direction? Why do I trust him?

Because he had healed her. That was one answer. Unless it had been someone else who'd fixed up her bullet wound and Smith was lying about it, but he didn't appear to be.

He had fed her, too, and he had saved her from Rich. And, what's more, he was kind. Yes, there was that incident with the frying pan, but he had done it to make a point, that was all. No harm done. In general Ajia wasn't getting any sort of rapey-creepy vibe from him. In fact, she rather liked him.

He seemed to know what was happening. That was another reason. Everything Smith had been saying made a wacky kind of sense. Especially that stuff about her speed. Ajia remembered how she had stopped running when she was in Willesden and had wondered how she could have got there from Hackney in record time. She'd thought she had simply got it wrong; she hadn't been in Hackney at all. But what if she had? And it wasn't even as if Hackney had been her starting point. The industrial zone where the policemen had tried to kill her lay further east. At a rough estimate, she had travelled thirteen miles in ten minutes. Which worked out at 78 mph.

No one could run that fast.

Nor could anyone come back from the dead.

Yet both things were apparently true of her.

They were walking beside a canal, along a towpath overgrown with buddleia and brambles, when Ajia said, "Smith, if I did die— and believe me, it's still a honking great if—might the fact that I can now move super fast have something to do with that?"

"It might," Smith replied.

"How?"

"The man we are going to meet will explain. I could paraphrase him, but it's better if you get it straight from the horse's mouth, as it were. He can articulate it far more neatly than I."

"Come on, give me a hint. Spoil the surprise."

"Really, you'll have to ask him."

"Okay, so who's Wayland the Smith? You called yourself that yesterday when you were putting that chair back together. I thought it was 'just Smith'."

Smith shrugged. "Smith is both name and job description. I prefer it. 'Wayland the Smith' is too formal-sounding, too ostentatious. But if you must know, Wayland the Smith is a character from folklore. Icelandic folklore originally, but he was adopted into Britain's. He was an elven prince."

"An elven prince? Like Legolas?"

Smith frowned.

"Legolas," she said. "From *Lord of the Rings*."

"I know who you're referring to," Smith said. "But you're confusing fiction and folklore, good fellow. Fiction is a mere trickling stream. Folklore is a river that runs much deeper, with more powerful currents. It is an artery in the nation's body. It holds the lifeblood. *The Lord of the Rings* is a story. Folklore is truth."

"Huh. Okay. So what did he do, this Wayland the Smith? What was his thing?"

"He was a goldsmith of unparalleled skill. One time, a king hired him, promising him his daughter's hand in marriage as the fee. The king reneged on the deal. He cut Wayland's hamstrings, to hobble him, so that he could not go anywhere, he could work only for the king at the palace smithy."

"Nice."

"Wayland got his own back. The king's sons wanted him to make weapons for them. Wayland killed the boys and made drinking vessels out of their skulls, which he gave to the king as a gift."

"Even nicer."

"Then he built himself some mechanical wings and flew away."

"And this guy was you?"

"No. I am an incarnation of him."

"Okay. Got it. In that case, who am I an incarnation of?"

"I have been telling you all this time," said Smith. "Good fellow."

"No, you've been calling me that, but that isn't telling me anything."

"That is who you are: Goodfellow. Robin Goodfellow."

Robin Goodfellow. The name was familiar to Ajia. Where did she know it from?

Then she remembered. *A Midsummer Night's Dream*. The

character, Puck, was also known by the name Robin Goodfellow. She even recalled a line addressed to Puck, in which he was referred to as "that shrewd and knavish sprite called Robin Goodfellow".

"I'm... Puck?"

Smith nodded. "The penny drops."

Ajia recalled another line from the play. "The same Puck who could 'put a girdle round the earth in forty minutes'?"

"You know your Shakespeare."

"Not really, but we did *Midsummer Night's Dream* for GCSE English. So I'm some sort of speed-demon fairy?"

"You have Puck's facility for moving faster than is humanly possible."

"He could turn into animals and take the form of a will-o'-the-wisp. Can I do those things too?"

"I don't know. Can you?"

Ajia thought about it. "No idea. I haven't tried. Why would I? Running is one thing. It's kind of an instinct. It feels natural, especially when I'm running from danger. But transforming into an animal?"

"Perhaps you can," said Smith. "You just haven't had the right stimulus. Or perhaps it is not among your suite of abilities. This isn't an exact science, being imbued with aspects of folkloric figures. Miracles seldom are."

"Is that how you were able to find me, back there at the park in Willesden? Because we're both a version of a folklore character, so we have some sort of instinctive connection? Like gaydar?"

"No, it was pure chance. I was out for a stroll and happened to see you leaving that shop. You tore down the road like the proverbial bat out of hell, almost faster than the eye could follow, and I intuited at once who you were. From the glimpse I got of you, you looked in a bad way, and I thought you could do with some help. Then it was a question of locating you. Had I not heard Rich yelling, I might never have found you."

"Hooray for Rich and his bench territoriality," said Ajia. "You said where we're going, there are more like us. How many?"

"Dozens."

"So, what's happened? Why are all these people dying and coming back as something else? Is it a recent thing or has it been going on for centuries?"

"Mr LeRoy has a theory, one that fits the entire phenomenon."

"And he's who we're going to see—Mr LeRoy."

Smith nodded. "He's a helpful soul. I think you and he will get on."

"How far?"

"To reach him? The last I heard, he'd pitched tent somewhere out by Oxford."

"Oxford!" she exclaimed. "But that's bloody miles! I thought it'd be, like, Hayes or Slough. We're not going to walk the whole way there, surely."

"It might take a few days."

"Let's catch a train."

"How much money do you have on you?"

He already knew her answer. "None," Ajia said. "What about hitchhiking?"

"A passing driver might well be willing to pick you up," Smith said. "But me?"

"Good point." Smith was big, intimidating-looking, male, everything she wasn't. Not to mention black-skinned, which, in today's Britain, made him a pariah. "And, although you could get there in no time by running, I doubt you could carry me."

Ajia eyed him up and down. "Someone my size give someone your size a piggyback? Hardly!"

They carried on along the towpath, Ajia sunk in thought.

Eventually she said, "One more question."

"You've asked plenty, but that's understandable. Fire away."

"How did you die?"

"Thereby hangs a tale. A long and sorry one."

"Well, you know about me and my run-in with the cops, so it's only fair. I've shown you mine, you show me yours. Come on," she cajoled. "It's not as if we're doing much else, and we've got hours of walking ahead of us. It'll help pass the time."

Smith sighed.

"But if I'm prying…" Ajia added.

"No. You're right, it is only fair. I was—"

He broke off, halting in his tracks.

"Did you see that?" he hissed.

Ajia followed the line of his pointing finger. It was aimed at the canal. A layer of duckweed covered the water's surface, and it was undulating gently where Smith indicated.

"So?" she said. "Did a fish just come up? Or was it a duck diving under?"

"Neither." Smith's expression had gone grave. He stared at the canal with an intensity Ajia found disconcerting. "It was no animal. Goodfellow, run. Run as fast as you can."

"What, leave you?"

"Go. Now!"

"No," Ajia said. "Not until you tell me—"

The next instant, a shape erupted from the canal, landing on the towpath amid a spray of water.

Crouching in front of them was just about the most hideous old woman Ajia had laid eyes on. She had a pointy nose and a liberal sprinkling of warts across her face, and her sodden dress clung to her bony form, revealing a pot belly, saggy breasts and scrawny muscles. She was festooned with water weed, her head in particular, where the slimy strands formed a kind of wig. The nails on her hands, and also on her bare feet, were crooked and long, like talons, while her eyes were the muddy brown of a brackish pond.

"Jenny Greenteeth," Smith intoned coldly. "Or is it Peg Powler? Or Nelly Longarms?"

The creature cackled. "Right first time." Her grin exposed two rows of teeth that were long, fang-like, and indeed distinctly green.

"I knew it was one of you wretched river hags, but now the Yorkshire accent gives it away. Leave us alone, Jenny. You have no business with us."

"I think I do," said Jenny Greenteeth. "You've shown your face, Smith. You could have stayed in Summer Land, where you know the likes of me will leave you alone. But no-o-o-o, instead you had to venture out into the big wide world. That makes you fair game."

"Back off," Smith warned. "I'll say it only the once. Get back into that canal, or else."

"Yeah," said Ajia. "Back the fuck off." She didn't have the faintest clue what was going on here, but she knew that siding with Smith was the safer option. Whoever—whatever—this Jenny Greenteeth was, menace radiated off her like heat from a bonfire.

Jenny Greenteeth snapped her head round to glare at her. "Keep a civil tongue in your head, child, or I'll bite it out." She sniffed the air, her damp nostrils flaring like a frog exercising its legs. "It's Puck, isn't it? Yes. Newly minted. The whiff of death still clings to you. Welcome to your second life, sprite. Pity it's going to be such a short one."

She moved towards Ajia, talons outstretched.

Not taking her eyes off the hag, Ajia said to Smith, "And now you're going to do your thing."

"My thing?"

"You know, with your..." She tipped her head in the direction of his hammer. Even if Smith preferred not to use the implement for violent purposes, he could still intimidate Jenny Greenteeth with it, the way he had Rich.

Somewhat reluctantly, Smith drew the hammer from his belt. "Last chance, Jenny," he said, hefting it in his hand.

The bluff wasn't nearly as effective as it had been at the park. Smith's heart wasn't in it. He clearly didn't think it would work on the hag.

He was right. Jenny Greenteeth glanced at the hammer and sneered.

"Hit me with that? Not likely. Everyone knows that tool is sacred to you, Smith. Everyone knows you've vowed only to create with it, never to destroy. Might as well wave a stick of celery at me, for all the good—"

That was when Ajia shoulder-barged her. While Jenny Greenteeth was distracted, she propelled herself forward with a kick of the legs, slamming headlong into the hag at blinding speed. Momentum lent her power. Jenny Greenteeth went flying off the towpath, arms windmilling, and landed in the canal backside-first with an almighty splash.

"Come on!" Ajia cried to Smith.

They began running along the towpath.

The river hag pursued them in the water. Head down, arms by her sides, body writhing, she slithered along just under the surface with the suppleness of a sea snake.

She was quick. Water seemed to be her natural element. She was moving as fast as a shark. Still, Ajia could easily have outpaced her. Had she been on her own, it would have been no contest. Smith was no great runner, though, and Ajia was modifying her speed to suit his. She refused to leave him behind.

Jenny Greenteeth soon drew level with them. Just ahead lay a steel footbridge that crossed the canal, giving access to the towpath from an adjacent road.

"Up there," Ajia said to Smith. "We're screwed as long as we stay on the towpath. Nowhere to go. Cross that bridge and we've got some wiggle room. We can lose her."

Smith was panting hard. "Good plan," he gasped. "You first. I'll be right behind you."

"No way." She grabbed his arm and pulled him along. "You're coming with."

They had just made it to the base of the steps leading up to the bridge, when the river hag burst out of the water, springing lithely onto dry land. She pounced on Ajia, raking her talons down her back. Ajia tumbled to the ground, crying out in pain.

Rolling over, Ajia found Jenny Greenteeth standing astride her. Water sluiced off the river hag's clothes and hair, dripping onto her. A foot was placed on Ajia's chest, pinning her down. Ajia squirmed but couldn't break free.

"Rip your pretty face off, you little runt," Jenny Greenteeth snarled. "Dig out your guts and eat them. Feast on your eyeballs."

"Smith!" Ajia yelled. "For fuck's sake! If you can't hit her, make something. Make something to stop her."

The river hag leered. "Don't look to him for help, Puck. He's useless. Oh, I'm going to take my time over this. I'm going to have my fun."

She lowered her taloned hands towards Ajia.

Clang!

It was the dull chime of a hammer striking metal.

Jenny Greenteeth looked up.

Clang! Clang! Clang!

A blunt metal spar shot out, lancing between Ajia and the river hag.

It was followed by another, running crosswise to the first.

Smith was hammering the footbridge steps, and with each carefully angled blow a section of steel was reshaped, elongated, bending to his will.

Clang! Clang! Clang! Clang! Clang!

In swift succession, dozens of steel spars surrounded Jenny Greenteeth, forming a jagged cage around her. Several of them were bedded deep into the ground; others were anchored by the steps from which they extruded. The river hag rattled the bars of this impromptu cage but they held fast. She was securely confined.

By now, Ajia had managed to lever herself out from under her opponent's foot. She slithered away, pushing herself up into a sitting position.

Jenny Greenteeth hissed and howled in frustration.

"Smart thinking," Smith said, holstering his hammer into his belt.

"Yeah, well," said Ajia, "desperation leads to inspiration. Nice job yourself."

He helped her to her feet. "How are you doing?"

Ajia winced. "She got me good with those nails. Obviously she's never heard of a mani-pedi. How's it look?"

Smith inspected her back. "Superficial."

"Doesn't feel superficial. Can you heal me, like you did with my bullet wound?"

"I will. Fix your torn clothing, too. But first, we should make ourselves scarce. That's quite a caterwaul Jenny is setting up. People may come."

"So we're just going to leave her there?" Ajia said, eyeing the trapped river hag. "Won't it look odd? I mean, the Wicked Bitch of the West, stuck inside what looks like an Antony Gormley installation? It's going to end up on the TV news, that's for sure.

Questions are going to be asked."

"Not our problem," said Smith. "You'd rather I freed her?"

"No…"

"Besides, this is far from being the first time Jenny Greenteeth and her ilk have shown their faces in public."

"Yeah? Then how come there's not been a big old hoo-hah about it? Look at her." Jenny Greenteeth continued to rage and gibber like a madwoman, the water weed on her head flailing to and fro. "That's not normal. That's internet-viral right there. Stick a clip of her on YouTube and you'd get a million hits within an hour."

"Jenny has allies," said Smith. "Don't you, hag? Friends in high places. Influential friends who have the power to cover up your existence and the existence of others like you."

"Piss on you!" Jenny Greenteeth growled in reply. "I shan't forget this, Smith. Next time we meet, you're dead, I swear it. You and that pathetic, simpering little latecomer. Does she know about you? Does she know the truth? Does she know what sort of man you really are?"

"We should go," Smith said, turning on his heel.

"You haven't told her, have you?" the river hag said, laughing triumphantly. "She has no idea. Wayland the Smith is a murderer, Puck. Yes! He has blood on his hands. He may not be willing to harm anyone nowadays, but there was a time. Oh yes, there was a time when he killed."

Ajia was torn. She wanted to go with Smith, but she felt a dark urge to listen further to what Jenny Greenteeth had to say.

"Ignore her, Goodfellow," Smith called out over his shoulder. "Come on."

Ajia hesitated a moment longer, then turned and followed him. The river hag shrieked at her but she tuned it out.

THEY HAD PUT half a mile between them and Jenny Greenteeth when Ajia said, "She was talking about the princes, wasn't she? The ones whose skulls you turned into mugs. That's what she meant by 'murderer'."

Smith sounded weary. "Yes."

"But that wasn't you. That was the original Wayland the Smith. You personally had nothing to do with it."

"Of course. Now, if you don't mind, I would like to drop the subject. Let's just walk."

They continued on in silence, but Ajia's mind had not been put at ease. When Smith first mentioned the princes to her, he had sounded dismissive, as though any connection between him and the perpetrator of that atrocity was tangential at best. He'd been talking about someone else. This time, by contrast, he seemed evasive. There was something he wasn't letting on.

I still trust him, Ajia thought.

Just not as much as she had half an hour ago, before Jenny Greenteeth came along.

EIGHT

THEY WALKED FOR four days.

Four days of backroads and backwaters.

Across the brow of the Chilterns, through villages and hamlets and clusters of houses too small to be called even a hamlet.

Footsoreness became Ajia's constant companion. So did hunger.

One evening, a group of travellers took them in and fed them handsomely. They slept that night in a caravan vacated specially for them. The hospitality was so generous, Ajia almost couldn't bear to leave. There were tears in her eyes as she said goodbye.

On another occasion, as they paused for a rest outside a pub, the landlady brought out sandwiches. It was a kind gesture but it carried a condition. She asked them to eat somewhere else, out of sight of the pub's clientele. The implication was clear: people like them—like Smith especially—might put off the lunchtime crowd.

Otherwise it was a case of relying on indirect charity. They helped themselves at food banks, taking whatever was available, even if there was nothing on offer except a tin of peas or a packet of rice cakes.

As for sleeping, the night in the caravan was the exception. They had to huddle under bridges or in bus shelters.

They were rained on. The sun glared down on them.

They walked.

This is what my life has come to.

The thought circled around in Ajia's head constantly.

At a stroke, through a combination of bad timing, her own bloodymindedness, and police brutality, she had lost everything. Not that she had had that much to begin with, but her world had been, if nothing else, stable. Now it was off-kilter, all certainties vanished.

Smith was sympathetic. "I appreciate how difficult all this is for you, Goodfellow, adjusting to your new reality. You wish things could go back to the way they were. For what it's worth, I felt the same."

"Felt? You don't any more?"

"I have acclimatised. I was a successful professional once. An architect, with my own practice. I had money. I had respect. You wouldn't suspect it, would you?"

"I don't know. You talk like an architect might. Proper sentences. Longish words."

"Well, that vestige of my former life remains. Everything else— gone. But the compensation is, I can still build. Just not in the way I used to."

Ajia rolled her shoulders, feeling the slight stiffness from the scars on her upper back. Smith's repair work, conducted with a few light taps of his hammer. Her new reality. This.

ON THE MORNING of the fourth day they descended into a long, shallow valley. Dawn mist was draped across the landscape in wisps, like shreds of dreams.

"Not far now, I reckon," Smith said.

From hints he had dropped during conversation, Ajia had the impression that this Summer Land place was a haven for people like them. A community of the dead-and-reborn, gathered together for safety and self-protection under the aegis of Mr LeRoy, whoever he was. She pictured a camp, somewhat like the travellers'. A field of tents, caravans and motorhomes. Ramshackle, bustling, chaotic. She could live like that for a while, she thought. Until she got some equilibrium back and could make sense of things again. Time to recoup, acclimatise—and, of course, lie low. Maybe, eventually, the police would give up looking for her. Assuming, that was, they were looking for her. And if they weren't, it still wouldn't hurt to stay out of sight for a few weeks or even months, until the whole fuss blew over.

Would she ever return to London? Would that ever be an option?

She doubted it. In the long term, her best bet was to see if she could make it to India and track down her mother and grandparents. The hardest part of that journey would be getting out of the UK with no money and no passport, but she reckoned if she could somehow cross the Channel—borrow a boat, or stow away on one—and get to France or the Netherlands, somebody there would help with the rest. Since Britain had successfully ostracised itself from Europe, numerous charitable organisations had sprung up on the near continent offering financial and practical assistance to British citizens who wished to relocate, with the tacit approval of the governments concerned. Depending on your viewpoint, this was either compassion or a calculated snub. Derek Drake certainly considered it the second of the two, accusing Europeans of facilitating an exodus that was both illegal and immoral and that was motivated by nothing other than spite. Hence checks at exit and entry points on the UK's border were more stringent than they ever had been.

Ajia and Smith arrived at a small market town, one where modern housing estates encircled a quaint, picturesque core as though the new world were laying siege to the old. A poster pasted to a disused telephone box caught Ajia's eye.

"SUMMER LAND," it declared in looping, fanciful capitals. "WHERE THE SUN NEVER SETS AND THE JOY NEVER ENDS."

She tugged Smith's sleeve. "That's not it, is it? That's not the Summer Land we're looking for."

"It is the very one," said Smith.

"Seriously?"

"Yes. Well spotted."

He squinted at the poster. To Ajia, it looked like a flyer for a travelling funfair, the kind that used to set up near her home—in West Ham Park, say, or Mile End Park—for a week or so. Her father, the grumpy sod, had always thought them a rip-off and refused to go, but her mother had taken her a couple of times and watched, smiling, as Ajia enjoyed the rides and negotiated the mirror maze. The funfairs still came, but Ajia couldn't remember when she'd last visited one.

"It's here for the next three days," Smith said, running a finger down the dates printed on the poster. "All we have to do is find where this 'North Common' is."

They got directions from a postal worker out on his rounds, and shortly they were approaching North Common, a large meadow on the town outskirts which had been designated public land. A funfair was not what Ajia had been expecting, but she was obscurely excited by the prospect. It was a lot more appealing than the image she had conjured of a rag-tag campsite inhabited by a bunch of displaced randoms who might, or might not, have powers like Smith and her. Funfairs were, well, fun.

She was quickly disabused of that notion when the fairground came into sight. Above the entrance, an arch-shaped hoarding spelled out SUMMER LAND, or would have if the placards sporting the "U" and the "L" hadn't been missing.

Summer Land itself consisted of some of the grottiest-looking attractions Ajia had ever seen. Even the word "attractions" was a misnomer. Admittedly it was early in the morning, the sun barely up, the sky still pearly grey. The funfair wasn't open, and the rides and stalls were unattended. There were no flashing lights, no jaunty music, no laughing punters, not even the smell of candyfloss to enliven the atmosphere.

But still, as she and Smith made their way through the site, traipsing along muddy paths worn by fair-goers' feet, Ajia's overriding impression was of seediness and grubbiness. Everywhere, there was rust and rotten timber. The paint on the carousel horses was peeling. The wavy slides were riddled with splinters. The shooting gallery looked like a fire hazard. The dodgems could not have been dodgier.

The artwork adorning the rides was just as bad. It was tricky deciding whether the animals airbrushed onto the sides of the waltzer were dogs, cats or unicorns. Whoever was responsible for the panels on the central column of the swinging chairs, which depicted famous buildings from around the world, he or she appeared to have only the most basic grasp of perspective, proportion and colour harmony. As for the faces on the helter-skelter, meant to convey delight, these were so cack-handedly done that they looked more like portraits of dismay.

"The artist in me is dying, just being here," Ajia remarked. "Plus, I think I'm getting tetanus."

"It isn't the most salubrious of venues," Smith said, "but you'll find, after a while, it grows on you."

"Like mould," Ajia muttered.

They came to an area at the edge of the funfair where an assortment of lorries, cars, vans and caravans were parked, higgledy-piggledy. These matched the attractions in decrepitude. The newest of them looked at least twenty years old, and Ajia lost count of the number of bald tyres she saw and the number of windows patched with gaffer tape. In some instances the vehicle's bodywork was so dirty, it was hard to tell what colour it was supposed to be.

A man was sitting on his haunches outside a Volkswagen camper van, shirtless, washing in a bucket of water. He was squat, pallid and thickset, with a bulbous nose and tiny eyes. The hair on his head was thin and lank, but his back, chest and upper arms were covered with so much of it, and so densely, it resembled fur.

Warily the man looked up at Ajia and Smith.

"Smith," he said, scowling. "You're back."

"Morning, Vic," Smith replied. "Is Mr LeRoy up yet?"

"Doubt it. Likes a lie-in, he does. You know where to look for him."

Vic resumed scrubbing his armpits with a tattered flannel.

"Friendly," Ajia murmured to Smith as they strolled on.

"You'll have to make allowances," Smith said. "Everybody here has had their share of traumas. These are damaged individuals. Outcasts, to a man and woman. A positive outlook, if they ever had any, has long since deserted them, and with it the social graces. Mind you, Vic is a boggart, and they, of course, are famously grouchy."

"Boggart? Right. I remember them from *Harry Potter*. They can change shape to resemble your worst fear."

"Fiction again. What did I tell you about fiction?"

"It's not the same as folklore. A stream, not a river."

"Precisely. Boggarts like to cause mischief, somewhere at the malevolent end of the scale. If your milk goes sour unexpectedly, or your dog goes lame, or your horse bucks you for no discernible reason, chances are a boggart is to blame."

"If only he was called Humphrey rather than Vic."

"Humphrey?"

"Humphrey Boggart."

Smith remained stony-faced.

"Not funny?" Ajia said.

"It's not that I don't get it. It's just that you shouldn't make fun of boggarts."

"He couldn't hear me."

"All the same, they don't have a sense of humour, and if you mock one, it could go badly for you. So, as a rule, it's best to play it safe."

"Okay," Ajia said. "Message received and understood."

The largest of the caravans was also the most dilapidated. It was box-shaped, with sides clad in corrugated aluminium that was coming away at the corners and that someone had daubed in a shade halfway between oatmeal and diarrhoea. Thin cotton curtains hung askew in the windows.

Smith knocked and, after a long wait, knocked again.

The door was opened, eventually, by a slender, beautiful young man wearing just his underpants.

"Oh, it's you," he said, running a cursory gaze over Smith. His eyes were perfect ovals, like polished gemstones, and his long hair, tied up in a man bun, was silvery white.

"Perry," said Smith. "Always a pleasure. I take it Mr LeRoy is still asleep."

"Bron, are you still asleep?" Perry called into the caravan's interior.

"Wide awake, dear boy," came the reply. "Who is it?"

"Smith."

Ajia liked the V-shape of Perry's torso and the way his abs flexed as he spoke. She chose to think that her admiration of his physique was purely pragmatic. One person who kept in shape appreciating another person who kept in shape, that was all.

"Smith?" said Mr LeRoy. "The Smith? My goodness! The prodigal returns. Give me a moment, Smith. I'll just pop some clothes on. You can come in when I'm decent."

A couple of minutes later, Smith and Ajia were invited in. Mr LeRoy, in a towelling bathrobe and stripy silk pyjama bottoms, made a great fuss of Smith, shaking his hand warmly and embracing him. He was a rotund man with a halo of curly golden hair and soft, cherubic features that made his age difficult to gauge. He could have been anything from forty to sixty.

"We've missed you, Smith," he said. "Is this a passing visit or are you back to stay?"

"To stay, I suppose."

"For good?"

"For a while. Can't promise anything."

"Well, a while is better than nothing. Wonderful. So many things round here need mending. Proper mending, not the bodge jobs we've had to make do with. Not that having you back isn't a delight in itself, of course, but still... I can give you a list, if you'd like."

Smith shrugged. "It won't hurt to make myself useful. Earn my keep."

Mr LeRoy turned towards Ajia. The moment he laid eyes on her, the air of warmth and affability he gave off intensified.

"Good grief!" he exclaimed. "I do believe... It can't be. But it is. It's you."

Ajia frowned. "Do we know each other?"

"Not as such," said Mr LeRoy slyly. "And yet we do, don't we?"

Ajia had to admit, there was something familiar about him. Was he an actor? Someone off the TV? He had the over-loud voice and the slightly camp thespian manner. But then, if that was the case, how come he was claiming he knew her?

"Bron LeRoy," he said, clasping Ajia's hand in both of his. "But to you, I'm more than that, and I think you realise it, my girl, don't you? You and I, we have had a relationship."

Ajia looked askance.

"Not like that!" Mr LeRoy said. "Definitely not. Which isn't to say there's anything wrong with you. You're attractive enough—for a female. But you were once my... Well, I hesitate to call it servant. Sounds so lordly. My messenger. Weren't you? You ran errands for me. And, when my spirits were low, you would sing to me, or dance, to cheer me up. You were my Puck, and I your king."

"Bron," she said. "Short for Oberon."

"Yes. Mine's the Auberon that's spelled with an 'AU' instead of an 'O', but otherwise, he and I are one and the same. Like him, I am ruler of the faery folk. Unlike him, I am also ruler of the funfair folk."

He was still holding Ajia's hand, but only now seemed to realise it.

"I do apologise," he said, letting go. "I didn't mean to make you feel uncomfortable."

"It's okay."

"My lively, lovely Puck. After all this time, we meet, or rather we meet again. It feels like fate. Please, sit down, both of you. Perry? Would you be a love and make us coffee?"

Perry busied himself in the caravan's tiny kitchenette, bashing around the kettle and the mugs with a somewhat surly expression on his face. Ajia could only assume he was Mr LeRoy's significant other and was used to being bossed about by his lover, but didn't necessarily like it.

Mr LeRoy ushered her and Smith to a bench seat which was upholstered in some coarse fabric that felt marginally softer to the touch than sandpaper.

"How good of you to bring her to me, Smith," he said, sitting opposite them.

"I thought you'd be glad."

"And you, Puck..."

"Ajia," Ajia said. "I'm not used to being called Puck, and I'm not sure yet whether I like it."

"Ajia, then, if you prefer. You have only lately joined our ranks. A relative babe in arms. If it's asylum you seek, or somewhere simply to stop awhile and take stock, you're more than welcome. Summer Land can be your home."

"Thanks," she said uncertainly.

"No pressure. Just know that you're amongst friends. Everyone here has been through what you've been through. They've known the disorientation you're feeling, the sense of dislocation, as though you've woken from a long sleep to find yourself in a foreign country. We're a family, in a strange kind of way, because of it. That doesn't mean we all get along. Some of us don't see eye to eye at all. Nevertheless there's a bond that unites us. I hope you'll come to realise it and cherish it, as we do."

"Okay." Truth be known, Ajia was feeling a little overwhelmed just then. Partly it was exhaustion after four days on the road, and partly it was Mr LeRoy's sheer, unbridled openness. People never normally were this kind unless they wanted something in return.

"There is a catch, though," Mr LeRoy said.

Here it comes.

"You'll be expected to work. Everyone at Summer Land has to pull their weight. There are no free rides. That's the rule for the punters, and that's the rule for us too. No free rides. We'll find you some sort of job, whatever suits your talents best."

"That's it?" she said. "To stay, all I have to do is work?"

"That's it. Staffing the stands, or helping out with the practical nitty-gritty like cleaning and cooking. Anywhere there's a vacancy."

Ajia thought for a moment.

"I know exactly what I can do for you," she said.

"My dear, I am all ears," said Mr LeRoy, leaning forward.

NINE

THE REDECORATING BEGAN the very next day.

Mr LeRoy supplied her with paints and brushes, none of them good-quality, but serviceable. Ajia set to work, starting with the animals on the hoardings of the waltzer. Whatever those abominations were supposed to be, they were as ugly as sin. It was almost painful to look at them.

Perching on a stepladder, she covered them over with a wash of white, sketched in fresh outlines and filled in the spaces with colour. She had decided on an undersea theme, and it was all clownfish and dolphins and lobsters and mermaids, cartoony but with a degree of polish and sophistication. For the background she depicted a coral reef set against layers of deepening blue.

Halfway through the process she thought, *Hold on a moment. I have super speed. Can't I get this done a bit faster?*

She tried, but the results were shambolic. Her hand moved too quickly for the paint to lay itself down with sufficient thickness and precision. Her brushstrokes were scratchy smears.

Better just stick to running fast.

She worked from morning until mid-afternoon, when the fair opened for business. Throughout, her constant companion was the tolling of Smith's hammer, sometimes close by, sometimes further away. He was moving around the fairground from ride to ride, repairing.

The next day, she started again, this time repainting the gallopers—the carousel horses. She chose a pastel palette, giving the horses a makeover that she thought might be garish, a bit too My Little Pony, but in the event was pleasing to look at. She added plenty of texturing and dappling, for a semblance of realism.

She couldn't finish all of them in the time available. By the following afternoon, however, the job was completed.

In the meantime, she was learning about the different beings who made up the funfair folk, as Mr LeRoy had called them.

There were perhaps sixty people in all working at the fair, and they comprised various types of faery, each with its own abilities and affinities. There were the boggarts, like Vic. They weren't exactly a barrel of laughs, and mostly they kept themselves to themselves. They ran the game stalls, such as the hook-a-duck and the shooting gallery. If a punter was doing too well, they would exert some of their malign influence, and all at once the person would experience a streak of bad luck. It kept them amused and saved money on prizes.

Then there were the elves, of which Perry, Mr LeRoy's lover, was one. They could be quite charming when they wished to be, and so they worked primarily as barkers on the rides, luring punters over with catcalls and come-ons, a talent known as glamouring. The females were as beautiful as the males, and they all preferred to wear their hair long. Often it was hard to tell one gender from the other.

The brownies were the friendliest of the lot—helpful and industrious—and their duties were mainly in the catering and cleaning departments. Brownies cooked the hamburgers and hot dogs and supervised the candyfloss and toffee apple stalls.

Pixies were small and childlike. Some of them could even pass for children. Therefore they were put in charge of the "juveniles"—the rides designed for the under-tens.

Goblins were small too, but lumbering and muscular, and not

very bright. Menial labour suited them best, although they took it in turns to manage the high striker, the machine which permitted you to test your strength by hitting a lever with a mallet to send a puck shooting up towards a bell. A goblin was strong enough to make the bell ring every time, with scarcely any effort, and punters, seeing someone small achieving this feat, thought it easy to replicate and would keep paying for yet another go until they succeeded.

Another area of responsibility for the goblins was security. They patrolled the fairground after closing time, like sentries, and if there was trouble during opening hours, they dealt with it. Ajia witnessed this for herself on her third evening with the funfair folk—the last before Summer Land decamped to another site— when a gang of local lads with a bit too much cider in them got lairy. The youths abused other fair-goers, but it was the funfair folk they were particularly offensive towards, swearing at them, spitting at them and calling them "gyppos" and "pikeys". The goblins stepped in. When the youths would not leave quietly, as invited, the goblins evicted them by force. It was not pretty to watch but it was immensely satisfying. The goblins stopped short of causing serious physical harm, which might result in police involvement, but they roughed up the troublemakers just enough to deter them from returning.

The next day, Summer Land moved on.

THE SMALLER RIDES could be folded up, becoming self-contained towable trailers. The larger ones had to be dismantled and the pieces stowed in the backs of lorries. The caravans were then hitched to the lorries.

The entire procedure, which the funfair folk had down to a fine art, took less than eight hours. By mid-afternoon, a convoy of vehicles was winding its way out from the site, leaving behind a field criss-crossed with muddy ruts and dotted with geometrical-shaped patches of flattened grass.

On her first night, Ajia had been assigned a bunk in a caravan occupied by three female brownies. The brownies were hospitable.

They were also house-proud, and the interior of the caravan was spick and span, always smelling like fresh flowers. She felt fortunate to have them as roommates.

She thought she would be travelling with these three, up front in the cab of the lorry pulling their caravan. However, Mr LeRoy asked if she would come with him instead.

"I imagine you have plenty of questions," he said. "I've been too busy to answer them. You've been rather busy yourself. That or too polite to come and pester me. Now's your chance. Captive audience."

She joined him in the back of a beaten-up old four-door Land Rover Defender, to which his large caravan was attached. Perry drove.

Mr LeRoy helped poured cups of tea for her and himself from a tartan Thermos flask. "You've done a terrific job repainting the rides, by the way," he said. "I so appreciate it."

"You're welcome. Can't say it's not been fun."

"I'd be happy for you to carry on, if you care to."

"Don't see why not."

"Wonderful. And now, those questions. Fire away, dear girl. Whatever you'd like to know."

"It's hard to know where to start," said Ajia. "So, everyone here at Summer Land, they've all died and come back to life as faeries? Yeah?"

"That's about the long and the short of it."

"How? How is this happening?"

"I have a theory," replied Mr LeRoy. "I'm not sure how correct it is, but it's the best I can do. Britain is suffering. You don't need me to tell you that. Under Derek Drake this country has gone to the dogs. We have sunk into a mire of intolerance and scapegoating. Foreigners are no longer welcome, nor is anyone who doesn't meet the criteria of white, straight and nominally Christian. We have segregated ourselves from the rest of the world, both diplomatically and economically. Our officials are corrupt and venal, part of a wealthy elite who prosper while the vast majority struggle along in increasing poverty. We are like some first-world banana republic, barely scraping by, a laughingstock to the rest of the globe. True?"

"No argument."

"You could say Britain is sick. What does the body do when it's sick? It reacts. There is inflammation. There is a fever. And I would say that we, us funfair folk, are symptoms of the sickness. We are the inflammation. We are the fever."

"What?"

"A balance has been disturbed and something has bubbled up from deep within the national psyche. Britain's collective consciousness is sending out alarm signals, and we are the heralds of that."

"That's crazy."

"Is it?" said Mr LeRoy. "Well, if you have a better explanation..."

"I don't," Ajia admitted.

"Consider, if you will, the rash of UFO sightings across America during the Cold War, particularly in the 'fifties and 'sixties. One can think of it as reflecting the paranoia of the times, the fear of being overrun by hostile external forces. In that instance, it manifested as airborne craft of great sophistication, seemingly from another planet. Were the UFOs real? Some seem to think so. Perhaps they were conjured up from some great wellspring of imagination, ideas given a sleek, technological tangibility. And in our own case, perhaps the same thing has occurred, only in a different guise. People used to tell one another stories about faery folk all the time. They were cautionary tales, but they were also a means of quantifying abstract concepts such as bad luck and explaining natural phenomena for which there was no scientific rationale as yet—storms, nightmares, crop failure, blight, disease. These myths and legends once suffused daily life at every level. They were a way of making the world make sense, and they were widely held to be the truth. You might even say they were the truth, until science supplanted them. And now here we are, with our nation on its knees, so many people needing reassurance, looking to understand why things can have gone so wrong. Some primal, organising power has responded by turning to the past, dredging up these thought-forms which once provided succour and justification, and giving them corporeality."

Ajia mulled it over.

"You're not convinced," Mr LeRoy said. "The main plank of my theory is the timing. It all follows on immediately from Prime Minister Drake's ascent to power. Everyone at Summer Land was transformed after Drake and the Resurrection Party began their campaign, myself included. I would count myself among the first, in fact. I'd only just heard of the bloody man when I had my fatal heart attack. He'd been in the news for barely a month, starting to make a name for himself, and one day I was in the company of a nice young chap, in the throes of—shall we say exertion?—when I began to experience severe chest pains."

Ajia saw Perry dart a glance at Mr LeRoy in the rearview mirror.

Jealous much? she thought. *Don't like it when he mentions previous boyfriends?*

No. The look, she decided, was concern. Perry genuinely cared for Mr LeRoy and didn't relish hearing about him at his most vulnerable.

"All at once the pain receded and I felt darkness closing in around me," Mr LeRoy continued. "I knew I was dying. It felt very peaceful, I remember. I was lying on the bedroom floor, staring up at the ceiling. I knew my time had come, and I was fine with it. But, as it turned out, my time hadn't come. I was gone, but then paramedics arrived and defibrillated me back to life. And like you, like all of us, I came back different. Altered. It took me some time to realise what about me had changed."

"What was it?" Ajia asked.

"I was aware of others. Others the same as me. I was conscious of their whereabouts. I knew where to look for them, and when I found them, I was able to counsel them and help them through the period of adjustment. It became a kind of mission for me, locating the faery folk as they appeared and taking them under my wing."

"You brought them to Summer Land?"

"I didn't own Summer Land back then, at the beginning. I was a folklorist—a professor of history specialising in early modern Britain, pre-Christian religion, paganism and suchlike. I had a tenured position at one of the lesser provincial universities. Summer Land came later, as the number of waifs and strays I was gathering around me grew and I couldn't find accommodation and employment for them all. I needed somewhere where they could shelter together, these poor lost souls who had come to rely on me for direction and leadership. A funfair happened to arrive in town, and I caught wind that the family who owned it were considering selling up. It seemed the perfect solution. I pooled together my savings, sold my house, and bought them out. So began this peripatetic lifestyle of ours."

"Do you think that's the reason you're ruler of the faery folk? Because you were a folklorist?"

"A good question, and you're right," said Mr LeRoy, nodding. "There is invariably an element of suitability in the case of each of us who becomes an eidolon."

"Okay, I have no idea what that word means."

"Eidolon. Comes from the Ancient Greek. It has several connotations. A spirit image. A simulacrum. Something which lives on after death. I've taken to applying it to everyone who has died and been returned to life imbued with faery folk characteristics."

"Right. And where does suitability come into it?"

"We weren't simply properties which were temporarily vacant, waiting for someone to come and take possession. We were each of us chosen as an eidolon for specific qualities we already had. Goblins, for example, tend to be those who were somewhat lumpen and thuggish in former life. Elves—well, they're more the aesthete sort, aren't they, Perry? Perry was an arts graduate. A ceramicist of considerable talent. Then there was some business with drugs. I don't think he wants me to go into it any further, judging by the way he's hunching his shoulders and gripping the steering wheel; so I shan't. Another factor in the eidolon selection process is nominative determinism."

"Nominative what now?"

"Determinism. The influence one's name has on one's destiny. Look at me. Auberon LeRoy. LeRoy is a version of the French le roi, meaning 'king'. Essentially I was King Oberon long before I became the eidolon of King Oberon. And you. You who have become the eidolon of Puck. Smith tells me you used to work as a bike courier, is that correct?"

Ajia nodded.

"So you've long been about going places fast," LeRoy said. "It's there in your surname—Snell—which is derived from an Old Norse word, snjallr, meaning quick and lively. I looked it up. As for 'Ajia'…"

"Urdu for 'swift'. My mother called me that because I was a month premature. Her idea of a joke."

Mr LeRoy clapped his hands. "Precisely."

"So both my surname and my given name mean the same thing? Shit. I never realised. Doubt my parents did either."

"Whether you're aware of it or not, nominative determinism selected you from the start to grow up to become someone who nips around on a bicycle delivering packages and latterly, in this new phase of your existence, Puck. You could not have been anything other than what you are, Ajia. It was written in the stars."

"Or in my birth certificate."

"That too. If you conduct a survey of the funfair folk, you'll find similar examples. One of the elves is called Faye, and another, believe it or not, Elvis. There's a brownie with the surname Neate, a goblin who goes by Hobb, and among the boggarts, tricky little devils that they are, you'll find a Rook and a Crooke." Mr LeRoy smiled with an almost childlike glee. "It's really rather fun, and it does seem to confirm my hypothesis that there's some sort of intelligence at work here. I spoke of an 'organising power', didn't I?"

"You mean, like a god?"

"No, more in the sense that nature likes patterns. Physics likes patterns too. The structure of crystals. The symmetry of a snowflake. The spiral of a snail's shell. The way the wind can sculpt sand dunes into symmetrical waves. Bees and their honeycombs. Subatomic forces in balance. Things, left to their own devices, tend towards configuration and orderliness. So it is with us. Whatever brought us back to life and recast us as folkloric beings, it wasn't random. It acted with a will. A design."

"A design," Ajia echoed. The idea was outlandish, but then her ability to run several times faster than the fastest human was outlandish, so the one thing kind of cancelled out the other.

Outlandish was her new normal. "Doesn't that imply a purpose?"

"There is a purpose. It's like I said, we eidolons are alarm signals from the collective consciousness. Canaries in the coalmine. Britain is in distress and we're its cries of pain made flesh."

"Nothing more than that?"

"Not that I can think of."

"So where does someone like Jenny Greenteeth fit in?"

"Yes, Smith told me that the two of you had a run-in with her," said Mr LeRoy. "He praised your resourcefulness and your quick thinking. Said you saved the day. Jenny and her ilk, Ajia, are incarnations of the darker side of our nation's folklore. There's us, the more or less respectable entities, and then there's them, our shadowy counterparts. I suppose you can't have the one without the other, just as you can't have day without night or light without shade. What's that saying about taking the rough with the smooth? And they are a very rough lot. They despise us funfair folk, and they'll attack us at any opportunity. That's another reason why it's useful to be on the road, constantly moving from place to place. We're less at risk that way."

"Smith mentioned other river hags."

"That isn't the end of it. Far from it. There are worse creatures out there than Jenny Greenteeth. Much worse."

"Ugh. You're kidding."

"I wish I were. Black Annis. Rawhead-and-Bloody-Bones. The Shug Monkey. The list goes on."

Ajia found even just the names unsettling. "And someone else knows about them, don't they? Smith was talking to Jenny Greenteeth after we captured her, and he said she had 'influential friends'."

"Someone in power certainly knows about Jenny and her kind," said Mr LeRoy. "How could they not? You can't have horrors like that roaming the land without it coming to the attention of the authorities. I've long harboured the suspicion that there's a conspiracy to keep the fact of their existence out of the public domain, but how high the conspiracy reaches, I couldn't say. The intelligence agencies, at the very least, have to be in on it. Does it go any further, perhaps all the way to the top? Maybe, but Derek Drake seems too much of a reactionary buffoon to be trusted with that kind of information. If he did know, his first instinct would be to have all of the monstrous eidolons eliminated. Since they continue to be at large, one can only assume he has been kept in ignorance."

"If the intelligence agencies know about those other eidolons, surely they know about our kind as well." Ajia was surprised to hear herself say "our kind". Even after only a few days, she was beginning to realise she belonged with the funfair folk. Whether she was comfortable with this was another matter.

"They might do," said Mr LeRoy, "but then we can pass for ordinary humans, can't we? And Summer Land enables us to slip around the country practically unnoticed. Who looks twice at the people operating fairground attractions or doling out candyfloss? Provided we don't draw undue attention to ourselves, we can continue to go undetected and unmolested by the people in charge. Long may that situation persist."

TEN

ONE OF THE great drawbacks of being a national leader was that you got very little time to yourself. You were obliged to attend meetings, play host to dignitaries from overseas, sign countless documents and make the odd appearance on broadcast media and in public, not to mention show your face in parliament most days. Rarely did you get home before midnight. In fact, Derek Drake wished someone had told him in advance just how much damn work was involved. He might have thought twice before launching his bid for political supremacy.

Then again, his country had been in its hour of greatest need. Britain had been crying out for someone like him—another Churchill, another Thatcher—to pull it out of its death-spiral. He could not have refused to heed the call. His conscience would not let him.

Nonetheless, in order to maintain his sanity and his sense of self, Drake made sure there was always room in his daily schedule for three morning engagements. They were sacrosanct.

The first was his session with his cosmetician.

The second was breakfast with Harriet. He never missed that. They might not talk much at the table, but at least they were together in the same room. It kept alive a marital connection which even he had to admit was held together by the slenderest of threads these days.

The third was his visit to his collection of holy relics. This was an opportunity for Drake to reflect on the greatness of God and remind himself that his position of power was nothing short of divinely-appointed. Although it wasn't just that. It was much more.

The interior of the converted stable block which served as his private museum was a self-contained microclimate. Air conditioning held the temperature steady between 16 and 20°C, the chilly side of warm, while dehumidifiers maintained a constant relative humidity of 30%. Certain artefacts, the parchments ones in particular, needed a dryer atmosphere than that to preserve their integrity and so were kept in vacuum-sealed cases.

In all, the relics numbered nearly a hundred, the product of three decades of assiduous collecting. In his younger days, when Drake had had more spare time, he would travel far and wide across the world to source and buy the items. Later, he had relied on commissioned agents to do the legwork for him, although more often than not he would fly in to make the actual purchase himself. There was nothing quite like the thrill of authorising a bank transfer on his phone, or sometimes handing over a suitcase full of cash, and holding his new acquisition in his hands for the first time.

The collection included numerous body parts of saints. Drake owned fingers belonging to canonised individuals; a couple of whole mummified hands, one a man's, the other a woman's; a few skulls; a nose; a toe; even what looked like a shrivelled hoop of beef jerky, which he had on good authority was a foreskin. Most of these treasures were contained in reliquaries—caskets made of silver, gold or varnished hardwood.

There were phials of blood, ornate things of crystal and filigreed metal, more than one of which had been officially venerated by a pope.

There were several splinters of the True Cross and a brittle twist of twig which had formed part of the Crown of Thorns. There was a rusty nail reputed to be one of those driven into Christ's hands when He was crucified, and a flake of iron from the blade of the lance with which the Roman soldier Longinus pierced His side, the so-called Spear of Destiny.

There was a tiny fragment of linen which had been cut neatly from the Turin Shroud, and another similar shred of material from the Sudarium, the cloth used by the Saint Veronica to wipe sweat and blood from Christ's face as He made His torturous way towards Calvary.

There were effigies of Christ and the Madonna which were reputed to have wept blood, and there were a number of ikons and Bibles which had performed miracles for people who had prayed before them, curing ailments or bringing financial windfalls.

The collection had cost Drake a significant chunk of his personal fortune. The prices of the relics themselves had been steep, of course, but there were additional expenses. More often than not, Drake had to supply a replica of the artefact as a substitute for the original, a plausible fake that could be put on display so that the faithful would still have something to worship. Church officials had to be bribed, as did customs officers, and in neither case did the turning of a blind eye come cheap. It wasn't a poor man's game, amassing the most extensive private showcase of religious artefacts on the planet. Far from it.

But it was worth every penny.

Derek Drake was an unswerving believer. He had been since boyhood. It wasn't fashionable for a kid growing up in the 1970s to go to church, study the Bible, and openly espouse Christian values. His parents weren't religious, or rather they were Church of England, which was much the same thing as being not religious, and it surprised them that their son, their only child, should be quite so devout.

He'd got quite a bit of stick for it from his peer group, too. He wouldn't go so far as to call it persecution, but his Christianity had set him apart from his friends and schoolmates, no doubt about that, and made him the butt of their jokes. "The Reverend Derek," they would jeer. "Say a prayer for us, will you, your holiness? Sing us a hymn!" Rising above their teasing had been one of his great achievements. In accordance with our Saviour's advice in the Sermon on the Mount, no less, Drake had turned the other cheek, and had felt pleased with himself for doing so.

Nor was it easy working in the City and having faith, especially during the 'eighties when the mantra was greed and Mammon was the deity adored by all. Drake had joined in the orgy of money-making with enthusiasm. The Bible's admonition about the rich man and the eye of the needle didn't apply to him, he thought. There was no harm in wealth as long as you weren't vulgar with it. There were plenty who roared around the Square Mile in Porsches, drank only the best champagne, and bragged about their brick-sized mobile phones to anyone who cared to listen. Drake did not mind having the good things in life, but he did not make them the centre of his existence and never let them distract him from the Lord. Faith was his rudder, material belongings just the cargo he carried.

Besides, by then he had started buying holy relics. A good proportion of his disposable income went on those. That surely was some kind of compensation, wasn't it? An indulgence in both the secular and the religious sense. A way of balancing the scales of his soul, by turning excess profit into tangible representations of faith.

Still, there had been times when Drake had felt conflict within himself and wondered whether he shouldn't quit his job and find some worthier form of employment. It even occurred to him to take a degree in theology and see where that led. Might the man who, as a boy, had been mocked as "Reverend Derek", one day be ordained as a genuine priest?

It was Emrys who helped reconcile Drake's inner struggle.

Emrys Sage was a senior partner at Thurlow, Sage, Wright Ltd., the hedge fund management company Drake joined in the late 'eighties. From the outset, Emrys and Drake had hit it off, even though they came from very different backgrounds. Emrys was a softly-spoken Welshman, son of a coalminer, state-educated, who had left the pit-scarred valleys of Merthyr Tydfil in 1961 and come to London with nothing but a few pounds in his pocket and a molten core of ambition.

On the face of it, he and Drake—English, middle-class, public school, twenty years his junior—had little in common. What they shared was faith. Emrys was a Methodist. "Not practising but not lapsed either," he would say, adding with a laugh, "Can't even conform to being a nonconformist, can I?" But he retained a firm belief in a divinely-ordered world. God had not only created life, He had laid down the precepts by which it should be lived, and they were simple. You did what your inner promptings told you do, because those were messages from the source of all truth, the Lord. Each person had that voice within them and should listen to it. Anyone who didn't was no better than a beast.

"My own late father is a perfect example," Emrys once told Drake. "A man who knew he shouldn't get drunk and beat his wife and children, yet did just that on a regular basis. I could see the pain in his eyes as he took his belt to my mam and my sisters and me. It was deep in there, almost buried, but I could see it. He knew he was doing wrong and he hated himself for it, but he couldn't stop. The animal in him took over. I see it in so many other people too. They crash around, doing harm to themselves and others, all because they have lost touch with their God-given purpose."

Emrys's worldview was eschatological. Even after the Cold War sputtered to a close, he worried that humankind would sooner or later destroy itself. Throughout the 'nineties and into the new millennium he saw portents of inexorable corruption and decline everywhere. The environment deteriorating. Rogue states gaining weapons of mass destruction. Terrorist bombings. Increasingly unreliable and unstable national leaders. Banking crises. It all seemed to be coming to a head, events building to an apocalyptic climax.

"Somebody needs to take things in hand, Derek," he said. "Somebody needs to stop the rot, before it's too late."

By then, Emrys had become more than a friend to Drake. He had become a mentor, a surrogate father. He often accompanied Drake on his relic-buying trips, and the two of them would spend hours just talking, discussing the global situation and what might be done to put it right.

"It has to begin here," Emrys said, "in this country. You can't hope to effect worldwide change without getting your own house in order first. Britain should set the example for others to follow. We should show everyone how it can be done."

Drake had never harboured any political aspirations. He was content making the company's investors and himself richer, all the more so since Emrys had helped quell his misgivings. Drake's inner voice, the voice of God, consistently told him it was okay to earn his living this way. In submitting to his own will, Drake was submitting to God's will too.

But gradually it was becoming clear to him that Emrys had some grand project in mind and that he, Derek Drake, was instrumental in it.

"Derek, you have a charm about you," Emrys said. "You have a confidence that falls just the right side of swaggering. Somehow I think you could, should, be more than merely a hedge fund manager. You are meant for a higher calling."

By that time Drake had begun experiencing problems in the bedroom department. He and Harriet had been married for over a decade and he loved her dearly but no longer was able to prove it physically. The anguish of that, coupled with a sense of the loss of his masculinity, was a continuous background throb in his mind. He was feeling the desperate need to prove himself somehow, to show that he was still potent in some way.

He and Emrys began putting together thoughts about a new political movement, one which would reject the modern fad for inclusiveness and diversity and return Britain to the values of yore. The time for a multicultural nation was over. That experiment had failed. The proof lay everywhere: in the grumbling discontent of the disenfranchised white working class, in the restless ethnic ghettos which were springing up in cities all across the land, in the fear of causing offence to others that was inhibiting people's right to free speech, in the rapid decline of Britain's standing on the world stage. What was needed now was a shake-up. A purging of interlopers and other detrimental elements. A reassertion of the qualities which had once made the country a global power and the envy of others.

A resurrection.

On a journey to Madrid, Drake and Emrys thrashed out the details of their vision for a new Britain. This was the relic-buying trip to end all relic-buying trips, since Drake was about to hand over a seven-figure sum to a fairly shady individual in exchange for the Chalice of Doña Urraca, an onyx cup which was widely considered to be the Holy Grail. A facsimile of the cup currently sat in the Basilica of San Isidoro in Léon, in northwest Spain, while the original had been withdrawn from display and was supposedly kept under lock and key in a safe location, a vault somewhere. This was because the popularity of the chalice had been drawing crowds too big for such a relatively small church to cope with. The replacement, which everyone knew to be a copy, remained an object of curiosity, but no longer were worshippers queueing out the door and round the corner.

In fact, unbeknownst to the church authorities, the original cup had itself been supplanted by a counterfeit. It had fallen into the possession of an industrialist with underworld connections who, like Drake, had an abiding interest in holy relics and few compunctions about how he obtained them.

The man, José Molinero, was also an inveterate gambler and had got deep into debt with Branimir Stojanović, boss of one of the Serbian gangs operating an illegal football betting syndicate in Spain. Molinero needed a lot of money, fast, or else Stojanović was going to exact his pound of flesh—probably literally—from Molinero's two teenage sons. The chalice was perhaps Molinero's most valuable single asset and one he could liquidate without alerting the tax revenue service, since they were unaware he owned it in the first place. That was as long as he could find a buyer with a relaxed approach toward legality.

Drake had arranged for the chalice's provenance to be verified by an expert in religious antiquities who had that admirable combination of qualities, a taste for the high life and a tendency not to ask awkward questions. The cup was, the expert said, the real thing, in as much as it matched perfectly pictures he had seen of the Chalice of Doña Urraca and the jewels which encrusted it were not fakes. As for its age, the onyx could be dated back to the early

Christian era at least—the jewels had been added later—and the manufacture matched that of other carved vessels from first-century Jerusalem. The cup was authentic to the period and place it was said to originate from, although whether it was the actual Holy Grail remained open to debate.

Drake knew that the chalice had been associated with several miracles during its history. That was good enough for him.

He and Molinero met at the man's gated compound in Pozuelo, an affluent suburb of Madrid. Funds were transferred. The chalice was handed over. Both Molinero and Drake heaved a sigh, the one of relief, the other of something approaching ecstasy.

It was as Drake and Emrys were flying home in Drake's private helicopter that the crash occurred. The crash that was to prove fatal and, indeed, fateful.

THE MOMENT DRAKE first laid eyes on the chalice at Molinero's house, snug in its bed of pre-cut foam inside a steel briefcase, he had a clear sense that it was meant to be his. The cup had a long and storied past. It had travelled far and wide, from Jerusalem to England courtesy of Joseph of Arimathea, from there to Cairo and on to Castile, where it had been given as a gift to King Ferdinand I of Léon. He in turn had bequeathed it to his daughter Urraca of Zamora, from whom the chalice derived its nickname. Finally, after a few further twists and turns, it had wound up in the hands of Derek Drake, and a more deserving owner there could not be. The cup was the ultimate goal of a relic collector like him, a holy grail in more ways than one.

Now it resided in a special chamber in his museum at Charrington Grange, and Drake never approached it without reverence and awe. Anything else would have been disrespectful. There was not a shred of doubt in his mind that it was genuinely the Holy Grail, the cup which Christ had drunk from at the Last Supper and which Joseph of Arimathea had used to catch drops of His blood at the Crucifixion. This was not even an article of faith with him. He knew it to be fact because he had seen the Grail's divine power in action. He owed everything to it. Everything he was. Everything he had become. Everything.

Today, on a brisk, sunny morning in late April, Drake made the usual jaunt over from the house to the museum. The code for entry was two, zero, six, four. The pattern described by his moving finger on the door's numerical keypad mimicked someone making the sign of the Cross. Spectacles, testicles, wallet and watch, as the old joke had it.

Inside, Drake sauntered past the lesser items in his collection, making for the Grail chamber. Access to this subsidiary room entailed a much more sophisticated procedure than the outer door. Full biometric data input: retinal scan, fingerprint confirmation, voice identification.

Sitting on a pedestal lit from above by a single spotlight, the chalice gleamed. The chamber—cylindrical, concrete-walled, soundproofed, as impregnable as any panic room—was some eight yards in diameter and four high, and the Grail's presence filled every cubic inch of it. Drake felt a familiar crackle in the air, like static electricity. He could hear a faint, omnipresent humming, similar to tinnitus but deeper, more resonant.

As the door slid shut behind him, he knelt in front of the pedestal and bowed his head. Minutes passed, Drake praying in silence, as though sharing some intimate communion with the Grail.

Then, at last, the Grail spoke.

"Derek."

The fact that the Grail addressed him in the voice of Emrys Sage no longer surprised Drake, if it ever had. He was accustomed to hearing those forthright Welsh cadences emanating from the chalice. He couldn't think of anyone whose voice he would rather it used, or whose voice was more fitting.

"I bend the knee in supplication," Drake said, still genuflecting.

"You are a good and faithful servant," the Grail said.

"And you, the bringer of hope and realiser of dreams."

"With you, I am shared among the people."

"And without you, I am nothing."

This was their habitual greeting, a kind of call-and-answer liturgy.

It had evolved over the years, almost of its own accord, and was, to Drake, the most purely solemn act he participated in, akin to being freshly baptised every single day.

"Tell me your news," the Grail said.

In this room, kneeling before the Grail, like a congregant in the confessional, Drake was only ever truthful.

"The economic figures aren't encouraging," he said. "There's further evidence of capital flight. Just this week, two more international banks have said they're mothballing their UK operations. Three national retail chains have posted profit warnings. The FTSE index dropped another fifty points yesterday. Manufacturing output is still on the decline. There've been riots outside a number of hospitals. Not enough doctors, not enough medicine, patients not getting treated."

"There will always be troubles. You have to accept that."

"Still? After nearly seven years? I thought we'd be past that."

"Britain stands firm, does it not?" said the Grail. "The country endures."

"But..." It pained Drake even to consider the idea that the Resurrection Party administration—the project he and Emrys Sage had concocted together—might be failing in its aims. "We did everything right. We got rid of the undesirables. We pulled out the weeds by the roots. People should be reaping the benefits. This should be the Promised Land. Instead, all we have is discontent and disruption."

"Sounds a lot to me like you're whining, Derek."

One thing Emrys had never been able to abide was a whiner. Neither, it seemed, could the Grail.

"I just want to know, when is it all going to come good?" Drake said. "All the effort I've put in, the sacrifices I've made—when is it going to pay off? I keep putting on a brave face for the media. I tell them everything's terrific, nothing to worry about, Britain is booming, happiness and prosperity for all. When can I say that without it being a lie?"

"Change takes time. Nobody said this would be easy. I certainly did not. There was always going to be a period of adjustment. You just have to tough it out."

Drake gave a hesitant nod. "Then there are those awkward characters."

"Protestors?"

"No. Oh no. We've got a handle on them. The police are very keen on clamping down on anything that carries the slightest whiff of subversion or opposition. Over the weekend they broke up no fewer than five demos. Baton charges, CS gas, water cannon, the works. They love it. No, I'm talking about the... you know, imaginary beings."

"Hmmmm." Like Emrys, the Grail was fond of a sustained, wordless murmur. Emrys had had a beautiful singing voice; it made a sound like a bass chorister holding a low note. "Any of them in particular been difficult?"

"One of the river hags. Annie Greenteeth?"

"Jenny."

"That's it. Jenny Greenteeth. Someone walking their dog beside a canal came across her. She was stuck inside some sort of metal contraption. It required firefighters with cutting equipment to free her. Then we had to implement the usual containment protocols. Paladins convinced the dog walker and firefighters that what they had seen was nothing more than a piece of performance art. A journalist from a local rag came sniffing around the story. She was disincentivised from pursuing it further. Rather easily, it must be said. She's single, no partner, no kids of her own, but she has a beloved sister and a nephew and niece she dotes on. Everyone has their pressure points. As for the creature herself, she has been taken into custody."

"So?" said the Grail. "It would appear your people had everything under control."

"But they're not under control, are they?" said Drake, grimacing in frustration. "That's just it. There are so many of these things on the loose and they're so damn elusive. My Paladins snag one or two of them and lock them up at Stronghold, but most of them get away or simply won't be found. We're constantly playing catch-up, and it's an absolute bloody nuisance. And who put the Greenteeth monster in a makeshift cage? That's what I want to know. How did that happen?"

For a time, the Grail was silent.

Then it said, "You know as well as I do why they exist, these legends. Why they have assumed flesh."

Drake lowered his head in acknowledgement. "Yes," he said softly. "You've told me before. It's for the same reason I am still alive and I am Britain's saviour."

"It was spontaneous. It was unstoppable. So much power was released at once, it could not go into you, not all of it. It had to be dispersed."

"And we're stuck with a mess we have to clean up."

"You overstate the case," the Holy Grail said. "It's an inconvenience, that's all, and you must not let it distract you from your mission. You still have much to do. You have a reputation to live up to. The role you are fulfilling is one of the most important, if not the most important, ever. You must continue to prove yourself worthy."

DRAKE LEFT THE museum chastened and reinvigorated. The Holy Grail had just given him a salutary lesson. Buck up your ideas. Stop being a wimp. At Thurlow, Sage, Wright Ltd., Emrys had often been a harsh taskmaster. He wanted the best from people and he got it through cajoling, coaxing and the occasional bit of well-intentioned bullying. His man-management skills were one of the traits Drake had most admired about him.

The truth was, Drake and the Grail did not always agree on everything, just as in their City days he and Emrys had not agreed on everything. Emrys, while alive, had more than once called him reckless and said that his wilder impulses needed curbing, usually after a trade went wrong and Drake had lost money for the company. Even when Drake went into politics—a decision bolstered by Emrys's urging—there had been instances of tension between them. The Summer of Terror was a case in point: Emrys had not been happy about that at all. He had understood why Drake had exploited it as a stepping stone to power. He had been less certain about other aspects of the event. "Ask yourself what you have gained," he had said, "and whether the price is worth it." To which Drake had replied, using the kind of economic terminology that Emrys should have appreciated, that simple cost-benefit analysis would prove him right in the long run.

Even in his new incarnation as the Grail, Emrys had sometimes openly doubted Drake's judgement, and now and then had become somewhat exasperated with him. The frequency of such instances, however, had declined noticeably over the past two or three years. If anything, Emrys had been getting milder in his reproofs, becoming a mellower proposition all round. Drake took this to mean that he, as Prime Minister, was getting things right more often than wrong.

On his way back to the house, Drake allowed himself a small grin. There were some who might say that the Grail did not actually speak to him. That he only imagined it. That its voice was inside his head. There were some who might even think that he was in some way schizophrenic and that the conversations he was holding with the Grail were in fact conversations with himself.

Anyone who thought that, knew nothing.

As his Bell 407 plummeted to earth in a field just north of Portsmouth, Drake had clutched the steel briefcase containing the Grail, praying harder than he had ever prayed before. Above the screaming of tortured metal, the grinding of the broken rotor and the shrill alarms from the dashboard, he had heard himself begging for life at the top of his voice. Emrys, in the passenger seat to his left, had been clinging on to the armrests, teeth gritted. Captain Unsworth had been grappling with the cyclic and the collective and pumping the anti-torque pedals for all he was worth, battling to keep the aircraft horizontal and stable. If either of the other men had been beseeching God for help, Drake had seen no sign of it. Only he, of the three aboard, had been invoking divine intervention.

And the Grail had answered.

It was the only explanation.

At the moment of impact, the power of the Holy Grail had spilled out, enfolding Drake and cocooning him. He alone had survived the crash because he alone had been begging God to save him.

It was, everyone said, a miracle that he had not been killed. Drake had seen pictures of the crash site. The helicopter's fuselage was like a shattered eggshell. Pieces of debris were strewn across a whole acre of prime arable land. Air accident inspectors determined that the cause had been a faulty main rotor gearbox. Bearings inside the second-stage planet gear had come loose, resulting in a sudden, catastrophic failure. Shards of metal had hurtled outward. One had collided with a rotor vane, resulting in significant damage. The vane had sheared off, striking the tail boom and compromising the rear rotor. From then on, the Bell had been hopelessly crippled and utterly doomed.

Drake himself was hauled from the wreckage by a couple of Polish-immigrant farmworkers who had been cropping an adjacent field with combine harvesters. He was barely conscious but, by all reports, he would not let go of the briefcase, which was itself unscathed. He was comatose for a week, and the first thing he asked about when he came round was where the briefcase had got to. It turned out that it had been handed to Harriet for safekeeping, along with the rest of his personal effects. He demanded that it be brought to the hospital and placed by his bedside. The next time he was alone, Drake opened the lid and inspected the Grail. The chalice in its foam insert was intact, as he had hoped and expected. He vowed there and then that he would not let it out of his sight until he could find a secure home for it.

It was during the ensuing weeks of convalescence that the Grail first spoke to him. To begin with, Drake assumed the chalice was addressing him in Emrys's voice because he missed his dear friend. He had been unable to attend the funeral service. Doctor's orders. Although Drake was in surprisingly rude health for a man who had just spent a week in a coma, he was told it was medically unadvisable for him to leave hospital. Maybe it was guilt about that, or a more general survivor guilt, that was making him hear Emrys talking.

But the voice from the Grail persisted. And Drake listened. And he learned that, as he suspected, the Grail had engineered his survival. The Grail had given him a new lease of life.

"You prayed to me," the Grail said. "Never have I been prayed to with such sincerity or such need. You awoke me from dormancy. You summoned out of me all the power that is mine to bestow."

The upshot of this was that the Grail had inadvertently distributed its blessings elsewhere at the same time. As Drake understood it—and even he would have to admit that his grasp on the principles was shaky—too much mystical energy had been released at once for one body to contain. It would have destroyed him, like a balloon being filled with air until it popped. In a great outpouring of God-given might, the Grail had sent sizzling tendrils of its essence in all directions, arbitrarily touching people other than him and altering them.

In many ways it was Drake's own fault that all manner of strange, awful beings now infested Britain. Not that he could have known that that would be the consequence of his actions. He had just wanted to live, and thanks to the Grail he had managed to. But he'd been left with a permanent inconvenience, like a hangover that would not go away.

Hence the Paladins. They weren't merely bodyguards. Drake had put together a special unit of service personnel and MI5 operatives not only to provide him with protection but to tidy up the fallout from the Grail's activation. Each of them had been handpicked and personally vetted by Drake, and each could be relied on for loyalty and discretion.

Not least their leader, Major Dominic Wynne.

MAJOR DOMINIC WYNNE, who at that very moment was supervising the transfer of the bedraggled hideosity known as Jenny Greenteeth to a secure location: Stronghold, the Paladins' headquarters five miles outside Swindon.

And who was very much looking forward to the next time he could fuck his boss's wife.

He was in the back of a Paladin rendition vehicle, a ten-wheeler truck with an integrally-built containment unit. The rear doors of the containment unit were half-inch-thick steel, as were the sides and roof, which were reinforced by tungsten carbide ribs. Wynne shared the space with five other Paladins, all fully armed, and the creature known as Jenny Greenteeth.

Jenny Greenteeth, bound with enough chains and padlocks to restrain an elephant, hissed and snarled at her captors. When that didn't get a rise out of them, she called them foul names, and when that didn't work, she spat.

Eventually Wynne said, "Do you want me to use this again?" He held up an electric prod.

That cowed her. He had delivered a shock with the prod once already, just to let Jenny Greenteeth know who was in charge here, and she seemed to have no desire for a second helping.

"Yeah, thought so. They're all piss and vinegar till they get fifty thousand volts up the arse."

Next to him on the bench seat his second-in-command, Lieutenant Noble, sniggered.

The rendition vehicle entered the Stronghold compound via its one and only gate, bypassing three layers of electrified fence with landmined strips of ground in between. A short access road led to the main building, which was large, circular and divided internally into wedge-shaped sectors. Purpose-built, the structure served multiple functions: command post, barracks, detention centre and more. It had cost the taxpayer a little under £20 million and been constructed in record time by a workforce consisting largely of East European labourers on temporary visas, who had been summarily deported the day after completion of the project.

In a basement level, Jenny Greenteeth was borne by forklift truck past a guard station and along a broad corridor lined on both sides with solid steel doors, each the entrance to a cell. Wynne and the five other Paladins marched behind. Still seething about her captivity, she managed to keep from speaking again until the forklift arrived at the door marking the windowless, ten-yard-square chamber where she would be spending the rest of her days.

"Why don't you bastards go after the other lot?" she said.

"Shut it," said Wynne, waving the prod under her nose.

Jenny Greenteeth was not to be deterred. "It's always us, isn't it?

The obvious ones. Never the ones who pretend they're normal."

"The fuck you rabbiting on about?" snapped Lieutenant Noble.

"You mean you don't know?" the river hag said with a kind of preening puzzlement. "Surely you must. All this time you've been persecuting my kind, harassing us, rounding us up, you haven't realised there are others out there? A different breed?"

"Sir, want me to zap her?" Lieutenant Noble asked Wynne. He too was carrying a prod. "Or I could just..." He patted the sidearm holstered at his hip, a Glock 17. "Double-tap to the head. Save us a whole lot of bother. Plus, get us some payback for Hemmings."

Hemmings was one of the Paladins who'd been involved in the operation to secure Jenny Greenteeth. While he and three others had been subduing her and putting on restraints, she had caught him sidelong with her talons, dislodging his helmet and slashing open the lower portion of his face. The wounds were not life-threatening, the doctors said, but Hemmings would be permanently disfigured.

"Hold on," said Major Wynne, pensive. "These others. Can you tell me anything useful about them? Such as perhaps where we could find them?

"Hee hee hee!" Jenny Greenteeth cackled like something demented. Her body shook hard enough to make her chains rattle. "I don't believe this. You Paladins, so puffed-up, so proud of yourselves. Think you've got it all sorted, with your weapons and your stupid uniforms. But you haven't even heard of Summer Land."

"Isn't that a supermarket chain?" said Noble.

"I thought it was a rock festival," said another Paladin.

"It's where they all gather," said Jenny Greenteeth. "Their safe space. The piece of shit who trapped me in that cage, Smith, he lives there most of the time. He was headed there when I ran into him—him and the tricky little bitch with him. I overheard the two of them talking. Smith was bringing her to meet LeRoy. LeRoy's the man who runs Summer Land. King of the fucking faeries."

Wynne rolled his hand in the air, a keep talking gesture.

"No," said Jenny Greenteeth. "If you want more, you're going to have to offer me something in return."

"Such as?"

"Freedom."

"Not a chance."

"Worth a try," said Jenny Greenteeth. "How about a room with a view?"

"Down here? I don't think so. What if I let Lieutenant Noble shoot you instead?"

"Any time, sir." Noble drew his Glock and chambered a round. "Just say the word."

Jenny Greenteeth eyed the gun speculatively. "Then you've got nothing to bargain with."

"Apart from your life," said Wynne.

"My life is over anyway. I'll fester down here forever, won't I? Might as well be put out of my misery."

"Name one thing that might make incarceration more tolerable for you."

"Water," Jenny Greenteeth said straight away. "Plenty of water. Soak me daily. Douse the floor of my cell with it. Water is treasure to me. It's my home. If I'm never to know the caress of a river current again or the warmth of a summer pond, the slipperiness of a stream or the pounding of a waterfall, let me have the next best thing."

Her expression was plaintive. She was even trying to smile, although all this did was show off those repulsive teeth of hers, grey-white fading to green at the gum line, like a row of leeks. Wynne felt a pang of something that was not quite sympathy; more a kind of detached pity. It reminded him of some of his one night stands, how they'd look at him the morning after with eyes cloyingly full of hope. They honestly thought he might want to see them again. As if.

"All right," he said. "You have a deal. Once every morning and evening, we'll hose you down."

"Thank you. Oh, thank you!"

"Now tell me more about this Summer Land."

LATER, WHEN HE was upstairs and could get a signal, Wynne phoned Drake. He relayed the information Jenny Greenteeth had given him.

"Did you have any idea about this, sir?"

"These 'others'?" said Drake. A momentary pause. "No. Is she telling the truth?"

"It isn't the first time I've heard mention of a secondary group of creatures, distinct from the likes of Jenny Greenteeth. Most of the things occupying the cells at Stronghold are incapable of intelligible speech. They're monsters that can't do much apart from gibber and roar. There are several, though, who are more or less sentient, and a couple of them have muttered about a separate race. A superior race who keep themselves to themselves, stay aloof from the rest. I just thought they were rambling, or trying to deflect attention elsewhere. Now I'm not so sure. Besides, Jenny Greenteeth hasn't got anything to gain by lying."

"Except a concession to her comfort."

"You didn't see her, sir. She was desperate."

"Desperate people will say anything."

"At the very least, I think it's worth checking out."

"I agree," said Drake. "If there are significantly more of these creatures out there than we realised and they're all in one place, it seems too good an opportunity to pass up."

"So I have full sanction to track down this Summer Land funfair?"

"You do."

"And if they have numbers and mount a resistance...?"

"You know how to handle it, Dominic."

That tacit confirmation was all he needed. Wynne was being invited to use his discretion. Should the people of Summer Land prove difficult, he and his Paladins were entitled to respond with lethal force.

This excited him almost as much as the prospect of another tryst with Harriet Drake.

ELEVEN

AJIA NOTICED THE four of them strolling around Summer Land—three men and a woman. They were different, not the typical punter. The way they moved, the way they looked around them, made them stand out. They were smiling, enjoying themselves, but there was a tenseness about their body language, as though despite all the entrancing lights and jaunty music they were on the alert.

She was helping out at the candyfloss stand that evening. Maya—one of the brownies who ran it, and a roommate of Ajia's—was feeling under the weather, so Ajia stepped in to replace her. It was no chore. Working the candyfloss machine was fun. She found it deeply satisfying to dip a stick into the whirl of sugar strands and stir it against the flow to create a pink cloud, almost like making something out of nothing. And who didn't love candyfloss? Even grownups grinned as they took their first bite and felt feathery sweetness in their mouths.

The four people ambled past the stand several times. Usually it was all of them together, but they split up into pairs for a while. The pair which consisted of a man and a woman appeared to be a couple. They had an arm around each other and were chatting flirtatiously as they went by.

The men had roughly the same haircut, severely short at the back. The woman's hair was scraped back in a tight ponytail and she had plucked her eyebrows almost to nonexistence. They all walked with straight backs, chests out. Two of them wore remarkably chunky spectacles.

Ajia could not help but think they were military. This wasn't so surprising, however. Summer Land had made its way to Wiltshire, a county peppered with army and air force bases. Some of the punters were bound to come from those.

What nagged at her about these four was how they spent a long time at each attraction just watching before they paid their money and took part. She saw them do this at every ride that lay within view of the candyfloss stand. They would hang back, sizing things up, as though unable to make up their minds whether or not they wanted a go. If they were military, she doubted they were too bothered about being subjected to the g-forces of the pendulum ride or hurled around in the double centrifuge of the orbiter. With their training they must be able to take that kind of physical stress in their stride. They wouldn't be short of nerve, either. So why the hesitation? It was odd.

It occurred to Ajia that she should mention the four to Mr LeRoy. She decided not to. Her doubts about them just weren't strong enough. She didn't want to trouble him needlessly.

Later, she would wish she had gone to him with her suspicions. It might have made a difference. It might have prevented a massacre.

BY THIS TIME, Ajia had been with Summer Land for nearly a month, and she was starting to feel right at home. The funfair folk were a tight-knit community and the prevailing attitude was very much "us against the world", but she was used to that. For the past couple of years, since her father's suicide, she had been living with a similar attitude, although in her case it was just her against the world, her and nobody else, an army of one. Where she had been alone in her defiance, however, now she was in the company of dozens of others who felt likewise.

She was still busy repainting the rides. She was making friends. She was also testing out her speed, seeing how fast she really could run. Mr LeRoy permitted these trials as long as they were conducted out of sight of the general public. Anything that drew undue attention to Summer Land was a bad idea. He likened the fair to a low-flying jet that didn't leave a vapour trail. For much the same reason, phones were forbidden to the funfair folk, an edict which carried the penalty of expulsion. Calls could be spied on by the authorities, texts intercepted, data harvested and collated, conclusions drawn. Ajia missed having a phone—it felt like losing a limb, or a friend— but had adjusted to the absence. A small price to pay for safety.

On one occasion, Ajia timed herself running circuits of the fairground site. She did this at dawn, when there was nobody around. She completed the first circuit, which she estimated as being four hundred yards, in twelve seconds flat. By the fifth attempt, she had shaved the time down to ten and a half seconds.

On another occasion, she roped Maya in to time her. Summer Land had pitched camp beside a school which had its own athletics track, and on a bright moonlit night, an hour after the fair closed, Ajia and Maya sneaked past the goblins on guard duty and hopped the fence. Maya stood at the finish line with a stopwatch. Ajia ran the 100-metre straight track several times, covering the distance in an average of 2.9 seconds.

"Blimey, Ajia, that's incredible," Maya gushed. "You're just a blur. You're like a flipping rocket! The rest of us must look like snails to you."

"Snails in treacle," Ajia said. "But not all the time. Only when I'm in 'Puck mode'."

"You should go on telly. Or be an athlete. You'd be famous."

"Probably not wise. I told you about those cops, didn't I? The ones who killed me?"

"Oh yes." Maya, bless her, seldom thought through the consequences of anything. She was tirelessly enthusiastic and a hard worker, but she seemed to live in a perpetual now. It was a common failing among brownies, Ajia had noticed, this gnat-like attention span. "But couldn't you, like, wear a disguise maybe? And you wouldn't have to show off your full speed. You could just be, you know, a bit fast."

All Ajia could think of to do was hug her. "You're as daft as a brush but I love you, Maya," she said, and Maya giggled.

What amazed Ajia was how natural it felt, being the eidolon of Puck. The gift of extraordinary speed took very little getting used to. It was as though she had been practising half her life in readiness to receive it. She had always been fairly proficient in sports events at school, if not quite a medal winner, but once she got her first bike, a present from her parents on her ninth birthday, there'd been almost literally no stopping her. She'd been at home on the saddle, a perfect symbiosis of human and machine, capable of speeds impossible on foot. She had continually pushed herself to go faster, further, longer. She'd had a fair few spills along the way, but the odd bruise, the odd bit of road rash, was a fair price to pay for the sublime sensation of shooting along London's streets like a human bullet.

And now, without a bike, she was virtually as fast as an actual bullet. Not that she hadn't earned it. She had had to die, after all, brutally, in order to be reborn as Puck. But there were worse trade-offs. She could, instead, be just plain dead. Whereas this was death plus. Death deluxe. Death with benefits.

THE FOUR-STRONG TEAM of Paladins who had reconnoitred Summer Land reported back to Major Wynne with their findings.

"Funfair itself's a shithole," said Lieutenant Noble, who had headed up the recon. "Seems to have had a lick of paint recently, but that can't disguise the fact that half the rides are deathtraps. If Mr Drake hadn't repealed EU health-and-safety regulations, the place'd be out of business tomorrow. As for the people running it, they seem normal enough all right. You mightn't think there was anything out of the ordinary, just to look at them. But you know, after all this time dealing with so many of these weird fuckers, you get an instinct, don't you? A prickle at the back of the neck. They're not right."

"I was at the shooting gallery," said a Paladin called Stirling. She was slight of stature but hard as nails. Wynne had slept with her once. Grossly unprofessional behaviour, without doubt a sackable offence, and they'd both known it and they'd both agreed never to talk about it again, ever. But it had been well worthwhile, at least as far as Wynne was concerned, even if the scratches and bite marks she'd inflicted on him had taken weeks to fade.

"I wasn't doing badly either," Stirling continued. "The airgun was rigged, of course, but once I'd adjusted for the sights being off and the slight bend in the barrel, I was scoring bullseyes every time. And then... I wasn't." She gave a perplexed shrug. "I couldn't hit the target, no matter how I tried. It was like my eye and my trigger finger just weren't coordinated any more. And you know me. You know my rifle range stats."

Wynne did. Stirling was the Paladins' top marksman.

"The guy manning the gallery, ugly-looking little runt, just kept giving me the evils," she said.

"Put you off?"

Stirling snorted. "It'd take a lot more than that. But the way he was staring, it was like he was willing me to fail—and then I started failing. Had my heart set on nabbing a prize. A massive stuffed panda. I'm pissed off I didn't win it."

"And the people in charge of the actual rides," said Noble, "they were all alike. You've seen the footage."

Wynne had. Microcameras concealed within the spectacles worn by the other two Paladins on the team had recorded the entire op. Pretty much without exception, the fairground rides had been run by tall, slender men and women with long hair, pointed chins and bright, fascinating eyes. Even just watching the video, Wynne had found their come-ons beguiling. They sweet-talked and flattered the punters and made the idea of parting with a couple of quid to get hurled around mindlessly for a minute or so the most enticing prospect there ever was.

It was a judgement call. Wynne had no firm intel that the funfair was, as Jenny Greenteeth asserted, home to faeries, elves and the like. The river hag might just be settling a score, getting revenge for some insult perpetrated on her. Perhaps she had once worked at

Summer Land and been thrown out, and had nursed a grudge ever since.

Then again, he had done some background research on Summer Land's current owner, one Auberon LeRoy. It seemed LeRoy had once been a successful academic until, following a near-fatal heart attack, he'd had some kind of breakdown, jacked in his university career and gone into the funfair business instead.

This was a pattern familiar to Wynne. Rigorous interrogation of the various creatures imprisoned in the basement level at Stronghold—the ones which could speak, that was—revealed a common thread. Each had undergone a near-death experience which had left them altered, mentally and in most cases physically, so as to resemble something from folklore. The whys and wherefores of these transformations were unknown to Wynne, but then he didn't really want to know, or need to. That sort of thing was above his pay grade. Prime Minister Drake clearly had some idea but wasn't divulging. All that mattered, where Wynne was concerned, was that Auberon LeRoy fit the bill. He had almost died and the experience had left him changed. And if the person in charge of Summer Land matched the profile, why not the people who worked for him, too?

The balance of probabilities was that Summer Land was a travelling refuge for a whole tribe of misfit beings who did not belong in Drake's Britain. There they had been, right under everyone's noses, moving from place to place, hiding in plain sight. As bad as any illegal immigrants. Worse, in many ways. Folkloric creatures with eerie supernatural abilities who could pass for human.

To Wynne, this was repugnant. Summer Land's very existence was a provocation, and he resolved to deal with the situation in the most extreme manner possible. Drake had given him carte blanche. He had a battalion of Paladins under his command. Time to mobilise.

TWELVE

THE PALADINS LAUNCHED their attack during the small hours of a Monday morning.

Summer Land was ensconced that week in a horseshoe-shaped valley on the outskirts of a provincial town in southern Dorset. Steep forested slopes enclosed it on three sides. For Major Wynne's purposes, this could not have been more ideal. The terrain advantage was all his.

The weather proved to be on his side, too. The night sky was overcast, no moonlight, and just after midnight a heavy rain started falling.

The fairground people were in bed, all of them except a handful of gnarled, husky little men who were performing sentry duty. A hundred Paladins began infiltrating the surrounding woodland, padding stealthily between the ashes and elders. What little noise they made, the rain masked. A couple of dozen of them held back in reserve positions on the ridge of the hills. The rest halted just inside the treeline.

Stirling and three other sharpshooters arranged themselves at predetermined vantage points, equidistantly around the fairground. Each had an AW50 Accuracy International long-range sniper rifle fitted with bipod, suppressor and thermal imaging night scope.

Each had a clear, unimpeded view of the site.

When he had confirmation that everyone was in place, Wynne gave the go command. The instruction was transmitted to earpieces in the Paladins' helmets on a dedicated shortwave band.

Stirling picked off the first of the sentries. Three hundred yards. No wind adjustment necessary. Her gunshot was little louder than a cat's sneeze. Through her night scope, she saw her target's head jerk back and his body crumple.

In rapid succession, the other sentries were downed.

"All right, ladies and gentlemen," said Wynne. "You know the drill. Keep it clean and keep it quick. The longer we can hold off the unsuppressed gunfire, the better. And remember, these bastards are likely to have 'abilities', so I want everyone on their game. Don't take any chances. If you don't like the way something looks, don't hesitate, eliminate."

Paladins moved out from the trees, combat knives and silenced pistols at the ready, stalking towards the cluster of caravans where the fairground people slept.

AJIA WAS AWOKEN by a shout, just audible above the drumming of the rain on the caravan roof. It was a guttural cry of surprise and indignation, and it was abruptly cut short.

She slid out of her bunk, levered up the window blind and peeked out.

In the doorway of the next caravan, two figures were engaged in violent struggle. One was darkly dressed and positioned behind the other, with a hand clamped over the other's mouth. Through the downpour Ajia glimpsed a metallic flicker passing across a throat. Immediately, the other figure went limp. The dark-dressed figure lowered the sagging body to the ground.

Ajia shrank back from the window, letting the blind drop back into place. Her heart was racing.

When she next peeked out, the dark-dressed figure had been joined by another person, similarly clad. Paladins. She identified them by their helmets—that distinctive crest on top like a fish's dorsal fin. The two were conferring. One pointed towards Ajia's caravan. The gesture obviously meant go deal with anyone in there.

Ajia scrambled over to the bunks. She shook Maya awake, placing a finger on her lips to shush her.

"Get the others up," she whispered.

"What is it?" Maya whispered back, eyes wide in the darkness.

"I think we're under attack."

As Maya woke the other two brownies, Ajia crept over to the door. Pressing her ear against it, she detected a faint footfall on the upturned plastic crate they used as a front step. The bolt on the door had been slid shut but was neither large nor sturdy. A good, solid kick to the door would snap the bolt free from its mountings.

She could only assume their neighbour—one of the boggarts, Dennis—had heard the Paladin outside his caravan and come out to investigate. That had been his fatal mistake. She wasn't going to get caught out the same way.

The three brownies were gathered in an anxious huddle.

"We're going out through the bathroom window," Ajia said to them. The bathroom lay on the opposite side of the caravan from the door. "Whatever you do, don't make a sound."

The brownies nodded.

The Paladin gently tested the door. Ajia made an urgent ushering motion towards the bathroom, a tiny cubicle where there was just about enough floorspace for one person to stand. Maya went first. Ajia watched her ease the window open, while at the same time keeping a wary eye on the door. As soon as Maya slithered out, Ajia silently exhorted the next brownie, Alice, to follow.

The door began to bow inward. The Paladin was applying pressure with a shoulder. Even if the bolt didn't give under the strain, the hinges might.

Genevieve, the third brownie, was crawling out through the bathroom window. The door creaked, then relaxed back into its frame.

Ajia didn't believe for a moment that the Paladin had given up.

She heard a panicked gasp outside the bathroom window. There was a series of swift, snippy hisses which could only have been silenced gunshots.

Oh shit. The Paladins had had the caravan surrounded. They had been staking out all the possible exits. Ajia had just sent the three brownies out to their deaths.

Next instant, a booted foot rammed the door open. The owner of the booted foot charged in, brandishing a combat knife. Rainwater dripped from his uniform onto the floor.

Ajia darted towards the kitchenette. All at once, the intruding Paladin was a crippled octogenarian, his every movement arthritically slow. In the time it took Ajia to open a drawer and select a paring knife, he had turned his head only a few degrees. He was just bringing his knife round as she ran back and jabbed her much smaller but no less sharp knife deep into his leg. He hadn't even collapsed to his knees before Ajia had skirted past him out of the door and was rounding the corner of the caravan.

Two handgun-toting Paladins crouched over three bodies sprawled in the grass. They were checking their victims' necks for a pulse—not that they would find one, given the bullet holes in the brownies' foreheads.

Ajia still had the paring knife. Maya, diligent domesticated creature that she was, had always made sure the cutting edge was kept keen.

She buried the blade up to the hilt in the back of the nearer of the Paladins. She stabbed the other Paladin in the gut, just to the side of the padded panel that covered most of his front torso. Neither had reflexes anywhere near quick enough to stop her.

Then she was off across the campsite at full pelt, making for the caravan Smith was staying in.

SEVEN MINUTES ELAPSED before an uproar arose.

The Paladins fanned out between the various kinds of mobile home, moving smoothly, ultra-efficiently from one to the next and effecting ingress. The doors gave way quite easily, on the whole. Some were little more than pieces of plywood with a skin of aluminium and would break in half if shoved hard enough. The windows were a doddle to open, too. Slip a knife blade through the rubber trim, slide the catch aside, job done.

Nearly a quarter the funfair folk were dispatched inside their caravans, many of them while they still slumbered.

Then a couple of goblins proved trickier to kill than hoped. They fought back against the uniformed interlopers who had broken into their sleeping quarters. A brutal hand-to-hand brawl rocked the caravan on its suspension. Bodies thumped around. There were yells and cries of pain.

This alerted everyone in the vicinity, and an anxious hubbub spread like wildfire across the campsite. All of a sudden funfair folk were emerging into the open air in their nightclothes, squinting through the rain, trying to fathom what the hell was going on.

The time for subtlety was past. The Paladins, at a command from Major Wynne, transitioned from stealth to full-frontal offensive. Knives were sheathed. Stubby L85A3 assault rifles were unshipped. Suppressors were removed from pistols, to permit greater accuracy. Gunshots crackled. Muzzle flashes lit up the dark. A storm had come to the campsite, a relentless, destructive force bringing death and terror.

AJIA HAMMERED ON the door of Smith's caravan.

"Smith! Smith!"

Smith shambled out in a string vest and a pair of longjohns. "Goodfellow. Do you know what time it is?"

"How can you be sleeping through this?"

"I can sleep through anything. What's going on?" He frowned down at the knife in Ajia's hand. "That blood..." he began.

"It's not mine. Grab your hammer. They're killing people. We've got to get the fuck out of here."

"Killing? Who?"

"Paladins. There are Paladins fucking everywhere. Now, just shut up and do as I say."

As Smith ducked back indoors, Ajia turned to see if the coast was clear.

It wasn't. A trio of Paladins were zeroing in on the caravan in a V-formation. Their rifles were at their shoulders, barrels trained on her.

Without a second's hesitation she started running straight at them. Two of them fired. The shots were deep, soft booms, like explosions underwater. She saw flame slowly bulge at the barrel ends. The bullets sailed towards her at an almost leisurely pace. She perceived the rounds' whirling flight, the paths they sliced through the rain, which itself seemed in no hurry, each individual droplet falling to earth with the same casual grace as thistledown. Dodging the bullets was like dodging a couple of tennis balls lobbed underarm.

Then she was sliding across the sodden turf on her side, the knife in her outstretched hand. She slashed at the leg of the Paladin on her right, behind the knee. Switching the knife to her other hand, she did something similar to the Paladin on her left. She skidded to a halt just past them, rolling over with her momentum until she was crouching on all fours.

The rain returned to normal speed as she paused for the briefest of moments to assess. The two Paladins she had wounded were sagging to the ground, while the third was pivoting on his heel, looking to his comrades. His jaw was slack with astonishment. Ajia could only imagine how it had seemed to him: the girl in front of them had somehow disappeared, and next thing he knew, he was the only Paladin still standing. The other two were, for some inexplicable reason, down.

Then, like a sprinter bounding away from the starting block, she set off again. She hurtled towards the uninjured Paladin through the fluttering rain, knife to the fore. At this point she was past caring whether she was simply putting the Paladins out of action or killing them. Back at her caravan she had used the knife indiscriminately. She didn't think any of the damage she had inflicted so far, either there or here, was fatal, but she wasn't much fussed even if it was. She only had to recall the bodies of the three brownies lying lifeless on the ground, murdered without mercy, without scruple. Maya among them. Sweet, guileless Maya, who hadn't a bad word for anyone.

The Paladin didn't have time to squeeze off a shot. Ajia's knife tore through his sleeve, gashing the underside of his forearm, severing tendons. The rifle began to tumble from his grasp. She swung back and buried the blade in his inner thigh. When she pulled it out, an arc of blood jetted from the cut, looking to her accelerated perceptions like a worm squeezing its way out of the soil.

She was back at Smith's caravan to meet him as he came out, with shoes on his feet now and his hammer in his hand. He blinked as he saw the three Paladins rolling around, clutching knife wounds and groaning.

"No time to gawp," she said, panting for breath. "We've got to move."

"Yes," Smith said. "Where?"

"Doesn't matter where. Anywhere but here."

"What about Mr LeRoy?"

"What about him?"

"We can't just leave him."

"Smith, the site is overrun with Paladins," Ajia said, exasperated. "It's a fucking slaughterhouse. I think the rule 'every man for himself' applies."

"I disagree. You came for me, didn't you?"

"Yeah, but that's different."

"No, it isn't. Mr LeRoy is my friend. He is the heart and soul of Summer Land. Without him, this place wouldn't exist and everyone here would have nowhere to go to."

"And Summer Land is getting the shit kicked out of it," Ajia insisted. "Look around you. Listen."

From everywhere there came a chaotic cacophony of gunfire and screams. Figures flitted to and fro through the rain-curtained dark. It was hard to tell if they were friend or foe, but Ajia reckoned they were more likely to be the latter. It was only a matter of time before more Paladins ventured this way.

"There isn't a Summer Land any more," she went on. "The Paladins are on the warpath. Can't you tell? They're not going to stop until absolutely every one of us is dead."

"No," said Smith, adamant. "Mr LeRoy."

"Fucksake," she hissed through gritted teeth. "Okay. We make our way out past his caravan. But if they've already got to him, we don't hang around. We motor on by. Deal?"

"Deal."

Furtive, keeping low, Ajia and Smith pursued a circuitous route through the campsite. At one point they stumbled across a group of Paladins who had lined several pixies up against the side of a lorry. The little childlike creatures were sobbing and snivelling, powerless to resist. Ajia immediately poised herself to intervene, but too late. Gunshots rippled. The pixies collapsed like scythed wheat.

Ajia bit back a cry of anguish and started forward. Smith seized her arm, pinning her to the spot.

"No," he murmured. "We missed our opportunity. We can't do anything for them now."

"But they… they executed them. Like a firing squad."

"And you confront those Paladins now and you could wind up getting shot too, and for what? Revenge? Do you want that?"

"Yes!"

"No, you don't. Neither do I. Come on."

Smith strode off. Ajia trudged after him.

A minute later they arrived at Mr LeRoy's big box of a caravan. Paladins were milling about at the entrance. As Ajia and Smith looked on from behind Mr LeRoy's dilapidated Land Rover Defender, more Paladins filed out from inside the caravan. One of them shrugged to the others who'd been waiting. The gesture clearly implied that the caravan was empty.

"Seems Mr LeRoy and Perry had enough warning and got out in time," Smith observed. "Good for them."

A soft rap on the inside of the Land Rover's nearest window attracted their attention.

It was Mr LeRoy. He beckoned frantically to them with a hand, mouthing the words, "Get in."

Casting a glance towards the Paladins, Smith eased open the backseat door and slid into the car. Ajia was close behind.

"Stay down," Mr LeRoy whispered from the front passenger seat as Ajia pulled the door to. Perry was in the driving seat next to him. Both of them were hunkering in the footwells, keeping as low as possible.

The four crouched in silence, breathing hard. Mr LeRoy lifted his head just high enough to peer out over the bonnet, bobbing back down immediately.

"Still there?" Smith enquired.

"Yes. More of them than before."

"Damn it. We're trapped."

"As long as they don't head in this direction, we should be fine," said Perry. "They might not think to look inside a car. They'll assume we're all in the caravans."

"It was Perry's idea," said Mr LeRoy. "Soon as the ruckus started, he dragged me out to the Land Rover. Very clever of him."

"But if they do head in this direction, they're bound to spot us," said Smith. "We'll be sitting ducks."

"You didn't have to get in," Perry said tartly.

"Seemed like a good idea at the time," Smith muttered in a gruff tone.

"Why?" said Mr LeRoy, after a moment's silence. "That's the question I keep asking myself. Why this attack? Why now, when we've managed to stay under the radar for so long?"

"It was never going to last," Perry replied. "I think we all knew that. Sooner or later, the powers-that-be were going to cotton on to what Summer Land really was. It was inevitable."

"They came the other day," Ajia confessed. "I saw them. Four soldiers in plain clothes. They looked like soldiers, at any rate. They were wandering around the fair, going on the rides and stuff. I didn't think anything of it. Well, I didn't think *enough* of it. I thought I was maybe being paranoid. But I wasn't, was I? They were scoping us out. They were a scouting party. This is my fault. I should have said something. If I had, we'd have been prepared. They wouldn't have taken us by surprise. We'd have stood a chance."

"My dear girl, you mustn't blame yourself," Mr LeRoy said. "I won't hear of it. You can't be the only one to have seen them. Others of the funfair folk must have too, and they didn't twig to who those four were, any more than you did."

"Still, I should have at least mentioned it."

"You weren't to know better. What's happened has happened, and we must deal with things as they are."

A worse thought occurred to Ajia. "What if the bastards are here because of me? What if the police ID'ed me and put them onto us, because I'm a fugitive or whatever?"

"Really, that's enough," Mr LeRoy snapped as vehemently as he could without raising his voice. "If this were all about you, Ajia, it wouldn't have been Paladins deployed against us, it would have been just policemen. Paladins are for special circumstances, and I think we funfair folk rate as special. The fact that they're killing us systematically also points to this being supra-judicial. It's got nothing to do with the law and everything to do with genocide. Prime Minister Drake is behind this. He must be. He's found out about us somehow and he's having us exterminated. Like so many others, we don't fit in with his vision of a new Britain."

"Jenny," said Smith. "Jenny Greenteeth. She could have told the Paladins about Summer Land."

"She or any other of the monsters," said Perry. "That's what I meant when I said it was inevitable. I warned you this might happen, Bron, didn't I? A number of times."

"Yes, my boy." Mr LeRoy patted his cheek. "And I refused to listen, because I'm a stubborn old fool. And also because what else could I do but carry on as before? I couldn't just abandon Summer Land. It would have been like abandoning hope."

He dared to sneak another look up over the dashboard.

"Oh dear God," he gasped, shrinking back down.

"What is it?" said Smith.

"Two of them. They're heading this way. Everyone, stay absolutely still. Keep your hands and faces out of sight. Try as much as you can to look like just a bundle of clothes. We may get lucky."

Ajia buried her face against her knees, making herself as small as possible. She knew it would be futile if the Paladins should happen to glance into the Land Rover. A human being was very easy to distinguish from a bundle of clothes. Her pulse was pounding in her ears, so loud she could hardly hear anything else.

Please pass on by. Please pass on by.

There was a sharp, metallic tap on the windscreen. A voice said, "You lot in the car. Out."

Ajia raised her head to see one of the Paladins aiming his assault rifle at them, its muzzle inches from the windscreen. The other Paladin was making a summoning gesture to his colleagues over by the caravan.

She was still clutching the bloodstained paring knife, but suddenly it seemed a pathetic weapon. A piece of kitchenware against an assault rifle levelled at point blank range. Absurd.

She looked through the gap between the two front seats to Mr LeRoy. His expression was resigned and weary.

"Best do as they say," he said, starting to rise. "Maybe they'll spare us."

He didn't believe it any more than Ajia did.

"Let me deal with this," said Perry, reaching for the door handle. "No one's immune to my charm if I really pour it on."

"Perry, no," said Mr LeRoy. "You're not glamouring punters here. This lot won't succumb nearly as easily."

"I can try anyway. If nothing else I can buy the rest of you some time."

"Perry, my love…" Mr LeRoy implored. His face was a rictus of anguish.

"Don't argue. Just get ready to start the car." Perry climbed out. "My, my," he said to the Paladins, drawing himself up to his full height and tossing back his hair. "What have we here? Two fine, strapping fellows. Have we met before? I feel like I know you."

The Paladins had their guns pointed at him but all at once they didn't appear too concerned about using them.

"Yes," Perry continued, "you should probably lower those weapons." His voice was like honey and silk. Ajia thought she could have listened to him talk all day. "There's no need for all this aggression."

The assault rifles drooped. One of the Paladins half-smiled.

"It's working," said Smith. "Mr LeRoy, start the car, like Perry said. Once we get rolling, he can dive in."

Mr LeRoy fumbled the car keys from his pocket and slid across to the driving seat. Ajia, sitting up, saw more Paladins approaching. She knew what would happen once the engine fired up. A hail of bullets, surely. Yet there was a chance, just a chance, that they could get out of here unscathed. The Land Rover had thick metal panels which might absorb some of the gunfire.

The windows were another matter, but...

"Smith," she said. "I need you to make something."

Smith drew his hammer. "What?"

"Armour plating. To shield the windows. Can you do that?"

Smith gave a slow nod. "I believe I can."

Perry, meanwhile, was continuing to bewitch the two Paladins beside the car. However, the other Paladins were close now, and one of them expressed surprise that the two did not have full situational control.

"What the bloody hell is this?" he barked. "Why are your weapons down? Why are you just standing around chatting with this bloke? And there's still three others in the car. They should be out here."

Ajia was 99% certain the man who had just spoken was Dominic Wynne. She recognised the voice.

Confirmation came when one of the englamoured Paladins said, "But he's a nice guy, Major Wynne."

"It'd be a shame to shoot him," said the other.

Major Wynne, without even hesitating, put a bullet in Perry's chest and another in his head.

"No!" Mr LeRoy shrieked.

"I told you they were tricky," Wynne said. "I told you to take care. Weren't you fuckwits listening?"

The two Paladins shook their heads in a baffled manner, as though they couldn't understand what had come over them.

"Now," Wynne said, turning towards the Land Rover. "The rest of you in there. You know what's coming. Let's make this as straightforward as we can, shall we? Get out. Save yourselves, and us, a hassle."

"Cunt!" Mr LeRoy roared. Ajia was from the East End, where that particular expletive was used by certain people pretty much as punctuation. It was oddly more startling to hear it from the lips of someone usually so erudite and refined. Tears were streaming down Mr LeRoy's cheeks. He slotted the key into the ignition and twisted it hard. The Land Rover coughed into life.

Smith took this as his cue to act. He whacked his hammer hard against the inside of the driver's side door. Instantly a latticework of bars criss-crossed the window, springing like tentacles out of the surrounding bodywork. He repeated the process with the window directly next to him.

Mr LeRoy threw the car into first and slammed his foot down on the accelerator. The Land Rover skidded into the life, lurching forwards.

Rifle reports rattled outside. Bullets thudded into the vehicle.

Mr LeRoy drove straight at a Paladin who was in the way, a blurry silhouette through the rain-streaked windscreen. The Paladin leapt to one side, narrowly avoiding being hit.

Smith reached across Ajia and armoured the windows on that side. The Paladins raked the Land Rover with gunfire from the rear. Mr LeRoy slewed the car between two caravans, heading for the gate which afforded access to the fairground site from the B-road beyond.

Paladins converged from elsewhere to intercept the escapees, firing as they went. Rifle rounds starred the windscreen. Smith leaned forward from the backseat and repaired the glass with hammer taps, adding a row of thick metal strips to reinforce it against further salvoes.

The gate itself was shut, but it was just a five-bar wooden thing, elderly and none too robust. The Land Rover rammed into it square-on. The chain which secured it snapped and the gate was flung wide open. Mr LeRoy threw the Land Rover into a sharp right-hand turn. The tyres skidded across wet tarmac, the rear of the car drifting leftwards. Mr LeRoy corrected, and the Land Rover hared off along the road. He shifted up through the gears, gaining speed.

"Is everyone all right?" Mr LeRoy sai without looking round. "Nobody hurt?"

"Uh-uh," said Ajia.

"Me too," said Smith. "You?"

"Fine," said Mr LeRoy. "Not a scratch. But…" He thumped the steering wheel with his fist. The tears were still flowing fast. "Perry, you wretched idiot. You didn't have to do that. Not like that."

"He saved us," Smith said, laying a consoling hand on Mr LeRoy's shoulder. "He saved you."

"He could be a right vicious little bitch sometimes, Smith, but I loved him."

"I know. And he knew, and I think, in his way, he loved you back. He must have, to sacrifice himself for you like he did."

"Yes. Yes, he must have," Mr LeRoy said with a grimace.

The Land Rover struck the verge shudderingly and veered across the road. Mr LeRoy fought to regain control.

"Would you like me to drive?" Smith offered.

"No." Mr LeRoy ran a thumb across each eye. "No, I can manage. Windscreen wipers would help. Headlights too."

In all the commotion of their getaway, he hadn't turned either on. He did so now. As the wipers flopped to and fro, dual cones of illumination from the headlights picked out high hedgerow-topped banks on either side of the road and the silvery shimmer of the rain. Shortly, the Land Rover approached a T-junction, with a fingerpost indicating the nearby town. Mr LeRoy turned left, away from the town, heading deeper into the countryside.

"So," said Ajia, "where are we going?"

"Where is there to go?" said a forlorn Mr LeRoy. "Summer Land is no more. There's nowhere safe. The Paladins will probably have noted down our numberplate, so we can't expect to keep driving indefinitely. Even if they haven't, the car's riddled with bullet holes, and that and Smith's customisations will make it stand out. We'll have to ditch it somewhere, and then what?"

There was a pause, then Smith said, "How far are we from Nottingham?"

"I don't know, a couple of hundred miles maybe. Why?"

"I know someone up there, someone who might help."

"Ah. Ah yes," said Mr LeRoy. "I know who you mean. Him. But didn't the two of you…?"

"Have a falling-out? Yes."

"So won't he be…?"

"Not best pleased to see me? Yes. But," Smith added, "when your back's against the wall, there's no better person to have by your side."

THIRTEEN

THE NEXT MORNING, Derek Drake received two calls in quick succession on his personal phone while he was being chauffeured from home to Downing Street.

The first was from Dominic Wynne, informing him that decisive action had been taken against Summer Land.

"How decisive?" Drake asked.

"Very, sir."

"Do I want to know more?"

"Not if plausible deniability means anything to you."

"So no potential blowback?"

"One or two loose ends remain to be tied up," said Wynne, "but we're on the case. We're throwing every available resource at it."

"Good man, Dominic. Thank you."

"Send my regards to Mrs Drake."

"I shall."

The second phone call was an unscheduled communication from none other than the Russian premier.

"*Dobroye utro*," said Drake, doing his best to hide his surprise.

"And good morning to you, Derek." President Vasilyev, unlike any of his predecessors, spoke very creditable English. He had studied international politics at Oxford.

"I must admit, I didn't realise you had my private number."

"You don't recall giving it to me at Davos last year? Well, perhaps not, but my foreign intelligence service is very efficient."

"I imagine so. To what do I owe the honour, Vasily Vasilyevich?" Drake used Vasilyev's given name and patronymic of out both politeness and deference. He considered the Russian a friend but was less certain if the two of them were equals.

"Can the leaders of great nations not pick up the phone and call one another when the mood takes them?"

"Don't see why not."

"And Britain, now, she does not have so many comrades, does she?" Vasilyev said. "The old relationships have failed her and she has had to form new ones."

This was a truth that could not be denied. Drake's domestic policies had proven unpalatable to the countries Britain had once been able to count on for support. Shunned on all sides by former allies, even by longstanding pal America, Britain's only option had been to turn to states it had previously dealt with only at arm's length and with a certain amount of nose-holding, states whose regimes had an elastic approach to democracy and whose human rights records were, to put it mildly, questionable. Russia was foremost among them. If anything, Russia was now Britain's staunchest affiliate. Tariff-exempt trade flowed between the two, their militaries undertook joint training exercises, and in UN Security Council decisions, the UK's representative was apt to vote whichever way his Russian counterpart voted.

"Relationships," Vasilyev continued, "which she would do well to cultivate, no?"

"Is that what this is?" said Drake. Vasilyev was a shrewd operator, and Drake knew he should tread with caution. "Relationship cultivation?"

"Yes. Why not? Of course, above all else I am keen to congratulate you on your television interview. It has gone down very well over here."

"Thank you. You'll note I said nice things about you."

"About Russian leaders in general."

"Surely the subtext was apparent."

"And Ms Bazanova, she sang your praises."

"Did she?" said Drake, recalling the lubricious journalist. He glanced towards the glass partition which separated him from the Paladin driving the limousine. It was not only tinted but soundproofed. Nonetheless he lowered his voice somewhat. "Well, she was... a nice surprise. It was a pleasure making her acquaintance."

"I have no doubt."

"I wish I could reciprocate one day, but I'm not sure I could find a television presenter here quite so accommodating."

"I understand," said Vasilyev. "The British woman does not have quite the same grasp of what is meant by service to the motherland as the Russian woman does. It can't be denied that you have, Derek, something of a way with the ladies. At Davos, you and that hostess. Remember?"

"How did you...? No, never mind." *My foreign intelligence service is very efficient.* In other words: I have spies everywhere.

"And then the waitress at the G7 summit."

A bitter occasion, that summit. The other nations in the group had voted unanimously to strip the UK of its membership of their elite club, and at the same time had reinstated Russia in its place. The waitress had been a consolation prize from Drake to himself but also an act of defiance, a way of mitigating the humiliation he'd felt.

"At least with Ms Bazanova there will be no need to pay her for her silence," Vasilyev went on. "You can rest assured on that front."

"Never crossed my mind," Drake said. "I imagine she has been amply rewarded for her work by you."

"Yet there is still, as so often, a price to be paid."

"I'm not sure I follow."

"How is Mrs Drake?" Was this a change of subject? "Such a remarkable-looking woman. My Viktoriya, though much the same age, cannot compare. Dumpy as a pig, is Viktoriya, whereas your Harriet—exquisite, still. And yet she is clearly not enough for you."

It sounded like locker-room banter, and Drake decided to treat it as such. "Well, you know how it is, Vasily Vasilyevich. The comforts of a home game versus the excitement of an away fixture. One can enjoy both."

"Quite so. You may expect a text from me shortly, with an attachment. Goodbye, Derek."

Vasilyev hung up before Drake had a chance to respond. Rather rude, but then Russians weren't renowned for their manners.

For two minutes Drake waited, curious to know what the attachment Vasilyev had referred to might be. Perhaps a picture of Viktoriya Vasilyeva, to remind Drake of her porcine charms? Or maybe it was some silly gif or a cat video. Even leaders of superpowers weren't above sending one another such nonsenses.

He felt a vague apprehension but could not quite put a finger on why.

At last his inbox pinged. The text came from the same number as the call, unrecognised by his contacts directory and prefixed with the international dialling code for Russia.

It said, simply, "Just a taster. Best wishes to yourself and Mrs Drake." Attached to it was a 500kb jpeg, around thirty seconds of video footage. Drake opened the file.

He stared at his phone screen, first with perplexity, then with mounting dismay.

Drake's extramarital flings, of which he'd had several since becoming prime minister, had often been tawdry but they had never been cheap. He'd always offered sizeable amounts in hush money, with the implicit threat that if a six-figure sum didn't suffice, then the woman was too greedy for her own good and her avarice would come round to bite her. It was a good thing he was a very rich man, and so far the bribes had been effective.

This, now, was something else. Something new. This was a predicament he could not spent his way out of.

The clip showed him and Tatjana Bazanova in the Downing Street master bedroom. The quality was poor—the image grainy, the lighting murky—but there was no mistaking what was going on or who the participants were.

He remembered Tatjana's Louis Vuitton handbag and the way she had placed it on a side-table. She had, now that he thought about it, been oddly fastidious with regard to its positioning. And no wonder. She'd had to get just the right angle for the camera concealed in it. The camera which would have recorded their tryst in its entirety, from its brisk beginning to its frenetic, thrashing, taking-the-Lord's-name-in-vain climax.

He watched the clip a second time, remarking on the fact that Tatjana's facial expressions did not really match the enthusiastic noises she was making. He hadn't noticed this at the time.

Then he called Vasilyev back.

Somehow he was not surprised to discover that the number had been disconnected.

So, the bastard wanted to play games, did he?

But Drake knew there was more to it than that. This wasn't a joke. This was blackmail, pure and simple. The famous Russian *kompromat*. President Vasily Vasilyevich Vasilyev now had absolute power over him. He could use the video as leverage to ensure Drake did his bidding at all times. He was the puppetmaster and Drake the marionette.

Or so he thought.

Drake, however, was determined to remedy the situation, maybe even turn it around to his advantage. All he had to do was think.

The queasy, tightening sensation in his stomach, however, made it very difficult to think—and very easy to panic.

FOURTEEN

THE PLAN WAS to drive through the night, but that was scuppered by the weather. The rain went from merely heavy to downright torrential, beyond the power of the Land Rover's disproportionately small windscreen wipers to cope with. Mr LeRoy grew more and more fretful at the wheel. "Can't see a damn thing," he complained several times. "Especially with half the windscreen covered up with metal."

Nor was he sure whether they were going in the right direction. Signposts on those Dorset country lanes were few and far between, and whichever way Mr Le Roy turned, the car seemed to be getting no nearer a major road. In the end he was forced to admit that he was lost.

"Fuel situation is looking a bit unhappy, too," he said, tapping the gauge. "Do you know what? I reckon we should find somewhere to park and carry on at first light."

He diverted down a track that meandered through woodland, drawing to a halt in a densely forested section. When he killed the engine, the sound of the rain battering down on the Land Rover's roof rushed to fill the vacuum, so loud it was almost deafening.

The three of them—Ajia, Smith, Mr LeRoy—sat there in the dark, each lost in morose thought. In time, Smith dozed off, snoring softly. Ajia was so wired, she didn't think she would ever sleep again. She crawled forward into the passenger seat next to Mr LeRoy.

"I'm sorry about Perry," she said. She was well aware how paltry such commiserations sounded. She had heard enough of them in the wake of her father's death. They might be sincerely meant but they were also, to the bereaved, virtually meaningless.

Mr LeRoy grunted something resembling a thank-you.

"I was wondering," she went on. "There's something I don't understand."

"And what is that?"

"About what happened to me, to all of us. We were brought back from the dead, right? All of us, the eidolons, the brownies and boggarts and elves. So…"

Mr LeRoy anticipated her question. "So why doesn't whatever is behind our resurrection simply bring us back to life when we die again?" His voice caught. "Why doesn't the power bring Perry back?"

Ajia nodded, watching Mr LeRoy as he shook his head, mystified.

"That is something that has sorely vexed me over the months, girl. We had one or two deaths at Summer Land, accidents involving the boggarts, and the first time one happened… Well, I wondered the same thing." He shrugged his his great shoulders. "But the dead remained dead, so I could only surmise that whatever is responsible for what is happening has limited… powers, let's say. And can only bring the dead back to life the once."

Ajia nodded. "I see."

He smiled at her. "So don't go thinking that you're invincible. Life is precious, so take care."

"I'll do that, Mr LeRoy."

She fell silent, but a little later said, "I'm sorry about Summer Land too. For what it's worth, I haven't felt as at home anywhere in a long time as I did there."

"You're kind to say such things, Puck," said Mr LeRoy, absently patting her arm. "I mean Ajia. I mustn't forget. Not Puck. Ajia. Although," he added, "Smith gets to call you Goodfellow, doesn't he?"

"I've asked him not to but it seems, with him, it's too late to change," Ajia said. "Maybe, I don't know, some of the others got away." The remark carried far more hope than conviction.

"It would be nice to think so, but the Paladins seemed rather too thorough for that."

Ajia, recalling how Paladins had lined up and shot that group of pixies, nodded grimly. Who could do such a thing? Who could do it, moreover, to people who resembled children? What kind of cast-iron callousness did that take?

She glanced round at Smith, who'd prevented her exacting revenge on the pixies' killers. In hindsight, he had been right to do so. She might otherwise be dead herself. She almost certainly wouldn't be in this car now, miles clear of the site of the massacre. Yet she still seethed inwardly at her own inaction.

"What is it with Smith?" she asked Mr LeRoy.

"What do you mean?"

"He won't kill. He won't hurt anyone, even in self-defence. Is it because Wayland the Smith was a murderer? Because I'm not convinced by that."

"Is that what he said? That his pacifism is connected to the original Wayland the Smith's behaviour?"

"Well, not in so many words…"

"It isn't," Mr LeRoy said. "And it's not my place to tell you his story if he hasn't told you himself. What I will say about Smith is he finds it hard to settle anywhere. He always has since becoming an eidolon. At Summer Land he would come and go. Sometimes he'd stay for weeks, other times just a few days. His life before was good, you see—right up until it wasn't. Tragedy befell him, and it shook him to his core, leaving him the sensitive but broken creature that you know. Smith is looking for redemption but he seems unable to find it anywhere."

"I am listening, you know," Smith intoned from the backseat.

"Shit!" said Ajia, startled. "Sorry, Smith. Thought you were asleep." That wasn't an excuse in itself, so she added, "I was only making conversation."

"You were prying."

"Yes. Yes, I was."

"You could just come straight out and ask."

"When the subject came up last time—just after Jenny Greenteeth—you pretty much shut me down."

"Maybe I'd be more prepared to talk about it now."

"And are you?"

"No," said Smith. Then: "Perhaps. There isn't much to tell. Some people died. I was responsible. I carry that burden around my neck. I refuse to add to it by causing any further harm to anyone."

"You were not responsible," said Mr LeRoy.

"As good as," said Smith. "Here's how it was, Ajia. My architectural practice was working on a social housing project. Affordable accommodation. Developing a brownfield site in Bermondsey, in fulfilment of a government contract which pre-dated Derek Drake. We'd designed the housing to be sustainable, accessible and aesthetically pleasing, with plenty of green space. It was a big deal for us. The practice wasn't huge—ten of us in all—but we were eager and competitive. Everything was going swimmingly, but then the time came to start building. We had the groundbreaking ceremony, and three days later Drake won his landslide victory, and all at once our budget was slashed. To the bone. Social housing was no longer a priority for the Resurrectionists. You know them. 'Waste of taxpayers' money' and so on. 'No one should have their rent subsidised by the state.' What they meant was—"

"People on low incomes can go fuck themselves," said Ajia.

"And the majority of people on low incomes were people only recently arrived in the country. We soldiered on anyway. We did what we could. Sourced the cheapest building materials, hired the lowest-bidding contractors, scrimped, skimped. I was damned if I was going to let Derek Drake and his minions destroy this project. Maybe if I hadn't been so pig-headed, everything would have been fine. I should have just given up. That was what the Resurrection Party wanted. I should have admitted defeat and walked away."

"You say pig-headed," said Mr LeRoy. "I would say determined."

"I knew we were building substandard accommodation," Smith said. "I knew we were taking risks. But we got it done, and to me, in my arrogance, seeing those houses and blocks of flats finished and having people who needed them move in, that was the most important thing. That was a victory. There was a fire a month later."

Smith did not speak for a while. The rain pounded down on the Land Rover with renewed ferocity.

"It was in one of the flats," he went on at last. "A faulty microwave spontaneously caught alight. The fire suppression system could have handled it—would have if it hadn't malfunctioned. There was a leak in the pipes due to incorrect installation and cheap couplings. Most of the sprinklers didn't receive any water and so couldn't operate. Eighteen people perished, including seven children."

"Jesus, yeah, I remember that," said Ajia. "Bermondsey. It was on the news."

"The accident investigation report laid the blame squarely with my practice," Smith said, "and I could hardly disagree. We had screwed up calamitously. For all the right reasons, we had done everything wrong. There was talk of legal action but I decided to pre-empt it. I wrote a note exonerating my employees. It was me, I said. All me. I had made the judgment calls. I had sanctioned the corner-cutting. Then I took myself to Tower Bridge, climbed up onto the parapet and threw myself off."

He laughed bitterly.

"Couldn't even get that right. Or so I thought as I came to, washed up on the Thames foreshore somewhere out by Wapping. Couldn't build a safe building, couldn't kill myself. Totally useless. It wasn't until much later that I learned I had died and been brought back to life. At the time I simply felt I was every kind of failure, and so I took myself out of the world. I took myself out of it by living rough, drinking whatever alcohol I could lay my hands on, and not caring what happened to me. I got into a few scrapes, got out of them. If it hadn't been for this man..."

He indicated Mr LeRoy.

"He found me. Summer Land had pitched close to where I was then shacked up—a shelter on the promenade in a seaside town—and one day Mr LeRoy paid a visit. Just sidled up with a smile on his face and told me he'd been looking for me. I thought, at first, he was a vicar or something."

"Hah!" Mr LeRoy snorted. "Hardly."

"Wanted to share with me the word of God," Smith continued. "The way he was talking about being reborn, a new life, all of that."

"Funny, I thought the same about you," Ajia said.

Smith gave a wry nod. "But then he began to explain, and things just sort of fell into place. I had been having these dreams, you see. Dreams about being a metalsmith, a master craftsman. About smithing for giants and kings. About being married to a swan maiden, as my two brothers were likewise married to swan maidens, until our wives tired of us and stole back the coats of white feathers which we'd stolen from them so that they had to remain in human form. Dreams of a life I'd had never had, a surreal life that felt real. Naturally I blamed it on the booze."

"The dreams are the subconscious trying to communicate with the conscious mind," Mr LeRoy cut in. "Every eidolon has them if they aren't reconciled with their new selves soon. You would have too, Ajia, if Smith hadn't found you so early on after your transformation and explained to you who you were. My own dreams were terrible. Feverish visions of castles and glades and flying above treetops and waylaying unwary travellers and taming wild beasts…"

"Mr LeRoy told me about Wayland the Smith," said Smith. "He told me that was who I was now. What clinched it was when he gave me a hammer to hold. This hammer."

"Just some old hammer that had been lying around the funfair," Mr LeRoy said. "Nothing special."

"But it felt special in my hand," Smith said. "All of a sudden I knew I could do anything with it. Make anything. Repair anything. Mr LeRoy picked up one of the empty bottles I'd left lying on the floor of the shelter. He dropped it. It smashed. 'Put that back together,' he said. And I did. I couldn't believe it even as I was doing it, but I fused the broken pieces of glass back into a single bottle, label and all, completely intact, with just a few light taps of the hammer. I knew somehow where to hit and how hard, as though by instinct."

He chuckled wistfully.

"And that was that. I was no longer who I had been. I was this new entity. From that day on, there was no more drinking. By then, though, there was also no possibility of going back to my old life. I'd had a partner, Lianne. A son, Jacob. I'd been drinking in order to forget about them, to avoid even thinking about them. Now, a year and a half on, too much time had passed and I was too different. I could never re-join them. They would assume, anyway, that I was dead. They would have mourned me and moved on. I couldn't just waltz back into their lives and hope we could pick up where we had left off. Mr LeRoy was offering me a new home, a new family. What could I do but accept?"

"You were always free to return to your true family, any time," Mr LeRoy said.

"And I tried. Often I would drift away from Summer Land with vague ideas about going to my old house and turning up on the front doorstep, but sooner or later I'd always drift back."

"You could still go back to Lianne and Jacob," Ajia said. "Why are you looking at me like that? It's not impossible. Bloody hell, if I had the chance to be with my mum again, I'd take it like a shot. And my dad, although that would be a bit harder to organise, on account of he's dead."

"You haven't spoken much about your former life, Ajia," said Smith. "And of course, we've none of us enquired. It's your business." He looked at her pointedly.

"Fair's fair." Ajia shrugged. "You've shown me yours. My turn to show you mine. And it's not as if the mood in this car could get any more depressed. You guys want the full grisly tale? Brace yourselves."

She told them about the forced repatriation of her mother and grandparents, and about her father's subsequent suicide.

"I was parentless at sixteen, but just too old to be taken into care. Occasional checks from social workers were all I got, and their funding was being cut month by month. After a while they didn't have the staff numbers to keep up the visits. I seemed to be getting along okay so they left me to it. I needed money so I ditched college and got a job bike couriering, but even then I couldn't keep up the rent on our flat without digging into my dad's savings. When the money ran out, I moved into a bedsit. Street art was about the only thing that kept me sane. If it hadn't been for that, I might have taken the same option my dad did, and you, Smith. And then the cops shot me and beat me to death. But hey"—she faked a breezy, tra-la-la laugh—"what can you do? One minute you're up, next you're down. Life's crazy like that."

SHORTLY BEFORE DAWN, the rain relented. As the sky lightened, Smith got to work ridding the Land Rover of its bullet holes and the bars he had forged over the windows until it looked like a normal, if still veteran, car again.

With Mr LeRoy at the wheel once more, they drove northward, keeping to minor roads. There were too many cameras on motorways with numberplate recognition technology, and too many unmarked police patrols.

They filled up with diesel at a small, out-of-the-way petrol station, where Mr LeRoy bought a selection of fairly unappetising snacks for breakfast. He paid cash. He told Ajia that since founding Summer Land he hadn't used debit or credit cards or carried out any kind of electronic transaction, so as not to give the government financial spoor to track.

"Luckily I had the presence of mind to grab the week's takings as Perry and I sneaked out of my caravan," he remarked as they pulled onto the road again. "A decent sum but it's not going to last forever. I don't suppose either of you is carrying any money?"

Ajia was in a T-shirt and a pair of soft cotton tracksuit bottoms, nightwear which could just about pass for daywear but lacked pockets of any sort. Not that it would have mattered even if she had been in her daytime clothes. She didn't own a wallet any more and didn't have a penny to her name. Smith was just as cash-strapped.

"Well," Mr LeRoy said, "perhaps Smith's friend in Nottingham will help us out."

"Wouldn't bet on it," Smith muttered.

"I thought he was all for donating to good causes."

"As far as he's concerned, there isn't a better cause than himself."

Summer Land had confined its operations to the south of England, principally the Home Counties, where there was still relative prosperity and people had a few spare quid to spend on entertainment. As the Land Rover wound its way up into the Midlands, signs of neglect and deprivation were more and more in evidence. Out of the window Ajia saw fallow crop fields overgrown with poppies, thistles and tall grasses, and farm machinery sitting idle, succumbing to rust. Here and there, smoke from fires smudged the horizon. Verges were choked with litter and played host to the occasional broken-down vehicle, long since abandoned and stripped of salvageable parts. Manufacturing plants stood derelict, walls scrawled with slogans about Derek Drake and the Resurrection Party, as many pro as anti. A few wind turbines stood wreathed in ivy, unmaintained, their static blades like arms raised in supplication. Several of the towns the car passed through didn't have a single shop that was open for business, and even at this early hour gangs of youths hung around at war memorials and other municipal monuments, drinking from cans, scuffling with one another and harassing passers-by. Other towns had barricades across the roads which led into them, guarded by people dressed in army-surplus gear and toting shotguns and pistols. Part survivalist, part concerned citizen, these municipal militias had rallied in defence of their homes against both a lawless society and what they perceived as a government hostile to their interests.

To Ajia, groggy from lack of sleep and horrified by the events of the previous night, this part of the country looked as lousy as she felt. Like her, England was shellshocked and desolate, and she knew that the further north you went, the worse it got. Of course she had seen images of the nation's ailing regions on the news and social media, but it was one thing to look at video on a screen, another to watch the sights themselves roll by in an endless sorry parade. Eventually her eyelids drooped and she drowsed off. It wasn't so much exhaustion as a defence mechanism, her mind saying enough.

She awoke to find that the Land Rover had halted. Mr LeRoy had pulled into a lay-by—one of the rare ones that wasn't a dumping ground for defunct white goods and items of broken furniture—and was poring over a dog-eared road atlas.

"We nearly there?" she asked, but Smith shushed her.

"He's concentrating," he said.

Mr LeRoy's eyes were half-closed and his lips were pursed. He raised a hand over the open page of the atlas, palm down, and began moving it around and around in a figure of eight.

"What's he up to?" Ajia whispered.

"Divining," said Smith. "He's using the atlas to help him locate my friend. He can sense he's close by. The map—any map—allows him to refine his search."

Ajia had heard about certain people who could find underground water sources and mineral deposits using a map and a pendulum, a form of dowsing. Mr LeRoy, it seemed, could do something similar for eidolons.

"Where are we anyway?" she said, looking outside. "Looks like the middle of nowh—"

"I am," said Mr LeRoy loudly and sternly, "quite busy here. If you don't mind."

"Okay, okay. Sorry."

As quietly as she could, so as not to disturb him any further, Ajia opened the car door and got out. Smith looked questioningly at her. She crossed her legs and bobbed up and down, mime for I need a pee. He gave her a thumbs up, then tapped an imaginary wristwatch, mime for don't be too long.

She scaled the steep roadside bank in search of a secluded spot. Thick forest lay before her, with bushy undergrowth that came up to her thighs. She waded into the greenery, steering clear of the clumps of stinging nettles. Everything was still damp from the overnight rain and beginning to steam in the sunlight. A few dozen yards from the road, the sound of traffic was dimmed, just the occasional muted whoosh of a passing vehicle. Raucous birdsong and the rustle of leaves engulfed her. She found an oak with a massive, gnarly trunk, broader than she was tall, and squatted behind it.

She was just finishing up when she sensed something was amiss. All at once, the birds had stopped singing.

She tugged up her tracksuit bottoms and stood. As a city girl born and bred, she didn't know if sudden hushes like this were common in the countryside, but somehow it didn't feel normal. The forest seemed to be offended by a presence in its midst, cringing from it as if in revulsion. Not her presence, she thought. Someone else's.

Could the Paladins have caught up with them already? Were they about to spring an ambush?

She tensed, ready to flee. She could be back at the Land Rover in under a second.

She scanned around. Maybe she was just imagining things. After all she'd been through, not least the slaughter at Summer Land, nobody could blame her for getting spooked.

Amid the tree shadows, dead ahead of her, something glowed.

A pair of eyes.

Blood-red eyes at waist height, staring at her.

She discerned a shape around the eyes, a patch of ragged darkness. The silhouette of some sort of dog. Large, shaggy and with fur as black as night.

Then teeth. A sickle grin of white fangs, and an accompanying growl which was so deep it was almost subsonic.

The dog padded out from the shadows, making for Ajia. She twisted to her left, only to find an even more alarming-looking apparition stalking towards her through the undergrowth. It was a scrawny, human-like thing, going on all fours, haunches in the air, with two large tusks sticking up from its lower jaw. Scraps of animal fur were attached to its body, glued in place with blood, and the skin left exposed was criss-crossed with scars, much as if the creature had been torn apart and stitched back together again. Its eyes were glassy and full of horrible glee.

Ajia was almost too terrified to tear her gaze from this monstrosity, but she did, swinging to her right, the only direction that still offered an escape route.

Except, it didn't any more.

A tall, muscular man stood there with his long arms dangling by his sides. He was naked and exceptionally hairy, and he had a tail which twitched and coiled behind him like an irritated cat's. His brow was Neanderthal-large, a jutting ledge from beneath which a pair of small, gimlet eyes peered.

He grinned. He knew, as Ajia did, that she was surrounded. She had the oak at her back, to the south, and the hairy man, the scrawny beast and the black dog were closing in on her from east, west and north respectively. She wished she had the paring knife with her, but she had left it back at the Land Rover. She'd had no idea she might need it.

Still, her three opponents weren't necessarily quicker than her.

She dug her feet into the soft, loamy ground and darted into the gap between the hairy man and the black dog.

The dog pounced to the side, intercepting. Ajia skidded to a halt so as not to collide with it. She swivelled through a quarter turn and sprinted again. Again the dog jumped into her path, checking her.

The black dog had reflexes to match her speed. Its glowing eyes, bright with triumph, said it knew this and knew Ajia knew too. Whichever way she ran, the dog could obstruct her. Right now it was toying with her, but its bared fangs were a promise that in the near future, at a moment of its choosing, it would rend her to pieces.

Then the bony thing with the animal fur stuck to it began to sing. The melody was simple but sinister, with the repetitive cadences of a nursery rhyme:

> *Rawhead-and-Bloody-Bones*
> *Steals naughty children from their homes,*
> *Takes them to his dirty den,*
> *And they are never seen again.*

Its voice was guttural, and the words themselves were slurred, those two tusks creating a speech impediment.

"Are you a naughty girl?" it asked Ajia, drool leaking from the corner of its mouth. "Would you like to come back to my dirty den? We can play together. I know games. You won't like them but I do. One is called 'Which Body Part Shall I Eat First?'"

Ajia recoiled, retreating until her back was against the oak once more. The hairy man now loomed large over her, his tail more agitated than ever. She noticed—*How could I have missed that?*—a compact digital camera strapped to his shoulder, the lens peeking out through the thick tufts of his pelt. He was recording this? Either that or someone was monitoring proceedings remotely. Somehow the second possibility seemed the likelier. The hairy man didn't look intelligent enough to know what a camera was, let alone how to operate one.

As if to confirm her suspicion, the hairy man let out a throaty chortle—"Hurrgh hurrgh hurrgh"—which was as moronic a laugh as Ajia had ever heard. He spread his arms wide, waggling long, spatulate fingers in the air. He wanted to seize her, and no doubt not to give her a friendly hug.

There was one option still open to her: going upward. She spun round and began clambering up the oak at full speed. A couple of large knobbly burrs near the base of the trunk provided footholds from which she sprang to grab one of the lower boughs.

The black dog, seeing this, hurled itself after her. Its claws missed her by a hair's breadth, raking the rough bark instead and digging furrows. It growled in frustrated fury and tried leaping to catch her, only to keep slithering back down to the ground. Ajia hauled herself from the bough to an equally thick branch above, and then to another less thick branch above that one.

She paused there, straddling the branch. Should she shout for help? The Land Rover wasn't far away. Smith and Mr LeRoy could be there in moments, and Smith could fashion cages out of the trees to corral the three creatures.

That was assuming the creatures didn't kill him first, and Mr LeRoy.

She didn't want them to die rescuing her. But she didn't much fancy dying herself. Again. What should she do?

She heard scuffling sounds below. The hairy man was swinging his way up the oak towards her, as agilely as any monkey.

Ajia immediately started climbing again, fast as she could. The hairy man followed, only slightly slower than she was. He seemed quite at home in trees, even using his tail, prehensile-fashion, as an additional limb.

Soon Ajia was near the top of the oak, higher than she wanted to go, vertiginously high. She had to halt. The branches here were barely able to support her. And still the hairy man kept coming.

The moment his looning face was within reach, she lashed out at it with her foot. He avoided the kick and swung round the trunk. He continued clambering upwards on the opposite side of the tree until he was level with her, then began approaching her laterally, shinning from branch to branch. He kept up that low chortling of his throughout, while down on the ground the black dog barked and the bony, scarred abomination—Rawhead-and-Bloody-Bones? Was that its name?—crooned that sordid song.

Ajia backed away along the branch she was on, as far as she dared. The tree limb bent beneath her with a worrying groan. It bowed all the more when the hairy man joined her on it, adding his weight to hers. Either he was too stupid to realise the branch was in danger of breaking or he didn't care. The blank deadness of his gaze was matched by the blank deadness of the camera lens on his shoulder. Ajia wondered if whoever was watching the feed from the camera was getting off on her distress, or was just some dispassionate observer who didn't give a damn.

The hairy man edged closer along the branch. He looped his tail around a parallel branch for extra support, sliding it along as he went. If this branch should snap, he had given himself a safety rope. Maybe he wasn't as dumb as he acted; or maybe he just had an ingrained, animalistic instinct for self-preservation.

Now he was almost within touching distance. The branch, meanwhile, was making deep splintering creaks at its junction with the trunk. Ajia reckoned it could part company from the rest of the oak at any second.

Then the hairy man stiffened. He frowned, looking utterly flummoxed. His gaze went to his flank, from which a slender wooden rod several inches long now protruded. An arrow, with feather flights at the end. It was embedded in the hairy man at an acute angle, clearly having been fired from below.

A second arrow joined it, thudding into the hairy man's belly. He let out a yawp of pain and shock. His dull eyes grew duller, his tail relaxed its grip on the parallel branch, and he keeled sideways, plummeting through the oak's leafy crown and striking several other branches on his way down to the forest floor. He hit the ground with an almighty thump.

Rawhead-and-Bloody-Bones gave a cry of dismay. "Who's there?" he demanded. "Who did that?"

Then, snarling, the black dog shot off through the undergrowth. Ajia, from her precarious vantage point, watched the animal streak between the trees, an ebony blur. It was homing in on some target she couldn't see.

Then the dog was rolling over and over, legs flailing. It managed to regain its feet but it was whimpering now and trembling terribly. There was an arrow shaft in its hindquarters, the end splintered.

The black dog limped on, as determined as before to reach its quarry, but it was barely able to walk. Its head sagged. Its tongue lolled.

An arrow transfixed its skull, right between those bright crimson eyes. The black dog let out a sharp yipe and fell.

Rawhead-and-Bloody-Bones started prattling incoherently. The swagger he'd shown when Ajia was cornered was all gone. He was scared almost to the point of inarticulacy.

"Please," he burbled. He cast his gaze this way and that, looking for whoever it was that had slain his two allies. "I didn't mean it. I'm sorry. I'll be good. I swear. I'll be a good boy from now on. I won't eat anyone ever again. Please don't—"

An arrow pierced his throat from the front, its tip emerging from the back of his neck. With a wet gargle, Rawhead-and-Bloody-Bones slumped to the ground. His gaunt body twitched and shuddered, then lay still.

The forest was silent for another full minute. Then, gradually, a chirrup here, a twitter there, the birds resumed their chorus.

Ajia waited. Whoever had killed the three monsters didn't seem ready to show his or her face. She had no idea whether or not the person was going to kill her too. Perhaps the archer was even now lining up another shot. Had she just been rescued or was she fourth on the hit list? Until she knew the answer, she was going to stay put in the oak, whose foliage at least afforded some cover. Not much, judging by the ease with which the archer had picked off the hairy man, but it was better than nothing.

"Goodfellow?" It was Smith, calling out to her from by the road. "Goodfellow, where have you got to?"

She didn't reply. With luck, he might head in the wrong direction. If he came this way, he could wind up as the archer's next victim.

"Goodfellow?"

His voice was a little louder. He was getting closer.

She had to warn him away, even if it was at the expense of her own life.

Before she could open her mouth, however, a male voice said, "Smith?"

The speaker appeared as if from nowhere, rising sleekly out of the undergrowth some thirty paces from the oak. He was dressed in jeans, olive-drab combat jacket and desert boots. His hairline was receding but he had plenty of stubble on his chin, as if to demonstrate that some of the follicles on his head still functioned. Green and black camouflage cream streaked his forehead, nose and cheeks, and there was a longbow in his hand and a quiver full of arrows on his back, similarly coloured.

Smith came crashing into view.

"It *is* you," the archer said.

And he nocked an arrow and took aim.

FIFTEEN

"No!" Ajia YELLED, even as Smith came to an abrupt halt and raised his hands.

Both men glanced upward into the tree, Smith in surprise, the archer with an ironical smile.

"Don't shoot him," Ajia said, starting to clamber down. "Don't you dare. I'll fucking kill you if you do."

The archer archly arched an eyebrow. "Who's the girl, Smith?"

"A friend," Smith said.

"Well, I'll have you know I just saved her life, this friend of yours. See these three creeps lying dead on the ground? They were going to have their wicked way with her. I recognise two of them—Black Shuck and Rawhead-and-Bloody-Bones—and the hairy bastard's the Lubber Fiend, I think. Three of the finest bogeymen Britain has to offer. You'll note that each has an arrow or two sticking out of him, courtesy of yours truly."

"Thank you for that," Smith said. "It's much appreciated."

The archer bowed his head a fraction, neither taking his gaze off Smith nor lowering his bow. "You're welcome. Nice outfit, by the way. String vest and longjohns combo. Fetching. Now give me one good reason why I shouldn't plant an arrow in you too."

"Because you're showboating. You wouldn't really kill me. You don't hate me that much."

"Don't I?"

The bowstring twanged. The arrow shot past Smith's head, thudding into a tree behind him.

One of Smith's dreadlocks twirled to the ground. It had been severed just half an inch from his scalp.

The archer already had another arrow in place, bowstring drawn, primed to fire.

By now, however, Ajia was back on the forest floor, and she was fuming. Without hesitating she raced towards the archer. His eyes tracked her. Even though she was going at Puck speed, he was able to follow her movement with his gaze. But he still couldn't move quickly enough to prevent her snatching the arrow out of his grasp and snapping it in two over her knee.

She held up the broken halves to show him.

"Try that again," she said, "and I'll shove these where you least want them. Sideways."

The archer studied the sundered arrow, then burst into laughter. "Fuck me. I thought I was fast."

"You have no idea. Now, don't get me wrong, I'm grateful for what you did. You're also, I'm pretty sure, the person we've come to see. But even if you and Smith have some kind of history, which you seem to, you're just going to have to set it aside. We've travelled quite a long way to get here, wherever 'here' is, and speaking for myself, I'm tired and I'm pissed off and I don't have time for any bullshit. Do you understand?"

The archer seemed more than a little amused. "You're a feisty one, and no mistake."

"Don't call me feisty," Ajia said. "That's so bloody patronising."

"I do beg your pardon. What would you prefer? Spunky? Spirited? Go-getting?"

"What I'd prefer is you putting down that bow."

"There's no arrow in it."

"I've seen how quickly you can reload. And when I say put it down, I mean on the ground."

The archer deliberated, then bent and set the bow down at his feet.

"Good," Ajia said. "Maybe, at last, we—"

The archer hooked a toe under the bow, flipped it up, caught it and nocked a fresh arrow, all in one swift, fluid movement.

"Seriously?" Ajia sighed.

The next instant, both bow and arrow were in Smith's hands. He looked somewhat bemused to find them there.

"You are fast," the archer said wonderingly.

"When I need to be," Ajia said. "Now that I've confiscated your toy, can we just have a civilised conversation?"

"Well, okay. But there is one thing I'd like to do first."

The archer strode over to the hairy man and snatched the digital camera off his shoulder. He held it up to his face, frowning into it. Then he raised a middle finger to the lens, dropped the camera on the ground and stamped on it until it was in smithereens.

"Paladins are after you, yeah?" he said. "Must be. This wasn't some random attack. The Three Fucketeers here were released from Stronghold and sent to take you out. The camera says as much. It also says the Paladins don't care if you know they're after you. Because they're like that, the arrogant twats."

Ajia masked a smile. In spite of his hostility towards Smith, she found herself warming to this man. It wasn't just that she owed him her life. He had attitude.

"I'm not happy, though," he added. "I'm trying to stay off the grid, and the two of you have brought trouble right to my doorstep."

"Three," said Smith. "Auberon LeRoy is with us."

"Mr LeRoy? So Summer Land has finally deigned to come up this way? Wonders will never cease."

"No. There isn't a Summer Land. Not any more."

"Paladins?"

"Yes."

The archer took the information on board. "Shiiiit. All right. I'm sorry to hear that. That's bad. Then you'll be looking for somewhere to lay low for a while, won't you?"

"Any chance you can help with that?" said Ajia.

He grinned. "As it happens, lass, you've come to the right place."
He spread his arms wide. "Welcome to Sherwood Forest, home of
the professional hider-outer."

"Sherwood…?" said Ajia. The penny, belatedly, dropped. It might
have sooner if she hadn't been busy climbing trees and disarming
the archer. "Oh God, don't tell me. You're…"

"Robin Goodfellow," said Smith, "meet Robin Hood."

AT THAT MOMENT, some 150 miles due south, Major Wynne sat in
the operations room at Stronghold and began reviewing the footage
which had just been beamed back from the camera attached to the
Lubber Fiend.

The op itself had not gone wholly to plan. Three assets lost, with
not a single casualty on the other side. However, if Wynne had
learned anything during his stint in the army and his years heading
up a counterterrorism unit at MI5, it was that nothing was a waste
as long as you gleaned some useful intel from it. And he definitely
had.

He rewound to the point where the Lubber Fiend, along with
Black Shuck and Rawhead-and-Bloody-Bones, homed in on their
target. The jerky footage showed the black dog questing eagerly
through the undergrowth. The lumbering Lubber Fiend could
barely keep up. Audio captured his panting breaths and the grisly
mutterings of Rawhead-and-Bloody-Bones beside him.

Then the trio had their quarry cornered against a tree. A young
woman, maybe eighteen, nineteen. Dark, straight hair, olive-tinged
complexion. Wynne recognised her from Summer Land. She was
one of the three who had escaped in the Land Rover Defender. He
watched as she darted to and fro in an attempt to evade Black Shuck.
She was little more than a blur. With a few mouse clicks, he slowed
the footage down to twentieth speed. Even then the girl was just a
roughly human-shaped smear sliding across the screen. The outlines
of Black Shuck in motion were, likewise, almost indecipherable. His
glowing eyes registered on the screen as zigzagging lines, like bolts
of red lightning.

Reverting the playback to normal speed, Wynne watched the Lubber Fiend pursue the girl up the tree. The Lubber Fiend almost had her, until suddenly the footage became a whirling chaos of leaves and branches. The image juddered and went still. The camera was now on its side, as was the Lubber Fiend, lying on the ground. Black Shuck disappeared offscreen, and the audio track relayed faintly the sounds of his death. Wynne was then able to make out the death of Rawhead-and-Bloody-Bones, just. The angle was not good but it was clear that the creature got skewered through the neck by an arrow.

Shortly afterwards, there was a conversation between the girl and a man with a bow and arrow, whom Wynne could only assume was the person responsible for eradicating all three assets. The dialogue was muffled—the camera's microphone was probably buried in the forest leaf litter—but it was apparent that some kind of standoff was happening and that there was a third party involved, somewhere out of shot. The girl disarmed the archer, there was more talk, then the archer stooped to pick up the camera, leered into it, gave it the finger, and dropped it to the ground. The image degenerated into ragged, overlapping fields of colour, while the audio was a maelstrom of static. Then blackness and silence. Signal lost.

Wynne leaned back in his chair, folding his arms behind his head.

So. The survivors of the assault on Summer Land had sought refuge in, of all places, Sherwood Forest. That was the first tick in the plus column. The Paladins now had a good idea where they were, although whether or not they were going to stay put was another matter. The forest wasn't that big. If they had any sense, they would get the hell out of the area ASAP.

The second tick was that the footage contained decent shots of the girl's and the archer's faces. Wynne would send the file down to Stronghold's tech department, who would run matches against the national ID database and pull up names and background details on both.

The third tick was that Wynne now knew that the girl possessed preternatural abilities. She could move as fast as Black Shuck—and that was fast. The dog had been clocked at over a hundred and fifty miles an hour.

The biggest tick in the minus column, Wynne reflected, was the loss of Black Shuck. Of the three assets involved in the op, the dog's destruction was the only one that was in any way regrettable. All three were monsters, but there was something so repellent about the two human-looking ones that in a way Wynne was glad to be rid of them. Prisoners at Stronghold, they had agreed to take part in the op on the promise of various special privileges. In the case of the Lubber Fiend, this meant the opportunity to molest horses, one of his peccadilloes. Rawhead-and-Bloody-Bones, meanwhile, had demanded a living child to feast on as his fee, in addition to consuming the flesh of at least one of the targets the three of them were assigned to kill. Wynne had had no intention of granting either's wish, but both had been too dumb and gullible to realise that. They were cannon fodder and he had few regrets about expending them.

Black Shuck, by contrast, had been useful, and it was a shame he was no longer alive. Developing the dog as an asset had not been easy. A police K-9 unit trainer had spent months working on him, on the Paladins' behalf. The man had managed to tame him up to a point, although he had admitted to Wynne that the beast would never be fully obedient. "I don't know where you found him," he'd said, "but that's the fiercest fucking hound I've ever encountered, not to mention the fastest. And don't get me started on those eyes. I mean to say, what breed has eyes like that?"

Earlier in the day, Wynne had arranged for Black Shuck to sniff pieces of clothing from several of the caravans at Summer Land, shortly before the Paladins set about torching the entire place. One item in particular had excited the dog: a Justin Bieber T-shirt, of all things. Once Black Shuck had indicated he had caught a scent trail, Wynne had unleashed him.

A computerised subdermal implant in Black Shuck's neck not only emitted a GPS signal but permitted some control over him by means of electric shocks. The Paladins had tracked him via satellite as he'd streaked northward and, when his circling movements had indicated that he was closing in on his target, a sequence of jolts from the implant had brought him to a standstill. This was one of the behavioural curbs the K-9 trainer had instilled in him. Black

Shuck had waited patiently while the Lubber Fiend and Rawhead-and-Bloody-Bones were choppered up-country to join him in the field. The rest of the op had played out as recorded on the camera footage, all the way to its less than satisfactory outcome.

The question facing Wynne now was whether or not to dispatch Paladin teams to apprehend and kill the fugitives. Sherwood Forest covered 450 acres: a large space to get lost in, with plenty of cover. Paladins could scour the woods extensively and still fail to find them, especially if they were on the move.

The more prudent tactic would be to contain them. Put up a cordon around the forest, blockading all the main points of ingress and egress. Rather than flush them out, wait for them to break cover. They would have to sooner or later, and then the Paladins could pounce.

Several factors inclined Wynne towards the latter alternative. He was exhausted, for one thing. He hadn't slept in thirty-six hours. He was keen to supervise the elimination of the fugitives himself, to make sure it was carried out with all due diligence, and for that he needed to be rested and refreshed.

For another thing, Harriet Drake had sent him a text just half an hour ago, informing him that she required urgent close protection. Tired or not, it was a summons he was reluctant to ignore.

Wynne found Lieutenant Noble and told him to mobilise every available Paladin. "I want Sherwood Forest surrounded. Nobody gets in or out. Ring of steel. You have full autonomy."

Then he picked up his phone and texted Harriet back, making arrangements for a rendezvous.

Wynne was under no illusion. If the prime minister discovered their affair, he would almost certainly have him killed.

And if that wasn't the icing on the cake, the cream in the coffee, the dash of tabasco in the Bloody Mary, then Wynne didn't know what was.

THE WEEKLY CABINET meeting, normally a chore, today turned out to be worse: an ordeal.

Drake looked round the Cabinet Room table at the couple of dozen ministers who held senior positions in his government. All had document folders and tablets in front of them and were looking as efficient and officious as humanly possible. He could divide them up into three categories. There were the ones he trusted implicitly because they shared his values. There were the ones he trusted but only because they were spineless and unimaginative. And there were the ones he didn't quite trust because they were ambitious. They wanted his crown. They were waiting for the moment they could take over, jockeying for position to be his successor. Drake had no intention of retiring yet, but someday he would, and there was no shortage of candidates poised to step up when he stepped down. They were dogs nipping at his heels, but for the time being he knew he could browbeat them into submission if need be.

Every one of these meetings was little more than a series of formalities. One after another, the ministers would deliver brief reports on the business of the sub-committees they chaired. Drake would yea or nay the policies being put forward. His word was final. There was no argument.

This morning, he could scarcely concentrate. Voices washed over him like white noise. Now and then a question would come through loud and clear, like a lighthouse beam penetrating fog.

"Prime Minister, this proposal for increasing the budget for security at our ports is modest and reasonable. What's your view?"

"Do you think, Derek, that we should trim unemployment benefit by a further ten per cent? The Treasury coffers are hardly brimming."

"We at the Digital taskforce reckon the police should have greater powers to crack down on cyber-protest. Don't you?"

Drake responded to each query as appropriate, albeit on autopilot. Mostly, he was thinking about the video clip. Him and Tatjana Bazanova on the bed upstairs in this very building. The sight of his own bare buttocks pumping up and down, while Tatjana writhed beneath him, feigning ecstasy.

Just a taster. Best wishes to yourself and Mrs Drake.

Vasilyev could not have made it more plain. He would have no compunction about sending the clip—perhaps even the entire video in all its pornographic glory—to Harriet if he felt the situation warranted it.

But what situation would that be? What would Drake have to do to deserve that penalty? So far he had been a staunch and vocal supporter of the Russian premier, and he had not foreseen this stance changing any time soon. Clearly Vasilyev wanted extra leverage over him. An insurance policy should Drake's enthusiasm ever wane.

Doubtless Drake was not the only national leader whom Vasilyev had compromised in this way. This wasn't much consolation, though. He had an image in his head he couldn't get rid of: Vasilyev watching the video, perhaps in the company of a select few cronies. Chuckling at the sight of Derek Drake caught with his pants down, literally. Rubbing his hands with bawdy glee.

The utter bastard.

Drake fumed.

He was still fuming an hour later as he conducted a press conference outside Number 10.

"It is," he said, "a terrible tragedy." The subject was the devastating fire which had broken out at a funfair in Dorset overnight, resulting in extensive loss of life. Decorum demanded an official statement. "It's too early to say yet what the cause might have been, but poorly maintained machinery is thought to be at the heart of it, although arson is not being ruled out."

He inclined his head to one side in a manner that could be construed as sympathetic.

"We must thank God," he continued, "that disaster struck after the fair had closed and that the only victims were fairground workers and not members of the public. It could have been a lot worse. I feel moved to point out that the employees of Summer Land were, in all likelihood, part of the cash-in-hand economy which is undermining the fiscal fabric of our nation. Nonetheless, brave firefighters, funded by the taxpayer, stepped in to combat the blaze and bring it under control."

A question was lobbed at him from the mob of journalists across the road. "Do you think, Prime Minister, there were illegals working at the fair?"

In spite of everything, Drake almost smiled. The reporter was from the *Daily Mail*, a paper that could be relied on to toe the Resurrection Party line. It, the *Daily Telegraph* and the *Sun* were practically part of the government machinery.

"It's not beyond the realms of possibility," he replied. "Of course I am not saying anyone deserves to die because they are resident in this country illegally, nor am I condoning violence of any kind towards undocumented citizens. I would, though, like to remind your readers, and everyone else"—he swivelled his head from left to right so that every camera present could catch the lofty, statesmanlike expression on his face—"that it is their civic duty to report those whom they feel may not have a legal right to remain on these shores. Britain is for the British."

He returned indoors, having done his bit to help draw an obscuring veil over the Paladin assault on Summer Land. And still he fumed.

Fucking Vasilyev.

Brooding on the problem, Drake decided he had two options. One was untenable, the other was unpalatable, and neither was desirable.

The untenable option was to try to recover the *kompromat* footage somehow. He could, for instance, make Vasilyev an offer he couldn't refuse. The Russian was already a multibillionaire, thanks to his rigorous plundering of state-owned corporations and the nation's cash reserves, but there was surely some form of financial inducement that could persuade him to part with the video. A controlling stake in Britain's nuclear industry, perhaps. Some juicy contracts for his armament companies. Or maybe a huge swathe of the Scottish highlands. Yes. Drive a few lairds and crofters off their land and give it to Vasilyev in perpetuity, to add to his burgeoning property portfolio. Let him build hotels, golf courses, even air force bases there, and in exchange he would hand the footage over to Drake, deleting any copies he himself had.

The unpalatable option was coming clean to Harriet about Tatjana. Then Vasilyev's hold over him would be considerably lessened. Harriet might learn to forgive him, eventually. But she would have questions about his ability to achieve a hard-on for another women but not for her. Questions which might prove tricky to answer honestly.

The problem with either option was that Vasily Vasilyev was a shifty son of a bitch who had risen up the ranks of the State Duma with eel-like slipperiness, squirming through the grasp of every political opponent who tried to impede his progress. "Vaseline" Vasilyev, as one US TV satirist had nicknamed him. He would surely not bother sending the clip to British media outlets, knowing that Drake had those more or less in his pocket. But what was to stop him releasing the footage into the public domain any time he liked? He might do it just for kicks. Even if Drake managed to bribe him off, there might still be a leak, accidental or otherwise, and suddenly Derek Drake Giving Russian TV Journalist a Good Seeing-to would be the top search on the internet and the #1 trending topic on Twitter, proliferating faster than the country's cyber-monitoring services could shut it down. Drake's humiliation would be universal rather than merely marital. It would be the kind of public relations shitstorm even the soundest political career might not survive.

However you looked at it, Vasily Vasilyevich Vasilyev had him over a barrel.

Drake needed help. He needed advice.

Luckily, he knew where to turn to for that.

He cancelled all of his appointments for the rest of the afternoon, summoned a limo and headed homeward.

AN HOUR AND a half later the prime ministerial motorcade passed through the gates of Charrington Grange. Drake leapt out of the limo before it had fully come to a halt and, rather than entering the house, hurried off in the direction of the museum.

From the point of view of Major Wynne and Harriet Drake, it was just as well he did.

"Fuck fuck fuck fuck fuck," Wynne hissed, peering out from behind the bedroom curtain while his tumescent penis slowly wilted. The moment he had heard cars crunching along the drive, he had rolled off Harriet and scuttled over to the window. "What the hell is he doing back?"

Harriet was as nonplussed as he was. "How should I know?" she said, reaching for her clothes which, like her lover's, were strewn all over the bedroom floor. "Usually he rings me if he knows he'll be home earlier than scheduled."

"At least he's not coming inside."

"Where's he going?"

"The museum of holy bits and bobs, looks like." Wynne snatched up his uniform and began tugging it on. He found his hands were clumsy. He kept fumbling with the zips and buttons. "Can you give me some help here?"

"Bit busy myself," Harriet said, slipping on her floaty Givenchy summer dress. "We're okay, Dominic. You have every reason to be at the Grange. It's not as if you aren't here practically every day. Just calm down."

"I am calm."

"You're not acting it. You're acting flustered. I thought you got off on this as much as I do, the sense that we could be found out at any time. I thought that was part of the attraction."

"It is, but I don't like being taken unawares," Wynne said, smoothing the Velcro fastening of his high-necked collar into place. "I try to take all the possible contingencies into account, and then something like this happens."

"What is it you military types like to say? 'No plan survives contact with the enemy.'"

Wynne knelt to lace up his boots. "Still no excuse."

Harriet took his head in her hands, clasping it firmly. "Go downstairs," she said. "Wait for Derek to come in. Front it out. You're here to report on your mission, the one you told me about, the funfair. You wanted to deliver the latest update in person. By great good fortune, your boss has come home sooner than expected. Hooray. Less time spent cooling your heels. Meanwhile, I'll go over and catch him as he leaves the museum. 'Darling, what a pleasant surprise! Didn't expect you till much later.' I can lay it on just the right amount. He won't suspect a thing, and you'll have more time to compose yourself."

Wynne looked up at her with frank admiration. "I so want to shag the arse off you right now."

"I know. Me too. And you were doing such a good job of it before Derek arrived."

HARRIET LEFT WYNNE and sauntered out across the grounds, for all the world like a loving, dutiful wife delighted at the return of her husband from work.

She envisaged loitering near the poolhouse, then just so happening to bump into Derek as he exited the museum. In the event, when she reached the pool she saw through the gap in the yew hedge that the door to the museum had been left slightly ajar.

This surprised her. Derek always shut the door.

Should she go in?

It wasn't as though he had ever explicitly forbidden her from entering the museum. On the other hand, he had made it crystal clear that it was a place for him alone and that others were not welcome. The fact that he hadn't shared the door code with her, or anyone else, was proof of that. It was his glorified man cave, and to be frank, Harriet had never seen the attraction of visiting it.

Until now.

The open door seemed almost an invitation. Derek wouldn't have left it like that on purpose, but she could always pretend she thought he had. And if he got shirty with her for trespassing on his holy ground, so much the better as far as she was concerned. She could use his anger against him. It would mean he wasn't thinking straight and was less liable to notice anything awry. He might be oblivious to any odd behaviour by Dominic Wynne.

She crossed the threshold, venturing into a space which, although part of the home she had lived in for nearly two decades, she had never entered before.

Harriet had seen most of the religious artefacts in the collection individually. Whenever Derek bought one, he would often show it off to her before depositing it in the museum.

It was different seeing them all in one place, however. They were a motley assortment of objects, some of them richly wrought treasures and obviously valuable, others rather tatty-looking, grotesque, even repellent, yet no less expensive for that. She supposed this was a hobby equivalent to stamp collecting or trainspotting, what the wealthy religious zealot did with his spare cash and his spare time. She didn't much mind that Derek had squandered a considerable percentage of his fortune on the relics. He had plenty left over, and her monthly spending allowance was more than generous. As long as her lifestyle was unaffected, he could do what he wanted with his money.

But still, it was overwhelming, in a way, this jealously husbanded and guarded hoard. As she passed through the museum—here a sliver of ancient wood, there a bejewelled casket—Harriet wondered whether there wasn't a streak of madness in Derek Drake.

She could have been forgiven for wondering it more, when she heard Derek's voice emanating from the far end of the room. He was talking. Holding what appeared to be a one-sided conversation.

Following the sound, she came to a chamber the door to which was also open. It was some kind of inner sanctum, brightly lit. She saw her husband kneeling in front of a pedestal at the centre. His back was to her. He gave no sign that he had heard her approach.

What he was talking to was a jewel-encrusted onyx chalice which Harriet recognised instantly. It was the cup Derek believed to be the Holy Grail, the relic which he'd purchased the same day he had his helicopter crash and which he had begged her to bring to him at the hospital, the first thing he had asked for after emerging from his coma.

He was talking to it as though it could hear him. He was speaking low and Harriet could not make out what he was saying but, as she listened, she became aware of a second, softer voice, one that filled the gaps between Derek's remarks.

Was there someone else in the chamber after all?

She couldn't see anyone. Derek was alone in there. Yet somebody was definitely replying to him.

Was he on the phone? No, his hands were interlaced together in front of him. No phone in sight.

A hidden speaker, perhaps? Harriet couldn't see any.

Nevertheless the second voice was coming from somewhere.

And, my God... It wasn't just any voice. It was one Harriet knew. Knew well. One she hadn't heard in a long while.

All of a sudden, Derek looked round.

It was hard to say which of them was the more startled, her or him. Each gaped at the other in consternation.

"Derek," she said eventually.

"Harriet."

"What are you doing?"

"I could ask the same of you. You shouldn't be in here."

"The door was open."

"Was it?" He looked perplexed. "I must've... Distracted. Hell of a day. But still. You know this is my private place."

"Never mind that," Harriet said. "Answer me this. How come that cup is speaking to you, and why does it have Emrys Sage's voice?"

Her husband's alarm turned to astonishment. He stared at her as though scarcely able to comprehend what she had just said.

"You mean," he said in a hushed, incredulous whisper, "you can hear him too?"

SIXTEEN

ROBIN HOOD'S LAIR was not some arboreal fantasy of treehouses, ropes and catwalks, like in the old Kevin Costner movie. If she was honest with herself, Ajia hadn't expected it would be, but if she was even more honest with herself, she had rather hoped it might.

Robin Hood's lair was, instead, a bunker built along the lines of a World War II Anderson shelter, with walls and roof of corrugated iron. It lay mostly below ground and, from the outside, looked like nothing more than a small grassy hillock in a glade in the middle of the forest. The entrance door was disguised under a layer of turf. Until the archer grasped a concealed handle and opened it, Ajia had had no idea it was there.

"Welcome to my bijou residence," he said, hanging up bow and quiver on a hook inside the door. "Make yourselves comfortable. I'll get a brew going."

"No Merrie Men?" Ajia asked, sweeping her gaze around the cramped accommodation. There was an area for food storage and cooking in one corner. The furniture comprised a plastic picnic table with a couple of matching chairs and a rickety cot, which together occupied almost entirely what little square footage of floorspace there was. The only illumination came courtesy of a pair of battery-powered lanterns. The air reeked of dank earth and male musk.

"Just me." The archer busied himself lighting a Primus stove while his guests squeezed around one another to sit down. He served the tea in chipped enamel mugs. "No fridge, so milk's the powdered stuff only. Not that powdered milk did me any harm when I was in the Paras. If you add enough sugar, it'll take the taste away."

They drank in silence. Smith kept giving Robin Hood glowering looks. The tension simmering between the two men was palpable.

"So," Robin Hood said to Mr LeRoy, "Summer Land's gone, eh? They finally caught up with you."

The king of the funfair folk gave a morose nod. "Our luck ran out."

"Luck?" Robin Hood sneered. "You'd have been a whole lot luckier if you'd taken steps to protect yourself."

"We had the goblins."

"Those guys? Thick as pigshit. Nothing more than glorified bouncers. I kept telling you you should arm yourselves. The Paladins were going to find you sooner or later, and you'd have stood a better chance against them if you'd been all tooled up. You might even have seen them off."

"And I kept telling you," Mr LeRoy replied sternly, "that that is not my way. With Summer Land I wanted to create a safe haven for our kind, not a fortress. Somewhere we could just be ourselves."

"And look where that got you."

"Violence isn't the answer to everything, Fletcher," Smith said. "You seem to think it is, but it isn't."

Fletcher, Ajia thought. *Robin Hood's real surname. Nominative determinism rearing its head again.*

"It isn't the answer to everything," Fletcher replied, "but sometimes, depending on the question, it's the right answer. That's why I couldn't stay with you people. You were just so... passive. It was like you were waiting for the Paladins to come and get you. In many ways you did the hard work for them, Mr LeRoy, by gathering a bunch of eidolons together under one roof. You did the corralling. All the Paladins had to do was turn up and start the slaughter."

"This was not my fault," Mr LeRoy said.

"Keep telling yourself that."

"It was not!" Tea slopped from Mr LeRoy's mug onto his hand. He didn't seem to notice. "I did the right thing. I needn't have started Summer Land. I could have left all those eidolons to fend for themselves. A few of them might have coped with their new identities. They might have carried on with their lives and been able to pass for normal. Most would not have. Wasn't it better to bring them together, so that they could share the burden with others? Wasn't that the more sensible approach?"

"Only if your plan was to make a ghetto."

"If Summer Land was a ghetto, it was at least a peripatetic one. The proverbial moving target, much harder to hit. And everyone had a choice about being there. People were free to come and go as they pleased. Smith is proof of that, as are you."

Fletcher chuckled mirthlessly. "I came and went within the space of a week, because I could see what was coming down the line, even if you couldn't. Our kind, the only way to stay safe is by keeping as low a profile as possible. There you were, practically flaunting yourselves. Disaster waiting to happen."

"This isn't at all helpful," Smith growled. "As usual, Fletcher, you're letting your mouth run off. Can't you see Mr LeRoy is grieving? We all are. We've lost friends. Close ones, some of us. We only just survived. Show some consideration."

But Fletcher, it seemed, was incapable of tact. "You, Smith, you're a fine one to talk. Did you show me any consideration when you lit out on me in my hour of need? Huh? I thought we were partners. I thought you had my back. But when it came to the crunch, noooo, Smith was too prissy to do what needed to be done. Smith would rather scarper and leave me dangling. And now here you are, you and Mr LeRoy, crawling back to me after your policy of non-aggression comes round and bites you on the arse. There's irony. What is it exactly you want? You want me to reassure you that you're still in the right? That you still have the moral high ground, even though the Paladins fucked you five ways to Sunday? Because if so, you've come to the wrong place."

"Yes," Smith said, rising to his feet. "I knew this was a mistake.

I knew we shouldn't have bothered. I'd thought you might at least be sympathetic."

"Oh, don't get me wrong," Fletcher said. "I'm sorry about what's happened with Summer Land. Truly I am. But I can't tell you I'm surprised and I can't tell you it wasn't inevitable."

"There's no point in us staying if all you're going to do is act all superior."

"You can go," said Fletcher with a sweeping gesture. "Door's right there. Feel free. Just bear this in mind. The Paladins know where you are. They know your approximate location. If I were Dominic Wynne—and say what you like about him, the man's no slouch—I'd be overflying the forest with drones and setting up a grid-pattern search."

"At the risk of sounding naïve," Ajia said, "you don't think they'll just give up on looking for us, then?"

Fletcher shook his head. "Bless you for hoping that, girl. No, they expended three of their captive eidolons tracing you this far. Wynne's got a honking great hard-on for finding you lot and he's not going to stop now. You pissed him off by getting away."

"I think we also pissed him off by taking down a few Paladins."

"You did?" Fletcher raised an eyebrow. "So it wasn't a complete rout?"

"I can't speak for anyone else but I know I stabbed five of them."

"To death?"

"Not sure. Maybe. If I did, it wasn't intentionally. I just wanted to stop them." Hurt them, she added, to herself. Get them back for what they did to May and the others.

"What did you use?"

"A paring knife."

"You'd have done a better job with something bigger."

"It was all I had. I made do."

Fletcher let out a low whistle. "Well, it's impressive, still. One of you's got some balls at least."

"If you mean that as a compliment, it really isn't," Ajia said. "Blokes believe the world revolves around their genitalia. Hate to break it to you, but it doesn't."

Now Fletcher laughed loudly and lustily. He even threw back his head, and for a moment Ajia caught a glimpse of the Robin Hood of legend, the devil-may-care brigand, full of joviality.

"I really like you," he said. "I'd be prepared to give these two mopey twats the benefit of the doubt, simply because they've introduced me to you. Not only can you move like greased lightning, you're not afraid to speak your mind. I didn't catch your full name. You're Puck but you're also…?"

"Ajia Snell."

"Reed Fletcher." He shook her hand. "Pity we're not going to be acquainted that long, since you lot appear to be about to bugger off."

"I suppose we are," Ajia said. "Not sure where we're planning to bugger off to, though."

"Anywhere but here," said Smith. "This was a waste of time. If we hurry, we can probably get back to the Land Rover before the Paladins arrive in force. We can keep driving north and be in Scotland before nightfall. Up there, there's plenty more space to lose ourselves in."

"Plenty more open ground, too," said Fletcher, "making it a damn sight easier to track you by satellite or drone. Just pointing out the slight flaw in your plans. Don't let me stop you."

"What's the alternative? You've not been the most hospitable of hosts. But then it's always all about you, isn't it, Fletcher? What you can get out of something. What's in it for you."

"It's how I've managed to keep going. I didn't ask to become an eidolon."

"None of us did," Mr LeRoy interjected.

"But since I am one," Fletcher went on, "I'm going to make damn well sure it doesn't ruin me. I'm settled here. I've built my little hidey-hole and I've been living off the land, scrounging whatever I can get. I'm managing."

"Barely." Mr LeRoy subjected the bunker to a sceptical once-over. "I'd call this subsistence at best."

"It's worked for me so far, and it beats running away from the Paladins with my tail between my legs."

"Isn't that exactly what you've done?" Smith barked. "Isn't lurking underground all day long like a mole just another form of cowardice?"

"Says the man who turned and ran when he was meant to be providing backup."

"Because you were willing to kill in order to get your way, and I wasn't. It's that simple."

"And I could have died because you were such a pants-wetting wimp. It's that simple."

Fletcher was now on his feet as well, and he and Smith were leaning towards each other, glaring, fists clenched. They were pretty much the living epitome of the phrase at loggerheads.

"I can't believe this," Ajia said. "You're acting like spoilt brats. Whoever did whatever to who, now isn't the time to rake it up. We've got bigger things to worry about."

Each man jabbed a finger at the other. "He—" they both began.

"I swear to God," Ajia cut in, "if either of you says 'He started it', I'm going to grab two of those arrows and stab you both in the eye."

"Yes, well," Smith grumbled. "I was all for bygones being bygones, but obviously I'm alone in that. Here's your tea back, Fletcher." He tipped the mug, pouring the contents onto the bunker's earthen floor. "Powdered milk or not, it's too foul to drink."

"I wouldn't want to drink tea with you anyway," Fletcher retorted, and tipped his onto the floor as well. He tossed the mug aside, thrust the door open and stormed out of the bunker.

AJIA JOINED HIM outside.

"Did that really just happen, Reed?" she said. "You and Smith had a hissy fit and poured away your tea? The words 'toys' and 'pram' spring to mind."

"They send you out to make peace?" Fletcher said. He was leaning against a tree not far from the bunker, with a disgruntled air. "Try and butter me up?"

"No. I came out of my own accord, because I've just watched

two grown men behave like huge babies and I find it ridiculous. It's obvious you two were best buds at one time, and still are, in spite of everything. Smith's even been referring to you as his 'friend' all along. That's why you're so annoyed with each other. You're actually annoyed with yourselves for falling out."

"You have no idea what that man did, Ajia. How badly he screwed me over."

"Does it matter what he did? Way I see it, what matters is he came all this way to find you because he needs help—we need help—and he thought you'd be the person to provide it. That must tell you something."

"Tells me he's desperate."

"All the more reason to feel honoured. Smith didn't turn to just anyone in his desperation. He turned to you. If you could get over yourself for a moment, you'd see how it's your duty to do what you can for him. And for Mr LeRoy."

"I don't owe either of them anything," Fletcher stated adamantly. "Besides," he added with a shrug, "they're keen to leave. Who am I to stand in their way?"

"Look," Ajia said, stepping closer, "you can pretend you're a tough nut, you can act all hard-case and don't-give-a-shit, but you shot three hellbeast eidolons to protect me. You took your life in your hands on a stranger's behalf and I don't think you thought twice about it."

"They were in my forest," Fletcher said. "I was out hunting squirrel and they came crashing past and I won't have their sort in my forest."

"You saved me and you didn't know me from Adam."

"Don't get ideas. I'd have done it for anybody."

"You're Robin Hood. Steals from the rich, gives to the poor. That's your code of ethics, isn't it? You're a good guy. Everybody knows that."

"But I don't actually see what I can do here," said Fletcher, with a touch of petulance. "Paladins are after you. Why should I get in the middle of that? I can happily hide out in my luxury underground condo until all this whole mess blows over, and I can do that far more easily on my own. So you should get going while you still can, all of you. Head for Scotland. Maybe you'll make it."

"Or you can let us hide out in your luxury underground condo with you. How about that?"

"Four of us in there?" He waved towards the grassy mound. "Talk about close quarters. How long do you reckon we'll last before I throttle Smith or he throttles me? Anyway, it may already be too late."

"What do you mean?"

Fletcher caressed the tree trunk beside him, looking ruminative. "Sherwood Forest talks to me, you see."

"It does?"

"Nothing happens in these woods that I don't know about. And the forest is telling me…" He cocked his head to one side, as though listening to voices Ajia could not hear. Around them, a myriad leaves chattered busily, like gossips' tongues. "It's telling me Paladins are moving in to surround it. They're closing the place off. No way in or out. So you three are trapped. I guess if you started out straight away, you might get back to your car in time, but I don't rate your chances."

"That's it, then," Ajia said. "We have to stay."

"Maybe you do," Fletcher said ruefully. Then he burst into laughter. "Come on, you didn't really fall for it, did you? 'Sherwood Forest talks to me'? I'm bullshitting."

"Oh." It wouldn't have surprised Ajia if Reed Fletcher, given that he was the eidolon of Robin Hood, had some sort of mystical connection with the forest. She was somewhat disappointed, in fact, that he didn't. She knew now, from experience, that far stranger things were possible. "So, that stuff about the Paladins isn't true either?"

"No, it's true all right." He produced a phone from his pocket and waggled it in the air. "I was just checking the BBC news feed. Can't get a signal inside the lair but out here there's a couple of bars. Major-league Paladin operation under way around Sherwood Forest, apparently. Whole area's cordoned off to the public until further notice. Details are sketchy, but it doesn't take a genius to figure out they're setting up a perimeter. After that, they'll either move in to search or they'll sit tight, hoping to starve you guys out, like it's a siege. One or the other, depending on how pissy or patient they're feeling. My money's on pissy."

Ajia took him by the arm and dragged him back to the bunker.

"Tell them what you just told me," she said.

Fletcher did.

"Great," said Smith. "We're trapped. The forest has become a prison and all we can do is wait for the Paladins to find us."

"If Reed lets us hang out with him here," said Ajia, "maybe we can stick it out. They won't keep hunting for us forever. There's got to come a point when they say enough's enough and give up. We just have to outlast them."

"Easier said than done," said Fletcher. "There's the supply situation, for starters. We don't have to worry about drinking water. There's a spring I use nearby. But food's limited. I have a few tins, some dried stuff, but mostly the forest provides. Squirrel, rabbit, the odd deer. Wild mushrooms, chickweed, sorrel, horse parsley, dandelion leaves. Beech nuts, blackberries and hawthorn berries in season. I get by. But that's me alone. Four of us, that'll be a whole lot harder to cater for and it'll mean more time spent outdoors foraging, which'll mean more chance of getting spotted. I'm not saying we couldn't make this work. I'm just saying it's going to be damn near impossible."

"At least you're not turfing us out," said Mr LeRoy. "That's something."

"Yeah, well, I'm not a total wanker."

Smith grumbled something inaudible. Ajia suspected he was disputing Fletcher's assertion.

"So that's that," she said, slumping down in one of the picnic-table chairs. "We're living here until further notice. Not ideal but it'll have to do. I just…"

"What?" said Mr LeRoy.

"No, nothing."

"Come on, out with it, Ajia."

She took a deep breath. So much had happened over the past few hours, she was having difficulty processing it. Yet certain thoughts were starting to crystallise in her head, the events of last night bringing a whole host of things—emotions, ideas, memories—into focus.

"I'm fed up, that's all," she said. "It shouldn't have to be like this. I've been on the run pretty much constantly since the police arrested me and I died and came back to life. Even at Summer Land, it felt like a respite but it wasn't, not really. It was just a different kind of being on the run. I'm sick and tired of it. I'm tired, full stop. That'll be why I'm having a moan. You can tell me to shut up if you like."

"No, you're entitled to vent," said Mr LeRoy. "Get it out of your system. No one minds."

"I'm not just venting, though," Ajia said. "I'm feeling... Well, resentful doesn't begin to cover it. I hate the fucking Paladins. I hate Derek Drake. I hate what this country's become. Everything keeps getting worse and worse. There's a part of me wants to go outside and walk up to the nearest Paladin and let the bastard shoot me. Put me out of my misery."

"Don't say that," Fletcher said. "Don't *ever* say that."

"Don't worry, because there's another part of me that wants to bring them to their knees—the Paladins, the Resurrection Party, dickhead Drake, the whole lot. It's a larger part. An angrier part. And it's the part that's speaking now. I wish there were some way we could tear down the government, undo everything Drake's done, make it all better again. Britain wasn't perfect before but it wasn't shitawful either. It functioned. It tried to be tolerant. If you didn't like something, you could at least protest about it, maybe change it. There was hope. We hadn't all turned on each other like rats in a dumpster. We weren't bullying the weak and chucking out the unwanted."

"You're not the only one who feels that way," Mr LeRoy said, "but it's too late, Ajia. The damage is done. I don't think there's anything you or I or anybody can do about it."

"Isn't there?" Ajia said. "When you told me your theory about why eidolons came to be, what did you compare us to?"

"I don't recall the precise metaphor. Was it canaries in the coalmine?"

"It was. And I asked you if that was all. Because it seemed to me—still does—that that's kind of underwhelming. I mean, look at us. I can run faster than a Bullet Train. You can find other eidolons as if by magic. Smith can build things practically out of thin air and heal injuries. Reed here's super accurate with his arrows. Am I right about that? I saw how you clipped off one of Smith's dreads."

"I was aiming for his face," said Fletcher.

"No, you weren't. We've all got these abilities, these powers. Calling us coalmine canaries is selling us short. You also, Mr LeRoy, said that we're signs of a fever. That the country's sick and we're the symptoms. I've been thinking about that, and I reckon it's wrong."

The three men were quiet. Ajia took this as carte blanche to carry on.

"What if our purpose isn't to be a human warning system?" she said. "What if it's something more?"

"In what way?" said Mr LeRoy.

"My feeling is, if you're going to liken us to anything illness-related, it should be antibodies. You know, white blood cells and all that. We have a specific purpose. We're designed to oppose, to fight back, to fix things."

Fletcher shook his head slowly, warily. "This is sounding very much like insurgent talk. The sort of talk that ends up getting you killed."

"You could sound more disapproving."

"Well, as long as it remains just talk…"

"Please hear me out, at least," she said. "I find it hard to believe that we've got the talents we have and we're not using them proactively. We've run, we've hid, we've been on the back foot. We've let the authorities hound us. Just now, Reed said he found Summer Land passive. I have to say, on balance I agree with him. I didn't realise it at the time but I can see it now. Summer Land was a wonderful idea, Mr LeRoy, but it was, all said and done, a defensive tactic. Perhaps, with all those eidolons gathered in one place, we could have achieved more. We could have stood up and made a difference."

"Perry stood up," Mr LeRoy said. "He stood up to those Paladins, and you saw the result."

"It was horrible but at least he tried. We should draw inspiration from his example."

"What are you proposing here, Ajia?" said Smith. "That the four of us should somehow try and take on the government? Smash the whole Resurrection Party apparatus, Paladins and all? Be Britain's liberators? A noble sentiment, undoubtedly, but preposterous."

Ajia sighed. "I am probably talking out of my arse, and you can blame it on exhaustion, grief, outrage, whatever. However, it's making sense, if only to me. So, Reed is Robin Hood. Folk hero who fought against the Sherriff of Nottingham and wicked King John. Those two were his big bads, as far as I remember. I'm not an expert. But they were the oppressive forces back then, the Derek Drakes of the day."

"I hope you're not trying to recruit me for something," said Fletcher. "Three tours in Helmand Province, one in Sierra Leone. I've had enough of the whole putting-your-life-on-the-line-for-others thing. Been there, done that, got the bloodstained T-shirt."

"What I'm getting at is that Robin Hood has pedigree, more so than Wayland the Smith or Oberon or Puck. Robin Hood is a bona fide big name in anti-establishment resistance."

"Robin Hood might have been, but Reed Fletcher isn't."

"You could at least be a figurehead we could rally around," Ajia said. "The core of something much larger."

"No. No." Fletcher was shaking his head vigorously. "I live in a hole in the ground. Like a mole, as Smith said. It suits me."

"And there you were, criticising Summer Land for being passive. But this is my point. Why don't we put together a new band of Merrie Men? The four of us can be its nucleus. There might be others out there willing to join. In particular, other eidolons. We just have to find them, and for that, conveniently, we have Mr LeRoy. There must be more folkloric figures than just us and the generic faeries who made up the funfair folk. I don't know enough about British legends to be able to come up with a comprehensive list, but off the top of my head I can think of at least one big name, up there with Robin Hood in the recognisability rankings. King Arthur? Yeah? If there's an eidolon of Robin Hood, there must be an eidolon of King Arthur. It'd be weird if there wasn't."

She looked to Mr LeRoy for confirmation and got a shrug of the shoulders which implied he didn't disagree.

"He would be a good place to start," she said. "You can't go wrong with an actual, for-realsies, sword-wielding king on your side. I don't suppose you know where he is."

"Not a clue," Mr LeRoy said.

"Well, we can figure it out. And I remember this TV programme I saw once about British paganism. My dad was watching it, actually, on one of those documentary channels way up the planner, the ones you only look at when you're bored and there's nothing else you fancy. I was just faffing around in the living room while it was on. But there was this one bit about a nature spirit called the Green Man. His face appears in carvings on churches, and loads of pubs are named after him. Kind of a god of vegetation, I think. Mightn't there be an eidolon of him too?"

"I don't see why not," Mr LeRoy said. "He's a deity associated with fertility and the harvest. He's also known as Jack-in-the-Green, and someone dressed as him often appears alongside Morris dancers at May Day festivals. As it happens, I do know of a couple of similar eidolons whom I came across during the early days of Summer Land. Like Reed, they didn't want anything to do with me. They just got on with their own lives. Both were fairly special, though."

"There!" said Ajia. "So that's four potential team members already."

"You're proposing that we go looking for these others?" said Smith.

"Look for them, find them, convince them to join us. Once they see we're serious, they'll jump aboard."

"Ah, the optimism of youth," said Mr LeRoy.

"What would you prefer we do?" Ajia replied hotly, her temper overcoming her usual deference towards him. "Sit on our arses? Let Derek Drake carry on running this country into the ground? Thanks to his policies my mother was kicked out, exiled to a place she'd never been to before even though it was her"—air quotes

—"'homeland'. My father fell into a depression and killed himself because of that. Drake fucked my life as surely as he's fucked Britain, and I'm getting to the point where I've taken enough of all this shit. In fact, I may be past it. Last night I saw Paladins kill people in cold blood. Makes me feel sick even just thinking about it—not only what they did but the fact they can get away with it and there won't be any comebacks. Don't tell me you haven't wanted to retaliate against them. Thought about it, at any rate. Don't tell me they don't deserve justice, them and the regime they protect."

"And we're the ones to deliver it?" said Smith.

"If not us, who? Nobody else seems willing or able. We're not just your average citizens. For some reason, by some process we don't understand, we've been made extraordinary. What's the good of that if we don't use it?"

"Use it and wind up dead ourselves," said Fletcher.

"So what? If that happens, at least we'll have tried. But if we don't even try, how can we hold our heads up? It'd be a complete waste of the gifts we've been given."

She sat back, breathing hard.

"Well? I've said my piece. Your thoughts, gentlemen?"

There was silence in the bunker, the three men exchanging glances. Ajia knew they were going to dismiss everything she had said. They weren't going to call her a hysterical girl, not openly, not to her face, but it was what they were thinking.

Never mind. I've spoken passionately. I stand by every word.

If her scheme was ever to be enacted, however, she would need them with her. She couldn't do it on her own.

"Quite the rabble-rouser," Mr LeRoy said eventually.

"But you've no intention of following up on what I'm suggesting," Ajia said. "Right? You think it's a ridiculous idea."

"Not necessarily." Something glinted in his weary, red-rimmed eyes, like a spark being kindled. "I think it's a long shot, dangerous, and very possibly doomed to failure. But like it or not, you've struck a chord. I'm no firebrand, Ajia, God knows. As an undergraduate I was the straight-down-the-line sort, never once going on protest marches, never even handing in an essay late, and my academic career was all about plodding towards tenure and not making waves. Summer Land was the most radical thing I ever did in my life. It's time that that changed. After all, what's the point of Perry sacrificing himself for me—for us—if no good comes of it?"

"You're in?"

The ghost of a smile flitted across his careworn face. "I'm in."

"And you, Smith?"

Smith ummed and ahhed.

"No one's asking you to kill, if that's what you're worried about," Ajia said. "But you've been with me from the start. You've helped me this far. I probably wouldn't be alive if not for you. I'd really love it if you'd carry on as my number one go-to guy."

She knew Smith felt protective towards her and she was using that, or rather abusing it. She thought that maybe she had laid on the appeal to his paternalistic side a little too thick, but in the event it worked.

"All right," he said. "I'm not hopeful, but you've made a good case."

"And you, Reed?"

"Nuh-uh." Fletcher folded his arms. "You three do what you want. Count me out."

"Oh, come on," she chided. "Deep down you know this is the right thing. You can feel it inside. Your blood's stirring. I don't know how long you've been hibernating in this bunker, living off squirrel meat and dandelions…"

"Year and a half."

"And that's far too long. It's about time you lived up to the person whose eidolon you are. The dashing outlaw, battling on behalf of the common people against tyranny. Put that marksmanship of yours to good use."

"Still a no. Maybe you can wrap these two around your little finger, but not me, Ajia."

"Okay. Pity, but there you go. What I'd like, though, is for you to help get us out of Sherwood Forest."

"I might be able to do that," Fletcher said. "Assuming you have some sneaky plan in mind for getting past the Paladins' cordon, because I sure as fuck don't."

"Actually," said Ajia, "it just so happens I might."

SEVENTEEN

HARRIET FALLON WALKED into Derek Drake's life at a lavish Christmas party thrown by Thurlow, Sage, Wright Ltd. at the Savoy Hotel, a celebration not so much of the festive season as of the company's projected annual pre-tax profits, which were in eight figures, edging towards nine. This was in the early 1990s, and while the boom years of the previous decade were fading into memory, there were still fortunes to be made in the City of London, not least by hedge fundies.

It was Emrys Sage who introduced them to each other, and for that, as for so many reasons, Drake would be eternally grateful to him.

"I think the two of you should get along nicely," Sage said, with a hint of a smile and the merest suggestion of a wink, before leaving them alone.

Sage had told Drake beforehand about Harriet. She was the daughter of a friend of his—Robert Fallon, recently deceased— and was enjoying a modestly successful career over in the United States as a model, although her willowy, slightly haughty looks made her best suited for the covers of the higher-brow women's magazines and adverts for, of all things, cat food and feminine sanitary products. She was also an heiress, albeit sole beneficiary of a much-depleted estate and a large, crumbling house in rural

Gloucestershire, Charrington Grange, a white elephant of a place which she was trying to sell in order to pay off death duties and her father's various debts. That was why she was over in the UK, and she informed Drake that she had no intention of staying any longer than she had to.

"As soon as I've got everything sorted financially, I'll be on the first plane back to New York," she said.

Drake's reply was characteristic. "Not now you've met me, you won't."

"Confident, aren't you?"

"No one's ever said I am deficient in that quality."

Over flutes of Krug Grande Cuvée they sounded each other out. They discovered a shared interest in classical music, particularly Mozart, and a mutual inclination towards religious faith, his being firmly entrenched, hers a faint but still tangible residue left behind after a Catholic upbringing and a convent education. Politically they were compatible. Humour-wise, his occasionally coarse jokes didn't offend her. By evening's end they knew they were destined to be a couple. A month after that, they knew they were destined to marry.

By then Drake had already agreed to buy Charrington Grange off her, and they were planning its renovation.

ON HER SIDE, Harriet considered Derek Drake to be the right man at the right time. In Manhattan she had had a string of boyfriends and numerous flings. In fact, she'd built quite a reputation for herself: sexually voracious, with a penchant for alcohol and recreational drugs, a party girl through and through. She had begun to tire of all that, however. The lifestyle was exhausting, not to mention expensive. She mightn't necessarily have been ready to settle down, but she had reached the age when she was on the lookout for something else, something more.

Derek was physically unprepossessing, not least after some of the toothy, all-American Adonises she had slept with. He was not the best endowed man she had ever had, nor the best in bed. He was, though, a man who was going places. Emrys Sage kept talking him up to her, praising his verve and ambition and hinting that a glittering future awaited him outside the City, in a wider sphere. Harriet did not need Emrys's approval of Derek, and didn't seek it, but she welcomed it nonetheless. Her father had always said that Emrys was no fool, and if he was championing Derek, it weighed heavily in Derek's favour. Above all else, what Harriet was looking for in life just then was stability, and Derek appeared to represent just that.

His wealth didn't hurt, either. By purchasing Charrington Grange, he made her financial headaches disappear with a finger-click. Harriet knew that as Mrs Derek Drake she would never have to work again if she didn't want to and would always be comfortably off.

Did she love him? Absolutely. Would she have loved him if he'd been poor? Probably not. She was, aside from all else, a pragmatist.

Now, AFTER NEARLY a quarter of a century of marriage, some of it contented, some of it less so, Drake and Harriet sat on the floor of the museum of holy relics, facing each other. The door to the Grail chamber was shut. Drake had ushered Harriet out of the little room as soon as he had overcome his surprise at her intrusion. He had also closed the main door to the museum. In the several minutes since, each had been waiting for the other to start speaking.

"So," Harriet said, finally breaking the thorny silence, "is it some kind of trick?"

"Is what some kind of trick?"

"You don't have to use that politician's technique of repeating back the question to give yourself time to think. Honest answer, Derek. First thing that comes into your head. The voice that comes from the cup, Emrys's voice—is it a trick?"

"No. No trick. How could it be?"

"I just wondered if it was something you'd set up, using a voice synthesiser or something like that. Some sort of clever software, like Siri only you've made it sound like Emrys."

"What would be the point of that?" Drake said.

"I don't know!" she snapped. "Because you miss your old friend?

Because you wish he was still alive so you've re-created him using computer jiggery-pokery? You tell me!"

"No. It's nothing like that. I wouldn't even know how to begin to do that."

"You could have hired some tech whizz-kid who does. If that's what this is, then frankly, Derek, it's bloody peculiar. Borderline crazy. Especially since you were on your knees in front of that thing, like you were grovelling."

"I was just... talking to it. Did you... Did you happen to hear what I was saying? Or what the Grail said to me?"

"No. Does that matter?"

"No, no," he said hurriedly. "It doesn't. We were just having a conversation, that's all."

"But that's just it. That's the issue. You were having a conversation with an inanimate object."

"But it isn't simply an inanimate object," Drake said. "I have no idea how to explain this to you, Harriet. The whole thing's incredible. Impossible. There were times when I even thought it might all be in my head. That's why I was so stunned when I realised you could hear Emrys too. With hindsight, I shouldn't have been. Because it's a miracle but it's also quite real. I know that. I've always known that."

"Listen, darling," Harriet said, choosing her words with care, "I'm being very patient here. I could be having a fit of the screaming abdabs right now and no one could blame me, but I'm staying calm, I'm being reasonable, I'm trying to parse this whole thing. Are you telling me that that cup—?"

"Not just any cup. The Holy Grail."

"Yes, I know it's the Holy Grail, or alleged to be. I remember you going off to buy it. I remember how excited you were. And I remember you begging me to fetch it for you when you were in hospital, after the crash. It obviously meant a huge amount to you."

"A huge amount? It meant everything. It still does."

"But back to my question. That cup—I'm sorry, the Grail—is genuinely speaking back to you? It's sentient?"

Her eyes were wild with disbelief. Drake wondered if his own eyes had looked like that, the first time the Grail spoke to him.

"I can see that this is hard to accept," he said. "I don't know the whys and wherefores of it myself. I can only tell you that the chalice has power. Divine power. It once held our Saviour's blood, and His essence still resides within it."

"If that's the case—and I'm going along with this for now but I'm not buying into any of it—how come it's using Emrys Sage's voice? Why him, of all people? Not that he wasn't a great man, in his way, but he wasn't exactly Jesus. Why isn't the Grail speaking to you in the voice of Christ instead, or even God?"

"I've thought about it long and hard," Drake replied, "and the only conclusion I can draw is that the Grail chose to take the guise of someone from my own life whom I loved and admired."

"Why?"

"So that it wouldn't scare me. So that it would be comprehensible to me. If it had boomed at me like a voice from on high in an old Hollywood Biblical epic, or if it had gabbled away in authentic Aramaic, I'd have been baffled and probably terrified. I might have rejected it. Instead, it presented itself to me in a familiar, relatable guise. As Emrys." He spread out his hands. "And just like Emrys did when he was alive, the Grail advises me. It's my guide and consultant. It's helped me throughout my political career. It wouldn't be an exaggeration to say it's got me where I am today."

At that moment, Drake paused to ask himself why he was coming clean with his wife about the Holy Grail. Could he not have lied? She had given him what was practically the perfect get-out clause. He could simply have agreed that it was all a cunning trick. Computer jiggery-pokery, just as she'd said.

Yet hadn't the Grail itself told him, just minutes earlier, that he should place his trust in Harriet? This had been in relation to Vasilyev and the video clip. "Don't underestimate your wife's capacity for forgiveness," it had counselled. "She might surprise you."

Moreover, for a while now Drake had been experiencing a deep-seated desire to share the miracle with someone. For years he had kept the Grail to himself, and at times the strain had been almost unbearable. Everything happened for a reason. There were no accidents. Perhaps he had left the museum door open today on purpose, without realising it. Perhaps he had been hoping someone would come in and find him genuflecting before the Grail. It wasn't that he had been distracted by Vasilyev's implicit threat of blackmail. Secretly, subconsciously, he had left himself open to discovery.

And who better to share all of this with than Harriet?

It was almost a relief to be able to bring her in on it. She was his wife, after all. She had been part of his world for nearly half his life. She had a right to know everything about this integral aspect of his existence.

Well, almost everything. If this was to be a confession, it wasn't going to be a full confession. But Drake was willing to give her enough of the story to satisfy her and shrive himself of the burden of being the only one in the world who communed with the mightiest religious artefact of all time.

Harriet shook her head slowly, wonderingly. "I still think this is all a fraud. You've engineered the whole thing. Fitted the Grail with some sort of bespoke AI device."

"I swear to you, I haven't. I could pretend I had, Harriet, and that would make me look like a demented lunatic in your eyes. Instead, I'm telling you the truth, even though it risks making me look even more like a demented lunatic."

She half laughed. "You have a point. You know, Derek, don't you, that I'm going to have to check this out for myself? If that is the actual, authentic Holy Grail in there, I can't just let it be. I may not be as devout as you, but I'm no atheist either."

"I had a feeling you might say that."

"Well? The very least you can do is allow me an audience with it."

Drake mulled it over, then nodded. He got stiffly to his feet and extended a hand to Harriet. "Come on, then."

HARRIET ENTERED THE chamber with trepidation. She told herself it was silly to be nervous. She still half believed it was all some elaborate contraption Derek had devised for himself, a means of coping with his grief over Emrys Sage. She herself had been fond of Emrys but hadn't had the deep love for him that Derek had had. Perhaps he blamed himself for Emrys's death, even though the helicopter crash had been nothing but mechanical failure, nobody's fault but fate's. Perhaps Derek had gone to great lengths to bring his mentor back from the dead, as it were, in order to expiate guilt, or else torture himself.

Perhaps, unbeknownst to her, her husband had been functionally insane for years. Driven mad by self-reproach and the pressures of his political position.

The thought sent a chill of horror through her which she struggled to dispel.

The Holy Grail sat before her, its onyx body and attached jewels glistening splendidly. She felt the hairs on her arms stand up. There was a crackle in the air like static electricity. Maybe it was just static electricity. The air was dry in here, aridly climate-controlled.

"What should I do?" she asked in hushed tones.

"I don't know," Derek replied. "I just try to be respectful."

"Should I kneel?"

"Do you want to?"

"Not really."

"Then don't. Just talk."

Harriet gazed at the chalice. How did you address a relic imbued with heavenly power? If, that was, it really was the Grail and really did possess some sort of divine intelligence.

She cleared her throat. "Umm, Grail? This is Harriet Drake. But I'm guessing you know that, if you are the Holy Grail."

"Harriet. It's been a while. How good to see you again."

She almost screamed. The voice was emanating from the chalice but seemed to shiver through her head like the ringing of a gong. And it was Emrys, right down to the heavily aspirated "H" and the rolled "r's" of her name, which Emrys had always made a meal of.

"Are you... Are you real?" she stammered.

"As real as you, my dear, if not quite as lovely-looking."

In life, Emrys had never shied away from unctuous flattery towards women. It seemed the Holy Grail version of Emrys was keeping up the habit.

"How is this even possible?" she said. "How can it be happening?"

"God moves in a mysterious way, His wonders to perform," the Grail said. "It's well past time that Derek introduced you to me. A husband should withhold nothing from his wife, and vice versa. Marriage is man and woman becoming one flesh, indivisible. Don't you agree?"

"Yes," Harriet said hesitantly. "Are you still Emrys Sage, then, or are you the Lord speaking through the medium of Emrys Sage?"

"Which do you suppose?"

"I don't know. This is so far outside my normal experience, I'm not sure what to think."

"What do you believe, Harriet?"

She had her hands clasped to her chest, as if in prayer. She wasn't aware of putting them there.

"It's all too much. I don't think I can take it in."

"I understand," the Grail said.

"I need air." Feeling dizzy, she turned and stumbled out of the chamber. Derek followed.

Outdoors, she breathed deeply until her head settled. Derek stood beside her, a solicitous arm around her waist.

"Better?" he said.

"Yes. It's… My God, Derek, it's extraordinary. Whatever's happening in that room, whatever's causing that phenomenon— extraordinary. It makes me think anything is possible. And all this time, you've known about it and I haven't."

"I should have shared it with you sooner."

"Better late than never."

She turned to him. Her heart was pounding and she could feel her face was flushed with excitement.

He was looking at her in a way he hadn't for ages. As if seeing her anew. As if it was the first time he had laid eyes on her at that Christmas party at the Savoy, all over again.

On impulse, she leaned in and kissed him. Hard. Passionately.

He reciprocated. This was no bedtime peck, nor a delicate public display of affection for the TV cameras. This was a kiss Harriet felt, tinglingly, all the way to her toes.

"Derek. Oh my God, Derek…"

Prodding into her thigh was the unmistakable, forthright outline of an erection. Her hand groped down to touch it, clasp it.

"The poolhouse," she breathed. "Quick."

There wasn't a moment to waste. They scurried to the poolhouse. Harriet wrenched the gauzy drapes shut. She struggled out of her clothes. Derek was fumbling with his shirt buttons. She tore the garment off him, then unlashed his belt and dragged his trousers down.

The erection was still there, tenting the front of his underpants.

They fell together onto the cushioned wicker settee. Harriet was wet, desperate, ready.

It was glorious. It was sublime. One long hymnal hallelujah.

AFTERWARD, THEY AMBLED back to the house, hand in hand.

In the hall, Major Wynne was waiting in a chair, checking his phone. He snapped to attention as Drake entered.

"Sir."

"Wynne."

"Ready to report on last night's events, sir."

"Not now, Major," his employer said. "It's a lovely evening. Harriet and I are going to have cocktails out on the terrace. You look tired. Go home, get some rest. We'll talk again in the morning."

"Yes, sir."

Harriet Drake did not catch Wynne's eye as she and her husband sauntered past. Wynne was used to this. It was important she and he gave away nothing. They were cordial but formal with each other at all times, unless they were alone.

What struck him as strange, though, was the dishevelment of her clothing. And, come to think of it, of Drake's. His shirt was missing a couple of buttons. Both he and Harriet had a bit of colour in their cheeks, too, and their hair was mussed.

It was almost as though…

No. Couldn't be.

But as Wynne drove to Stronghold, he couldn't shake the thought that Derek and Harriet Drake had just been having rampant sex.

EIGHTEEN

NIGHT HAD FALLEN over Sherwood Forest, and the moon was high and full.

"Okay, I've been doing the maths," said Fletcher. "If Puck can put a girdle round the Earth in forty minutes…"

"Ooh, look at you with the literary references," said Ajia.

"I was a soldier. Doesn't mean I'm a moron. Now, the Earth's circumference is twenty-five thousand miles at the equator. That works out at a mean speed of around six hundred miles a minute. Is that how fast you can go?"

"You know I can't. If I did, I'd probably suffocate or explode or something. I think Shakespeare was using a bit of artistic licence there."

"Well, you're going to have to be quick, girl. No two ways about it. Are you ready for this?"

He was bantering in an attempt to keep her spirits up and her nerves at bay. He wasn't quite succeeding but Ajia appreciated the effort.

"Ready as I'll ever be," she said, "even though I look like a baglady." She was wearing clothes borrowed from Fletcher: a pair of jeans and a black hoodie. The jeans were cinched at the waist with rope, to hold them up, and rolled at the cuffs. The hoodie was as baggy as a balloon.

"Got to blend in," Fletcher said. "Everything you had on was too light-coloured. You'd stand out like a sore thumb in the dark."

"I know, but still. Also, this facepaint stinks." Her face was smeared with stripes of black and dark green in a camouflage pattern.

"What do you expect? It's made out of wild spinach and dirt. Look, are you going to whinge all night or are you going to recce?"

"Recce."

"Right answer. You can do this, girl. Just don't take any stupid risks. Run, pause and look, keep running."

"And don't get seen."

"Most important of all. Don't get seen."

"Good luck, Goodfellow," said Smith.

"Come back safe," said Mr LeRoy.

Ajia looked at the old man and thought, If now isn't the appropriate moment, I don't know when is.

"I go, I go," she said, as Puck to Oberon in *A Midsummer Night's Dream*, "look how I go, swifter than arrow from the Tartar's bow."

"Or from my bow," said Fletcher.

"Yeah, because it's all about you."

Fletcher smirked.

And Ajia ran.

SHE RAN THROUGH moonlit woodland, through a dapple-flicker of silver and black.

She moved away from the bunker in an ever widening spiral, testing her footing over the uneven terrain before launching herself into full Puck mode. As she ran ever faster and her heart pumped in a measured, even rhythm, she felt more than just adrenalin coursing through her system. There was something else, over and above the fear-inspired hyperactivity. A resolve born of determination to help the those she was coming to think of as her people.

Solid, static immovable objects flickered by her, while moving things like the occasional owl and bats were caught in slow motion. Sounds were protracted, slurred: the ululation of an owl sounded like the long drone of a foghorn.

She saw no sign of the Paladins that Reed Fletcher said were surrounding the forest. She was wondering if the news report had been mistaken when she heard the rumble of a vehicle to her right. She veered and sprinted through dense woodland, covering two hundred yards in a little over five seconds, and reached the lane before the vehicle passed by. As she slowed, the world returned to normal, the vehicle's engine noise crashing towards her.

She crouched and watched as a Paladin Humvee appeared round a bend on the lane. A helmeted figure stood tall in an open hatch, clutching some kind of thermal imaging device. Ajia ducked back into the cover of the ferns as the vehicle swept past.

She counted ten seconds as the engine noise died in the distance. A mile along the lane, to the south, was the lay-by where they had left the Land Rover.

Her plan hinged on whether the Paladins had found the vehicle.

She emerged from behind the ferns and switched immediately into Puck mode. The even surface of the tarmac made running at speed a joy. The world slowed around her. She wished she had the ability to slow everything down, even when she wasn't sprinting. She'd be able to show the bastard Paladins a thing or two, then.

She came to the lay-by and slowed, moving into the undergrowth at the side of the lane and approaching the Land Rover cautiously. She slowed and made a tentative circuit of the vehicle, ensuring there were no hidden goons in the vicinity.

Then she pulled Mr LeRoy's car keys from her pocket and slipped in behind the steering wheel.

This was the most dangerous phase of her grand plan, of course. It had taken all her powers of persuasion to convince Smith and LeRoy that her scheme made sense, and wasn't suicidal madness. Fletcher had just looked on, silent, with a cynical curl of his lip, while her friends had tried to dissuade her.

She'd fought her corner and ended up telling them that she was doing it, whether they liked the idea or not.

She wound the window down and listened.

Five minutes later she heard the distinctive engine noise of a Humvee, heading south. She wondered if it were the vehicle she had seen earlier, making a return trip.

When she judged it was just a couple of hundred yards away, she started the engine and accelerated out of the lay-by, heading south ahead of the Paladins.

She felt vulnerable. It was all very well when she was protected by her ability, but now she was, when all was said and done, a sitting target.

She glanced into the rear-view mirror. Fifty yards behind her, the Humvee came into sight. The Paladins would be on the alert for any vehicle active in the area, but they knew that Ajia and two others had fled Dorset in a Land Rover. The car would red-flag the bastards like nothing else.

Ajia accelerated, and on cue a dazzling searchlight lit up the interior of the Land Rover. She ducked, half-expecting a hail of bullets. But the Paladins, murderous thugs though they were, would still have to exercise a little caution. The killing of an innocent farmer wouldn't look good splashed across the front pages of the local paper. Even smarmy Major Wynne would have difficulty explaining that.

The Humvee was closing on her. Ajia increased speed, drawing away. The Paladin's vehicle was built for endurance, not speed. The advantage was with her. She would lead them a merry dance for a few miles, then ditch the Land Rover as planned and sprint like crazy back to the bunker.

That was the plan, at least. But she had thought without the possibility that the pursuing militia would summon cohorts. With heart-thumping alarm, she saw a blaze of headlights up ahead as an armoured car rounded a bend and bore down on her.

Reflexively she spun the wheel—a quick twitch to the left and then to the right—and she chicaned past the Paladins without ending up in the ditch. She rounded the bend at speed, glancing in the rear-view. The curving hedge obscured the lane to the rear, and she was unable to see whether the vehicles had collided. There was no sound of impact, but at least the oncoming vehicle would have impeded the progress of the Humvee.

She reckoned she had travelled about three or four miles from Fletcher's bunker.

Now for phase two.

Ajia slowed, waiting until headlights showed perhaps half a mile behind her, then slewed the Land Rover into the side of the lane and jumped from the cab, leaving the driver's door wide open. Moving at speed, she opened the back doors to give the impression that more than one person had fled the vehicle, then jumped over the ditch. She crawled through a hedge, found herself on the margin of a ploughed field, and ran in the direction of the oncoming vehicles.

They passed on the other side of the hedge as if in slow motion, engines moaning like tortured banshees. The field had been ploughed north to south, as neat as corduroy, and this helped her progress as she sprinted north, parallel with the lane.

When she judged she had reached the lay-by, Ajia slowed and pushed her way through the hedge, continuing north over the even surface of the lane. Seconds later she heard shouts, multiple voices so slowed that they sounded almost sub-aquatic. Through the trees on the other side of the lane she made out flickering torches illuminating the forest. She approached them, still running, and made out a cordon of Paladin goons moving through the undergrowth with glacial and almost comical slowness.

She thought of Maya and the two other brownies, lying dead outside the caravan. All the others slaughtered by the Paladin, Perry and the elves and goblins who had sought refuge at Summer Land. She fingered the knife in her pocket as she ran. It would be easy to take out one or two of these wankers, in revenge, to show Drake and his fascists that he wasn't having everything his own way. But she stayed the impulse. It would be foolish, just when she'd achieved the object of her plan and lured the Paladins south.

Later, she told herself.

She continued along the lane for half a mile, then veered into the forest.

Five minutes later, when she hauled up the lid on Reed Fletcher's cut-price Hobbit house, she found Reed and Smith going at it hammer and tongs.

Almost literally, in Smith's case.

He towered over Reed at the far end of the cramped bunker, his hammer raised above his head in a show of unSmith-like aggression. Mr LeRoy danced futile attendance, fingers fluttering at his chin as he carolled, "Boys! Boys!"

Fletcher looked up from where he cowered on the floor, affecting a defiant nonchalance he obviously didn't really feel. "Go on, then! Do it! For once in your life, be a man!"

Smith saw Ajia, staring at him, and his aggression withered. He lowered his hammer and let go of Fletcher's shirtfront.

"Chrissake," Ajia said. "So while I've been out there risking my fucking neck, you two cretins… Honestly, words fail me."

"Reed has had a change of heart," Mr LeRoy reported, clearly relieved at Ajia's intervention.

She frowned. "You're coming with us, Reed?"

Smith grunted. "Hardly. And he calls *me* a coward. He's decided he'd rather not, all things considered, guide us out of the forest."

Ajia stared at Fletcher. "Is that right?"

Fletcher fussily rearranged his collar. "I said that if you were successful in drawing the Paladins away, then you wouldn't need me."

Ajia felt like asking for Smith's hammer so she could do what he'd left undone. She took a calming breath. "Reed, we need you. Your expertise. You know this forest like the back of your hand. I might have drawn a few vehicles, but… But the place is still crawling with the bastards." She hesitated, staring at him. "I mean, how would you feel if we left here without you, and a day later you found us slaughtered out there?"

"Well said, Ajia," Mr LeRoy put in.

"We're not asking you to come with us. Or join the fight," she went on. "Just guide us out of the fucking forest, okay? An hour, two. Chances are we won't come across any more patrols, but just on the off-chance…"

She told them about her flight south in the Land Rover, and the pursuit of the Paladins.

Fletcher looked at her, considering. At last he said, "For you, okay? I'm doing this for you, not Smith here."

Ajia nodded. "Thank you," she said. "Right, let's get the hell out of here, okay?"

"MY REASONING IS that they'll have regular checkpoints on all the major roads surrounding the forest."

"Your reasoning?" Smith said. "Or is that a guess?"

Fletcher stared him down. "I was in Helmand, remember? I've been on patrols. I know how these things work."

"Ignore Smith," Mr LeRoy said. "Go on."

"They'll back up the checkpoints with patrols. I reckon that's what you came across earlier, Ajia. I'll take you north, for five or six miles, to the old Haxley road. I'll see you across, dodging the patrols."

"And then you'll turn tail," Smith said.

"And then I'll have discharged my duty, Smith. Done what I said I'd do. You'll still have a couple of hours till dawn. My advice is to travel at night, hole up during the day. Find transport of some kind as soon as you can. Which way will you be heading?"

Mr LeRoy said, decisively, "North."

Ajia looked at him. He sounded certain. She wondered if he'd been consulting his map while she had been out there.

Fletcher went on, "I'll give you what I can spare in the way of food and water. But that isn't much."

Ajia nodded, surprised by his generosity.

They set off.

They travelled by the light of the moon and the stars. The night and the forest seemed magical to Ajia, a city girl born and bred. She wondered if it were the Puck in her, responding to nature.

She scouted ahead, using her speed to dart forward half a mile then zigzag back towards the trio as they made painstakingly slow progress north. Smith and Fletcher were relatively fit, but on his own admission Mr LeRoy was more accustomed to chomping than yomping. Every few hundred yards he demanded they stop so that he could regain his breath. Smith accepted the situation with good grace, but Fletcher was not so tolerant.

At one point, when Ajia returned to the fold to find Mr LeRoy sitting on a fallen trunk mopping his brow, Fletcher was striding back and forth, chuntering. "We need to get a shuffle-on. We're still an hour from the road. You'll want at least that long to put as much distance between yourselves and the closest Paladin patrol before sunrise."

"The way's clear for another half a mile," Ajia reported.

"Good," said Fletcher. "Come on, you two!"

Smith helped a groaning Mr LeRoy to his feet and they struggled on.

For the next half a mile they followed the edge of a low ridge, which Fletcher reported was a deer run. It was concealed to the west by the forest of beech, and to the east by a wild tangle of hawthorn, elder and blackberry brambles.

Ajia sprinted through the forest on a course parallel with the deer run. From time to time she crossed the run, fought her way through the shrubbery, and surveyed the land beyond, just to be thorough. There was neither sight nor sound of Paladin patrols.

At last the deer run petered out into dense woodland, and Ajia re-joined the others. In the splintered moonlight falling through the treetops, she made out Mr LeRoy's sweating, cherubic face. He smiled at her bravely.

Fletcher said, "We're about a mile and a half from the road. I suggest you scout ahead, Ajia. Mr LeRoy needs a breather, but we'll set off again in two minutes."

"A breather! Never a truer word uttered, my friend," Mr LeRoy said, sinking into a bed of dried leaf mould at the foot of an oak tree. "But would you be generous and grant me perhaps five minutes?"

"Two and then we're off!" Fletcher snapped.

Smith sat down beside a panting Mr LeRoy. Fletcher, muttering to himself, strode off a few yards and stared into the darkness.

Ajia set off.

She sprinted, and the world around her decelerated. She recalled the time, just a week ago, when her idea of speed was pumping the pedals as fast as her legs would work as she darted in and out of traffic along the Hammersmith bypass. What had she been travelling then? Twenty miles per hour, thirty at a push?

And now?

Little Maya—and oh, how the mere thought of her was painful!— had timed her at 2.9 seconds over a hundred metres. Sixteen hundred metres in a mile, roughly. So that was, give or take, fifty miles an hour. And that had been a few days ago. She was sure she was getting faster with practice.

She was so absorbed in her thoughts she almost failed to notice the hedge that bounded a main road, and the Paladin patrol just beyond it.

Only the rumbling-slow crackle of a two-way radio alerted her to their presence.

She skidded to a halt, sliding through the undergrowth and fetching up on her backside in the hedge. She lay very still, her pulse pounding, and listened.

If the soldiers had heard her, they gave no sign. A Paladin was still on the radio, perhaps ten yards away. "A-okay that," she heard.

Very carefully, Ajia untangled herself from the tenacious grip of a blackberry frond and moved, doubled-up, along the hedge until she came to a mildewed timber gate. She slid herself through a gap in the crossbars and peered around the hedge.

A Humvee stood twenty yards further up the lane. And they were certainly making a production of the roadblock, with flashing lights, a number of armed militia, and a portable boom to deter any adventurous wrongdoer.

She wondered how far away the next roadblock might be. She could go and recce, but what if Mr LeRoy and the others arrived here before she got back? The wisest course of action would be to go back and report the situation. She could always look for the next roadblock then.

She trod carefully back into the forest, loath to sprint so close to the hedge lest the sound alerted the goons. Well into the muffling woods, she kicked off.

She came across the labouring trio just twenty seconds later.

"Roadblock up ahead," she reported. "Some Paladins and a Humvee, twenty yards to the left of a gate."

Mr LeRoy looked agitated. "What do we do?"

Reed said, "Avoid the bastards. This way."

He veered right and led the way through the dappled woodland. Ajia and the others followed. She took Mr LeRoy's hand as he stumbled.

Ajia could have reached the road in a matter of seconds, but it took them ten long, slogging minutes battling through undergrowth before they reached the hedge.

Reed pushed his way through. Ajia followed. They stood on a high bank above a bend in the lane, the tarmac rendered pewter in the moonlight. She had a clear view of the lane to the left and right for a hundred yards, and there was no sign of the Paladins.

"Cross here," Reed said. "Get the others."

She hesitated. "Reed. You sure you won't come with us?"

"On Bron's fool's errand to defeat the massed forces of Derek Drake?" His voice was almost a sneer. "I know when I'm defeated, girl. I've done my bit. Get Smith and LeRoy."

She hesitated once more, staring at the man as he looked up and down the lane. Then she pushed through the hedge and found Mr LeRoy and Smith squatting in the shadows.

"Follow me," she whispered, and led them through the gap in the hawthorn to where Fletcher was waiting.

"I'll go first," Fletcher whispered. "I'll have a better view along the lane on the other side. Wait till I give the signal, then cross together, okay?"

He slid down the bank to the lane.

Looking back on the next minute or so, Ajia realised that it was sheer bad luck that accounted for why Fletcher never made it to the other side of the lane.

She heard the rumble of an approaching vehicle and called out.

The armoured slowed and appeared round the bend just as Fletcher slithered down the grassy banking and crouched in the lane.

He was caught in the headlights, frozen like a mesmerised rabbit.

"Halt!"

The Paladin was already out of the armoured car and advancing up the lane towards Fletcher, who turned and attempted to scramble up the incline.

"Back!" Ajia hissed, pushing Smith and Mr LeRoy through the gap in the hedge.

She turned, hoping to see Fletcher in close pursuit.

The Paladin pulled something from a side-holster and fired.

There was a faint electric crackle. Behind her, Fletcher groaned and rolled down the incline, stunned. The goon approached his prostrate form and unhooked the wires of his stun-gun from Fletcher's torso before returning the stun-gun to its holster. A second Paladin left the armoured car and joined him.

Ajia crouched in the hedge and watched them, her heart thumping wildly. The first goon reached out a foot and turned Fletcher over onto his back.

"What the fuck?" he said, bending down to pick up the bow that had fallen from Fletcher's grip. "Regular little Robin Hood we got ourselves here, sir."

The other grunted. "You might have spoken no truer word all day, Corporal."

The officer activated a lapel mic and spoke into it.

He nodded to his underling. "Right, let's get this tosser in the locker."

Fletcher moaned, coming to his senses. He tried to push himself upright on his elbows, but the corporal gave him a swift, deterrent kick in the ribs. "Oh, no, you don't, sonny boy."

He unshouldered his rifle, stood off a yard, and gestured at Fletcher with its barrel. "On your feet, hands in the air."

Ajia jumped in alarm as Mr LeRoy clutched her elbow. "What's happening?" he hissed.

She raised a finger to her lips, then turned back towards the lane. Already she had drawn her knife, knowing exactly what she was about to do.

As Fletcher climbed to his feet and stood swaying with his arms in the air, Ajia launched herself down the bank and into the lane.

The corporal didn't stand a chance. Ajia's speed mesmerised even Fletcher as she hit the tarmac, crossed the intervening five yards with the speed of a bullet, and slit the goon's throat with a quick backhand slash.

He sank to his knees in slow motion, arterial blood a frozen fan in the moonlight. Before the officer could react, Ajia crossed to him and slipped the blade of the knife into his lower abdomen, ripping upwards. His death cry was eerie and protracted as she ran back to Fletcher.

She stopped dead before him, gripping the bloody knife.

Behind her, the corporal hit the ground suddenly, followed a split second later by the officer.

For my father...

"Christ almighty," Fletcher breathed, staring from her to the corpses in the moonlit lane.

Arm in arm, Smith and Mr LeRoy slithered down the banking. Smith stared at the bodies and the blood—and then at the knife in Ajia's hand.

"What now?" He sounded sick.

Fletcher said, "If I were you, I'd take the armoured car. There's a turning up the lane on the left, heading away from the forest."

Ajia stared at him. "You're coming with us, Reed." It was not so much a question as a command.

"What the hell makes you think—?"

"I saved your fucking life there!"

"Then we're quits, remember? I saved yours too."

"But Sherwood Forest isn't safe for you any more. I've just killed two Paladins. The others will want payback, and they'll turn the place upside down to get it."

"I'll manage. I'm no slouch when it comes to looking after myself." Fletcher turned and approached the bank.

She took a step forward. "Reed, we..."

"Let him go," Smith said, quietly. "We don't need him."

"But..."

"Smith is right," Mr LeRoy put in, "we don't."

Ajia watched Fletcher scramble up the bank without a backward glance. A second later he vanished through the hedge.

She turned to Smith. "Can you drive that thing?"

He nodded, and they hurried up the lane towards the vehicle.

Smith took a minute to familiarise himself with the controls while Mr LeRoy sat in the back, exhorting them to make haste. Ajia sat beside Smith, staring at the dark shapes of the corpses in the lane, too stunned to speak.

She was still gripping the knife, the Paladins' blood sticky on her fingers.

The armoured car roared into life, and Smith performed an almost perfect three-point turn and accelerated along the lane.

"There!" Mr LeRoy called out, pointing to a turning on the left.

Smith took it, and Ajia sat back, feeling an almost childlike sense of relief as they motored away from the scene of the... crime? Revenge, more like.

She found her voice. "The Paladin officer. He reported finding Reed. The other patrol will be suspicious when they don't turn up."

Mr LeRoy said, "How long before dawn?"

"Two hours," Smith said. "We'll abandon the vehicle before then and continue on foot. We should make good progress." He turned and stared at Ajia, and she didn't like the look in his eyes.

"Should I have left Reed to be taken and interrogated?" she asked. "Probably tortured and killed? How long before he broke, and told them where we were?" She shook her head, angered. "I had to do it."

Smith looked away, and Ajia wiped her bloody hand on her tracksuit bottoms.

The armoured car raced on into the night.

NINETEEN

AJIA WOKE WITH a jolt to find Mr LeRoy and Smith arguing. Whether it was the sound of their voices that had woken her, or the fact that the car had come to a stop and with it the comforting, lulling motion, she was unable to say.

They were parked on a rutted track, with the first light of dawn glimmering through the foliage.

"We need to ditch the car and continue on foot," Smith was saying.

"But I fear that would be a grave mistake, my boy," Mr LeRoy countered.

Smith gripped the wheel. "A mistake? It'd be a greater mistake to continue in this damned thing and have the authorities trace us. They'll be looking out for a stolen armoured car, you know?"

"I am well aware of that possibility," Mr LeRoy said. "But I am not suggesting we continue in broad daylight; that would be foolish. I suggest we rest during the day, get all the sleep we can, and continue during the hours of darkness."

"And risk being apprehended?"

Mr LeRoy shrugged his meaty shoulders. "We will take the back roads and lanes. How many Paladin patrols do you fear we'll come across in rural Derbyshire? We run just as great a risk if we proceed on foot—three disparate souls, ill-equipped for walking in the middle of nowhere. Now *that* would be a recipe for disaster."

Ajia cleared her throat. "Can I say something?"

Mr LeRoy beamed at her. "Why, of course."

Smith remained staring straight ahead.

"First off, where exactly are we heading, Mr LeRoy?"

"A village called Dawley, on the edge of the Peak District, Derbyshire."

"And where are we now?"

Mr LeRoy rummaged around on the back seat and produced a tattered, spiral-bound map book. He passed it to her, open to the page showing the National Park as a big splotch of green.

His sausage-like finger indicated the village of Dawley. "And Smith estimates that we are here, perhaps thirty miles away."

She regarded the king of the fairies. "And what—or rather who—is at Dawley?"

"An old acquaintance. I think she will be a worthy addition to our cause. If, that is, we can recruit her."

Ajia studied the map. "Thirty miles is a long way to walk."

"And time is of the essence, my girl."

"All the more reason," Smith put in, "to set off on foot now, walk through the day and arrive at nightfall."

"Walk thirty miles," Mr LeRoy said, aghast, "without having hardly a wink of sleep, and on a practically empty stomach?"

Ajia looked at Smith, who avoided her gaze. "I agree with Mr LeRoy," she said. "We might as well rest today and set off again tonight. We can ditch the car when we get to Dawley, okay?" She waited. "I said okay, Smith?"

"It would appear I'm outvoted," he muttered.

"Excellent!" Mr LeRoy declared. "Now, perhaps it would be wise to drive a little further into the forest, and then we can eat. We don't want to be obvious to the prying eyes of passers-by, do we?"

With ill grace Smith did as instructed, accelerating the armoured car along the track then veering and ramming it into the thick cover of ferns and brambles. He forced the driver's door open and, instead of waiting for Mr LeRoy to dole out the meagre provisions donated by Fletcher, he jumped from the car and stomped off through the wood.

"I wonder if I should go and talk to him?" Ajia said.

"I doubt it would do any good, my child," Mr LeRoy said. "In modern parlance, Wayland Smith is conflicted."

"You mean, he's pissed off at what I did back there?"

"You put it with characteristic succinctness. Our quest is deeply troubling to Smith. He can see our motives, and to a certain extent applaud them—he, after all, has been affected by the execrable Drake just as much as you and me—but our methods disturb him."

"I'll go and have a chat," she said, opening the door.

"You wouldn't care to eat, first?" he asked, opening the hessian bag and frowning at the dubious feast of dried roots and berries within.

"I'm so tired I feel nauseous," she said. "I couldn't eat a thing."

She slipped from the car and pushed her way through the foliage until she found where Smith had gone before her. She followed his trail through the trampled undergrowth and heard the stream before she saw it, a plashing murmur in the dawn quiet. Seconds later dancing glints of silver showed through the vegetation.

She emerged on the bank and saw Smith a little further downstream, crouching and splashing his face with water.

She looked down at her hands.

She washed off the blood in the icy cold water, then examined the result. Most of the blood was gone, but a little remained, ingrained in the lines of her palms. She reached into the water, took a handful of grit from the riverbed, and vigorously rubbed her hands together.

That did the trick. Clean.

"You might be able to wash the blood from your hands," Smith said, "but not from your conscience."

She looked up. Smith towered over her. She went back to washing her hands, needlessly now. "I know you have a thing about violence, okay? And I respect that you want nothing to do with it. But I'm different. Sometimes you're pushed to it, right?"

"There is always another way."

"Another, less effective way, yes. A way that would have ended up with Fletcher, perhaps all of us, dead." She looked up at him, fighting back the tears. "Fucksake, look what the bastards did back at Summer Land. My friend Maya. All the others. *Your* friends. Slaughtered."

"So an eye for an eye. Revenge for revenge's sake? I always thought the Bible a little suspect there."

She shook her head. "Not revenge for revenge's sake, no. This isn't about revenge. It's about what's right, and fair." She stared down at the swirling water. "Look, I heard what you told us the other day. About the building, the fire. What happened to those people. And I understand you have their deaths on your conscience."

"You understand nothing, Ajia."

She sighed, exasperated. "What I don't understand is, you feel responsible for their deaths, okay? I get that. But when it comes to opposing the people really responsible for what happened—Drake and the government—don't you see that we have to fight him using his rules? That might be dirty, but it's necessary."

"I've done with killing," he said, "with death."

"But what if it came down to you defending, say, your wife? If someone was threatening her? Or your children? Or yourself, come to that? You'd fight in self-defence, wouldn't you?"

Smith shifted his gaze away from her, staring into the distance.

She said, "You know what, Smith? I think all this isn't about the right and wrong of killing. I think, if you can't even consider using violence in self-defence, then for some twisted reason you hate yourself."

She wondered if she'd said to much. Feared, paradoxically, that he'd attack her.

He loomed above her, silent and brooding.

Quietly, he said, "The fire was just the end, Ajia. The final straw. Lilliana and me... It was over. She'd met someone, told me she was leaving."

"I'm sorry."

"So when the fire happened, it just seemed the right thing to do. Throw myself off the bridge." He smiled, bitterly. "Couldn't even do that right, could I?"

She stood up and took his big, calloused hand. "You were saved to do a better thing," she said. Then smiled. "Come on, let's get something to eat."

THEY SAT SIDE by side next to the armoured car and chewed on tasteless, anonymous roots, and slightly more flavoursome berries, slaking their thirst with river water in canteens found in the vehicle.

Later, Smith found camping rolls in the car, and he and Ajia unfurled two of them on the forest floor, in the dappled shade of an elder, and slept. Mr LeRoy elected to remain in the vehicle, settling his bulk on the back seat. Within seconds he was snoring.

Ajia awoke in the early afternoon and went for a pee by the river, then slept again until five. She was awoken, this time, by hunger pangs. She wondered when she had last eaten a really nourishing hot meal.

In the armoured car, Mr LeRoy was weeping.

She slid off the mat and hesitantly approached the vehicle's open rear door.

Mr LeRoy sat hunched over his map book, his palms pressed flat on the page. His eyes were squeezed shut and his huge frame wobbled with sobs.

She reached out and touched his arm.

"My child," he exclaimed, dabbing at his eyes, "you apprehend me in a moment of weakness."

She shuffled onto the back seat and sat beside him.

"I know what it's like, Mr LeRoy. I told you about my father."

"I miss Perry so much, and feel such hatred for the people responsible."

"It's like a cut," she said. "A wound. It heals over, gets a bit better in time. But often the pain is still there, and the scar is always there, reminding you." She shrugged. "But it gets so that you can live with the grief, Mr LeRoy."

"Ajia, you're quite the philosopher on the quiet, aren't you?"

"I don't know what I am," she said. "An angry girl, wanting what's right, and wanting to see those responsible pay for their crimes."

"A woman," Mr Le Roy smiled. "A woman imbued with pluck. And Puck."

She stared at him. "So what happens when we find King Arthur? What will he be able to do for us?"

"Rally the forces of good in such a way as I have been signally unable to do, my child." He shook his head. "But they are just words. I don't honestly know what he can or will do. I suspect we'll find out when—if—we locate him."

"Do you have any idea where…?"

He stared down at the map book. "We have work to do in the north, Ajia. In Derbyshire, then Yorkshire, then the Lake District. We have people to petition, forces to rally."

"And then?"

"And then we head south," he said. "Everything tells me that in time we will head south and with our king confront the forces of darkness." He pressed his palms down against the pages of the map book. "I feel it in the book," he murmured.

An hour after sunset they left the cover of the forest, Mr LeRoy taking his turn at the wheel and heading north west into Derbyshire.

TWENTY

"MY MOTHER WAS a wonderful cook," Ajia said. "Still is, for all I know."

She lay on the back seat, her head pillowed on the furled-up camping roll. She had slept and awoken to find that three hours had elapsed and that it was now two in the morning. Smith had taken over at the wheel.

Mr LeRoy had starting talking about his favourite meals, no doubt in reaction to the lack of such during the course of the past two days. Ajia's stomach rumbled as she listened. Then Smith joined in with childhood tales of roast beef and Yorkshire pudding with rich oxtail gravy. Ajia had counted with details of her mother's samosas, tarka dhals and vegetable sabzis. "Oh, I could murder a curry now," she said. "Sorry, Smith."

"Apology accepted."

Mr LeRoy was peering through the side window, examining whatever was reflected in the wing mirror.

They had kept off the main roads and wound their way across country on minor roads and lanes, coming upon next to no traffic.

Ajia made out the dazzle of headlights in the wing mirror. Someone was following.

"I don't want to sound a note of alarm," said Mr LeRoy, "but the vehicle behind us has been on our trail for the past half hour."

"Since the last turning?" Smith sounded worried.

"And before that, yes. But it's keeping its distance."

There was no rear window in the armoured car, or Ajia would have squirmed around for a better look. "But if it was the Paladins, or the police... surely they'd stop us, right?"

"You'd think so," Smith said. "It's probably nothing to worry about."

"Perhaps we should go a bit faster?" Ajia suggested. "And if it accelerates as well, we'll know for sure."

Mr LeRoy looked across at Smith. "What do you think?"

In reply, Smith put his foot down on the accelerator and the armoured car picked up speed.

Mr LeRoy leaned forward, peeing at the wing mirror. His bulk obscured Ajia's view of the mirror. "Well? Is it...?"

"I'm afraid it is, my friends. It's keeping pace."

"Shit," Smith said.

"What do we do?" Mr LeRoy sounded more than a little panicked.

Ajia said, "Can you see what kind of vehicle it is?"

Mr LeRoy peered again, muttering to himself. "Confound it, but I can't make out a thing for the dazzle of its lights."

Smith consulted the map book. "There's a turning a mile ahead, and then another minor road off that one. If we take both, and it follows, then we know he means business."

"And if he does?" Mr LeRoy enquired.

Smith gripped the wheel. "Let's cross that proverbial when we come to it, okay?"

A mile further on they came to the turning. Smith slowed and swerved the car around the bend. Ajia leaned between the front seats, peering through the side-window at the wing-mirror.

"Shit."

The vehicle was still behind them.

The lane narrowed and the vehicle negotiated a series of tight bends which necessitated Smith shifting into lower gear and slowing down.

Mr LeRoy groaned.

"What?" Ajia said, seriously alarmed.

He pointed a trembling finger at the mirror. "It's one of those great big machines that belong to the Paladins," he quavered.

"I think Mr LeRoy means a Humvee," Smith said laconically.

Ajia's stomach flipped.

"So... what do we do?" Mr LeRoy asked.

Ajia looked at Smith, who gripped the wheel, his lips compressed and his gaze fixed on something dead ahead.

"I think," he said, "our options are limited. Look."

He nodded through the windscreen, slowing the vehicle.

The tarmacked lane had turned into a rutted track, which in turn came to an area of wasteland blocked with half a dozen huge boulders, half the size of a family car. A chain-link fence extended away from the opening on both sides.

"Our vehicle is armoured, right?" Ajia said.

"That's why it's called an armoured car," Smith responded.

"Right, so if the goons in the Humvee decide to open fire, you'll be safe?"

"I can tell you've led a sheltered existence," Smith said. "If they open up with everything they've got, they'll be sluicing out our minced remains with a high pressure hose."

"Ho-kay," Ajia said, thinking fast. "Right, Smith—turn us so that my side of the car is furthest away from the Humvee, okay?"

"What—?" Smith began.

"Just do it!" Ajia yelled.

Smith did it, slewing the car before they reached the boulders.

"But what are you going to do?" Mr LeRoy whimpered.

"This," Ajia said, cracking the door just wide enough for her to slip out. She hit the ground and sprinted towards the Humvee which had come to a halt behind them.

With the track hidden from the glare of the moon by overhanging trees, she was a high-speed blur impossible to track. She reached the Humvee in less than a second, slowed and moved behind the vehicle's camouflage-patterned bulk. She rounded it and paused on the driver's side.

Just as soon as the driver made a move, she'd be on him. She slipped her knife from her trainer bottoms in preparation.

And if the Paladins elected to open fire on the armoured car, and ask questions later?

She swore. In her haste to do something, be active, she'd not considered that eventuality.

The seconds ticked by and the bastards in the Humvee sat tight.

Come on... Move!

As a minute passed, she feared that Mr LeRoy might do something rash. She was sure that if he showed himself, then the Paladins would have no compunction about shooting him dead.

So why haven't they opened fire already?

She crouched at the rear corner of the vehicle, tensed for action and very aware of her heartbeat thumping in her ears.

Somewhere far off, an owl hooted, its call plaintive and haunting in the pre-dawn silence.

Climb down from the fucking vehicle and show yourselves!

The hilt of the knife felt slippery in her grip, as if her palm was already coated in life blood.

Sweat, she told herself. *Just sweat.*

She was as nervous as hell, and every passing second seemed like an eternity.

When the impasse finally ended, she nearly jumped out of her skin. The driver opened his door with a report like the crack of a rifle. A boot emerged and he kicked the heavy, armour-plated door further open.

As the figure jumped down, Ajia leapt.

And tripped on a rock and went sprawling, the knife slipping from her grip. On hands and knees she cast about for the knife.

Alerted, the driver turned to her, then raised his weapon and took aim. On all fours, defenceless and cursing her stupidity, Ajia looked up.

"Christ on a stick!" she exclaimed.

The familiar figure stepped forward, smiling at her. "What you doing down there, Ajia? Praying?" he asked, lowering his bow and arrow.

She leapt to her feet, beset by conflicting emotions. Shame at having been caught out. Relief that the cocky figure before her wasn't some Paladin but none other than Reed Fletcher. Anger that the bastard had given her such a fright.

"Reed!" she cried, embracing him. Then she stepped back and slapped his face.

"What the...?" he said, touching his cheek.

"That's for frightening the holy fuck out of us, Reed. What the hell were you playing at?"

"Nice," Fletcher said. "And there I was, expecting a hero's welcome."

"A hero? Last I remember, you turned tail and fucked off like a frightened rabbit."

He stared at her, and at least had the humility to look shamefaced. "Well, I was stunned, wasn't I? I'd just been shot. Wasn't thinking straight."

"What happened?"

Fletcher hesitated. "Had second thoughts. Saw you through the hedge, drive off in that." He pointed across to the armoured car. "And you didn't even think to take the Paladins' weapons, or check them for money. No, just nab the car and skedaddle without a strategic thought for what you might need. No sodding planning ahead. Typical of a bunch of amateurs! So..."

He reached back into the Humvee and pulled out three short-barrelled assault rifles, one of which he tossed to Ajia.

"What am I supposed to do with this?" she asked, holding the weapon gingerly.

"Use it as a golf club. Make it the centrepiece of a flower display. Or maybe, I dunno, shoot it at someone attacking you."

"How?"

Briefly he showed Ajia how to hold the rifle, how to toggle the cross-bolt safety on and off, how to select between semiautomatic and fully automatic fire, and how to replace an empty magazine.

"If the average British army recruit can handle one of these things, you shouldn't have any problem," he said. "It's not rocket science."

Next he produced a holdall. "Food," he said. "I thought Mr

LeRoy wouldn't be happy with the forage grub I gave you."

Ajia shook her head in wonder and kicked the front tyre of the Humvee. "And this?"

"After you left, I came to my senses and had second thoughts. Took the guns from the blokes you so ably knocked off and made my way along the lane to the checkpoint. In the end, I used this"— he patted his bow, now slung over his shoulder—"to despatch the Paladins. Just to show that, for all their high-tech kit, they had nothing over Robin Hood."

Ajia laughed, suddenly a little giddy with relief.

"You mad arsehole," she said. "Come and say hi to the others."

Mr LeRoy squeezed himself from the front of the armoured car and stared in frank disbelief at Fletcher, then laughed and approached him with open arms.

Smith's reaction, Ajia noted, was more muted: he gave Fletcher a cold stare, gave the assault rifles an even colder stare, then turned and strode away from the armoured car.

"But how on earth did you find us?" Mr LeRoy asked.

"Wasn't hard," Fletcher said. "I saw you with that map book of yours the other day, tracing a course into the Peaks. And you took the lane I mentioned as soon as you vamoosed. All I had to do was follow the same route, hole up during the day in case the Paladins were following, then set off again come nightfall. Not exactly difficult. Oh, and I thought you'd appreciate this. Dropped into a Co-Op on the way and stocked up provisions, using spondulicks looted from the Paladins."

He hefted the full hold-all at Mr LeRoy, who caught it with a quizzical expression, which turned to one of epicurean delight when he unzipped the bag and beheld its contents.

"Why," he breathed, "food..."

Half a dozen pork pies. A dozen assorted pre-made sandwiches. Three huge Victoria sponges and six bottles of beer. "That should keep us going for a little while," Fletcher said.

"My boy," Mr LeRoy said, near to tears. "A feast beyond my wildest dreams."

Smith stamped towards them. "If you've quite finished," he began, "there's the little matter of reaching our destination before dawn."

Ajia looked at Fletcher, wincing in anticipation of his possible reaction. To his credit, Fletcher refrained from answering Smith with the put-down she'd expected.

Instead he nodded. "You're right. We should be heading off. Drive the car into the undergrowth, one of you. We'll continue in the Humvee. It's armed to the teeth, and I stocked up with spare canisters of diesel on the way."

Smith drove the armoured car into the dense woodland to the right of the lane, ramming it into the undergrowth until the vehicle was lost to sight.

He came back and made a point of saying he'd be happier travelling into the troop-carrier section of the Humvee. Mr LeRoy, Ajia and Fletcher occupied the cab, with Fletcher at the wheel. The rifles lay at their feet.

They headed west as dawn washed the sky at their backs.

TWENTY-ONE

Major Wynne drove up to the imposing facade of Charrington Grange, slipped from behind the wheel and marched up to the front door.

He wasn't looking forward to what he had to tell Drake this morning. He had delayed breaking the news for over a day, but Drake would soon be asking for a progress report and would be suspicious if Wynne prevaricated any longer. For the duration of the drive from Swindon, he had been contemplating the best way to tell the Prime Minister that his elite Paladin forces had been unable to contain Ajia Snell, Bron LeRoy, and Reed Fletcher in Sherwood Forest. Worse, that the trio has somehow not only broken the cordon around the area but had inflicted significant losses on his forces.

Drake would be incandescent.

He found the Prime Minister and Harriet breakfasting in the conservatory.

He cleared his throat and stepped towards the table. To his consternation, Harriet looked away and pointedly busied herself with pouring tea into her china cup.

"What is it, Wynne?" Drake enquired.

"Report on Snell and the other renegades, sir."

"Can't it wait?"

"Ah..."

"Oh, very well. I presume it's good news?"

At his hesitation, Harriet said, "I'll leave you two to discuss this in private. See you later, Derek." She picked up her cup and swept from the conservatory without so much as a side glance at Wynne.

"Sit down," Drake said. "Tea?"

Wynne sat down. "No, thank you, sir."

"So... Snell and the others have been arrested, I take it?"

Wynne squirmed. "I wish that were the case, sir."

"Don't tell me. Your men haven't located them yet?" Drake absently bit into a slice of toast.

Wynne bit the bullet. "I'm afraid it's worse than that, sir. In the early hours of the morning, they broke through the cordon thrown up around the area and... and fled."

Drake stared at him. "Fled? How the hell did they manage that?"

Wynne felt his face colouring. "They attacked two Paladin vehicles, killing five personnel. The information I have indicates that they captured a Humvee and an armoured car and escaped in these."

Drake stopped chewing and stared at the major. "We're talking about an eighteen-year-old girl, an overweight circus impresario, and a reject from the British Army. And you tell me that these three misfits overcame an elite force of Paladins?"

"Misfits with... special abilities, sir. Snell runs like—"

Drake interrupted. "So the girl is fast and Fletcher can shoot a bow and arrow. Do you realise how pathetic this sounds?"

The major regarded his fingers. "Yes, sir."

"Put extra resources into finding them. They can't have got far—and in military vehicles that'll stick out like sore thumbs. I want them arrested by midnight. Do you understand, Major?"

"Yes, sir."

"That will be all."

Wynne saluted and left the conservatory.

All in all, he thought as he stepped from the Grange, he'd got away without suffering the tongue-lashing he'd excepted.

He was crossing to his car when his mobile beeped.

"Lieutenant Noble here, sir. Developments concerning Snell and the others."

His heart thumped. "Go on."

"A farmer reported seeing a Humvee in the vicinity of the Derbyshire village of Dawley at seven last night, sir. Also, and this might be significant, Dawley is where one Daisy Hawthorn has her nursery. It came to our attention after locals reported odd goings-on there over the months. I think we might have another Summer Land scenario on our hands, sir. Putting two and two together, I wouldn't bet against the possibility that Snell and the others have made their way to the sanctuary of Hawthorn's nursery."

Wynne smiled to himself. A breakthrough, at last. "Good work, Lieutenant."

"How would you like me to proceed, sir?"

"Get our best team to Dawley pronto, Lieutenant. I'll take a chopper up there and take command of the assault."

"Very good sir," Noble said, and cut the connection.

Wynne turned and made his way back to the Grange. He would report to Drake that Snell and her cohorts had been spotted, and that it was only a matter of time until they were apprehended. He would also ask if Drake wanted the trio summarily executed, or brought in for intensive interrogation.

He was crossing the foyer when a sound stopped him in his tracks. A coy giggle, followed by a gasp. He peered up the stairs to see Derek Drake and Harriet locked in a passionate embrace that left little to the imagination. And they'd started to undress each other even before reaching the bedroom.

Controlling his jealousy, Wynne turned on his heel and hurried from the house.

THE MARITAL BEDROOM of Charrington Grange had not seen such sexual callisthenics for a long time, at least not between the husband and wife who were its rightful users. Drake's new-found passion for Harriet, and the rampant escalation of his libido, brought to mind the carnal free-for-all that had characterised the first year or so of their marriage. Back then they had made love morning, noon and night, and even found time to slip in a little extracurricular sex between times. Now it was back to the good old days.

He wondered at Harriet's sudden renewed passion, and his reciprocal response. It had started the other day, when Harriet had discovered his communion with the Grail. Whatever her reasons, Drake had found himself rising to the occasion. And it wasn't, he reminded himself, merely a renewal of the physical aspect of their passion—along with that, he realised he truly loved Harriet.

They made love for an hour, a no-holds-barred coming together—in both senses—that included much sweat, a little blood, and on Harriet's part more than a few orgasmic exclamations.

Exhausted, they lay in each other's arms as morning sunlight flooded the room.

His mobile, on the bedside table, buzzed into life.

"Dammit!" He checked the caller: Symmons, his Defence Secretary. "I'd better take it," he said, moving into the en-suite bathroom.

Seating himself on the toilet, he took the call. "Symmons?"

"Sir, I've had a report from Rear Admiral Travers. There's been a spot of bother in the Channel."

"Bother?"

"A skirmish, sir, between a Royal Navy frigate and a Russian sub."

Vasilyev, the bastard...

"Go on."

"Apparently the sub tracked HMS *Fortitude* up the Channel from Portsmouth, against maritime protocols, and surfaced within fifty yards of the frigate just off Dover. Surfaced off the boat's bows, sir, dangerously impeding its progress. I understand that the captain was forced into some smart manoeuvring to avoid a collision."

"Very well. I'll get someone to haul in the Russian ambassador quick sharp. If you'd like a few stern words with him yourself, Symmons..."

"I'd be delighted," the Defence Secretary said. "But that's not all, sir. I'm getting reports of three Russian battleships steaming into the North Sea. On their current trajectory, they'll be entering our territorial waters within half an hour."

"Right. Keep an eye on the situation and report back to me."

"Very good, sir."

Drake was about to return to the bedroom, and Harriet—where business remained unfinished—when the phone shrilled again.

"Good morning, Prime Minister Drake," came the oleaginous tones of the Russian Premier. "I hear that sunlight bathes your green and pleasant land this wonderful morning."

"What do you want, Vasilyev?"

"Want? Merely to keep you up to date with the current situation— to keep you 'in the loop', as I think the saying goes."

"What are you playing at, Vasilyev? It doesn't look good, you know? Dogging our ships in the Channel. It's no more than pathetic sabre-rattling—"

Vasilyev cut him off with a low chuckle. "Sabre-rattling? Ah, another one of your quaint British phrases. I merely wanted to keep you apprised, in the best diplomatic traditions, of my intentions towards Estonia."

Drake's blood ran cold. He himself had signed a friendship pact with Estonia a couple of years ago that had entailed much in the way of beneficial trade benefits for Britain. The subtext had been that Estonia would expect protection from Britain in the face of possible Russian aggression.

"And those 'intentions'?"

"Military exercises on the border, with perhaps the occasional unintentional incursion. We are, after all, protecting the rights of ethnic Russians within Estonia, who have come under certain pressures of late."

"And your warships in the North Sea and English Channel?" Drake said.

He could imagine Vasilyev's disingenuous smile as he replied, "Merely exercises, Prime Minister, to keep you on your toes. Oh, and I have another little present."

He cut the connection before Drake could bring himself to protest.

The 'little present' came in the form of another jpeg—an extended version of his sexual peccadillo with the Russian journalist. Watching it, he assessed his performance and decided that, all things considered, the Russian had not elicited the best from him. That, he had saved for Harriet.

Speaking of whom... He looked down. The content of the jpeg, despite the threat it symbolised, had had a rousing effect.

He would put it to good use.

HARRIET HAD BEEN dealing with her own callers. Or rather, she had deigned not to deal with calls from Major Dominic Wynne. Four that morning. Really, he was becoming something of a pain. Did he really need it spelling out to him that it was over? Hadn't he realised that it had only ever been, from her point of view, a fling, to be enjoyed and then forgotten? Wynne was a plaything of the past.

She lay on the bed in a state of post-coital bliss and regarded Wynne's last text: *Please call me back. Urgent. I love you.*

Loved her? He loved the idea of shagging the boss's wife, more like: the delicious danger it represented. She was no more than an elicit thrill, though he'd tried to deny the fact. Well, it was over now.

And if he continued with his importunate hounding of her, she would have to take drastic action.

Drake emerged from the bathroom.

"Important business, darling?" said Harriet.

He told her about the call from his Defence Secretary, and then the one from Vasilyev.

"But what can he want?"

"To look good with his electorate in Russia. Baiting Britain always goes down well in Moscow. The man is no more than a tin-pot dictator."

Harriet squeezed his cock.

"He needs teaching a lesson. This reminds me," she smiled. "What about Trident?"

Drake lay back, his hands behind his head while Harriet took his manhood in her mouth and worked him to the edge of orgasm.

The Trident option had occurred to him the other day. In the nuclear stakes, Britain fought well above her weight. She had her own strategic nuclear defence force, both land and sea, and a couple of years ago Drake had taken a leaf from the American's book and initiated a chain of command that led straight from his own Nuclear Briefcase to the many missiles deployed around the globe. All he had to do was input a launch code, press the button, and atomic mayhem would be unleashed on his unwitting enemies.

There remained, of course, the small matter of Vasilyev's threat to make public his dalliance with the Russian bimbo.

But Drake had a scheme to neutralise that threat.

Before he came, he withdrew his cock from Harriet's mouth and spread her legs.

After all, it wouldn't do to spend his all ammunition too early.

TWENTY-TWO

THE HUMVEE RACED along the narrow, winding lanes with the craggy limestone peaks of Derbyshire looming on either side. Ajia had never felt more vulnerable or exposed. The sky was lightening by the minute and, though the lanes were deserted, she expected to come across a police patrol car at any second. And the coppers would be on the lookout for a stolen Humvee, of course, driven by desperate Paladin-killers. She told herself she was being paranoid and tried to concentrate on what Mr LeRoy was telling Reed Fletcher.

"...I think she will be a valuable asset to our little group—our band of Merrie Men, if I might be permitted to use the sobriquet."

"And she is?" Fletcher asked.

"One Daisy Hawthorn."

Ajia looked at Mr LeRoy. Daisy Hawthorn? The name was familiar.

Fletcher laughed. "Small world."

Mr LeRoy arched an eyebrow. "You know her?"

"You could say that. Me and Daisy, we were close, once."

"And by close?"

"Read: intimate. We had a fling, didn't we? Didn't last, though. Found me out for the loser I was, and got out. But it was fun while it lasted. You could say we had quite a lot in common."

Mr LeRoy smiled. "Yes, of course you did."

Then Ajia had it. Daisy Hawthorn! Daisy Hawthorn, TV presenter, gardening journalist, nursery owner and all round green-fingered expert. But she was quite bit older than Fletcher. They would have made something of a mismatched couple. Perhaps that's why it hadn't lasted.

The thought of Hawthorn's big, friendly, countrywoman's face brought back a slew of bittersweet memories. Even though her mum had never owned a garden—in fact, all she owned in the way of acreage were two window-boxes—she *had* been addicted to BBC's Sunday night gardening programme, *Gardener's Weekly*, presented by the motherly Daisy Hawthorn. Ajia had snuggled on the sofa next to her mum and watched Daisy, with her reassuring north country accent, talk the uninitiated through the best way to grown tomatoes, pot on dahlias, propagate hyacinths, and elucidate a million and one other arcane horticultural enigmas.

The memory filled Ajia with a feeling of desperate loss.

"And now she's one of us?" Fletcher asked.

"You didn't know?" Mr LeRoy said.

Fletcher shook his head. "We got together years ago, before I joined the army. I was a Jack-the-lad in my early twenties, Daisy the older woman." He grinned. "Taught me everything I know, and not just in the nursery."

"So Daisy Hawthorn's an eidolon like us?" Ajia said.

"She is," Mr LeRoy said, "and she will be a valuable recruit to our cause. If, that is, she will consent to be recruited. I might have my work cut out, though. Ah! Here we are," he said, pointing to their right.

High on the opposite side of the valley, a collection of small grey-stone cottages, with flint tile roofs, clung to the incline. "Dawley," Mr LeRoy pronounced. "Daisy has her nursery a couple of miles further along the valley, tucked away down a lane leading through what is known as Dawley Old Forest. Ancient woodland, I'll have you know."

Reed Fletcher smiled. "Coming home," he said.

They descended into the valley and left the village in their wake. The lane snaked along the valley bottom, criss-crossing a twinkling silver river with a series of tiny humpbacked stone bridges, river and lane entwining like a continuous pewter braid. Ahead, Ajia made out the dark mass of the ancient woodland.

Minutes later they reached the forest. Mr LeRoy indicated a gap in the trees to their right. Yet another rutted lane tunnelled into the woodland's sepulchral interior. A painted wooden sign, rotten and askew, read: HAWTHORN NURSERY 1 MILE.

Fletcher slowed down to walking pace. The Humvee bucked and shuddered along the uneven track.

Less than a mile further on, Fletcher braked. "What's that?"

"It would appear that dead-ends are the order of the day," Mr LeRoy commented.

The way ahead was blockaded. Great timber beams had been formed into giant crosses, and on these were placed crossbeams festooned with a tangle of barbed wire. Any gaps in the makeshift fortification had been filled with old tyres.

"This is very strange," Mr LeRoy said. "Why should Daisy wish to keep people from accessing her nursery?"

Ajia climbed from the cab and Mr LeRoy opened the back of the Humvee to release Smith. All four stood before the barricade.

Ajia said, "Do you feel it?" She shivered.

"We're being watched," Smith said.

The feeling was almost palpable. The dawn light was strengthening, spears of sunlight piercing the forest around them. The silence added to the sensation that they were being observed.

"Are you sure Daisy's still here?" Ajia asked Mr LeRoy. "The sign back there looked ancient. It's as if no one's been here for ages."

"I passed this way with Summer Land two years ago," Mr LeRoy said. "The nursery was flourishing then. I tried to get Daisy to join us, but she said she belonged here."

"It doesn't seem to be flourishing now," Smith said.

"Two years is a long time," Ajia said.

She heard something in the woods. She saw a swift movement, a flash of something dun-coloured. An animal, maybe. She stared into the undergrowth, alarmed. She could have sworn that she saw a pair of eyes staring back at her from the boscage. Then they were gone.

"I don't like—"

Something grabbed her, snatched her into the undergrowth. The transition from standing upright to being dragged through the vegetation by strong hands was so rapid she had no time to struggle. Then she was lying on her back, her arms and legs pinioned by the same powerful hands. She stared up at one of the most ugly faces she had ever seen in her life.

No, not one *of the most. Definitely the ugliest.*

It was sufficiently human-like to make the difference grotesque. A massive nose, deep-set tiny eyes, and a mouth sporting a snaggle of crooked green teeth.

Then a woman spoke—a reassuring tone Ajia recognised from many years ago.

"Let her go, and the others."

The ugly creature released her. Ajia jumped to her feet and fought her way back through the undergrowth to the track. The others had been assaulted, too. Smith was emerging from the woods at a stagger, flanked by two small, thickset uglies. Mr LeRoy was being pinned to the ground by three specimens of what she realised, belatedly, must be boggarts or goblins. Only Reed Fletcher had managed to maintain his autonomy by leaping up a nearby tree, notching his bow, and aiming it at the head of a boggart who was attempting, comically, to climb after him.

"You can get down now, Reed," said the woman.

She was small and plump, with a mass of auburn hair and a cherubic, ruddy-cheeked face. The sight of her filled Ajia with the warmth that had won the hearts of a million television viewers the length and breadth of the country.

She wore dungarees and green wellington boots and stood like a mother amid the boggarts, elves and brownies who were gathered around her in a protective phalanx.

Fletcher jumped from the tree. Mr LeRoy climbed to his feet, dusting himself down and looking somewhat chagrined.

"Nice welcome, Daisy," Fletcher said, slipping his bow over his shoulder. "I didn't think we parted on *such* bad terms."

Mr LeRoy interrupted him. "I think there might be a valid reason for our treatment, and for that," he said, indicating the barricade.

"Indeed there is," Daisy Hawthorn said. "And I'll tell you all about it over breakfast. I take it you're staying a while? First, though," she went on, frowning at the hulking shape of the Humvee, "we need to hide that. Back it into the forest would you, Reed?"

He did as requested, though the vehicle was still visible from the track.

As Ajia watched, Daisy stepped forward and knelt before the Humvee. She reached out and touched the ground. And something miraculous happened, something that made Ajia gasp with wonder.

At Daisy's touch, the ground appeared to come to life. Grasses writhed, tendrils snaked across the earth towards the vehicle. Flowers and weeds sent out runners and stalks that crept up the sides of the Humvee and over its cab in a great verdant tapestry. Within a minute the vehicle was covered in ivy, wisteria and assorted plant life.

Mr LeRoy noted Ajia's amazement. "Daisy is none other than the Green Man. Or, rather, the Green Woman."

Daisy blessed Ajia with a smile that warmed her heart.

"Now," she said, beaming around the group. "Shall we eat?"

AJIA HAD NEVER seen anything quite like Daisy Hawthorn's arboreal hideaway.

The house was constructed from halved logs which were largely hidden from view by the profusion of flowers that grew up its long, low facade. Sprouting from the logs, and working their way through the covering of blooms, were gnarled branches and boughs, bursting with leaves and obviously very much alive.

The magic continued inside the multi-levelled building. Trees sprouted from the packed-earth floor, and vines and lianas grew up the walls. Everything within the building was constructed from timber which still lived. Ajia was astounded to see a narrow, silver stream tinkling through the dining room.

They ate at a long timber table. Daisy sat its head, with to her left a brownie woman who reminded Ajia, painfully, of Maya, and to her right a charming young elf who bore more than a passing resemblance to Perry. She noticed that Mr LeRoy cast the occasional sad glance in the direction of the youth.

Bowls of porridge were followed by chunks of home-made bread with strawberry and raspberry jam. Even the herb tisane, Daisy proudly announced, was made in the nursery.

Daisy reached out and clutched Mr LeRoy's hand. "It's so good to see you again, Bron. If not for you…"

She hesitated, and smiled down the table at her guests. "But perhaps you'd better tell the tale, Bron?"

He dabbed his lips with a napkin. "I happened upon Hawthorn Nursery a couple of years ago, when I was in the area with Summer Land. The nursery was thriving, though the same could not be said of you, Daisy."

She beamed down the table at Ajia and Smith. "A month before meeting Bron, I had an accident. I was working in the woods, thinning the southern plantation." She winced. "Even the thought of it…!"

Mr LeRoy took up the tale. "The long and the short of it was that dear Daisy misjudged the fall of a pine and was struck a fatal blow as the tree toppled. Or fatal according to a nursery worker who brought her back here and called an ambulance. He was sure Daisy was quite dead, so imagine his astonishment when the paramedics announced that she was alive, though suffering concussion and a fractured skull."

"I have absolutely no memory of the incident itself, nor of my recuperation in the hospital. My first memory is returning home, to the nursery, and what happened next."

Mr LeRoy frowned. "Nightmares first, or was it the manifestation of your ability?"

"My ability," she said. "I'd always been green-fingered, of course, but things began to get a little ridiculous. Dead plants and trees and shrubs came back to life at my merest touch. Even timber was resurrected and took on renewed life." She gestured around her at the sprouting timber walls. "I had to hide my ability, lest it attract attention. I left the nursery work to my staff, and rarely ventured out. Then the nightmares began—terrible dreams of being lost in a hostile forest, prey to ravening beasts and monsters."

The other eidolons nodded in sympathy. Each had been through their own version of this metamorphosis. In retrospect, Ajia felt that she herself had got off rather easily. Doubtless it made a difference that she had had Smith there to help her through.

"I was making a rare visit to the local market-town one day," Daisy Hawthorn, the Green Woman, continued, "when I saw a rather large, irrepressibly cheerful fellow staring at me across the cheese stall. I recall you chased me to a cafe, Bron, took my hand and said, in that wonderful Thespian baritone of yours, 'My dear, but I can explain everything...'."

Mr LeRoy laughed. "I remember it as if it were yesterday."

"You explained, and I really thought I was going mad! Either that, or *you* were the lunatic."

"I took Daisy on a tour of Summer Land, pitched then just a mile outside the market town, and you met Perry and the others, Maya and all the brownies..."

He took Daisy's hand, and squeezed. "And when it was time for us to move on," he said, "I pleaded with Daisy to come with us, to join Summer Land and become part of the family of like-minded folk."

"But I had my life here. The nursery." She shook her head. "I was, I admit, a little tempted, but a year earlier I'd retired from broadcasting—I'd had enough of performing—and I couldn't see myself being part of Summer Land, and amazing people with my peculiar ability. My home was here." She smiled around the table. "But, saying that, I am looking forward to meeting the others again, Perry and Maya and Bostock..."

Daisy faltered as she sensed the atmosphere, and saw Mr LeRoy's pained expression. Ajia swallowed.

"What?" the Green Woman said, in barely a murmur.

"I am afraid to say that, on that score…" He could not go on.

Smith said, "Summer Land was attacked. Drake's thugs, the Paladins. They killed everyone, or almost everyone. The three of us, Mr LeRoy, myself and Ajia, we managed to escape."

Daisy Hawthorn lifted a plump, weathered hand to her stricken face. "Perry?"

Mr LeRoy shook his head, his lips compressed.

"Everyone?" Daisy echoed.

"It was an indiscriminate slaughter," Smith murmured.

Into the silence that had gripped the table, the elf to Daisy's right—the young man who so resembled Perry—spoke up for the first time.

"I told you we weren't safe," he said.

Daisy laid a hand on his arm. "Hush, Tonttu," she murmured.

Mr LeRoy eyed Daisy. "Safe?"

"Shortly after you departed with Summer Land," the Green Woman said, "I began to collect my little family, my waifs and strays. I'd been noticing them for some months, ever since the accident—quick flashes of movement through the forest out of the corner of my eye, manifestations in the ancient woodland. Then Tonttu came, requesting work." She smiled at the elf. "He claimed he came from Finland, an illegal immigrant without papers, but I sensed there was more to his story than that. A little later others began turning up, elves and brownies, and I noticed their talents; their glamour, their way with plants and animals. Finally the goblins and boggarts, who I set to work in the woods, clearing the paths, mending the fences. I'd saved enough from all my TV work to afford my little family…" She faltered.

Tonttu said, "And then we were noticed by the locals, the villagers."

Smith leaned forward. "What happened?"

The elf regarded his empty desert dish. "It was just insults, at first. They shouted at us when we were in the village and town, doing the weekly shopping. Calling us names. 'Ugly', 'queer', 'dwarf…'. We ignored them and went about our business."

"It's all down to Drake, the execrable Drake," Daisy said. "He grants anyone with a grievance the right to hate anyone not like themselves. When Drake's got rid of everyone of colour, and the gays, and the Jews, he'll find another target. Sometimes," she finished, "I despair."

"Just last week," Tonttu said, "Elvira was attacked by a crowd outside the pub. She was passing at lunchtime. They were drunk and took a fancy to her, and invited her to join them. And when she politely refused, and tried to leave, they grabbed her, pushed her around. If it wasn't for Constable Bruce..." He shook his head. "Who knows what might have happened to her?"

"The following day," Daisy took up the story, "a gang of them came here, local thugs, just lads in their twenties, drunk and looking for trouble. They got it, alright. They started messing up the shop, then overturning a few plant displays outside and breaking glass in one of the greenhouses. So Gregor set about them."

"Gregor?" Mr LeRoy enquired.

"The boggart who chased Reed up the tree," said the Green Woman, smiling. "He might be small, but he's built like an anvil. And he's phenomenally strong. They didn't know what had hit them. Not that he did any lasting damage, just roughed them up a bit and sent them on their way."

Tonttu said, "Then some of them came back and torched the potting shed. Daisy had to get Constable Bruce to send a couple of men round for a day or two, until tempers died down."

"Ah," said Mr LeRoy, "that would account for the barricade across the track?"

"We built it a few days ago," Daisy said, "along with one at the rear entrance. And I nurtured an especially strong hedge of briar and hawthorn along the southern edge of the property."

Tonttu exchanged a look with Daisy. "I suggested that we should leave Hawthorn Nursery," he said, "that we should get out before things turn seriously nasty. I can feel it in the air, every time I go into town. The hatred, the threat..." He shook his head. "We should get out now, while we can. We have the minibus we use for deliveries. It's old, but serviceable."

Mr LeRoy shifted his gaze to Daisy Hawthorn. "But...?"

The Green Woman sighed. "I must admit, Bron, that I'm torn. I lie awake at night, worrying. Thinking that perhaps Tonttu and Gregor are right, and that we should abandon the place before something dreadful happens. But I've put a lot of blood, sweat and tears into this place. It's home. I'm connected to the land, the ancient woods. It would seem like an act of cowardice, a giving in to Drake and his louts, if we fled. But now, after what you've told me about Summer Land…"

Mr LeRoy smiled, sadly. "You think it can never happen to you," he said. "Which I suppose is what the Jews thought in Nazi Germany, at first. And the analogy isn't cheap, or misguided, my dear. We are living in times that share certain correlations with earlier, terrible times. And we'd be wise to heed the warning signs."

As if in reflection, she looked from Tonttu to the girl on her left, and then around at the vibrant dining room. She said at last, in little more than a whisper, "But if we did leave here, then where would we go? Where might I take my little family? There are a dozen of us, all told."

Ajia looked at Mr LeRoy, who caught her eye and nodded.

"You could come with us," he said. "That is, we could travel together. We must needs leave the Humvee here. We could travel in the minibus Tonttu mentioned."

Daisy shrugged. "But to where?"

Mr LeRoy hesitated. "We are gathering forces, Daisy. In time we will confront Derek Drake and his hordes. We have our special talents, our abilities. Alone, we might not amount to much of an oppositional force, but in union lies our strength. At length we will head south, and…" He hesitated.

Smith said, "Tell them," he grunted, "or are you afraid it'll sound melodramatic?"

So Mr LeRoy, utilising all his oratorical skill, set out his scheme to locate and enlist the aid of King Arthur, or rather his eidolon, whose power would unite the disparate forces of opposition to Derek Drake and his Paladins, and bring the reign of terror and discrimination to an end.

And by the culmination of his little speech, Ajia could see the fire of enthusiasm in the eyes of many of those around the table.

"We could gather provisions," Mr LeRoy finished, "and leave tonight."

Daisy rose from the table and paced across the room. She stood before a window, her broad back to the company, staring out across the cobbled yard to an old greenhouse scintillating in the sunlight.

At last she turned. "It's a decision I can't make alone," she said. "We're all in this together. It's not a step to take lightly. Esther, call the others, Tonttu, fetch Gregor and Bogdan and Oleg from the woods."

Tonttu and Esther departed swiftly, and within minutes brownies and elves edged into the room, some garbed in kitchen wear, others in outdoor clothing, with mud on their boots and dirt on their hands. Last of all came the three boggarts and a goblin, brutish looking individuals who positioned themselves next to Daisy as if delegating themselves as her personal bodyguard.

Ajia counted a dozen souls in total, a mixture of boggarts, goblins, brownies and elves.

Daisy told them what had happened at Summer Land, and reminded them of the contretemps in the local town and village. She told them of her ambivalence, and finally of Bron LeRoy's grand scheme to seek the eidolon of King Arthur and confront the forces of Prime Minster Drake.

"And so, of course, the question is: should we remain, or leave? Whatever we do, I would rather we do it together. And nothing would please me more if we were unanimous in our decision." She took a breath. "Now, a show of hands. All those in favour of leaving with Mr LeRoy and his friends?"

Ajia looked around the little group of cowering brownies and elves, and the truculent quartet of goblins and boggarts.

Then, as if in telepathic communication, they lifted their hands as one.

Tonttu said, "And you, Daisy?"

The Green Woman laid a hand on the shoulder of the boggart to her right. "I could not remain here without my children," she said. "Everyone, gather your possessions and we will leave at sunset. I—"

She was interrupted by a hammering on the solid oak door.

Tonttu slipped from the room. Ajia looked across at Mr LeRoy, wondering at the interruption. He looked worried. Surely the Paladins had not traced them here so rapidly?

Tonttu returned a minute later with a reluctant police constable in tow. The bobby held his helmet in his hands and stared around the disparate gathering, his eyes flickering from the boggarts to the brownies, and alighting with seeming relief on Daisy Hawthorn's more quotidian figure.

"Ah, Ms Hawthorn, a quiet word, if you don't mind."

The pair moved to a corner of the room and conferred in urgent whispers.

Ajia heard one or two phrases from the tête-à-tête:

"I have it on good authority…

"Midnight, I understand…

"Imminent danger…

"Thought I'd better warn you, as you've always been right and law-abiding citizens…"

At length Daisy thanked the constable and escorted him to the door.

She returned, deep in thought. She looked around the group, shaken.

"PC Bruce informs me that we will be visited by a deputation of government officials tonight," she said. "That is, his superintendent told him to have a few men standing by in case of trouble. That is the official line. We are to be investigated by immigration officers seeking illegal immigrants. Unofficially, PC Bruce says that they resemble no immigration officers he's ever seen."

Reed Fletcher said, "They're here already?"

"Apparently, they arrived in the village an hour ago. In armoured cars. They will raid the nursery at midnight."

Feeling sick, Ajia rose to her feet. She inadvertently skittled her chair, and everyone looked at her. "Have any of you noticed… I mean, in the past few days…?" She was aware of the tremor in her voice. "Has the nursery been visited by strangers, men and women with a military bearing? Wearing thick black glasses?"

"Two days ago," a brownie said, her voice as light as air, "I saw a strange couple. They wandered around the nursery, but seemed more interested in the house, and my friends working in the hothouse."

Ajia swore to herself.

Fletcher said, "Plainclothes Paladins."

Mr LeRoy explained to Daisy. "A day or so before the attack on Summer Land, Ajia noticed a few men and women, scoping the place."

"Immigration officers my arse!" Fletcher spat. He looked at Mr LeRoy. "If they were here two days ago," he went on, "then they can't be after *us*. They must have got wind that you were harbouring folkloric characters. Or that you, Daisy, are an eidolon."

Tonttu looked across at Daisy, desperation in his eyes. "What do we do?"

The Green Woman looked pleadingly at Mr LeRoy. "Bron?"

"They'll have all the approach roads under surveillance, so we can't leave by vehicle. We could try to sneak out, in small groups, through the woods, though there's no telling as to their numbers, or whether they have the woods covered."

"And the alternative is...?" Fletcher wanted to know.

Mr LeRoy hesitated.

Gregor, a four-foot high mass of ugly muscle, stepped forward and looked around the assembly. "We stay and fight," he said. He looked up at Daisy, almost sheepishly, and went on, "Me and Bogdan, we have weapons, rifles."

"How many?" Fletcher asked.

"Four, in good working order."

"And I liberated three AR-80s from the Paladins," Fletcher said.

Ajia raised her knife aloft. "And I have this, plus I can run like fuck."

"But how should we go about defending ourselves against highly trained Paladins?" Mr LeRoy sounded almost desperate. "You saw what they did at Summer Land."

"They took us by surprise then," Fletcher said, "and we were unarmed. Now we have the advantage of knowing that they'll attack, and exactly when." He turned to Daisy. "We'll simulate a gathering in here, with lights on and figures around the table. Music playing."

Smith stood up. "This is madness. We don't stand a chance."

"What do you suggest we do, Smith?" Fletcher said, quietly. "We'd be foolish to leave along the tracks."

Smith looked around the gathering. "I could take those who can't fight into the woods come darkness."

"And the rest of us," Fletcher said, nodding to Gregor and Bogdan, "we take up positions outside and lie in wait."

They spent the rest of the day in frantic preparation. Fletcher took command, marking positions in buildings overlooking the central house: two armed boggarts would lie in wait in the loft of the potting shed, while two others would station themselves in an oak tree at the side of the house. Tonttu and another elf, Parisa, would hide in a tree-house to the west of the nursery, armed with rifles. Ajia would be a free agent, using her speed and her newly acquired expertise with a knife to wreak havoc. Fletcher prevailed upon Mr LeRoy and Daisy—hardly able combatants—to join Smith and two brownies in concealment deep in the woods. They would rendezvous at the rear exit of the nursery at two in the morning.

At eight o'clock they shared a last meal, then Daisy Hawthorn set about simulating a tableau of diners around the table. She set a dozen potted cactus plants on chairs around the table. Then she went from one to the next, touching each plant tenderly with her fingertips and standing back, her motherly face a mask of concentration as the plants, one by one, rapidly grew and miraculously took on the forms of seated human—and other—diners. Later, looking through the window from outside, Ajia was convinced that the room was inhabited, the charade enhanced by gauzy lace curtains, music and candle-light.

At nine o'clock, Wayland Smith led Daisy and two brownies, along with Mr LeRoy, into the woods.

Then Ajia and the others took up their positions in the darkness and settled down to wait.

TWENTY-THREE

Major Wynne's helicopter came down on the playing field of the village school requisitioned as the Paladins' command centre. Twilight was descending on the limestone crags surrounding Dawley. It wasn't yet ten o'clock, and he was on course to have Ajia Snell, Bron LeRoy and the others rounded up, or killed in short order.

Harriet might for some reason have turned her back on him, but he was determined that Derek Drake would soon be singing his praises.

Lieutenant Noble escorted Wynne through the downdraught of the chopper's rotor-blades and into the staffroom.

"Just had word from Corporal Evans, sir," Noble said. "He was on recce. In the woods surrounding Hawthorn Nursery, and he found a Humvee hidden in the undergrowth."

Wynne could not contain his smile. "So Snell and the others *are* hiding with Hawthorn."

"Looks that way, sir. And all reports from locals indicate that the workers employed by Hawthorn are, you know... of folkloric origin."

Wynne strode across to a map of the area Noble had set up on the wall. It showed an area of woodland and, outlined in red within it, Hawthorn Nursery. Also indicated, in blue marker pen, were two tracks leading into the woods from north and south.

"I have two Humvees with six men aboard each stationed here and here," Noble pointed to the northern track. "A mile from the nursery itself. I suggest we send in an initial force at midnight, followed by a second thirty minutes later." He smiled. "A mopping-up operation. All we need to decide is whether we eradicate everyone in there, or..."

On the flight north, Wynne had conveyed the news of the operation to the Prime Minister. Drake had ordered Snell, LeRoy and Fletcher to be taken alive. The others were to be killed in situ.

Wynne relayed the order to his second-in-command.

Noble led the way across to a picture window overlooking the widening valley. Two miles away the ancient woodland was a dark smudge in the gathering darkness, and buried somewhere in its heart was Ajia Snell's temporary sanctuary.

He would enjoy interrogating the girl. He had, after all, a score to settle. She was responsible for the deaths of five of his men. He would ensure that she suffered.

An underling fixed him a cup of coffee, hot and sweet. At eleven o'clock, with an hour to go before Mission Hawthorn was initiated, he ordered Noble to gather his men in the staffroom for a final briefing.

He gazed at the huge, imposing warriors with a sense of proprietorial pride. These were the cream of the cream, a merciless band of brothers culled from the finest that the SAS, the SBS and other elite commando forces had to offer and honed into a relentless killing machine.

That five Paladins had been brought down by a girl and a bootleg Robin Hood reinforced the fact that their opposition tonight was in no way to be underestimated—and this is what he impressed upon his men now.

"Let me remind you that this will not be the turkey shoot that Summer Land turned out to be," he said. "They might not be expecting tonight's attack, but all indications is that they will be armed and prepared to fight. Proceed with extreme caution. We are up against conscienceless killers who will take great delight in inflicting maximum damage. I want these three arrested, if at all feasible." He indicated images of Ajia Snell, Reed Fletcher and Bron LeRoy on the laptop. "The others are to be liquidated. Any questions?"

There were none.

"Very well, off you go. And good luck."

He stood with Lieutenant Noble before the picture window and watched the Humvees rumble into life and crawl from the playground.

HE SAT BACK in the armchair, sipped his coffee, and waited.

Midnight came and went.

Lieutenant Noble crouched over a radio on the table in the centre of the room.

Wynne always felt a soporific sense of lassitude in these situations. There had been times when, as a grunt on the ground, he'd been on the sharp end of similar missions. He'd distinguished himself over the course of a dozen years, and a hundred bloody sorties, and now he was reaping the reward.

He was expecting word from the ground any second now: *Mission accomplished. Snell and cohorts arrested. All others dead.*

Twelve-thirty came and went.

He rose from his chair and stared through the window. He could see very little past his own tall reflection. Somewhere out there, in the depths of the forest, slaughter was being committed.

He would relish inspecting the bloody aftermath.

TWENTY-FOUR

AJIA CROUCHED BEHIND a water butt across the cobbled yard from the house, ready to make her move. Earlier, a couple of boggarts had dismantled the blockade further along the track to encourage the Paladins to use that means of access. Not that they would, Reed Fletcher had warned the assembled fighters earlier. It was his guess that Drake's men would proceed only so far in military vehicles, then continue on foot through the woods. One thing he was certain of, though: some of their number would make a beeline for the illuminated house, while others hung back.

"I'll take out the Paladins who approach the house," Fletcher had said. "Then I'll leave my position and move to the potting shed. We don't know how many of the bastards they're sending in. Ajia, that'll be your job. Scout the area and report back to me."

Now she looked at the luminous dial of her watch in the light of the moon. 11.45. She set off.

She'd blackened her face with charcoal from the open fire and donned black gloves. Daisy had given her a navy blue anorak with a hood. In the darkness of the forest, she would be almost invisible.

However, the same darkness that was her ally would also be her enemy. The ground underfoot was uneven. She'd be risking her neck if she attempted to traverse the terrain in Puck mode. She would proceed through the woods with caution.

As she stepped through the forest towards the front entrance, she couldn't help thinking back to the Paladin attack on Summer Land. Their determination and ruthlessness, their unthinking butchery of innocents. That was the type of people she would be fighting tonight: conscienceless killers following orders from an elected politician little better than a dictator. She thought of Major Wynne, and how he'd put a bullet through Perry's head as a matter of course, almost without thinking about what he was doing. She wondered if the bastard would be leading tonight's operation. Oh, how she hoped he would be.

She gripped the knife in her right hand.

She came to the timber crosspieces of the barricade piled beside the track at the entrance and crouched next to a pile of tyres. The night was silent, still. There was no sign of the Paladins.

She listened intently, but there was no sound of engine noise from far or near.

She stepped onto the track and sprinted, heading towards the lane a mile away. Fifteen seconds later she approached the T-junction and slowed. She looked right and left. A half-moon and a scatter of stars illuminated the silent, patched macadam lane.

No Paladins.

She looked at her watch. 11.55.

The rear entrance?

She sprinted back to the dismantled barricade, then slowed as she made her way back through the wood to the nursery and the track beyond. She sprinted again, luxuriating in the feeling of her limbs stretching, her lungs expanding as she covered hundreds of yards in seconds.

A sound came to her, slurred by her accelerated progress along the track. She ducked into the undergrowth to her right.

The sound assumed its normal pitch: a vehicle's grinding engine. More than one vehicle, in fact. Two, three?

She peered along the track. In the distance, the glow of approaching headlights showed.

She swallowed, feeling suddenly sick.

Seconds later two armoured cars trundled into view.

Just two?

They could each hold no more than half a dozen Paladins. Was this the extent of their attacking force? If so, they were guilty of seriously underestimating the opposition awaiting them.

When the first of the vehicles was still a hundred yards away, Ajia stepped onto the track and sprinted back to the nursery, feeling vulnerable despite knowing that her speed and the darkness rendered her invisible.

Seconds later she arrived at the looming oak tree where Reed Fletcher was concealed.

"Reed!" she hissed.

He dropped from a branch, startling her.

"Two armoured cars, coming in from the north." She indicated along the lane.

"Nothing to the south?"

"Not that I saw."

"Tell the others," he said, and hauled himself back up into the branches.

She sprinted across the cobbled yard to the potting shed and relayed the message to the waiting boggarts, then crossed to the tree beside the house and found the elves. Tonttu stared down at her with big eyes as she spoke, an assault rifle clutched to his thin chest.

The yard before the house was illuminated by motion-sensitive lights, and the same went for the area behind the house. Whichever approach the Paladins chose, they would be lit up like sitting ducks.

She crossed the cobbles again, heading for the rear track. She heard music and voices issuing from the illuminated dining room. Daisy had switched on two radios before leaving, one tuned to a music station, the other to Radio Four.

The lights went out behind her.

She sprinted down the track until she made out the diffuse glow of the armoured cars' headlights, which suddenly cut out. Seconds later, the protracted slur of their engines ceased too.

They were coming in on foot.

She made out two Humvees, one behind the other. Their doors were opening in slow motion. She slowed and slipped into the cover of the forest beside the track, her pulse thumping.

Six armed and helmeted Paladins climbed from the leading vehicle, and the same number from the second. An officer spoke briefly to the group.

She watched as the first six touched gauntleted fists, two of them butting body armour in a sickening show of macho bravado. She heard grunts, something like a war-chant, as they set off towards the nursery. The second group held back.

Two Paladins remained on the track, another two veered into the forest to their right, and the remaining pair moved through the trees to the left.

Ajia took off again, sprinting back to the nursery.

"Twelve," she reported to Fletcher, "coming in two groups of six. The first lot are on their way, two on the track, the others in the woods."

She relayed the same information to the others, then sprinted back across the cobbles and ducked behind the water butt. Seconds later the motion-sensitive light cut out, plunging the forecourt into darkness.

She felt very vulnerable when not in motion, and worked to convince herself that she was well hidden here. She would play it by ear, allow the shootout to commence and then play the free agent, mopping up whichever stragglers remained and ensuring that not one single Paladin got out alive.

The first two soldiers emerged from the shadows, crouched and moving slowly towards the house. The motion lights kicked in, flooding the courtyard with silvery illumination. The pair froze comically. They waited five long seconds, then crept towards the house where to all intents and purposes a rather noisy party was in progress.

They reached the house and hunkered down to either side of the front door. One Paladin gestured towards the lighted window, and the other nodded and pulled something from the chest pocket of his flak-jacket.

A grenade?

Crouching, he duck-walked along the front of the house towards the window, paused and drew back his right hand.

It was his last conscious movement.

Ajia heard something, a low twang from the direction of the oak tree, and the Paladin with the grenade keeled over, the quarrel of an arrow emerging from his neck.

The motion light cut out and Ajia heard the second Paladin curse. He moved. The light flashed on again, illuminating him starkly as he crossed to his fallen colleague. He reached out, touched the arrow, then turned quickly in the direction from which the arrow must have come.

She heard nothing this time but the soldier's startled grunt as an arrow squelched through his eyeball and buried itself deep in his brain.

The light went out, obscuring the scene of silent carnage.

Two down, ten to go.

She took off. She reasoned that others must be planning to enter the house from the rear. She sprinted along the facade and turned the corner—barrelling straight into the solidity of a fourteen-stone Paladin. He went sprawling backwards, Ajia on top of him. Before he could react, she raised her knife and slashed it across his exposed throat. He grunted, gasped, and then the only sound was the gushing of his hot blood as it pumped out across the back of her hand.

Crouching, Ajia looked up and scanned the rear yard.

She took off like a sprinter from the blocks and crossed to the cover of a hedge.

A second later a Paladin emerged from the cover of the woods ten yards to her right, hurrying across to his fallen comrade. He was activating his lapel mic when Ajia ran up behind him and slashed her knife across his Achilles tendon. He fell with a cry, and she drove the blade into his abdomen below the protection of his body armour.

Four down, eight to go.

She took his ankles, dragged the body into the cover of the woods—no mean feat, with equipment and body armour adding to his already considerable bulk—then returned for the other Paladin.

She was hauling the corpse into the trees when a cacophony of sustained gunfire filled the night.

She abandoned the body and sprinted around the house.

She paused and peered around the corner.

She feared seeing Fletcher or the others lying at the foot of the oak, shot dead. The gunfire had ceased. The forecourt was in darkness. As she moved cautiously around the corner, the lights came on to reveal the bodies of two Paladins sprawled on the cobbles. One had an arrow projecting from his temple; the other was headless.

Six down, six to go.

Ajia sprinted across to the oak and hissed.

Fletcher hung from the bough with one arm, for all the world like a sloth. "I got one with an arrow," he reported, "but the other opened up on the tree. So Bogdan here let him have it. You?"

She indicated the pair before the house. "And I accounted for another two around the back. The other six'll be alerted now."

"They might assume the firing came from their own."

"I'll try to find them."

Fletcher hauled himself back up into the leaf cover and Ajia took off.

She sprinted along the track, within seconds coming across two Paladins moving cautiously in the margin of the forest towards the nursery. The remaining four, she presumed, would be somewhere deeper in the woods to either side.

She sprinted around the pair, then stopped and turned. She had misjudged her speed and overshot the Paladins by twenty yards. She followed them cautiously, crouching.

Take the one on the right, first, as he was lagging slightly behind the other.

She sprinted.

She slashed across the back of his knee, and when he fell backwards, squealing, she plunged the knife through his Adam's apple. Then she was up and away at speed, the Paladin's blood a slow-motion crimson gusher pumping into the ground.

The other had turned to stare in alarm. Ajia ran at him and slashed his neck.

Eight down, four to go.

She didn't hang about. The other four might be close by, somewhere in the cover of the forest.

She raced back to the nursery and awaited their arrival, squatting beside the water butt and breathing hard.

The motion-sensitive light went out, plunging the area into darkness. After its dazzle, Ajia found herself blinded. It was some seconds before her vision adjusted and she made out the cobbled courtyard in the moonlight.

All was still, quiet.

She savoured the respite. She was high and adrenalised, but she needed to calm herself, regain her breath and think things through. Everything had gone well, so far, but she wasn't going to allow herself to become over-confident. That way lay disaster.

Four deadly, highly-trained killers were somewhere out there, intent on murder.

She stared down at her hands, jet black and tacky with blood.

For Maya, Perry and all the others.

It was a beautiful night, balmy and calm, without the slightest breeze. A night to be admiring the stars, not killing fascistic thugs.

A second later, all hell broke loose.

The thunder of gunfire was deafening.

The remaining Paladins must have elected to come around the house and approach from the west, as the gunfire came from that direction. Tonttu and the others, she thought, in the tree beside the house. And judging by the duo-tone of the gunfire, it was being returned.

She sprinted around the house and stopped at the corner.

Two Paladins lay messily dead on the cobbles, one of them chopped in half.

Ten down, two to go.

At the foot of the tree, Tonttu and another elf lay very still.

Aware that she was taking a risk, she sprinted across to the elves. She knelt beside Tonttu and felt for his pulse. He was dead. She turned to the second, Parisa. There was no need to check her pulse. Multiple bullets had ripped a gaping cavity in her chest.

She slipped into the shade of the tree, knelt and scanned the area before the house.

The lights went out. All was still again.

Two Paladins remained. Maybe they'd seen the carnage, their dead colleagues, and decided to cut their losses and beat a retreat.

Not at all what she wanted.

She took off, sprinted past the house and along the track down which the elite Paladin force had approached the nursery.

She came across the remaining pair a split second later, and she was gratified to see that they were not retreating. Far from it. Assault rifles at the ready, they advanced through the forest to her right, separated from each other by ten yards.

One of the Paladins halted, gesturing back to the other to do the same. Ajia crouched, her pulse pounding.

The nearest Paladin spoke into a lapel mic.

She approached stealthily.

The Paladin said, "Do you read, Danny? Do you read?"

He turned to the other and murmured, "Nothing."

"Shit... What's happened?"

"Fuck knows. And Danny said it'd be a walk in the park."

"Some walk."

"Some fucking park."

"O-kay. Let's get in there. After me."

They set off again.

Ajia followed. These were the last two. No back-up called in, no pitiful pleas to a command centre asking what the fuck they should do now.

They were on their own.

And their days—their minutes—were numbered.

As she crept after them, she wondered if these two had taken part in the massacre at Summer Land.

She ran a fantasy. Before she killed the last one, she'd ask him: *Were you at Summer Land?* And if he admitted his part in that crime, she'd kill him very slowly.

She told herself to grow up and *concentrate*.

The Paladins came to the edge of the woodland and peered out at the nursery standing innocently in the moonlight.

From this angle, no bodies could be seen.

One of the pair gestured to the other: *You take the back, I'll go in at the front...*

Ajia smiled. They were playing right into her hands.

They split up. One crept from the cover of the trees and moved around the back of the house. The other sprinted across the cobbles and pressed himself against the gable wall. He approached the corner and peered round. Ajia set off.

She crossed the cobbles in less than a second.

Her first cut slashed the man's Achilles tendon. Her second, as he pirouetted, pierced his abdomen below his body armour. He lunged at her, catching her by surprise and knocking her backwards. She scrambled to her feet as he moved towards her in slow motion, blood falling in a stuttering cataract from his belly.

She leapt, knocked him onto his back, then straddled his chest as he lay on the cobbles. She stabbed down hard with the knife, into his face.

Her moment of victory was short-lived.

She heard movement behind her, but before she could move, arms encircled her waste like steel hawser and lifted her into the air. She kicked and struggled, but the last Paladin—the very last of the bastards!—pinned her to his body and hissed in her ear, "Don't move or you're fucking dead!"

And her incredulity was compounded when she realised that, somehow, the man had dispossessed her of the knife and was holding it against her throat as he backed across the cobbles.

She struggled, and the blade bit into her neck. She felt blood trickle down her chest.

"I said don't fucking move!"

She stopped struggling.

Across the cobbles, Reed Fletcher dropped from the oak tree and stood in the silver glare of the motion-sensitive lights, staring across at her and the Paladin.

Loud in her ear, the man yelled, "Drop your weapon or the girl gets it!"

Fletcher, like the soldier he had been, was careful when depositing his assault rifle on the ground. He ducked and laid it on the cobbles, then rose slowly with his hands in the air.

A grain of hope: he still had his bow slung across his shoulder, and his quiver on his back.

The Paladin's breathing was loud in her ear. The reek of his sweat was overpowering.

"You others! Show yourselves. One by one, and lay down your weapons. Now—or the girl dies! Come on—all sixteen of you!"

Sixteen. So they had the intel: the twelve inhabitants of the nursery, herself, Mr LeRoy, Fletcher, and Smith...

She managed to say, "Fourteen."

"What the fuck?" he hissed.

"Fourteen left. You killed two, over there, below the tree."

He yelled, "Update. Fourteen of you fuckers! Out, now!"

Bogdan and Gregor emerged from the tree behind Fletcher. They set down their weapons and stood with their stubby arms raised. Fletcher murmured something to them, perhaps counselling them to caution.

Others emerged: two elves and a boggart from the potting shed, their arms aloft.

"And the others!"

Fletcher called out, "They're in the woods."

"Then call them!"

Fletcher said, sounding amused, "I doubt they'd hear me."

"They don't have phones?"

One of the boggarts murmured something to Fletcher, who said to the Paladin, "He has a phone. He'll reach into his jacket..."

"Do it!" the Paladin yelled, deafening her. His grip on her tightened, the knuckle of his thumb pressing into her carotid.

One slice with the blade and she'd be dead.

A new voice said, "That won't be necessary."

Daisy Hawthorn.

The Green Woman stepped from behind a long greenhouse, flanked by Mr LeRoy and two brownies, and advanced with her arms in the air. She stopped five yards before Ajia and the Paladin and smiled.

Ajia felt warmth and reassurance radiating from the woman.

"Now, I suggest you release the girl and take off into the forest. We won't come after you."

"Like hell you won't!"

"You have my word. If you let the girl go, you'll live."

He was panting, desperate. He'd seen his dead colleagues. He pressed the knife against her throat. She felt the blade bite into her flesh. She cried out as hot blood trickled down her chest.

Daisy stepped forward, holding out a hand. Behind her, Mr LeRoy lifted a fearful hand to his mouth.

"Please, give me the knife," Daisy said.

"Like fuck!"

"Please, let her go, and you'll live. Keep this up, and you'll surely die."

"Go to hell."

The Paladin's arm around Ajia's waist tightened painfully.

Daisy reached out. "Give me the knife."

The Paladin backed off, dragging Ajia with him. "Any of you move, and she dies."

Ajia looked at Daisy's warm, motherly face, and she saw the woman wince.

She sensed movement behind her and the Paladin.

She heard a sudden, sickening crunch and the soldier grunted, released her, and slipped to the ground.

Ajia spun round, staring down at the remains of his shattered skull.

Then she looked up into the face of Wayland Smith. He stared down with stunned bemusement at the bloody hammer gripped in his right hand.

Reed Fletcher lost no time in issuing commands. He briefly clapped Smith on the shoulder, then turned to the others. "Bogdan, get the bus. Everyone else, follow me up the track. Ajia... If you're up to it, take off along the track and scout the way ahead. We can't leave here if they're scoping the place. Got that?"

Still stunned, either by the fact of her salvation or the nature of the intervention, she nodded.

She was about to set off when she heard the distinctive whump-whump of a helicopter's rotor blades beating the air above the woodland. A second later a jet-black Paladin chopper swept down and hovered above the cobbles.

Fletcher screamed orders, and he and the boggarts and elves retrieved their discarded weapons and took cover around the forecourt.

"Ajia!" Fletcher cried. "Move!"

The others scurried for cover but she just stood there, frozen. She felt her blood trickle down her neck and over her chest—and she was overcome with sudden and all-consuming rage.

Six feet above the courtyard, a Paladin leaned from the fuselage of the helicopter, raising a pistol and aiming at her as the helicopter came in to land. Ajia ducked swiftly, snatched her knife from the cobbles, and launched herself at him.

He fired. She saw the bullets hose towards her as she ran: she zigzagged, dodging the pellets of lead, and dived at the soldier. She sliced at his gun hand and saw the weapon drop, followed by a slow-motion fountain of blood. She yanked the man from the chopper, slashing at him on the way, then leapt at the pilot. Already he was attempting to take the helicopter up and away, and Ajia was aware of the retarded *whoomp-whoomp-whoomp* sound of gunfire from all around as she barrelled into him. Her momentum carried both her and the pilot out of the far side of the cabin as the helicopter climbed.

Oh, shit, she thought as she fell.

Then she hit the cobbles.

TWENTY-FIVE

WYNNE GLANCED AT his watch. One o'clock.

He turned to Noble. "No word?" he asked needlessly.

The lieutenant gave a terse nod.

At one-fifteen, the first symptoms of concern niggling in his back-brain, he said to Noble, "Get through to the pilot. Demand an update."

He paced the staffroom, nervous.

Noble looked up. "Nothing, sir."

"Christ!" Wynne strode to the window and stopped dead, shocked at what he saw down in the darkened valley.

It wasn't so dark, now.

The effulgent orange bloom of a raging conflagration lit up the surrounding night.

Could it be the nursery building itself, he wondered...

Or the helicopter?

Lieutenant Noble joined him and stared in silence.

"What now?" Noble said at last.

"We wait till dawn," Wynne said, his voice catching, "then we take six men and proceed with extreme caution."

* * *

As THE FIRST light of the new day seeped through the forest, Major Wynne stood at the northern end of the track and sent in Lieutenant Noble and four Paladins to secure the area around the nursery.

He waited tensely with the two remaining Paladins, pacing back and forth.

If he were honest with himself, it was not so much the loss of life that was concerning him right now. Uppermost in his mind was how he might report what was surely an ignoble defeat to Derek Drake. After the fiasco of Sherwood Forest, the Prime Minister had demanded the immediate capture of Ajia Snell and her cohorts. How would Wynne break the news that not only had he failed to capture *any* of the renegades, but had lost a fair few of his men in the process?

Because, surely, they were lost. What else might account for the ominous silence from within the ancient woodland?

He recalled his old shibboleth: *No plan survives contact with the enemy.* How true! His plans were in tatters. For the first time in his military career, he was having difficulty seeing the way ahead.

He heard the crackle of a radio. He turned to see a corporal speaking into a receiver.

"Lieutenant Noble, sir. Area secured. We can go in."

They climbed into the Humvee and trundled down the rutted track towards the nursery.

He would be lucky to emerge from the debacle without being demoted, of course. He'd had his chance, and failed. Drake's patience—always balanced on a knife edge—would teeter and tip, and Wynne would find himself publicly humiliated and kicked back into the ranks.

He needed a miracle, and quickly, if he were to survive.

Lieutenant Noble and the four Paladins stood in the cobbled yard outside the main nursery building. They looked stunned, as well they might. They were surrounded by a scene of such carnage as Wynne had not witnessed since Iraq.

He saw the helicopter first, or rather what remained of it. The mangled wreckage had fused with the bole of a mighty oak tree at the far end of the yard. The tree still burned, while the chopper smouldered. A choking reek of burnt-out circuitry and plastic filled the air.

Lieutenant Noble and his men were moving like zombies around the area, stopping from time to time to kneel beside the bodies of their fallen comrades. Wynne crossed to a dark shape beside the house and stared down at the remains with a mixture of revulsion and rage.

Corporal Johnson. A good, loyal man. One of the best. The left side of his skull had been stove in by what looked like a single blow from a heavy, blunt object. Nearby was another corpse. Captain Nicholls, a new recruit from the Marines. This had been his first active mission. He lay on his back, his throat slit from ear to ear.

Wynne made the round of his dead compatriots. Three of them had been shot dead, shredded by what looked like rifle fire. Three had been killed by arrows. Fucking *arrows*. The rest had had their throats expertly slit and had died within minutes. At one point, the soles of his boots meeting a tacky resistance, he looked down to see that blood had run across the yard and between the cobbles in a great reticulation, glistening in the morning sunlight.

He had no doubt who was behind the majority of these killings. His men were highly trained in every area of combat, with weapons or without. In close combat with most other opponents, they would have been unbeatable.

But not against Ajia Snell, who could run like the wind and strike like lightning. She was, in effect, invisible until she chose not to be. And by then it was too late for the hapless victim to put up any kind of fight.

And not against someone who, it appeared, was supernaturally gifted with a fucking bow and arrow.

The poor bastards hadn't stood a chance.

Wynne felt like weeping, but he had the sorry remainder of his men to consider. Tears were no response to this massacre, but rage—rage channelled towards tracking down and dealing with the perpetrators.

He crossed to the remains of the helicopter, and saw within the burned-out wreckage the twisted, charcoaled corpses of perhaps three or four Paladins. Two others had leaped from the vehicle as it had careered towards the oak, only to be minced by gunfire.

At the foot of a nearby tree was evidence that his men had not gone down without a fight: the ugly, bullet-riddled corpses of two elves.

Elves!

He closed his eyes, controlling his rage and shame.

Oh, make no mistake, Ajia Snell and the others would pay for this...

He looked across at Noble and the remaining Paladins. Never had he seen his men looking so stunned, defeated. He had drilled into his cohorts, day after day, in training and in briefings, that they were the best of the best, a handpicked, elite force of invincible warriors fighting for what was just and right for a leader whose motto was Britain First. They were Drake's protectors, his warriors, and his knights.

And now so many of them lay inert in their own blood, massacred.

Lieutenant Noble made his way across to Wynne, but was unable to bring himself to look his commanding officer in the eye.

"What happened, sir?" he asked in barely a murmur.

"We are fighting evil, Lieutenant," Wynne said. "What occurred here was not a fight against normal, civilised human beings, but the forces of evil."

Noble stared at him. "Ajia Snell, LeRoy and the others?"

"They are possessed, Lieutenant. Possessed by forces that know no order, no rules. They are a terrible enemy, but an enemy that we shall, I tell you, defeat. Given time, and more men, and superior tactics, we will overcome the forces of evil and the day will be ours!"

He gave Noble instructions to call in security and the mop-up brigade, and as the lieutenant moved off and spoke into his radio, Wynne smiled to himself. He was, all things considered, not a little proud of his extempore speech.

Even if he did know that it was nothing more, really, than so much hot air.

But how to break the news to Derek Drake?

He was rehearsing the phrases he would use to mitigate the extent of the losses when one of the Paladins called out from across the cobbled yard. He was kneeling beside the body of a comrade, which was partially concealed by shrubbery. And it was evident, from the urgent movements of the Paladin's hands, that he was attempting to give first aid to the injured soldier.

Lieutenant Noble sprinted over to the pair, soon joined by others. Wynne hurried across.

The first Paladin was working furiously to stem the flow of blood from the man's neck, while another joined in with a first-aid kit. The men worked tirelessly as Lieutenant Noble called in medical assistance.

The first-aider looked up. "I think he'll live, sir. He's lost a lot of blood, but I think he'll pull through. They didn't get his carotid."

"Good work, Corporal," Wynne said.

The injured man opened his eyes, reached out. He tried to speak.

Wynne knelt, watching the man's flickering eyes, his feebly moving lips.

His words were very faint.

"They… They—"

"Yes?"

"They… got… away…"

Wynne gripped the man's hand. "You saw them?"

"Saw them," the Paladin responded. "Drove off… Van… White van, painted with… with flowers."

Wynne looked up, triumphant. "Did you get that, Noble? A white van, decorated with flowers. Put out an alert."

He squeezed the man's hand again. "Good work, Captain."

He climbed to his feet, feeling a smidgen of hope for the first time that day.

Now to get through to Drake and put a positive spin on the events of the night.

HARRIET STOOD BEFORE the bedroom window and stared down the drive as her husband was chauffeured away in his armoured limousine, en route to an emergency cabinet meeting.

For the second time in as many days, their post-breakfast lovemaking had been interrupted by a telephone call.

Drake had taken the call in the bathroom, and had emerged minutes later crimson with rage.

"Derek… Why, what is it—?"

"Fucking Wynne!"

"Wynne?" Her heart leapt. Had the major let the cat out of the bag? "What about him?"

To her relief, Drake reprised the balls-up Wynne and his men had made of what should have been a relatively simple operation.

"So why wasn't it?" she asked.

Her husband had sat on the edge of the bed and told her all about the eidolons and the folkloric hordes unleashed by the power of the Holy Grail. It would seem that, along with all the good the Grail had brought about—and Harriet recalled her husband saying that it had helped him throughout his political career—the Grail had also manifested monsters best left where they had lain, in the deep recesses of ancient history.

Monsters like Ajia Snell, Reed Fletcher and others, who had massacred her husband's precious Paladins without mercy.

Harriet was thoughtful in the aftermath of Drake's hurried departure. She showered and dressed, still mulling over what he had told her about the eidolons and the figures from folk lore.

She recalled her husband's precise words when he had introduced her to the grail. *"It's helped me though my political career. It wouldn't be an exaggeration to say it's got me where I am today."*

And that was interesting. Very interesting.

After the helicopter crash, all those years ago, Harriet had noticed a subtle but definable change in her husband. Always thrusting and ambitious, he had become even more so, especially focused when he announced that he was entering politics for the good of the country. "What Britain needs," she recalled him saying, "is a leader who will lead, who will take the country forward with policies based on strong, righteous, Christian principles. There is no one in current politics prepared to do that… But I am!"

And that change had come after the crash, when figures of myth had risen to the fore and taken over unwitting individuals for who knew what motives?

Harriet hurried from the grange and crossed to the stable block.

She had memorised the codes the other day when her husband had ushered her into his sanctum sanctorum. She used them now to enter his relic museum and then, treading lightly but with a rapidly beating heart, to the cylindrical vault where Drake kept his precious Holy Grail.

The door swung slowly open and she entered the steel-ribbed chamber, approaching the onyx, jewel-encrusted cup on its stand with the hushed reverence of a supplicant.

It was as if she were thirteen again, and offering herself for her first communion.

She stared at the Grail and, feeling more than a little dubious, said, "Emrys?"

A silence. For a heartbeat, it occurred to her that everything her husband had told her was a lie—that the voice she had heard the other day was indeed no more than a gimmick of computer-generated wizardry.

Then she heard Emrys Rhys's mellow, Welsh cadences. She jumped.

"Harriet, how nice to see you again."

She stepped froward and murmured, "Emrys?"

"You appear… concerned."

She gestured. "Is it any wonder? Just the other day Derek drops all this on me. The Grail. You. The crash. Then today he told me about the eidolons and everything else."

"Ah yes, that would come as something of a shock, I fear."

"You can say that again. But…"

"Go on."

She hesitated. "Why?" she asked. "I mean, what's happening, Emrys? Why you? Why were you chosen?"

"Propinquity, I rather think. I did die within feet of the holiest of holy relics, after all. The power which resided in it—and as Derek mentioned the other day, the Grail once upon a time contained the life blood of our exalted Saviour—needed a channel through which to work."

Harriet stared at the cup. "A channel? To work?" She licked her lips. "But... what work?"

"Ah... That? As I told you the other day, Harriet, our Lord works in mysterious ways."

"But the eidolons," she persisted. "The creatures of myth that have been unleashed—"

Emrys interrupted, "Not myth, Harriet. Certainly *not* myth. You are very much mistaken if you think that the eidolons represent figures from mere legend. They might be the icons of folklore, Harriet, but the fact is that they existed. In their own time they were very, very real—just as real as they are again today, thanks to the Higher Power."

"Eidolons... Derek told me about them. Robin Hood, Wayland the Smith, Oberon and others. But..."

"Go on."

He heart pounded. "After the crash. Derek... changed. Became even more driven, focused. He told me he wanted to work for the good of the country."

"That is so, yes."

"But..." She leaned forward, staring at the glittering encrustations on the flank of the Holy Grail. "But did my husband, did Derek, become an eidolon? And if so, of whom?"

A silence greeted her words. She could almost see the Emrys of old, smiling tolerantly at her.

At last the warm, lilting voice replied, "Now whose spirit do you possibly think imbued itself in Derek, my dear?"

She gasped, almost fainted. She had been right! She had hardly dare credit her supposition, back in the bedroom, but Emrys—no lesser authority than the Holy Grail itself—had proved her notion correct.

She backed away from the Grail, almost genuflecting in her ecstasy. As she was about to turn and leave the chamber, Emrys said, "There is one more thing, Harriet."

She paused at the door, heart pounding. "Yes?"

"We live in interesting times, my dear. The country teeters on the cusp of hostilities. Hawkish voices whisper in the ears of those in power, and I would hate to think that Derek might be swayed, however much I might counsel him. But he listens to you, my dear, and I beg you to guide him in this time of strife, and steer him away from conflict."

The Grail fell silent.

When Harriet was sure that it would say no more, she stepped from the chamber, closed the door behind her, and hurried from the stable block.

So Emrys thought that he was losing control of her husband, did he? He wanted her to counsel him to caution?

She stifled a laugh.

Perhaps Derek had listened to Emrys a little too much in the past. Perhaps, now, it was time for Derek Drake to listen to his wife.

Derek Drake. Or what he had become.

Because, as Harriet entered the house and fixed herself a stiff gin and tonic, she was in no doubt as to the identity of the eidolon which had invested her husband with such power.

There was only one person Derek Drake could possibly be: Jesus Christ.

EIGHTY MILES AWAY at Number 10 Downing Street, Drake was chairing an emergency cabinet meeting.

"The three Russian battleships which entered our territorial waters yesterday show no indication of retreating," said the Minister of Defence, "despite the close attention of HMS *Edinburgh*."

"I had a call from our man in Tallinn this morning," the Home Secretary said. "Reports from the border indicate a build-up of Russian forces."

"The ambassador of Lithuania was on the line," said Laxton, the Foreign Minister, "reporting a similar Russian military build-up on *their* border…"

And so it went, his ministers chipping in with a list of Russian misdemeanours to which Drake listened with an outward air of equanimity. He leaned back in his chair, steepled his hands beneath his chin as if in prayer, and stared up at the ceiling.

The Defence Secretary finished, "All things considered, Derek, I urge caution."

"Caution?" Drake repeated. "Isn't our policy of caution the very reason slimy Vasilyev has been able to get where he is today, rattling his sabres as if his impoverished nation is still a super-power?"

"Nevertheless, sir—"

Drake cut across him and said to his minister for digital security, "Russia will stop at nothing now to undermine the sovereignty of our nation. High on their agenda will be cyberattacks. Vasilyev will increase his efforts to spread misinformation and disinformation. They will no doubt attempt to discredit member of this very cabinet, and even myself. We must be vigilant."

"Very good, sir."

"But about these dashed Russkie battleships, sir..." said the Minister for Defence.

Fifteen minutes later the meeting broke up, and Drake lost no time in contacting his secretary. "I want you to issue, with immediate effect, a report stating that Russia is planning to release so called 'compromising footage' to discredit government ministers and Resurrection Party politicians. Play it as yet another perfidious assault on the bastions of our cherished democracy, et cetera."

Next, this time on a secure line, he reached Rear Admiral Dorsey for a progress report.

"Everything running to plan, sir," Dorsey said. "The HMS *Nautilus* entered the Baltic at oh-three-hundred hours today."

"And...?"

"And it will be in range of Moscow before midnight."

Drake thanked him and cut the connection.

All in all, events were progressing smoothly. Even Major Wynne had sugared the pill of yet another Paladin humbling with news that the vehicle carrying Ajia Snell and her terrorist cell had been spotted heading north from Derbyshire that morning.

And now, home. Drake had some unfinished business with Harriet to attend to.

TWENTY-SIX

"What happened?" Ajia groaned.

She stared up at Mr LeRoy and Daisy Hawthorn. They smiled reassuringly down at her. Daisy was holding her hand, her touch filling Ajia with warmth.

"Where am I?"

She was flat on her back, jouncing up and down. She struggled into a sitting position and tried to make sense of her new surroundings, her head throbbing. A dozen semi-familiar faces regarded her. Some faces were small and beautiful, others big and ugly. Brownies and boggarts, she reminded herself. The nursery. The attack of the Paladins. The helicopter!

"You're a hero," Daisy Hawthorn said. "You accounted for most of the Paladins singlehandedly, and then brought the helicopter crashing down."

"Almost killing yourself in the process, I might add," Mr LeRoy said. "You landed on your head on the cobbles, and luckily the helicopter careered through the air before crashing."

"And you, my girl," the Green Woman went on, squeezing her hand, "had a nasty case of concussion. It's a good job we kept a first-aid kit aboard the bus. Smith could have healed you, but your injuries weren't life-threatening, and... Well, anyway, we've done the best job we can."

Ajia reached up and fingered the bandage on her head. She was lying on a makeshift bed in the back of the minibus, which had been cleared of seats to make room for crates of flowers.

Daisy saw her looking and explained. "I used this, when I had the nursery, to make deliveries. And I couldn't leave the place without bringing along a few plants, could I?"

Ajia smiled. Everyone else, the brownies and boggarts, elves and goblins, Reed Fletcher and Wayland Smith, sat around on sacks of compost and soil-improver, bouncing around with the motion of the minibus.

She recalled Smith, staring down at the bloody hammer, his expression an odd mixture of bewilderment and revulsion.

She had him to thank for saving her life.

Smith was slumped on a sack, staring morosely through the window.

"I need to talk to..." she whispered to Mr LeRoy.

He pressed her back down with a plump but firm hand, murmuring, "I'd leave him be for the time being, Ajia. Smith has much to think about. Maybe later, okay?"

She nodded, taking in the gallery of faces staring at her as the minibus jolted along. "I wonder, could you tell them to stop staring at me, please?"

Daisy laughed. "But they're in awe of you," she said, "Bogdan and Gregor and the other boggarts, especially. They're odd creatures. They think the normal run of humans puny when it comes to physical combat. But you taught them something last night."

"But I'm *not* normal, am I?"

The Green Woman whispered, "But the boggarts don't know that, love. Between you and me, they're none too bright upstairs."

Ajia smiled and peered through the window. "Where are we?"

"South Yorkshire, heading north," Mr LeRoy said. "We're about to find a suitable place to stop and hide up for the day." He saw her frowning, and forestalled her question: "It's almost dawn, Ajia, and you've been unconscious for almost twenty-four hours."

"Now settle back, my girl," Daisy said, "and rest."

*   *   *

AJIA WAS ALONE in the minibus when she came to her senses. The vehicle had stopped, and so had the throbbing in her head. Sunlight slanted in through the windows. She smelled cooking food and realised how hungry she was.

She sat up, kicked off the cocooning sleeping bag. Her old blood-soaked clothes were gone. Someone—Daisy?—had dressed her in leggings and a brown tunic that had obviously belonged to one of the bigger elves.

As she stood unsteadily, a boggart jumped up from where he had been sitting on the steps of the bus and came forward hesitantly, offering a big gnarled hand to assist her. Smiling, she took it, and stepped from the minibus. He watched her in silence, an expression like awe on his huge, ugly face with its Neanderthal brow and oversized, dumpling nose.

She thanked him and looked around.

What she saw resembled some woodland scene out of a storybook. Dying sunlight slanted in low from the west. In the centre of the clearing was a campfire, with a big pan bubbling over a licking flames. A brownie stood in attendance, stirring the pan. Elves and boggarts sat around chatting. Daisy Hawthorn and Reed Fletcher sat cross-legged, face to face. It was obvious by the intensity of their conversation that they were discussing old times.

Off to one side sat Mr LeRoy. He'd piled up three or four sacks of compost—or a boggart had done it for him—to arrange a seat that looked more like a throne. He was bent over his map book, his palms flat on the page and his eyes closed.

The boggart at her side seemed reluctant to release his grip on her hand. She smiled at him and murmured, "I'm fine, now, thank you. I'd like to speak with Mr LeRoy, in private."

She set off towards him, but the boggart followed. "In private," she said. "Alone."

The little man frowned at her.

"Perhaps you could get me a bowl of food, hmm? I'm very hungry."

"Food? You want food?"

"I do."

He grinned, showing her a set of spectacularly awry teeth, and scurried off.

She crossed to Mr LeRoy.

He sensed her arrival and opened his eyes.

"Ajia, my child. Awake at last. And how are you feeling?"

"I'm fine. Hungry. Where are we?" She nodded to the map book. Mr LeRoy indicated a sack of compost. She sat down.

"We are currently situated on the outskirts of Bradford," he said. "Caution is still the watchword. We travel by night, and rest up by day. After how we handled the Paladins back there, Mr Drake and his cohorts will be on the proverbial warpath."

She looked at him. "Why Bradford?"

"I am recruiting," he explained. "I hope to add another soul to our mismatched band, a character whose talents can only assist us on our venture. But..." He frowned. "I am being pulled by contradictory forces." He lay his flattened palms on the spread pages of the map book. His hands were covering a map of the entire country, not specifically this region.

"I am, on one hand, drawn to continue my own quest, north and then west, to pick up eidolons, but at the same time I feel a compelling force drawing me south."

The boggart arrived bearing her bowl of stew, and she took it with a smile.

The creature backed off, but paused a couple of yards away, watching her as she spooned hungrily. The thick vegetable broth was the first thing she'd eaten since the meal at the nursery, almost two days ago, and it tasted wonderful.

Mr LeRoy spoke gently to the boggart, and he moved away reluctantly.

"A compelling force?" she said. "From where? And why south?"

"From where? That, my child, is a mystery as vast as what is happening to us all. As to why south? That, I think, is not so great a mystery. Now, what is this quest all about, Ajia?"

"The overthrowing of Drake," she answered promptly.

"Precisely, but with whose assistance?"

"Arthur," she said, finding that she uttered the word with reverence. "King Arthur."

"And I am being drawn south by a force that tells me, with irrefutable logic, that we shall find the man we seek in his legendary—or not so legendary—stamping ground."

"Avalon."

"Or its modern equivalent."

"And where is this, precisely?"

"Aha! And that, my girl, is the question. Somerset? Devon? Experts are still divided on the issue." He flicked through the book until he came to a large-scale map of the south-west, and his plump hands hovered over the page. "I feel a nebulous force, but ill-defined, somewhere south of Bristol. But precisely where...? Glastonbury? At any rate, when we have done up here, and gathered as many to our number as we can, then south we shall head, in hope and expectation!"

She finished the broth and set aside the bowl. "And the person you're seeking next?"

"He lived with us in Summer Land, for a time—a brief while—before... Ah, before he left, under somewhat ignominious circumstances. I have his address. But whether he will still be there..."

"I want to come with you."

Mr LeRoy regarded her, considering. "Very well, you shall. But I must warn you that his manners leave much to be desired."

Across the clearing, Ajia saw Reed Fletcher hug Daisy, then move across to where Smith sat alone on a fallen log, looking beyond the clearing to where the woodland fell away down a twilit hillside.

Mr LeRoy turned his attention to his map book. She murmured her excuses and crossed to Smith and Fletcher.

"Hope I'm not interrupting anything? You two seem to be getting along fine now."

Fletcher and Smith sat side by side on the log. Fletcher shuffled up so that she could sit between them.

She looked from one to the other, wondering who might be the first to break the uneasy silence. "Well?" she said, nudging them both at the same time.

Fletcher said, "I buried the hatchet, after what happened back at the nursery."

Ajia turned to Smith. His expression was tortured, as if he were still wrestling with inner demons.

At last Smith said, in barely a murmur, "I'm not proud of what I did, Ajia. Certainly not proud. I don't know how I feel about it."

She laid a hand on his arm. "You saved my life," she said.

"By killing someone else," he replied, instantly.

She hesitated, thinking about her words. "Who's to judge what's right and wrong? You obviously felt, just then, that what you were doing was the right thing to do. And you did it."

It was a while before he spoke. "We'd concealed ourselves in the wood, Daisy and me, Elvira and Jasmine. Then we heard the gunfire."

He stopped, staring down at his big hands hanging between his knees.

Fletcher said, quietly, "What made you come back?"

"I don't know. I honestly don't know. I... I just couldn't leave you there, under attack. Maybe I thought I could be of some help, rather than hiding away in the woods. Daisy tried to stop me. She thought I'd get myself killed." He shrugged. "But I just couldn't sit there, doing nothing, with the Paladins... So I set off back through the woods. When I came to the house, I saw the Paladin capture you, hold his knife to your throat. Then the Paladin called out, and Mr LeRoy, Daisy and the brownies emerged." He stared into the distance. "And it would have been so easy for them to have kept hidden, not risked the danger they were putting themselves in." He turned and looked at her, bleakly. "So how the hell could I just stand there when I was the only one left, and the Paladin knew that? But he didn't know where I was. I had that advantage." As if unconscionably, he reached down and his fingertips brushed the head of his hammer hanging at his waist.

"It was him or me," Ajia said. "If you'd not... not attacked him, he would've slit my throat. You might not like what you did, Smith, but if you hadn't acted..." She looked at him. "Would you have been able to live with my death?"

He shook his head. "I don't know. Perhaps not. There was no *right* thing to do, Ajia."

"Or perhaps there was," Fletcher put in quietly. "If we go on to defeat Drake, make this country a better place. Then what you did in saving Ajia would be justified."

"So the end justifies the means?" Smith said bitterly.

"That isn't always so," Fletcher replied, "but in this case I think it is."

The two men were silent for a while, staring at each other, and Ajia felt that there was more being communicated between them than she was able to interpret.

"And back *then*, Reed?" Smith said at last. "What I did back then, or rather what I *didn't* do then? Was that justified? Did the fact that you survived justify my inaction?"

Fletcher opened his mouth to speak, but in the end just shook his head and looked away.

Ajia looked from one man to the other. "What did you mean, 'back *then*'? What happened?"

Fletcher and Smith were silent. After a while, Smith said, "Go on, tell her if you must."

"You sure?" Fletcher asked.

Smith just shrugged.

Fletcher looked from him to Ajia, then said, "We'd both been at Summer Land for a while, six months, whatever. This was a couple of years back. I was getting itchy feet, and I know that Smith here was. He never shut up about it. How he was tired of the place. Wanted to hit the open road. We'd always got along okay, hadn't we?"

Smith shrugged, grudgingly. "We rubbed along, I suppose."

"So one day we told Mr LeRoy we were grateful for his hospitality, but we needed time away from everything, and we set off. We lived rough for a while. This was summer, so pickings were sufficient. But when autumn passed and winter set in, we found the going tough. Even with my foraging, and this"—he tapped the bow slung over his shoulder—"we didn't have enough to eat. So one day we raided one of those emergency government food stores. But we'd reckoned without the place being guarded. And it just so happened that this guard was armed."

She winced. "What happened?"

Fletcher looked at Smith. "You want to give her your side of the story?"

Smith stared through the opening in the trees at the streetlights appearing as night fell over the city. It made what had been an ugly scene of mean terrace houses and narrow, potholed streets appear gaudily attractive.

"No, go on. I'll correct you when you get it wrong."

Fletcher smiled to himself. "To cut a long story short, the guard appeared from nowhere and cornered me. He aimed a handgun right at my head and told me to drop the food and get down on my knees."

Ajia looked from Smith to Fletcher. "But what could Smith have done, in that situation?"

Fletcher snorted. "Smith was on the other side of the warehouse. The guard didn't know there were two of us. So Smith, if he'd come up behind the guard, he could've incapacitated him." He flashed a look at Smith. "You wouldn't have had to kill the fucker. But oh, no, you thought of number one. Turned tail and ran, leaving me to face the sodding music."

Smith looked at Ajia, something like an appeal in his eyes as he said, "I could have acted, yes. I had my hammer. But... but I couldn't bring myself to use it, to injure the guard."

"You could have disarmed the guard without using your hammer," Fletcher said.

Smith just shook his head and stared down at his hands.

Fletcher went on, "So the guard cuffed me, called the cops, and I was carted off to the slammer. Did three months, and when I got out I went to ground. Went home to Sherwood and started a new life in the bunker. Alone."

Smith said, "Looking back, Reed, I admit it. What I did was cowardly. Even if I hadn't attacked the man, I could have helped.

But I panicked and ran."

Fletcher said, "It's over now. Spilt milk, and all that." He hesitated. "And anyway, what you did back at the nursery, saving Ajia, that took guts. Considering what you believe and all that. We're quits, okay?"

All three sat and watched the lights of the city glimmering in the gathering darkness far below.

"And what lies ahead?" Smith said a little later. "More bloodshed and mayhem. Daisy lost two good people back at the nursery. So far we've been lucky. More of us could've been killed back there. But if that luck runs out, and the Paladins have their way..."

"Then at least we'll have shown the bastards that some of us, at least, aren't taking Drake and his dictatorship lying down. Some things are worth fighting for, Smith." Fletcher looked at Ajia. "I think the girl's a good example of that, don't you?"

Before Smith could reply, Mr LeRoy called to her from across the clearing.

Mr LeRoy was preparing to venture into town in search of his latest recruit. They decided to leave the minibus in the cover of the spinney, rather than run the risk of driving into the city. Mr LeRoy, Reed Fletcher and Ajia were to break cover and head into an area of the city known as Idle—where Mr LeRoy's acquaintance, one Paul Klein, had last lived—while Daisy and a couple of brownies were to head to a nearby village and buy provisions and petrol.

They would meet back at the minibus in the early hours, then continue northwest under cover of darkness.

THEY LEFT THE spinney and followed a track over rolling moorland. Fletcher had elected to leave his bow and arrows back at the minibus. He would pass muster in his grubby army fatigues in the city, but might have aroused undue attention if armed with his bow.

They trooped through the bracken and emerged after fifteen minutes in a suburban council estate where the doors and windows of every other house were sealed with steel shutters. The gardens of those houses still inhabited were filled with either broken-down cars or abandoned fridges, and tethered dogs prowled back and forth with lunatic intensity. Ajia had last seen such indications of destitution in the sink estates of north London, and was well aware that poverty was the rich loam in which prejudice took root and flourished.

She recalled the news reports about Bradford from a couple of years ago. Prime Minister Drake's hate-fuelled policies had found eager adherents in the city which boasted a record number of members of the once-banned terrorist organisation known as National Action. The thugs had rejoiced when the first of Drake's repatriation laws was passed, and had helped the deportations on their way with some ad hoc and supra-judicial eviction of Pakistani and Bangladeshi families in the city.

These depopulated estates were the sorry result.

From time to time Mr LeRoy consulted his map, and pointed the way through litter-strewn streets. They left the council estates in their wake and came to wider streets of older, stone-built houses—small terrace houses, and larger Victorian edifices built for prosperous mill owners—every fifth one of which was a burned-out shell. She averted her gaze from these places, and marshalled her fear.

These fire-bombed properties stood in mute testament to the fact that hatred of the foreigner still festered in the hearts of English men and women.

They hurried on.

Curdled clouds were scudding across the face of a half-moon, fifteen minutes later, when they came to a terrace of back-to-back houses.

Fletcher sniffed and peered down the street. "Who could bring themselves to live in a shit-hole like this?"

"Some have no other option," Mr LeRoy said.

"And Paul Klein lives here?" Ajia asked.

"Well, this was the address he gave me," he said. "He'd fallen on hard times and took what he could get. His life wasn't exactly a bed of roses before his eidolon established itself, and he went through hell when it happened. Disorientation, terrible dreams. It was lucky for him that we were passing, a little north of here, and offered him sanctuary."

Ajia said, "Back in the clearing, you said he left in—what was the word?—*something* circumstances?"

Mr LeRoy smiled. "Ignominious circumstances. Yes, he did leave under something of a cloud."

"What happened?" Fletcher asked.

"Let's just say that he rather fell for one of the brownies—Maya, as it happened—and that his sentiments were not reciprocated."

"And he took it badly?"

"You could say that."

Ajia winced. "He didn't take it out on Maya, did he?"

Mr LeRoy shook his head. "No, nothing like that. Now," he went on, indicating the street, "shall we proceed? We're looking for number 42."

Ajia found the even-numbered side of the street and counted along the stone-built houses. Some dwellings were fire-gutted, others boarded up, and lights glowed in the windows of the few still occupied.

They came to number 42 and gazed at its soot-stained facade. It was neither fire-damaged nor boarded up, but no lights shone behind the squares of newspaper that passed for curtains in the downstairs windows.

Across the street, Ajia noticed a man working under the bonnet of a white van. His head was plunged into the innards of the vehicle, illuminated by a halogen lamp.

Mr LeRoy picked his way across the mouldy flagstone path, nimbly hopping around pert mounds of dog turds, and knocked on the door. Ajia remained at the gate, looking up and down the moribund street.

Mr LeRoy knocked again. There was no response.

Someone called out from across the street.

"I said, you looking for't little chap?"

The local had emerged from his tinkering with the engine and was wiping his hands on a rag. He was squat and balding, and reminded Ajia of a boggart.

The three crossed the road and approached the mechanic. Behind the windscreen, a hand-drawn sign read: £100 ONO.

"Friends of his, are y'?"

"We're business acquaintances, let's say," Mr LeRoy said, his Home Counties elocution clashing with the local's broad West Yorkshire brogue.

"Odd chap," he said. "Well-balanced, like."

"Well-balanced?"

"Aye. Has a chip on each shoulder. Well, you would, wouldn't you, if you were his size?"

"Is he at home?" Mr LeRoy asked.

"What're you wanting 'im for?" He looked the trio up and down. "You don't look like coppers."

"Has Mr Klein been in trouble with the police?" Mr LeRoy asked.

"From time to time. Little chap likes his booze, gets 'im'sen into trouble like. But we look out for him. Friendly lot round here," he added, though this quick glance at Ajia, taking in her colour, belied the claim.

The local pointed down the street. "Your chap's i'n't Idiot Hut, doing one of his turns."

"Idiot Hut?"

"That's what we called the Working Men's Club. The Idle Working Men's Club." He laughed at his joke.

"If you could perhaps direct us…" Mr LeRoy said.

"Aye, it's along't street, then first left ont't main road. Hundred yards along on't right. Can't miss it. Big building, all lit up. Tetley's, if you like a crap pint o' piss."

They thanked him and moved off.

The mechanic called out after them, "Not interested in buying a van, are y'? One hundred quid. Ninety for cash."

Mr LeRoy waved a cheery refusal and they continued on to the end of the street and turned left.

The Idle Working Men's Club was an impressive eighteenth-century building with a crow-stepped frontage and a long, arched window over the entrance. Loud music belted out into the night. Two huge bouncers, with the sinister bonhomie of their calling, vetted a line of punters at the entrance.

Fletcher said, "If I were you I'd sit this one out, Ajia."

"Like fuck I will. I'm coming in. It's a free country, as they used to say."

"Yes," said Mr LeRoy, "'As they used to say'. Are you quite sure?"

She bridled. "You don't think I can handle myself?"

"I have no doubt on that score, my dear. However, we don't want to draw attention to ourselves, do we?"

"I won't," she said. "It'll be fine."

Mr LeRoy nodded and led them across the road to the rear of the short queue.

When they came to the entrance, a bouncer said, "Members?"

"I'm afraid not," Mr LeRoy said.

"A tenner each, then," the bouncer said, then saw Ajia. "But the Paki lass can sling her hook."

"She's with us," Fletcher said, bristling.

The other bouncer joined his mate. "Trouble?"

"Paki wants in."

The second bouncer winked at her. "Better not. Won't be safe in there, luv."

"But we're together," Fletcher protested.

The first bouncer's already hostile expression hardened. "Then you can all piss off, right?"

"It's okay," Ajia said. "Go in without me." She smiled at Mr LeRoy and whispered, "See you inside."

Mr LeRoy and Fletcher handed over their ten pound notes and were duly processed into the throbbing interior of the club.

Ajia crossed the road, sat on a low wall, and waited.

She'd show those fuckwits.

She waited until there was no longer a queue at the door, then pushed herself from the wall, slipping into Puck mode and sprinting towards the entrance.

She was past the bouncers in a split second, and if they noticed a blur and a stir of wind they gave no sign. She stopped dead in the foyer and looked back. The two men were sharing a joke and laughing. She pushed through a pair of swing doors into the dimly-lit, smoke-filled interior, arriving just as the throbbing music stopped and an besuited MC took up the microphone on small stage opposite the entrance.

The room was filled with drinkers—men and women all dolled up for a night out—seated around a hundred small circular tables. Others patrons stood around the perimeter, leaning against the wall clutching pints and cigarettes. The darkness worked to Ajia's advantage: in the gloaming, the shade of her skin was not immediately apparent.

"Welcome back, ladies and gents. You've pulled your plonkers and had your pints pulled, and Wee Paul's back for the second half, the star turn who might be three foot nowt but knows how to please the ladies. You know what they say about short-arses, aye? And he can do magic tricks and tell a joke or three, an' all. Ladies and gents, let's hear it for Wee Paul!"

The crowd erupted in an explosion of applause and whistles.

Ajia saw Mr LeRoy and Fletcher standing against the back wall and edged through a press of drinkers towards them. Fletcher shuffled along and made room for her.

On stage, a midget in a white suit bounded on to the stage, thumped the air before him like a shadow boxer, then made a comical show of jumping up to reach the mic left at the top of its stand by the MC. After three futile leaps he called out, "Sod it!", kicked over the stand and retrieved the microphone from the stage to a round of cheering.

He was in his forties and running to seed, with dark receding hair, a chubby white face, and stubby hands. A star-shaped medallion hung on a silver chain around his neck.

He gripped the microphone and paced the stage.

"So there I am, having a quiet pint in the New Bee Hive, when this bloke comes up to me and says, 'Outside,' he says, and I says, 'Outside?' and he says, 'Outside,' and I says, 'What, you fancy a quickie?'"—loud laughter—"and he says, this huge bruiser built like a fucking brick shithouse, he says, 'Don't like your type in here. On yer bike.' So I says, 'Right, outside,' I says. So we go outside, ladies and gents, and you know what? You know how fast I am? I may only have little legs but I can shift. So I shifted, ran like the fucking blazes, round the corner and dodged a couple of bobbies on the beat. Only smart arse ain't so nimble, see, and he goes smack-bang into the coppers, knocking one flying, and gets his'sen arrested, didn't he?"

A round of applause, and Wee Paul strode back and forth, nodding and punching the air, the star-shaped medallion jouncing on his chest.

"Now this is where it gets political, like. Not that what I was just saying was very funny anyway. You had all your dirty jokes in the first half, and now I'm getting to indulge myself for a mo. Any Drake supporters in here?"

He peered out at his audience. Perhaps eighty per cent of the men and women in the room cheered and whooped.

"Well, you can fuck right off, 'cause you all know what I think of Mr Derek chuffing Drake!"

Heartened by this turn, Ajia exchanged a glance with Fletcher and Mr LeRoy. The latter looked uneasy.

A small section of the audience applauded, but no one—no Drake supporters—made to leave.

"Now what about his latest, eh? You all saw the news tonight? Mr Drake is waving his dick around, big style. Threatening that Russian, what's his name? Summat like Vaseline? Vasilyev, that's it. Now there's a fascist bed-partner for Drake if I ever saw one. And the way Drake's waving his plonker... Perhaps he does have a hard-on for the Russian leader? Russian subs in the North Sea, twenty Russkie diplomats sent home from the London embassy. And then Drake starts talking nuclear. Nuclear!" Wee Paul tapped his head. "Power? Power, it does for 'em all the time! You know what Pitt said, about too much power, et cetera."

He went on in this vein for another fifteen minutes, ridiculing Drake and his policies and earning cheers and jeers in almost equal measure.

"Anyway, enough of the execrable Drake for now. How about a trick? Who's for a trick, eh?"

Whoops and cheers greeted the question, and a tall blonde woman clad in a sequinned leotard wheeled a long box—more than like a coffin—on to the stage.

Ajia put her lips to Mr LeRoy's ear and murmurer, "What's all this about Drake and Vasilyev?"

"I must admit that recent events have rather kept me from world news, Ajia."

On the stage, to a fanfare of blaring music, Wee Paul and his assistant were opening the lid of the box to show its empty contents.

"Now I want six volunteers. Come on, you lucky ladies and gents, six of you lovely people. There we go!"

Duly six members of the audience were coerced by drunken friends to take up the offer. One by one they joined Wee Paul.

"Now I want you to stand around the Box of Death—that's what I call it, ladies and gents, and you'll soon see why—just to make sure that I don't get out. 'Cause once I'm inside, see, the glamorous Pamela here is going to kill me. That's right, ladies and gents! Pamela will set fire to the box and burn poor little me to cinders. This..." As the room erupted into ghoulish applause, he held up his arms for quiet. "This is a new act. Never done before. And I think it might very well be my last. A fond farewell."

He went around the six men and women, asking their names and positioning them equidistantly around the coffin-like box, which was propped up on two trestles.

While his assistant fetched a canister of petrol from the wings, Wee Paul came to the edge of the stage. His tone was less strident and jokey now, more confiding. "You know how it is, folks? Comes a time when it all gets just too much. You've had it up to here, and you think, Why bother? Why go on?" A deathly hush settled over the audience. "And in my case... Well, would you like to be three foot five in today's world where every evil fucker out there is just looking for an excuse to batter someone, anyone, because they're different? That's right, it ain't funny, folks. I've had enough, I really have. So tonight, right here, the venue where I made my debut more than twenty years ago, I'm making my fond farewell. Pamela?"

Wee Paul stepped towards the box. He handed Pamela the microphone. Around the box, the six onlookers fidgeted uneasily. A pre-recorded drumroll sounded. Ajia glanced at Mr LeRoy. She was alarmed to see that he was looking more than a little distressed.

Using a trestle as an improvised ladder, Wee Paul climbed into the box. He sat up, gave a last wave, then lay down in the box, disappearing from sight. In a touch both droll and comical, his small hand appeared over the edge of the box, waving. A few members of the audience tittered.

His assistant stepped forward and doused Wee Paul, and the coffin, with the contents of the canister. Then she closed the hinged lid, secured it with a padlock and stepped back.

The drumroll continued.

Pamela produced a lighter from the hem of her leotard, held it up for all to see, then flicked the wheel. A tall flame sprang into life.

She approached the box, held out the lighter—then had second thoughts and offered the lighter to the first of the six, miming that they should do the honours.

The woman demurred. Pamela passed on to the next, a cocky young man with a buzz-cut and bulging biceps. Someone from the audience egged him on drunkenly. He snatched the lighter from Pamela's hand and stepped towards the petrol-soused box.

All the while, Ajia had not allowed her gaze to leave the box. She examined the coffin-like oblong for any means of escape, but it seemed impossible that Wee Paul could exit the box without being seen. It was elevated from the stage on trestles, with fresh air visible all around. When the light was applied to the petrol, it seemed inevitable that Wee Paul would be granted his last wish and go up in flames.

She found Fletcher's hand and gripped.

The buzz-cut youth held up the flame for all to see, then lowered it and held the lighter to the wooden box.

The coffin exploded in flame and the young man stepped back precipitately.

Cries, applause, catcalls and screams erupted from the audience and Ajia stared in horror as flames licked the length of the box.

The six volunteers backed off, hands to mouths, while the youth who had initiated the immolation looked stricken, calling for someone to fetch an extinguisher.

No such salvation was forthcoming for Wee Paul Klein.

Amid a furore of distress from the crowd, the flames crackled and leapt—and with a touch of realism that might have been rehearsed, Pamela ran around the stage in distress, calling hidden stagehands in the wings for help.

A silence fell around the chamber. The only sound was the crackle of flames as they burned themselves out, but not before the supporting trestles were burned away and the remains of the box—presumably with the incinerated remains of the midget within—collapsed with a crash to the thick, fire-retardant mat laid out across the stage.

The six volunteers looked on abjectly.

A ghastly burnt stench filled the air.

Pamela stepped forward, a hand pressed to her mouth, and stared down at the shattered box. If her distress was an act, then she was more than convincing.

She cried out. A stagehand hurried onto the stage carrying a broom, which he reversed and used to prod at the blackened wood.

"But how could he have survived!" Ajia hissed to Fletcher. "I was watching all the time. I'm sure he didn't get out."

Fletcher just shook his head, looking on open-mouthed.

The only sound that broke the silence of the room was Pamela's hiccuping sobs as she watched the stagehand stir the mess of ash and blackened wood with the broom handle.

It was impossible to tell if Wee Paul's charred corpse lay amid the piled debris.

By now, much of the audience had left the tables and were crowding up against the stage, ghoulishly eager to see for themselves what had happened to Wee Paul.

Pamela cried out in distress. The stagehand poked the broom handle further into the now extinguished pyre, hooked it around something, and lifted it from the debris.

Wee Paul Klein's star-shaped medallion, tarnished now, hung high for all to see.

As if this were proof positive that indeed the midget had perished, pandemonium broke loose.

The subsequent mayhem would have kept a sociologist, studying the cause and effect of collective hysteria, busy for years.

Men and women alike fainted; others whooped and hollered in almost orgasmic frenzy; some wept; some made for the exit, or vomited—or both at the same time—while others resorted to a reflex primal response and resorted to violence. Fights broke out around Ajia, Mr LeRoy and Fletcher. Within seconds the hall was a madhouse—not quite the response the club's booking officer might have desired.

Someone saw the colour of Ajia's skin and swung a punch. Fletcher got in the way, blocking the upper cut with his forearm and jabbing the assailant in the gut.

Mr LeRoy took Ajia's arm. "I think you'd better make yourself scarce," he called out above the din. "Make your way to Paul's dressing room."

"You think he's alive?"

"I'm sure of it. Now go! I'll see you there."

Ajia went.

She sprinted towards the stage, vanishing instantly and drawing a startled cry of alarm from a youth who'd been preparing to punch her. Fletcher made the most of the lout's surprise to push him to the floor and dodge after her, Mr LeRoy panting in pursuit.

Everything seemed to be happening around Ajia in slow motion. What a second ago had been a chaotic mêlée of frantic movement, impossible to make out with any clarity, now became a series of retarded tableaux, each individual incident like a freeze-frame comic-book panel. As she flew past she caught glimpsed of stilled fists and punched faces wearing absurdly exaggerated expressions of pain and anger; faces frozen in tearful exhibits grief; men and women still in attitudes of running like sprinters caught in a photo-finish. She almost expected to see sound effects—Kapow! Ker-unch!—above the fracas.

She leapt on to the stage and hurried into the wings, where Pamela had disappeared to a minute earlier.

She slowed to walking pace. A shabby corridor led off into the nether regions of the club.

She came to a door, opened it and peered in. Pamela sat on a stool before a mirror, lighting up a cigarette and looking supremely unconcerned at the bedlam unfolding in the auditorium.

"Sorry!" Ajia said, and moved onto the next door, this one adorned with a star cut from silver Bacofoil.

She tried the handle but it was locked. A terse response came from beyond. "Piss off!" in Wee Paul's unmistakable Bradfordian brogue.

She looked along the corridor at the sound of approaching footsteps. Fletcher appeared, followed by Mr LeRoy.

"He's in here," Ajia said, "but he doesn't want autograph hunters."

Mr LeRoy squeezed past her and tried the handle. "Paul?"

"I've told you once, piss off! Go on, bugger off."

"Paul! It's me, Bron. Bron LeRoy."

Silence from within, followed by the snick of a bolt being drawn.

The door swung open. Wee Paul Klein, looking even smaller, and seedier, at close quarters, stood in his socks and a white dressing gown. He looked at Mr LeRoy with astonishment.

Ajia stared at the little man, wondering how he'd managed to save himself from the conflagration of his own devising.

She followed her friends into the room and watched as Paul Klein slumped on to a stool before the dressing table. He seemed at once incredulous at Mr LeRoy's appearance out of the blue, and almost—Ajia studied the man's expression—almost defiant.

Mr LeRoy found a vacant stool and settled his considerable bulk, while Ajia and Fletcher leaned against the dressing room wall.

Paul reached a shaking hand for a tumbler of what looked like whisky and took a mouthful.

He said, gesturing to the stage, "One of these days, Bron. You mark my word. Maybe not today, or next week at some other godforsaken fleapit north of here, but it'll happen."

"My boy, my boy," Mr LeRoy sympathised, clearly moved.

"Save yer crocodile tears, fatso. I didn't see them when you threw me out, told me to sling my effing hook!"

"I'm sure I never employed such vernacular!" Mr LeRoy protested.

Paul almost allowed a smile. "Not in so many words," he said. "But that's what you meant."

"But you must admit, in all fairness, I had a point."

Paul knocked back another slug of Scotch, wincing. "I had my reasons for acting as I did. The way she treated me! You've no idea what it's like, any of you." Here his gaze took in Fletcher and Ajia, his eyes lingering on her chest. "No idea. I was treated like shit before Summer Land, and it was no better when I joined your carnival of freaks."

"You complain about how Maya treated you," Mr LeRoy said, "but your own conduct was far from exemplary. You allowed your bitterness to blind your better instincts. But then I told you all this at the time. Maya... You should have seen that she was different, and treated her with respect. But no. You jumped into the relationship with the expectation of getting knocked back, as with all your other liaisons. And when she did reject you, because of your insistence, you took it to heart."

"I loved her!" Wee Paul wailed.

Mr LeRoy shook his head sadly. "That might have been so, but you were unable to show it."

Paul said, "And she turned out to be like all the others, nothing but a slut."

Mr LeRoy shook his head. "Maya was a brownie," he said. "She—they—were different. Are different. I told you that. She... Maya shared her love. She was guileless and loving, and if only you could have accepted her as she was, her free and open nature. But no, you wanted her all to yourself."

Wee Paul took another drink, not bothering to deny the charge. "Anyway, what're you doing here? What do you want?"

Mr LeRoy hesitated, then smiled at the midget. "I want you to come back, Paul, and join the people I've gathered around me."

The little man almost sneered. "And you don't think I've had a bellyful of Summer Land? I wouldn't come back for all the—"

Mr LeRoy said, "Summer Land is no more, Paul."

"What?"

"We were attacked. Drake's Paladins. One morning a week ago, under cover of darkness. They ran amok, killing indiscriminately."

Paul lowered his glass with a shaking hand. "Maya?"

Mr LeRoy shook his head, and looked at Ajia.

She said, "I saw a Paladin shoot Maya at point blank range. She was a friend, a good friend."

"Maya... *dead*?"

Ajia found it painful to watch the display of grief on Wee Paul's face. His features seemed to crumple, collapse, as he hung his head and sobbed.

"Maya? Poor, innocent, childlike Maya." He looked up. "And the others? Henri, Emanuel, Hector...?"

Mr LeRoy said. "Dead, all of them. Drake's Paladin's killed them all. Even..." he swallowed, "even Perry."

"Perry? Christ, Bron. I'm so sorry." He fell silent, staring into his drink, then looked up. "But you said 'join you'? Join who?"

"I've gathered together others, other eidolons like us. Fourteen of us. Fifteen if you join our merry band. Fifteen likeminded souls, against the world."

Wee Paul shook his head. "Join you *why*? It'd just be the same. The ridicule, the hatred."

"Paul, Paul... We have a mission. We are united against Drake and his forces of evil."

Paul stared at him. "United? What, all fourteen of you? Are you crazy? United against Drake's Paladins?"

Mr LeRoy looked across at Ajia, and nodded minimally.

She said, "Two nights ago, a force of Paladins, armed with assault weapons and backed up with a helicopter, attacked Daisy Hawthorn's nursery in Derbyshire. Reed and myself, ably assisted by boggarts and elves, we fought them off. Killed every one of them."

Paul looked from her to Mr LeRoy. "She can't be serious."

"Deadly serious," he said. "And Ajia, herself, accounted for most of the Paladins. Her small stature, like your own, conceals a wealth of... of ability."

"You have a plan?" Paul asked.

"We have a plan, which I'll tell you all about if you agree to join us."

Paul regarded his drink. "I don't know..."

Fletcher spoke for the first time since entering the dressing room. "You sounded bitter, earlier. Talked of topping yourself. Why not postpone that, and join us? Use your anger, your bitterness, to get back at the greatest ill in the land? Drake and his fascists."

"But... what you're doing is impossible."

"I don't think so," Mr LeRoy said. "You don't know us, our strengths. Join us. Add your ability own to ours. Avenge," he said, playing his trump card, "avenge Maya's senseless, barbaric murder."

Wee Paul drained his glass and set it down precisely on the dressing table. He looked from Ajia to Fletcher, and finally to Mr LeRoy. At last he said, "What have I got to lose, Bron? What indeed?"

"Attaboy," Mr LeRoy beamed.

Ajia said, "It's good to have you on our team." She hesitated. "But how the fuck did you get out of that burning box?"

"Yeah," Fletcher said, "that had me puzzled, too."

Paul looked across the small room at Mr LeRoy. "Shall I show them, Bron?"

"I think a demonstration will go down very well."

Ajia watched as Wee Paul scrunched his potato face up in concentration, lifted his right hand into the air, snapped his fingers—and vanished.

"What the...!" Fletcher gasped.

Ajia laughed. "How... how did he do that?"

Fletcher shook his head. "Where is he?"

A piping voice answered him. "Right here!"

Ajia heard the tiny voice. It seemed to come from the exact place that Wee Paul had occupied—though, manifestly, no one occupied that space.

Then she looked more closely.

Seated cross-legged on the pink brocade cushion of the chair was a tiny version of Wee Paul, garbed in a white dressing down and minuscule black socks, no more than two inches high.

He saw Ajia staring and gave a jaunty wave. "Hi, there, girl!" he piped.

"Ajia, Reed, meet Paul Klein, a.k.a. Tom Thumb."

The diminutive Paul snapped off a salute, then clicked his fingers and resumed his normal size in the blink of an eye.

"There was a tiny hole in the corner of the box," Wee Paul explained, "and when Pam was waving the lighter around, and everyone's attention was on her, I slipped through the hole, down the trestle leg, and legged it back here. Easy-peasy."

"And now I suggest we return to the minibus," Mr LeRoy said. "These days we travel by night, Paul, and rest up by day. And perhaps, for speed, it would be advisable if you were to assume Tom Thumb dimensions and ride in Ajia's pocket—that way finding out first hand her enviable talent."

"We'll be needing funds on our travels?" Paul asked.

Mr LeRoy agreed. "I would welcome any contribution."

"In that case we'll make a detour to my place and I'll dig out some readies."

He snapped his fingers and shrank instantly. Ajia bent down, held out a hand, and Wee Paul stepped on to her palm. Her only free pocket was on the chest of her shirt, and wondering at her wisdom she slipped the homunculus into it.

Her misgivings were justified a minute later as they left the club by a rear entrance and she prepared to slip into Puck mode.

"Hey!" she called out. "Let go or you're walking!"

"Sorry," came the piping reply. "Bit hard to resist, Ajia."

He unhanded her nipple and she sprinted.

AJIA SPIED THE glow of the fire long before she reached the wood.

She stopped on the edge of the estate and stared at the orange radiance pulsing above the darkened treetops a mile away.

"What is it?" Paul called. "Why've you stopped?"

"Shut it!" she snapped. She needed to think. Wait here for Mr LeRoy and Fletcher to catch up, or investigate the fire? The glow emanated from the dead centre of the woods where they had left the minibus, and she could think of no reason for the blaze—or, rather, she could think of one very good reason.

The Paladins had traced them here.

She scooped Wee Paul from her pocket and held him before her

face. "You need to stay here. Something's not right in the woods."
She indicated the distant fire. "That's where we left the minibus."

"What do you think is...?"

"That's what I'm going to find out. Wait here. I'll be back in a few minutes."

She lowered him to the ground and stood back as the diminutive man snapped his fingers and appeared instantly before her.

He peered at the fiery glow on the horizon. "A night of fire," he murmured.

"I should be back before Mr LeRoy and Fletcher get here, but in case I'm not, tell them where I went."

"If I can help—?"

"I don't think so. I'll be in and out of there as fast as I can. Later."
She sprinted.

She left the estate and sped over the moorland track. There was little movement around her to indicate how fast she was running, but down to her right, in the valley, the trail of red taillights from vehicles on the ring-road appeared motionless.

Ahead, the pulsing glow of the fire pulsed no longer.

She approached the trees with mounting apprehension.

She thought of Daisy Hawthorn, Smith and Elvira and the others. Had the campfire got out of hand and spread to the forest? It was summer and the ground cover was as dry as tinder...

Wishful thinking, she knew.

She came to a track leading into the woods, and slowed down.

A parked vehicle stood in the track, thirty yards away.

A Paladin Humvee.

How had the bastards tracked them here?

Tears stinging her eyes, she concealed herself behind a bush and considered what to do next.

When Mr LeRoy and Fletcher reached Wee Paul, they would know better than to risk proceeding to the woods. They would remain where they were and await her return.

The Paladins had obviously attacked the minibus. The question was, were there any survivors?

She made out the dim figure of a Paladin in the driving seat of the

Humvee, but no others were in sight. She'd sprint up the lane, into the wood, and take a look.

She slipped her knife from her pocket, sprinted from the cover of the bush, and raced past the Humvee.

She moved in spurts, ten yards at a time. Run. Halt. Assess the situation. The ground underfoot was uneven and she risked doing herself an injury if she lost her footing. Run. Halt. Assess the situation. The closer she moved into the heart of the woods, the brighter the glow became. There seemed to be no Paladins guarding the perimeter of the woods. They would be in there, of course, doing the killing. Run. Halt. Assess the situation.

Like this, in a series of stop-go stages, Ajia moved cautiously towards the clearing.

She came to a spray of ferns and hunkered down behind the curving leaves.

She stared into the clearing.

The minibus was on fire, sending bright flames high into the air along with a roiling churn of oily smoke and assorted debris. Even from a distance of twenty yards, she could feel the belting heat of the conflagration on her face.

Through the shattered windows, flaming bodies writhed and contorted. A great hole in the side of the minibus showed where a missile had entered and exploded. And as if not satisfied with bombing the bus and the innocents within, the Paladins had raked the length of the vehicle with assault-rifle fire.

A dozen black-uniformed soldiers stood around the pyre, talking amongst themselves, joking and laughing as they waited for the fire to die out. They knew how many fugitives they were seeking, so when they counted the corpses on the bus they would know there were three short.

But perhaps Daisy, Smith and some of the others had managed to flee the attack?

How likely would it have been that *all* her friends had been on the bus when the attack happened?

The alternative was too horrible to contemplate: that the Paladins had rounded up Daisy, Smith and all the others, forced them at gunpoint on to the bus, then bombed and riddled it with bullets.

She watched as the bodies in the bus twisted and contorted in a macabre dance of fiery death, and she was consumed by rage.

He first instinct was to attack.

She could do untold damage to the unsuspecting Paladins, knife them one by one.

But caution stopped her.

Why risk her life, and make it obvious to the Paladins in command that there were indeed survivors, when the bigger picture was to venture south and attack the source of all this evil, Derek Drake?

She turned and moved away from the clearing, hunkering through the undergrowth until she found a path leading from the woods.

She was about to sprint when a hand clutched her arm as tight as a tourniquet and pulled her backwards. Another hand clamped itself over her mouth.

She was dragged into the cover of an elder tree. A second figure stepped into view.

Daisy Hawthorn, as large and life and beaming at her.

The hands released her and she whirled around to see Wayland Smith.

She hugged Daisy, then Smith. "But... I saw... Back there... the minibus! Bodies!"

"Shhh," Daisy said, taking her hand. "It's okay, love."

"But the others?"

Smith murmured, "We're fine, all of us. We left the clearing before the Paladins found the bus."

Ajia found herself weeping with relief. "But how? What happened?"

"We were in a village over that way," Daisy said, pointing vaguely, "when Elvira found me. She was in a frantic state, weeping and wailing. She said she'd seen a man and a woman asking people in an off-licence if they'd seen a white minibus painted with flowers. And she recognised the couple: the very same pair who'd scoped the nursery last week. I found the others and we raced back here."

"But I saw bodies..." Ajia began.

Daisy smiled in the semi-darkness. She reached out, touched a bough of elder, and under the influence of her magical fingers the bough twisted, turned, and assumed a nascent human shape.

"I brought along some plants, remember? Not that I thought I'd be using them in quite that way, but they sufficed."

"And the others?" Ajia gasped. She found it almost impossible to believe that all her friends had escaped alive.

"While I was arranging the plants, everyone slipped away."

Smith interrupted. "We need to be moving. It won't be long before the Paladins realise that the corpses aren't exactly what they thought they were. I don't want to be anywhere nearby when that happens."

They hurried through the woods, making a detour to meet Mr LeRoy, Fletcher and Wee Paul. On the way, Ajia recounted the night's adventures and the recruiting of the Tom Thumb eidolon to their cause.

They hurried along the moorland path and came to the estate where she had left Wee Paul. Mr LeRoy, Fletcher and the midget were kicking their heels in the radiance of a street-light when Ajia turned the corner and ran to the trio.

"But we were worried sick!" Mr LeRoy cried when he saw Daisy and Smith. We thought..." He gestured vaguely toward the fiery glow. "But the others?"

"All safe," Smith said.

Daisy recounted the events of the evening, Elvira's sighting of the Paladin spies, and her horticultural simulation.

"You say that the couple knew of the minibus?" Mr LeRoy asked.

Smith said, "Either a survivor saw us leave the nursery, or more likely they've been tracking every vehicle seen at some point in the vicinity of the nursery after the attack."

Mr LeRoy made the hurried introductions of Wee Paul to Daisy and Smith, and the latter suggested they lose no time in making their way to a patch of woodland on the distant hillside.

It was almost an hour later by the time they reached the meeting point, having taken a circuitous route around the hill to avoid any lingering Paladins. When they reached the margin of the trees, Ajia looked around the bedraggled group, counting heads.

"Twelve, discounting Paul," she said. "Two missing."

"Ariel and Elvira," Daisy said.

Smith said, "Don't worry, they're safe. I saw them leave the clearing together."

"They knew where you were meeting?" Wee Paul said.

"I told everyone," Daisy said. "Elvira might be a little... away with the fairies, if you'll excuse the expression, but Ariel would take charge."

"We just need to wait," Bogdan the boggart said.

They were discussing their next possible move when, minutes later, Ajia was startled by a crashing through the undergrowth behind the fathering.

She jumped up and turned.

Ariel appeared through the shrubbery, distraught.

"They've got Elvira! She said she was going back for her charm. She'd left it on a log on the edge of the clearing. I argued with her, but she wouldn't listen." He stopped, gulping down great breaths.

Smith took his shoulder and shook the elf. "The Paladins have got her?"

Ariel nodded. "I tried to stop her, but she ran off. I followed. She'd reached the clearing, but... but a Paladin saw her. He knocked her unconscious with his rifle. I'm sorry, but I ran."

Fletcher touched his shoulder. "In the circumstances, you did the right thing."

Ajia looked across at Bogdan, who stood at ease with a stubby submachine gun slung over his shoulder.

"Give me that!"

Bogdan hesitated, looking at Daisy.

"I said give me the gun!" Ajia barked.

Grudgingly, the boggart handed it over.

"I'm going for her," Ajia said.

Mr LeRoy said, "Don't be a fool. There's nothing you can do."

Fletcher backed him up. "Listen to him, for Christ's sake! You'd be putting yourself in danger. And you'd be alerting the bastards the fact that there were survivors."

"Fuckwit!" she snapped. "Think about it. They'll know we got away when they see the bodies are fucking plants."

She stared back at their staring faces, daring them to oppose her.

"Good," she said. "I'll be back."

She shouldered the machine gun and took off.

SHE COVERED THE intervening mile and a half in under a minute, racing over moonlit moorland, leaping drystone walls, approaching the woodland where the minibus still burned.

Her objective was to reach Elvira before the Paladins killed her, and before the bus was safe enough for them to inspect. Once they knew of Daisy's duplicity, and that there were survivors, they would no doubt torture Elvira for information.

If they hadn't already killed her.

She reached the forest and made her way through the trees as before. Run. Halt. Assess the situation. She came to the clearing and ducked behind a bush. The Paladins were still gathered around the minibus. They stood at ease, some smoking, others vaping, laughing and joking amongst themselves. Killers inured to the bloody nature of their job. Doing their duty for King and Country. For Drake.

She moved from the ferns and sprinted clockwise around the clearing until she was on the other side of the bus.

And then she saw Elvira.

Saw her sprawled, naked body.

Saw what the Paladins had done to her.

Another innocent casualty.

She stifled a sob.

They would pay for this.

Unconsciously, she had pulled the knife from her trouser pocket and was gripping it in her right hand, the machine gun still slung over her shoulder.

She had the element of surprise. There was no need to rush. She had to get the job done quickly and cleanly.

But how best to go about it?

She could dart amongst them, slashing and cutting as before, taking them out one by one.

Or she could move into the clearing at speed and open fire with the machine gun.

She looked back at the elf's body and said to herself: *This is for you, girl.*

She moved around the margin of the clearing in the dappled shadows, counting the Paladins. There were eleven of them, with the twelfth still back at the Humvee, presumably. She would deal with him later.

Seven Paladins stood on the far side of the bus, in two groups. The other four stood a dozen yards from her, smoking and watching the vehicle burn.

As she watched, a Paladin strolled away from his colleague to relieve himself in the undergrowth, making her decision for her. She smiled.

You first.

She darted forward, caught the soldier around the neck, tugged, and pulled the knife across his jugular.

He was dead before he could cry out. She dragged the corpse into the forest and dumped it in the undergrowth.

Alerted by the noise, the remaining three Paladins turned as one and stared at where their colleague had stood. One of them called his name. He stepped forward, peering right and left, and then into the shadows of the wood. The others followed, bringing their weapons to bear.

Ajia unslung the machine gun, slipped off the safety catch, and sprayed a three second burst at the advancing soldiers.

She was surprised at how efficiently so many bullets could strip flesh from the bone.

She took off, back into the woods, and moved anticlockwise around the perimeter of the clearing.

Cries greeted the gunfire, and the first Paladin appeared cautiously around the burnt-out minibus. Ajia aimed at his head and squeezed off a one second burst. He fell without a sound. She set off again, moving around the bus—still in the cover of the trees—and the remaining six Paladins came into sight.

Two had dropped to their knees, weapons aiming into the

woods. Two others stood over them, covering their flanks, while the remaining pair backed off and slipped stealthily into the trees diametrically opposite her.

She backed into the trees and sprinted to meet them.

As she approached, she didn't slow down. Instead, she raised the butt of her machine gun and aimed at the head of the first goon as she passed. *Impact*, and she felt the skull crunch. She swung the weapon at the second, startled Paladin and connected with the side of his head. He went down without a sound. She checked that they were both dead—surprised at the extent of the damage done to their fragile skulls—then moved back to the clearing.

The remaining four Paladins had decided, in the face of this invisible opposition, to err on the side of caution and retreat. They were backing across the clearing, covering themselves, when Ajia stepped from the clearing and stood in open view.

Some urge had prompted the rash act. The desire for them to see and acknowledge their nemesis.

They turned as one, their expressions comical as they registered the unlikely fact that a girl had routed their elite force.

"This is for Elvira!" she told them before they could bring their arms to bear.

And she opened up.

"And for Maya!"

She kept the trigger squeezed for longer than was really necessary, until the four soldiers were reduced to shattered bone and meat scrags, and only then did she cease firing.

Blessed silence rang in her ears.

She was stepping around the bloody remains, and moving from the clearing, when something glinting silver in the grass caught her eye.

She knelt and picked up something on a fine silver chain.

Elvira's lucky charm.

Weeping, she slipped it into her pocket, next to her bloody knife, and ran from the clearing.

As she approached the Humvee stationed on the lane leading to the woods, she unslung the machine gun and readied herself behind a tree.

The last remaining Paladin had left the safety of the vehicle and was moving cautiously along the track, speaking into a lapel mic. She heard his frantic, "Sergeant Bryce, come in, come in..."

She smiled to herself.

Sergeant Bryce would never again come in.

The track passed within two yards of where she stood in the cover of the trees, and it would have been simplicity itself to kill the Paladin.

But something stayed her hand.

She would gain no satisfaction in killing just another mindless thug—but how wonderful it was to anticipate the man's fear, his terror, when he entered the woods and discovered the fate of his colleagues. He would creep back to the safety of the Humvee, in mortal dread that whatever occult force had accounted for the others would bloodily end his own life.

She allowed the Paladin to pass unharmed and, when he was well out of earshot, she took off.

She entered the woodland on the hilltop a minute later, and was aware of many sets of eyes on her as she approached the little group.

Daisy said, "Elvira?"

She handed Bogdan the machine gun, and shook her head. "I'm sorry," she said.

She pulled the elf's good luck charm from her pocket, wiped it on her shirt, and passed it silently to Ariel.

"We need to be moving," she told Mr LeRoy.

"We've been discussing that need in your absence, Ajia, but without—"

She interrupted, recalling the white van the Bradfordian had offered to sell them earlier that evening. "I have an idea," she said, "if Paul is willing to cough up a hundred quid."

TWENTY-SEVEN

THEY HAD MOTORED through the night, heading north-west towards the Lake District.

Shortly after leaving Bradford, Smith had suggested they ditch the van and buy another vehicle. He reasoned that the Paladins, on the warpath after suffering their second drubbing that week, would have investigators in the area who would soon learn about the suspicious trio—one of them brown-skinned—that had bought the van for cash with no questions asked.

At nine that morning, Smith and Fletcher had walked into the market town of Gargrave and bought what turned out to be a clapped-out, ex-council delivery van from a dubious second-hand dealership.

It was a tight squeeze, but Daisy had had the bright idea of making the ride more comfortable by coaxing a strand of Virginia creeper into the rear of the vehicle and, with her magic touch, having it proliferate lushly before cutting off the main trunk and standing back. "Hey presto!"

It wasn't exactly a luxury mattress, Ajia thought, but it beat the van's original oil-stained hardboard flooring.

Now they were parked up at the side of a muddy farm track,

resting for the rest of the day until they recommenced the journey at sunset. Ajia lay between a silent Ariel and a snoring Bogdan.

Wee Paul had proved himself a hit with the three remaining brownie girls. To aid the congestion in the back of the van, Paul had offered to shrink himself—though Ajia was pretty sure he had ulterior motives.

Now he lay on his back, hammocked in Persephone's crotch, with his hands laced nonchalantly behind his head and his tiny legs crossed at the ankles as he regaled the entranced brownies and elves with tales of his troubled life.

"That's the trouble with being different," he said, his piping tones reaching Ajia as she snuggled deeper into the ivy, "you find yourself being the butt of the frustration and anger of cowards and tossers with inferiority complexes."

"That's right," a brownie murmured, and a boggart grunted his assent.

"I played all the clubs in the north, and some of the bigger ones down south, but the pubs and clubs around Yorkshire and Lancashire were my bread and butter. But at every other gig some drunken lout, egged on by his mates, would have it in for me."

"It must have been terribly frustrating," an elf said with quaint understatement.

"Well, it was before I died and was reborn," Paul laughed. "I mean, think about it, there I was, three foot five and not exactly endowed with muscle. What could I do when a group of piss-heads decided to have some fun?"

"What did you do?" a boggart asked.

"What else? What I'm good at. The gift of the gab. I talked my way out of trouble. Joked and took the piss—often at my own expense. And it did nothing for my self-esteem, I'll tell you that for nowt. But it didn't always work. Some louts just wouldn't be pacified, and the number of times I was tripped up, grabbed and flung into the air…"

He fell silent. Ajia opened her eyes. His face was too tiny to make out clearly, but she saw him quickly rub tiny fists into his eyes.

Persephone asked, "What happened?"

"I was in Morley. Just finished a gig at the Con Club and was crossing the car park when this big ginger lout, backed up by his rat-arsed mates, decided to have a bit of fun. I'd seen him inside—couldn't miss him. He'd been heckling me all night, and I'd put him down a few times to the amusement of his mates. Now he wanted to get even."

The two brownies on either side of Persephone covered their faces with their tiny hands. "Oh, no!"

"So the ginger-nut yells that he wants my autograph. I was in two minds, make a dash for my car, or play along with the thug. I sensed things could turn nasty. But my car was on the far side of the lot, so I decided to face the music."

Wee Paul climbed to his feet, stretched, and walked up the incline of Persephone's thigh. On the summit of her knee, he sat cross-legged and resumed his story, looking around at his rapt audience.

"I was reaching into my jacket for the signed photos I always carried, when ginger-nut grabs me by the throat and throws me onto the roof of the nearest car. His mates surrounded the car and every time I tried to get down, slide over the bonnet or the boot, they'd punch me. After about ten minutes of this, they got a bit stalled. Then one of them had another bright idea and put it to ginger-nut, who liked it."

"What?" a brownie shrieked.

"A couple of them grabbed me and carried me over to an old banger belonging to one of the bastards, put me on the roof and told me not to move. Then ginger-nut climbed into the car, started the engine and drove off."

"But what did you do?" Persephone asked.

"What? After pissing me'sen?" Wee Paul laughed, self-deprecating. "Well, I did my best not to fall off—but try doing that on the curved roof of a car! And when ginger-nut, with his whooping mates following us around the car-park, decided to speed up… Well, I fell off and went arse over tit."

"Were you badly…?" an elf began in a whisper.

"Badly injured? You could say that. I hit my head on the tarmac and died."

A stunned silence filled the van.

Wee Paul went on, "To cut a long story short, the manager of the club had seen what'd happened and called the police and an ambulance. I was rushed to hospital and miraculously—according to the paramedics who attended to me in the car park—came back to life. Ginger-nut and his mates were arrested and charged with aggravated GBH. Ginger-nut got sent down for a year, his mates let off with fines. A year! I was angry, I can tell you."

Paul piped a laugh. "But then a strange thing happened." He looked around at his audience. "I started having dreams. I was the size of a mouse, being chased through a forest by ogres. I put it down to trauma from the attack, but the dreams persisted, and this is the funny thing. In them, I found I could control my size by simply snapping my fingers. And then one night, when I woke up from one of these dreams, I tried it. Snapped my fingers... and shrank. Like bloody magic, I shrank! After the shock, I found I could control how small I shrank to—though more's the pity, I couldn't make me'sen grow any taller than my original three foot five! Anyroad, I had an idea. Ginger-nut was out on bail, and I decided to have some fun. I knew his address from attending the court proceedings, and one night I followed him and his girlfriend home, shrunk me'sen and snook in before they closed the door. When they were in the bedroom having a bit of hanky-panky, I assumed my normal height and made a nuisance of me'sen—crashing about the bathroom, spilling things, then moving to the kitchen and doing the same there. When I heard him swearing upstairs, I made me'sen titchy again and watched ginger-nut's bewilderment and growing alarm. I kept this up for a week, and by the end he was begging the authorities to bang him up, I can tell you!"

Persephone clapped and laughed prettily.

"And then, when he did get sent down, I got to know his girlfriend—nice woman, too good for a thug like ginger-nut—and we had a bit of a fling, like. And I heard on the grapevine that ginger-nut went berserk when he found out I was knobbing his bird. Pardon my French.

"And then the dreams got worse—that old ogre was catching me every night. And just when I was thinking of topping me'sen, who should roll into town with his travelling circus but Mr LeRoy. He took me under his wing, told me all about Tom Thumb and eidolons and whatnot, gave me a job and introduced me to the wonderful Maya." He fell silent, then murmured, "And we all know how that ended, don't we? Poor Maya."

THEY HAD TRAVELLED throughout the night and were now in southern Cumbria.

Ajia finished chewing on an egg and cress sandwich and wandered over to where Wayland Smith was sitting at a picnic table. She sat beside him and admired the view. To the north, the rearing hills of the Lake District rose ever higher and ever hazier beyond each other until disappearing into the misty distance.

Daisy Hawthorn locked the van and she and Mr LeRoy led their troupe from the lay-by into a nearby spinney to lie low until sunset.

"We should join them," Ajia said.

Without replying, Smith leaned forward and, with his hammer, touched a piece of glass between his feet—one of a thousand green shards from a beer bottle. It reassembled itself before her eyes. Smith picked it up and placed it on the table. He did the same with another, this time a pop bottle, and set it on the table beside the first.

"It's very hard to explain," he said at last, "but the sense of satisfaction I get from repairing, recreating... It's responding to something fundamental deep within me. It's almost as if the need to create, to fix things, is encoded deep within my eidolon like DNA, and deep within me, too."

"I wonder if that's why you find it so hard to destroy? You're a creator, Smith, and always have been, and the opposite of that is against your nature."

They let the silence stretch. Smith said, "Do you fear what lies ahead?"

She thought about it. "I fear failing," she said. "I fear what will happen if Drake wins, if people like his Paladins are allowed to go unchecked. Yes, I fear that."

"But what about the confrontation ahead? Do you fear for yourself?"

She shook her head. "I was arrested by two coppers in London, and beaten up, and tortured—so bad that the bastards killed me. Then as if by a miracle I was given a second chance. No, I don't fear death any more." She glanced at him. "You?"

He pulled his handsome, brown face into a frown. "It's not so much death I fear, but finding myself, again, in a position where through necessity, I face the dilemma of having to cause it."

She watched him as he worked his magic on another broken bottle. "I think Mr LeRoy will have you use your ability to defend us, Smith. He wouldn't call on you to kill, and nor would I."

Smith sighed. "Perhaps the eidolon chose me because, at heart, it saw me for a coward."

"No you're not."

Ajia looked up.

It was Reed Fletcher. He stood beside the table, and she wondered how much he had overheard. Fletcher sat down across from them and shook his head. His bright green eyes looked from her to Smith.

"You're not a coward, Smith, because your actions are driven by principles. By fundamental beliefs. Not by fear of any harm you might come to. That's the difference."

Smith look up at Fletcher. "Just after what happened at the warehouse, after I ran. You called me a coward then, Reed."

Fletcher shrugged. "In the heat of the moment, and in the months following, that's what I might have thought. But I was wrong. I've had time to think about it, and perhaps I overreacted to what you did back then. I think I saw in what you did… something I didn't like in myself."

Smith looked at him. "Your insularity, the way you hid yourself away from the world in your little Sherwood Forest hobbit-house?"

Fletcher smiled, Ajia saw, and shook his head.

Smith tucked his hammer into his belt, stood up and nodded towards the spinney. "I think I'll join the others."

Ajia watched him as he left the table and wandered down the

narrow track, soon lost amidst the trees.

She turned to Fletcher. "What did you mean, 'something I didn't like in myself'?"

So Reed Fletcher told her what had happened in Helmand Province more than ten years ago. How a routine patrol had turned into a nightmare when a landmine destroyed two Humvees in their convoy and they'd come under sustained fire from the Taliban.

"My best mate, a lad from these parts as it happened... He'd been blown from our armoured car and lay on the far side of the road, perhaps ten yards away. There were plenty of lulls in the fire. I could have sprinted across and helped him, done whatever I could to stop his bleeding."

"But you didn't?"

"I was petrified. Frozen with fear. It was all I could do to shoot back at the fundies, but it didn't help that I couldn't see where the enemy was. It was hell. But I know I should have acted, instead of sitting tight and waiting for backup."

"What happened to...?"

"He died before backup arrived, Ajia."

Fletcher told her how he had been discharged with Post Traumatic Stress Disorder, and had tried to adapt himself to civilian life, burdened with guilt and shame he'd kept secret until now.

"But you lived with it," she said.

He laughed. "I didn't! That's just it. I even failed to live with it— because I killed myself."

She recalled that time a week ago when he had told her that she should never, ever, talk about taking her own life.

"One day the guilt became too much. I'd been stockpiling sleeping tablets and paracetamol, and one night I bought a bottle of whisky and necked the lot, the Scotch, the pills... And I died and came back to life in hospital, the medics calling it a ruddy miracle. Then the dreams began. Dreams of the greenwood. And something drove me to take up archery which gave my life some purpose, and I developed an affinity with the world. I mean the real world, the natural world. And then the dreams turned to nightmares. I was lost in a wildwood that was hostile to me, not the woods I knew and loved. I started drinking. Drinking heavily. Drinking so that I couldn't think. Wouldn't have to think. Until Mr LeRoy found me."

Ajia said, "He's the person we all have in common, Reed. Mr LeRoy. Our saviour. Our..." She smiled to herself. She had been about to say, *Our father*.

She said, "Have you told Smith about your time in Afghanistan, about what happened?"

He shook his head. "No."

"I dunno, but perhaps you should. It might help him a bit, don't you think?"

He nodded, staring into the spinney. "Yes," he said. "Perhaps it might."

TWENTY-EIGHT

WYNNE SAT BESIDE Lieutenant Noble and the pilot as the chopper headed north through the grey dawn light.

He had planned to be on hand last night to watch the slaughter in the woodland outside Bradford. In the event, the commander on the ground had deemed that an imminent attack on the bus and its passengers would achieve maximum effect. At eight yesterday evening, he had reported that the mission had been one hundred per cent successful: the bus was destroyed and every one of its passengers killed.

Wynne's triumph was tinged with only slight regret. He had really wanted Ajia Snell arrested. He had fantasised, for the past day, about just what he would do to the girl when he had her in his custody.

He stared down at the awakening countryside far below.

He had considered notifying Drake of his success immediately, but no doubt his boss would be busy shagging Harriet as if there were no tomorrow. What had suddenly got into the pair, he wondered. Harriet was no longer answering his calls or texts, and on the few occasions they had briefly met face to face, the bloody woman had cut him dead.

"ETA, Lieutenant?" he asked.

Noble conferred with the pilot. "Bang on six, sir. Ten minutes."

"Very good."

He sat back, enjoying the ride. He would enjoy, too, surveying the battleground. He would never forget the scene of carnage that had greeted him at the nursery in Derbyshire, the massacre perpetrated by Snell and her murderous terrorists. This was delicious payback.

And he would be once more in Derek Drake's good books.

Minutes later Noble pointed at a patch of woodland down below to their left. Wynne made out a drift of smoke rising from the centre of the woods and a Paladin Humvee stationed on an approach track.

They came down on a patch of level moorland a hundred yards from the vehicle. A dozen Paladins emerged from the back of the chopper, formed into two groups of six fore and aft of Wynne and Noble, and led the way across to the Humvee.

There was no sign of its driver.

Odd, Wynne thought, but not disturbing. He'd probably gone into the bushes to relieve himself.

Lieutenant Noble raised spoke hurriedly into his lapel mic.

"Well?" Wynne snapped.

Noble shook his head. "Nothing from Captain Hadley, sir."

Something fluttered in Wynne's stomach.

Christ. Not again.

No. There would be a simple explanation for his men's incommunicado. They were probably busy sifting through the debris of the burned-out minibus.

They followed the track into the woods.

An ominous silence greeted them as they made their way through the cool dawn air of the forest. Wynne would have expected to be met by Captain Hadley, high on the success of his mission and eager to report every last detail.

Noble strode ahead, clandestinely speaking into his radio. His lieutenant was spooked, and with good reason. Wynne himself was experiencing the beginnings of a terrible apprehension.

The stench of the burning bus reached them seconds before they saw the blackened carcass of the vehicle in the clearing.

And saw, too, what surrounded it.

"Oh, Sweet Jesus Christ…" Noble murmured.

His Paladins spread out in security formation and stationed themselves around the clearing like the numerals on a clock face, facing outwards.

Dazed, Wynne stepped into the clearing.

It was Derbyshire all over again.

Wynne counted eleven bodies, his stomach churning. You never got used to violent death, however often you saw it and, indeed, perpetrated it. Most of the corpses had been shredded by automatic gun fire, while others had had their throats slit. One belonged to a small, slender woman, unclothed. Her death had been no less brutal than the rest. She was clearly the victim of sustained physical abuse, and Wynne had a feeling it wasn't the terrorists who had been responsible for that.

All's fair in love and war, he thought coldly.

He looked across at the smouldering bus. So his men had conducted the missile launch on the vehicle, but then had been surprised by renegades hiding in ambush? Was that it? But why had the gunmen waited until the Paladins had launched their attack before opening fire?

Something was not quite right here—and he soon found out what.

Lieutenant Noble approached the minibus. With the muzzle of his assault rifle he tentatively prodded through a shattered window frame at the charcoaled head of a passenger.

It crumbled, quite unlike a normal skull.

Noble turned. "Sir!" he yelled.

Wynne stepped around the bullet-riddled corpse of a Paladin and crossed to the bus.

Noble was prodding at another blackened body, then another. They fell apart like burnt cardboard at the muzzle's gentle prodding.

"What the hell, Lieutenant?"

Noble shook his head. "They're not… bodies, sir. They… It looks like vegetable matter. Plants."

"Let me see." Wynne stepped closer to the bus and peered inside. Noble was right. Though the things seated in the back of the bus resembled human beings in shape, they were fashioned from fibrous matter, stalks and vines which—he saw as he peered closer—grew from the remains of compost bags placed in the aisle of the bus.

"I don't know how the hell they did it, Lieutenant, but this was a setup. And we fell for it."

"Sir!"

He turned, his heart thumping.

Two Paladins emerged from the undergrowth, assisting a third man between them.

"Corporal Smithson, sir," one of the Paladins said. "The driver."

The survivor of the terrorist outrage was in a bad way. He was shaking uncontrollably and tears streaked his face.

"What did you see, Corporal?" Wynne asked.

Smithson gestured pathetically towards his fallen comrades. "I saw nothing, sir. Not a thing. Just heard gunfire. I... I tried to reach Captain Hadley, sir, but not a thing. So I made my way into the woods and found..."

Wynne looked away. It galled him to see grown men reduced to tears.

"And you're absolutely sure you saw nothing?" he asked.

"Nothing sir. When the firing stopped, it was just silent. Deathly silent. Though..."

"Go on."

"When I couldn't reach Captain Hadley, sir, and went for a look-see. Just as I was setting off..." He shook his head. "I thought I saw something in the darkness. Something moving. Fast. A shadow. But then it was gone. I thought I was seeing things."

Ajia Snell.

Christ, but she would pay for this.

Wynne addressed Noble. "Secure the area. Get the local coppers to throw up a cordon. Keep reporters out. Get the mop-up squad in."

Again, he thought bitterly.

For the next hour Wynne paced the clearing, wondering how he would go about presenting this latest defeat to Derek Drake.

He would be lucky to still be in post, come noon.

At noon, he had still not contacted Drake.

Lieutenant Noble and the dozen Paladins who had accompanied him up here in the chopper had gathered at the far side of the clearing, their duties done for now. From time to time they cast glances across at Wynne, as if expecting him to address them with a few morale-boosting words.

He couldn't bring himself to do that, quite yet.

Noble left from the group and diffidently approached Wynne.

"What is it, Lieutenant?"

"The men, sir, they're…"

"Yes? They're what? They're shit scared? Is that it?"

"Sir, they're wondering what we're up against. That's more than thirty good men killed in just a couple of days."

"Thirty-three, to be precise, Lieutenant."

"And they want to know what the hell they're fighting. You see, sir, it helps to know the enemy."

Wynne sighed. "I know, Lieutenant. I do know that."

"And another thing…" Noble looked away.

"Go on."

"They—that is, we—we're wondering why we're being sent into these situations. We're up against things that aren't normal, sir. Supernatural things. And all we have are conventional weapons which, if you'll excuse my French, are fucking useless. Thing is, us Paladins were set up to protect the Prime Minister, sir, not fight these… these monsters."

Wynne considered his words. "And what would you say if I were to tell you that by fighting these so-called monsters, Lieutenant, we are fulfilling our duty to protect Mr Drake?"

Noble thought about it. "Then I'd say, with all due respect, sir, that Drake is ruddy two hundred miles away in the safety of his fucking great mansion, while we're risking our lives on a wild goose chase. But that's between you and me, sir," he added hastily.

Wynne smiled. "Between you and me, Lieutenant. Very well, you've made your point very clearly. And, if it's any consolation, I don't disagree with you. Go and tell the men that I'll address them presently."

"Yes, sir. Thank you, sir."

Wynne considered contacting the Prime Minister on his private line, but, all things considered, he decided to delay the call for a little while longer yet.

TWO HUNDRED MILES away in Derek Drake's mansion, Drake himself was awaiting the arrival of Dudley Fowler, his tame publicity officer.

He paced his study, going over the finer points of his scheme to spike Premier Vasily Vasilyev's guns.

Dudley Fowler was instrumental in this plan.

Young Dudley was undoubtedly a PR genius, adept at not only maintaining Drake's pristine image of Britain's saviour but blackening the reputations of the Prime Minister's opponents. Dudley could dig the dirt like no other and, when there was little or no dirt to dig, he was a whiz kid at fabricating it from thin air.

Dudley ducked into Drake's study thirty minutes later, somehow managing to combine the cocksure and the subservient in a fidgety, bobbing motion that never ceased. He looked like a schoolboy spiv in a tight suit, or an East End barrow-boy made good and constantly surprised that he'd done so.

"Dudley, my boy. How nice to see you again."

"Same here, boss. Nice place you got yourself here."

"You have never been to the Grange before?"

"First time," Dudley said, fidgeting. He looked uneasy, as if overawed not so much by the Prime Minister's presence as by the thick pile carpet, expensive leather armchairs, and works of art that hung around the room.

"You have the...?" Drake raised an eyebrow.

Dudley grinned and patted his breast pocket. "Right here, safe and sound."

"Excellent!"

Drake called the young man his press officer—and he did serve in that capacity—but Dudley's forte was in the arcane area of what he called "digital manipulation".

Drake indicated the 24" laptop on his desk. Dudley danced across to it, inserted a thumb-drive, and tapped the keyboard.

"And here we go!"

"I was afraid, Dudley, that you might have got rid of the... evidence."

The boy grinned. "Never do that, sir. Don't know when it might come in handy, do we?"

"We certainly do not, Dudley. Well done."

Dudley set the image rolling and stood back, grinning.

"You really are," Drake said admiringly, "an artist."

"Well, I do my best, sir."

The image on the screen showed a grey-haired old man slipping his engorged penis into the rear end of a young rent-boy, doggy style, and exhibiting an athleticism, and gusto, out of all proportion to his advanced years.

The British public would have been shocked at the predilections of one of the country's most respected politicians—had the footage ever come to light.

Edward Winterton had always been the longest, and thorniest, thorn in Drake's sensitive side. He had been one of those long-serving politicians who, after decades of distinguished duty on the backbenches, had earned the hallowed appellation of a "parliamentarian". He'd joined the Labour Party fresh out of university, risen through the ranks, and then fallen out of favour with the party's more radical elements, after which he had crossed the floor and joined the Liberal Democrats. A year later he crossed the floor yet again, this time hitching his star to Drake's emergent Resurrection Party, much to Drake's niggling suspicions.

Suspicions which, in time, were proved correct.

Last year the old parliamentarian had called at Number 10 and requested a "little word".

The politician had ensconced himself in a leather armchair across from Drake and proceeded to tell the Prime Minister that he, Winterton, was apprised of all the dirty details behind the so-called "Summer of Terror" a few years back, when a hit-squad of Daesh sympathisers had indiscriminately bombed three public venues in London, Birmingham and Glasgow, killing over three hundred British citizens.

The atrocities had proved that Drake's anti-immigrant, anti-Muslim, pro-British rhetoric had contained more than just a grain of common sense. And it was the act that had been instrumental in persuading the electorate to vote Drake's Resurrection Party into power a year later.

And Edward Winterton had sat in the armchair and, as calm as you like, purred, "The 'Summer of Terror', Derek. I know the truth."

Drake's blood had run cold. Blustering, he'd feigned misunderstanding.

"I know that the bombings had nothing to do with Islamic State activists," Winterton went on. "I know that certain of the more extreme elements in the secret services were responsible for planting the bombs. I know that this outrage was committed at your instigation, with your sponsorship, and that the suspects you rounded up and had summarily executed were illegal immigrants from Pakistan and Bangladesh whom no one would miss, or mourn. A truly despicable act, Derek, which helped to get you where you are today."

Drake had blustered, of course. He had denied everything and said that Winterton didn't have a shred of proof—but the backbencher hadn't taken the bait and disclosed his source.

"You haven't heard the last of this, Derek," Winterton had said, then swept from the room.

Drake had lost no time and ordered Dudley Fowler to fabricate a mock-up of Winterton with a rent boy. With the incriminating footage to hand—*kompromat* of his own—Drake had been about to confront Winterton with it, and demand his silence, when the politician had disappeared from his country retreat in Somerset.

Drake had hardly been able to believe his luck.

He had initiated his own private investigation into the disappearance, but to no avail. The politician had vanished off the face of the Earth.

Now he watched the pornographic footage with admiration.

"Yes," he said, "quite a work of art, Dudley."

"I try to oblige," said the man. He hesitated. "Just one thing I don't get. Winterton having vanished…" He pointed to the screen. "Why do you want it?"

Drake grinned at Winterton's strenuous pederasty, almost convincing himself that it had actually been the old man going like the devil at the rent boy's arse, and not a clever computer-generated image.

"That's not all I want. You have till midnight to create two further scenarios of a similar nature—using, let me see… How about that bloated writer I detest, Victor Shepperton, and that appalling socialist agitator who calls himself an actor, Dan Gerson?"

"Got it!" Dudley grinned, relishing the challenge. "Victor Shepperton and Dan Gerson."

Drake pulled a thumb-drive from his breast pocket and suggested that the youth take a look.

Dudley replaced his own thumb-drive with Drake's, then activated its only file.

Seconds later the boy was staring goggle-eyed at the grainy reproduction of Derek Drake shagging the arse off a beautiful blonde bimbo.

"It would appear, Dudley, that the Russians are attempting to emulate your own work of art—though it must be said they could learn a thing or two from you."

Dudley looked both flattered and relieved. "Phew!" he said, nodding at the screen. "For a second there, sir, I thought you'd been caught in the act."

"The very idea!" Drake laughed. "No, this pathetic effort is Premier Vasilyev's idea of a little joke."

"Ah. I'm beginning to understand where you're coming from, sir."

"You're quick on the uptake," Drake said. "Tomorrow, once you've had your people manufacture the dirt on Gerson and Shepperton, I want you to take this ridiculous mock-up of me and the young lady and release all four of the clips online, along with a press release along the lines of 'Russia up to its dirty tricks again'. Understood?"

"Loud and clear, sir. Leave it to me." Dudley took the thumb-drive from the laptop and slipped it into his breast pocket.

"That will be all, Dudley."

Smiling, he watched the nerdily eager young man skip from the room.

He looked at his watch. One o'clock.

Time for lunch with Harriet, with perhaps a drink or two afterwards, and then a spot of physical recreation.

If anything, Harriet's passion had increased in the last day or two. It was almost becoming, dare he say it, too much. And with the passion came a... How to describe her sudden, almost girlish devotion? It was almost as if she worshipped him.

Drake smiled to himself.

Well, she had that in common with a good percentage of the electorate, after all.

To lunch!

HARRIET LAID ON the bed, fuming.

She had had six calls from the bastard since breakfast. It was becoming too much. And the texts! The self-pitying, whining words begging her to take him back!

Her phone chimed again, and she snatched it up. The call was from an unrecognised number.

"Hello?" she said warily.

"Harriet, we need to talk."

"Wynne? For God's sake, can't you take a hint? Is your military skull so thick you can't see when it's over?"

"Over?"

"Over. Finished. Kaput."

"But, Harriet, I thought..."

"Well, you thought wrong, didn't you? You were only ever a fling, an amusement, pleasant while it lasted. But all things come to an end. Get over it."

"But I miss—" he began.

"You don't miss me," she sneered. "You miss the power trip, the danger, the illicit thrill of it all."

"Harriet!" he whined.

She cut him off.

A minute later her phone chimed again, this time with a text message. From Wynne. It had an attachment.

She opened it and stared at the selfie of Major Dominic Wynne's proud erection, accompanied by: *See what you're missing, Harriet.*

Typical of the man!

Well, he'd gone too far, this time.

She switched off her phone and stretched herself out on the bed, awaiting her husband's return.

When Drake finally emerged from the bathroom, minutes later, his face was almost as dolorous as his drooping member.

"Darling?"

He slumped onto the bed. "Wynne called earlier," he said. "I swear the man's incompetent. Another eleven Paladins, dead. Wiped out. And no sign of Snell and her mob."

She stroked his chest. "I think," she said, "that you ought to sack Wynne, or demote him, or whatever it is you do with incompetent soldier boys."

"Demote him? I'll have the bastard strung up by his balls!"

She twirled a strand of chest hair around her finger, considering.

"Speaking of Wynne," she said at last. "Derek, there's something you need to know."

He turned to her. "Concerning Wynne?"

"He... For the past month or two, he's been making... Let's say inappropriate suggestions, Derek."

He sat up, staring at her. "Inappropriate?"

"Touching me, whispering that what I needed was a... a real man. And," she went on, reaching for her phone. "I had this from him this morning."

She opened the text and showed him the selfie of Wynne's erection.

Derek turned purple as he read the accompanying text. "'See what you're missing, Harriet.' I trusted him." He paused, lost in thought. "I'll get him for this. I'll make sure the arsehole suffers."

Harriet smiled and reached out for her husband. "Forget about him for now, Derek. Let's enjoy ourselves, hmm?"

TWENTY-NINE

FLETCHER BRAKED THE van at the top of the pass and Ajia stared out at the view.

The sun was setting, laying long shadows over the valley and lakes. Ajia found the scenery awe-inspiring and a little hostile. The great soaring peaks looked to her more like mountains than the mere hills that Mr LeRoy assured her they were.

There was something eerie about the emptiness of the place, too. They had passed only the occasional house or cottage, whose isolation made obvious the fact that these wild hills were relatively uninhabited. Accustomed to the busy streets of London and the bustling press of humanity, she found that the emptiness and the silence gave her the shivers.

On Mr LeRoy's insistence, they had taken a risk and set off at five that evening. He had a feeling, he said—a deep intuition—that time was of the essence. They had kept to the back lanes, taking a circuitous route to the lakes, and now Mr LeRoy pointed to see the small town far below with a sense of triumph.

"Heelshead," he said, "and, if I'm not mistaken, the farmstead down there, a mile or so before the town, should be where our man resides."

Ajia made out the honey-coloured scatter of houses and cottages that was the town, gathered around a small square with a stubby cenotaph. On this side of Heelshead stood a tumbledown, whitewashed collection of farm buildings.

"Cuhullin the Hound," she said.

"Or rather his eidolon," said Mr LeRoy. "One Dustin Wolfson, the boxer."

Fletcher looked at Mr LeRoy. "The MMA title holder? I've seen a few of his fights on TV. Hell of a scrapper."

"None other," Mr LeRoy beamed. "Now Cuhullin—or Cú Chulainn—the Hound is famed in mythology as the youth who, in the form of a bestial hound, defended Ulster against Queen Medb."

Ajia stared at him. "And this Dustin can change himself into a hound?"

"I saw him transform once, when he had a drink or five inside him and his dander was up." Mr LeRoy shook his head. "It wasn't a pretty sight."

"Wolfson. Nominative determinism, right? But the 'Dustin' bit?"

Mr LeRoy explained. "From the Germanic, meaning brave fighter."

"And you think he'll be a worthy addition to our scrappy little band of rebels?" Fletcher asked.

"Indubitably, he is certainly someone to have on your side when your back's against the wall."

"Don't tell me," Ajia said. "Mr Wolfson is another waif and stray you happened upon while travelling with Summer Land?"

Mr LeRoy laughed and placed a pudgy hand on her knee. "And there you are very wrong, my girl. Mr Wolfson found *me*."

He told the tale of how, one autumn day when Summer Land had pitched itself over on the Cumberland coast, he had suggested to Perry that they have a romantic weekend in a cottage in the Lakes.

It was in a quiet public house in Ambleside, while they were enjoying an intimate candle-lit dinner, that a drunken bruiser had crossed to their table and pleaded with Mr LeRoy to help him. Whether the eidolon in Wolfson had intuited Auberon's own eidolon, and directed its host towards his saviour, Mr LeRoy would never know—but no sooner had the punch-drunk, whiskey-sozzled, cauliflower-eared, thick-lipped, Fenian prizefighter opened his mouth to claim that he was possessed by demons and plagued by nightmares, than Mr LeRoy knew he should take the poor man under his wing.

"I set him on labouring at Summer Land, and for a while all was well. But could I keep him away from the drink, and could my ministrations soothe his temper?"

"No to both?" Ajia guessed.

"How right you are. Wolfson soon slipped into his old ways, and drank to excess, and chose the fiercest, meanest boggarts to taunt—a dire mistake. Perhaps it was for the best, though a small part of me was sad to see him go, but he walked out of his own accord, a year ago now, and I haven't seen him since."

Fletcher let out the handbrake and they coasted down the winding road.

Darkness was falling as the minibus pulled into the cobbled courtyard of the dilapidated farmhouse. Fletcher swung round to face the house and kept the headlights shining to illuminate its mildewed frontage. "Doesn't look like anyone's at home, if you ask me."

Mr LeRoy climbed from the cab and Ajia joined him.

Gingerly, loath to soil his bespoke leather brogues, he stepped through slicks of chicken manure towards the front door. Ajia knocked and waited.

After a minute without response, Mr LeRoy said, "It would appear that no one is at home."

Ajia tried the handle and found it unlocked. She stepped into a narrow hallway that reeked of mould and cat piss.

"*Yeugh!* Are you sure he lived here?"

"This is the address he gave when he joined us. But he was never known for his salubrious lifestyle."

Ajia found a light switch and a feeble 40-watt bulb illuminated a bare, linoleum-covered corridor. She led the way to the first door, which opened onto a living room. A single settee proved the only item of furniture, pulled up before an open fire. She counted twenty empty whiskey bottles scattered across an ancient carpet stained with scabs of dried vomit.

The reek of stale whiskey vied for domination with the mildew.

They searched the rest of the house, finding only a soiled mattress in an upstairs room. Of Dustin Wolfson there was no sign.

"Looks like he's not been here for months, maybe years," Ajia said as they returned downstairs.

"Maybe. But just let me check." He led the way to the back of the farmhouse and entered the kitchen.

A rickety table against the far wall, a tiny fridge, and a cupboard that held—when Mr LeRoy opened it—six unopened bottles of Bushmill's red label.

"I think our bird has not flown the nest. Perhaps it might be wise to look for Mr Wolfson in the local hostelry."

They drove onto town and parked in the square. Mr LeRoy, Fletcher and Ajia left the others and crossed to The Ploughman's, an ancient coaching inn occupied by two cloth-capped pensioners staring into their pints as if in hope of divination. There was no sign of anyone remotely resembling an Irish boxer.

At television stood in the corner of the room. The portly publican leaned on the bar and watched the evening news.

Fletcher ordered a pint of Guinness, Mr LeRoy a half of mild, and Ajia sipped a half of lager and lime as Mr LeRoy chatted to the publican, who shot Ajia a suspicious glance from time to time. She assumed it was the colour of her skin.

The upshot of Mr LeRoy's enquiries about one Dustin Wolfson was that the "Paddy" was barred from the premises. "I run a respectable public house, sir. I don't tolerate trouble, and your Paddy is a handful. You know him?"

"I heard he lived hereabouts," said Mr LeRoy. "And once, in my youth, I was known as a pugilist, though to look at me now you would never guess that."

Ajia hid a smile behind her glass.

"Well, if you really want to meet him, he might be along at The Three Feathers, across the square and past the police station—if he isn't boozing at home."

Thanking the publican, they drank up and left The Ploughman's, making their way across the square to The Three Feathers.

This was obviously the town's preferred hostelry. The main bar was packed with customers, and the two smaller rooms to either side were similarly busy. Fletcher pushed his way through a crowd of drinkers to the bar and ordered the same again, a Guinness and halves of mild and lager.

Mr LeRoy slipped into a room off to one side, and Fletcher, clutching his pint protectively to his chest, moved to the other. Ajia glanced around the bar, looking for someone matching her idea of what a prize-fighter might look like.

A flatscreen TV above the bar, tuned to Sky News, caught her attention.

The Prime Minister was addressing journalists outside Number 10. Ajia filtered out the noisy drinkers and concentrated on what Drake was saying. "...and I repeat: Russian aggression will not be tolerated. Such unprovoked belligerence has no place in the modern, civilised world. I intend to contact Premier Vasilyev on the morning, when I will be having stern words."

Drake's sleek, silver-haired mugshot was replaced by a blonde newsreader. "Meanwhile, a build-up of Russian forces on the border with Estonia will be at the top of the agenda at tomorrow's meeting of European heads of state. Closer to home, Prime Minister Drake has repeated that hostile Russian military manoeuvres in the English Channel—where a submarine from the Russian navy was involved in a skirmish with a British navy frigate earlier today—will not be tolerated. The main news again..."

Ajia was about to look for the others when a still image on the TV screen rooted her to the spot.

Her blood ran cold. She looked up at her own face on the TV screen. Ridiculously, her first thought was to wonder where they had got the image. It must have been taken weeks ago during the police interrogation and confinement. The girl staring defiantly out of the screen appeared dazed and sleep-deprived, but recognisably her.

The anchor was saying, "...police have released a photograph of the suspect linked to the recent deaths of government security officers. Ajia Snell, eighteen, is described as an extremely dangerous terrorist who on no account should be approached by members of the public. Meanwhile..."

Her pulse pounding, Ajia stared around the bar. Miraculously, none of the drinkers seemed to have made the connection between the mugshot of the teenage terrorist and the scruffy girl self-consciously sipping her half lager.

The sooner she was out of here, she decided, the better.

The she recalled the suspicious glance of the publican in The Ploughman's. He'd been watching the TV news. He must have seen the lead story, and the image of the wanted eighteen-year-old terrorist.

She finished her drink in two gulps and was about to go in search of Mr LeRoy and Fletcher when someone touched her shoulder.

She jumped and turned, relieved to see Fletcher.

He stared at her. "What's wrong? You look like you've seen a ghost."

She made sure that none of the nearby drinkers could overhear her and said, nodding at the screen, "The news. The flashed up a fucking mugshot of me, didn't they? I'm officially a terrorist, responsible for the death of government security forces."

"Christ. Okay..." Fletcher looked away, thinking. "We've found Wolfson, only..."

"Let me guess. He's pissed?"

"As a fart," he said, leading the way to the next room.

Dustin Wolfson sat at a table by the window, swaying over a Guinness and whiskey chaser. He looked as if he had already been in a fight and come off second best. His hatchet face was puffy and blue with bruises, his right eye sulphurous with a day-old shiner. He was not alone. Two middle-aged, thuggish-looking men sat across the table from the ex-prize-fighter, occasionally jabbing a finger at him. Mr LeRoy sat at the end of the table, attempting to act as a mediator. "Now, now, gentlemen. I'm sure we can work this out amicably."

Fletcher laid a hand on Ajia's arm, restraining her from joining them.

Wolfson blinked at Mr LeRoy. "You're here, so you are," he slurred. "Or have I had one too many and I'm imagining you, Mr LeRoy? It's yourself, isn't it, in the flesh, as I live and breathe?"

"Indeed I am no hallucination, Dustin, my friend."

"Listen to me, fatso," one of the thugs said, leaning close to Mr LeRoy, "this little bleeder here owes us, so he does."

"But there you're wrong," Wolfson said, focusing with difficulty on his accuser. "I'm owing the likes of you nothing, not a penny."

"A bet's a bet," the second thug said. "Fifty nicker. In my palm." And so saying, he extended a meaty palm and held it before the sozzled pugilist.

"Mr LeRoy," Wolfson pleaded, "will you tell these gentlemen that I paid up me dues, so I have. And tell them... Tell them also that if they insist—*insist*—then I'll take them both outside and batter the both of 'em!"

Beside Ajia, Fletcher winced.

The first thug leaned forward. "Just say that again, Paddy!"

A strange transformation came over the Irishman then. Drunk and pathetic a second earlier, he seemed now to gather both dignity and strength as he sat up in his seat and faced the pair.

Mr LeRoy, perhaps sensing the danger, laid a hesitant hand on Wolfson arm. "Dustin, I have an idea. Why don't I pay these gentlemen what's owing and you come along with me?"

"But I owe the bastards not a single penny!" Wolfson roared. "And I'll prove it. Outside, the both of ye!"

Ajia touched Fletcher's arm. "I'm going. See you back at the farmhouse."

She turned to the door, and two things happened at once. Dustin Wolfson surged to his feet and tipped the table over the two thugs— and the publican of The Ploughman's appeared in the doorway. Mayhem broke out in the small room, the thugs laying into Wolfson and the fighter swinging like a windmill amid the shouts and cries of alarmed drinkers.

The publican pointed at Ajia and called out, "That's her!"

Two uniformed constables appeared behind the portly publican, squeezing past him into the room. Ajia looked for a way of escape.

JAMES LOVEGROVE

The snug was in chaos. Wolfson, raring like a demon, traded punches with the thugs, dodging their blows like the veteran fighter he was and dealing effective uppercuts that had the men's heads bobbing back comically.

Mr LeRoy danced nimbly to and fro, wincing and objecting, like a referee disconcerted that the Marquis of Queensberry rules were being flouted. Others had joined the affray. Someone broke a slate chessboard over Wolfson's head to no obvious effect. The fighter simply swung to face his assailant, sized him up, and jabbed him in the gut. The man went down. People fought in knots, as if the spontaneous outbreak of violence around them issued a carte blanche decree for old grievances to be resumed.

There was only one door in the room, and that was filled by the publican and a press of drinkers from the main bar come to witness the scrap. The first constable struggled through the mass of bodies towards Ajia. Fletcher, seeing the danger, worked himself between her and the policeman, buying her precious seconds. She dropped to all fours and scurried under a table. She peered out, trying to assess the situation. She saw the prize-fighter's nimble legs dance before her. He was taking on all-comers now. The constables stood in the middle of the room, turning in their search for her. The doorway was momentarily unblocked.

She rose like a sprinter from the blocks and slipped into Puck mode.

It was a mistake, and she knew it instantly.

She barrelled at speed into the publican from The Ploughman's, squelched into his padded bulk, and bounced off. The publican cried out in alarm, twirled like an outsized nine-pin, and in turn knocked down the curious gawpers behind him. Ajia bounced off the publican and fell down painfully on her rump.

She had a dazed view of what was happening. Someone had launched a table through the window, admitting a gust of fresh air, and drinkers were clambering through it. Mr LeRoy had captured and calmed a fuming Wolfson and was leading him towards the door.

Ajia tried to climb from her feet and launch herself at the window,

330

just as the constable dived at her and pinned her beneath his bulk. She struggled, but the fight was uneven, especially when he was joined by his colleague who—perhaps recalling the news reports that Ajia Snell, 18, was an extremely dangerous terrorist—pulled out his nightstick and clubbed her over the head.

As she slumped to the floor, she saw Mr LeRoy and Fletcher, with Wolfson between them, slip through the door. Her last thought was that at least they had managed to get away.

Ajia CAME TO her senses. She was in a cell. An old-fashioned police cell with a barred door, green-painted walls and a rubber mattress not quite thick enough to be comfortable.

She sat up and looked around. A small grille high up on the wall opposite the door showed the pale light of dawn. They had cuffed her, hand and foot, taking no chances. Well, she was a wanted terrorist, after all.

A constable showed himself in the corridor, come to stare. He recognised him as the one who had coshed her. He frowned at her, perhaps intrigued by the paradox she presented. That someone so slight, and feminine, could present such a threat. A terrorist. An extremely dangerous terrorist, responsible for the murder of security officers...

She looked away, and when she next glanced up he was gone.

An hour later she heard a commotion outside the cell, the beat of booted footsteps and a shouted command. She swung herself from the mattress and sat up, staring through the bars.

Two men in familiar uniforms showed themselves. Paladins. They were armed with assault rifles and, ridiculously, they aimed at her through the bars as if she presented a real and present danger.

She found herself laughing at them.

Another Paladin appeared, this one grey-haired and wearing a captain's uniform.

He spoke to one of the local policemen at his side. "That's her. Well done."

The sergeant puffed his chest. "All in a day's work, sir."

"Saved us a hell of a lot of bother, and saved untold lives. You'll be commended."

"Thank you, sir!"

The captain looked at Ajia. "Wouldn't think it, looking at her, would you? Slip of a thing. Butter wouldn't melt. And to think, a conscienceless killer…"

The sergeant shook his head sagely. "Who'd've thought it?"

"Right," the captain nodded to the two accompanying Paladins, "let's get her out of here."

One Paladin slipped into the cell and stood against the wall, covering her with his rifle. The sergeant and another constable took her upper arm and pulled her to her feet.

Between the local bobbies, with armed Paladins fore and aft, she was escorted from the cell, up a flight of stairs, and along a corridor.

A blue armoured van was drawn up to the rear exit of the station. The bobbies eased her into the rear of the vehicle and into a barred cage. The two armed Paladins sat on fold-down seats outside the cage. The rear doors were slammed shut and the vehicle set off.

Ajia squatted in the cage and closed her eyes.

THIRTY

Major Dominic Wynne needed a break, a decent roll of the dice, a smile from Lady Luck.

Because recently his fortunes had gone from bad to worse.

On a professional front, the last two operations he'd mounted had ended in abject failure, with the humiliating defeat of his finest men by a rag-tag band of folkloric renegades.

And Harriet Drake had decided, for some reason, to withdraw her sexual favours.

He missed her like hell.

Or did he? Did he actually miss Harriet, the person, or did he miss the psychological pat on the back he'd awarded himself for shafting the boss's wife?

The fact was, he wasn't getting any from that particular source, and his ego was bruised.

And, to put the tin lid on it, Derek Drake was being more than a little brusque with him of late. Was it possible, he asked himself, that the Prime Minister had got to know about his dalliance with Harriet?

Then, just when Wynne was expecting a call from Drake with word of his demotion, Lady Luck chose to smile on him.

Not once, but twice.

The first was in the form of a call from Lieutenant Noble.

"We've got her, sir!"

"What?"

"Snell. We've got her."

Wynne could hardly believe his luck. "Well done, Lieutenant. But how…?"

The trail had gone cold. Snell and the others had vanished after the massacre at Bradford.

"Well, it was couple of village bobbies up in the Lake District," Noble explained. "Arrested her at a kerfuffle in a pub."

"Village bobbies?" Wynne echoed, incredulous. "And what about the others?"

"Snell appeared to be alone, sir, and she isn't saying a dicky-bird about where the bastards might be. She's in a holding cell in Cumbria. I'm heading there as I speak. I'll soften her up for you, sir."

"Very good, Lieutenant. Do that. I'm on my way. And let's see how long she can keep schtum about the whereabouts of her friends, once I get to work on her."

The second phone call, a minute later while Wynne was arranging for a chopper to take him north, was from the commanding officer of Stronghold Two, the Paladins' secondary base situated on the outskirts of Manchester.

"Major Wynne? We have a creature in custody which claims he— it—might be able to assist you."

Wynne blinked. "A creature?"

"A phouka, sir. My men captured the critter in Northern Island a couple of days ago. And a nasty little phouka it is, too."

"And it claims…?"

"That it can help you, Major. It would like an audience."

"An audience?" Wynne hesitated. "And it's safe to approach this… phouka?"

"Oh, we have it well shackled, sir."

"But it doesn't say how exactly it can assist me?"

"It refuses to say anything other than it wants to see you, face to face."

Wynne thought about it. "Very well, Captain. I'm on my way."

*　　*　　*

WYNNE WAS MET at the gates of Stronghold Two by Captain Whiteley and escorted along the innumerable corridors of the concrete blockhouse.

They came to a cell with a door like that of a bank vault. Whiteley tapped the code into the lock and the door sighed open.

The cell was divided into two equal halves, separated by an inch-thick wall of bulletproof glass.

"Christ," Wynne said as he stared at the creature crouching behind the glass.

"Told you it was a nasty little phouka," Whiteley said. "Just knock when you've finished, sir." He stepped from the cell and the door sighed shut behind him.

Wynne approached the glass and stared at the monstrosity within.

It climbed to its feet and approached the glass, returning his gaze.

The manikin was vaguely familiar—and then he recalled where he'd seen its likeness before. Gollum in the film of *The Lord of the Rings*: the same thin limbs and swollen head, the same crouching, servile manner. It was dressed in rags and looked pathetic and ineffectual, and Wynne wondered how this creature had the gall to think it could help him.

"You wanted to see me," Wynne said.

The monstrosity blinked its huge milky eyes. "I can help you," it said in a broken croak.

Wynne smiled. "I very much doubt that," he sneered.

"You want Bron LeRoy, Reed Fletcher, Wayland Smith and the others."

Wynne tried not to look surprised. "How do you know?"

The phouka gave a sickly grin. "Oh, I know so much, Major Wynne. So much. When your men snared me, their minds were open, their every thought available to me. As are yours."

"Rubbish!" Wynne snapped, uneasy.

The phouka sniggered. A sly looked passed over its hideous features. "You miss the woman," it said, stunning Wynne. "Oh, how you miss her. You miss mastering her, making her submit to your desires."

Wynne felt himself colouring. "How the hell…?"

"And also you very much want to see the renegades dead for their crimes against your men, Major Wynne. And I can help you."

"How?"

"Watch," said the phouka.

Before his eyes the creature seemed to grow, expand. And as it did so, its appearance underwent a definite and substantial transformation. Its flesh flowed, filled out; no longer was it ugly. In fact, Wynne thought, little by little, it was becoming quite handsome.

A minute later he was staring at a very presentable simulacrum of himself.

The little phouka was a shapeshifter.

"As I said," the phouka repeated, "I can help you."

DRAKE LED HARRIET from their bedroom to his study.

He settled her on the leather sofa and booted up his laptop.

"This is exciting," Harriet cooed. "A film show?"

"You could say that," Drake said. "The Russians have been up to their old tricks again."

"Old tricks?"

He joined her on the sofa. "Watch," he said. "These went viral a little earlier today."

The first clip showed Edward Winterton rogering the rent boy. Harriet watched, goggle-eyed. "But I didn't think Winterton was into…"

"He wasn't," Drake said. "This is Premier Vasilyev's little joke. All part of bringing disrepute to my government, and to the country at large. It's a measure of the man that he'd try to defame someone who disappeared months ago." He waved at the screen. "This is a mock-up, needless to say. As are all the others."

Next he played a sequence showing the writer Victor Shepperton vigorously tonguing the dilated anus of a prepubescent schoolgirl. Drake had to hand it to Dudley. The youngster was a genius. The images were incredibly realistic.

"Ugh!" Harriet objected. "I really don't want to see any more."

"Just one more, my dear," Drake said. "I'd like you see it now, with me, rather than have some 'well-wisher' email it to you."

"Whatever do you mean by that?"

"Watch."

He played the clip of him and the Russian journalist bonking in an upstairs room at Number 10.

Harriet watched, her mouth hanging open. She leaned forward, peering intently. Still watching, her hand found his and squeezed.

At last, surprising him, she laughed.

"Harriet?"

She turned to him and stroked his cheek. "It's so obvious a fake, my darling, that you didn't have to worry about me seeing it alone. But I appreciate you showing it to me. That can't have been easy."

Drake smiled, relieved. He thought he might have had his work cut out convincing Harriet of his innocence.

She gestured at the screen. "Vasilyev might have captured your likeness, Derek, but he failed you in one very vital department. You're far, far more athletic than the wimpy stand-in they used as your double."

"Why, thank you, Harriet."

Her hand traced a line down his chest to his crotch. She was flushed and breathing hard. The little porn show had ignited the fires he thought he had quenched earlier that morning.

He should have known.

"Here?" he asked.

"Here," she panted.

Later, lying naked with limbs entwined, Harriet said, "I've been thinking."

"Mmm?" Drake was drifting into a delicious post-coital slumber.

"What you told me the other day, about those eidolons, and what happened after the helicopter crash."

He opened one eye. "What about it?"

"So, various souls around the land were brought back to life as these eidolons, Robin Hood, Puck, Oberon and others. All with special powers, abilities, strengths."

"Go on."

"I've been thinking about you, Derek, and how you were changed after the accident."

"Me?"

"It hasn't occurred to you?"

"Well, I was blessed with the Holy Grail, with Emrys Sage's transformation, his advice, counsel and leadership."

"No," she said. "More than that."

He propped himself up on one elbow and looked at her. "More? What do you mean?"

"Didn't it ever occur to you after the accident and your rise, the way you transformed the country, the way you restored national pride... Didn't it occur to you that you, too, were an eidolon?"

The idea rocked him. It was so vast a concept that he didn't, at first, know what to make of it—whether to be elated at the prospect, or dismayed that whatever greatness was in him was not innate but the result of some kind of supernatural takeover.

He shook his head, slowly. "No," he said. "No, Harriet, I must admit that it didn't. But..."

"Yes?"

"I think... Yes, I think I quite like the idea."

She stroked his cheek. "And the next, obvious question is...?"

He stared at her, then murmured, "Is 'Who?'."

"Exactly," she smiled. "Perhaps, Derek, you'd better ask Emrys for the answer."

Drake dressed and hurried to the stable block.

HIS HANDS TREMBLING, he entered the code to the chamber wherein sat the Holy Grail, then stepped inside.

He approached the relic and knelt.

"I bend the knee in supplication," he said.

"You are a good and faithful servant," said Emrys.

"And you, the bringer of hope and realiser of dreams."

"With you, I am shared among the people."

"And without you, I am nothing."

Drake stood and licked his lips.

"You seem… flushed," Emrys said.

"Vasilyev's been up to his old tricks, but I think I've spiked his guns."

"Ah, the compromising footage."

"You know about that?"

"I know everything, Derek."

"I got Dudley to beat Vasilyev with his own stick," Drake said. "Manufacture a few faked clips and pass them off as coming from Russia."

"And it has worked."

"Well, Harriet is convinced." He rubbed his chin. "I'm not so sure about the electorate, or some of my colleagues. Questions have been asked in parliament. Apparently there's an opposition journalist trying to dig the dirt."

Emrys spoke, and Drake was reassured as much by the warmth in his friend's voice as by the content of what he said. "Do not worry yourself on that score," Emrys said. "The end is approaching. The endgame, you might say. We must leave for Somerset in the morning."

"Leave?" Drake was nonplussed. "Why?"

"Because it is there that you will make your last stand, my friend."

Drake said. "Last stand?"

"Somerset," Emrys said. "Avalon."

Drake repeated the word, shaking his head. "Avalon…"

"You must surely see the connection. Especially," Emrys went on, "after Harriet's earlier… revelation. Avalon—Fairleigh Castle. Why do you think I suggested you buy the pile?" He hesitated. "Who do you think you are, Derek?"

A sudden heat passed through Drake's head. He felt dizzy. "I… I am…?"

"Who else?" Emrys said. "The leader that history claims will rise when our great nation is under threat; the warrior monarch destined to lead the people of Albion to safety, the man who will vanquish all enemies, no matter how powerful, and emerge triumphant. Our saviour."

Drake felt himself expand. "You mean…?"

"I mean," said Emrys, "that you are none other than King Arthur."

THIRTY-ONE

AJIA WAS TRANSFERRED from the armoured vehicle, marched down another long corridor, and locked into a cell. This one was modern, with vault-like doors. When it closed on her, with a muffled *whumph* of air, she felt suddenly, horribly, claustrophobic.

She sat on a narrow bunk and considered the events of the past few days. If it were to end here, then at least she had contributed something to the cause. She had saved the lives of good people, and assisted Mr LeRoy towards achieving his desired aim. She had succeeded, triumphed, even.

She was being selfish if she allowed herself to wish that she could be free, free to be with the others for the final fight, free to kill more Paladins and see Derek Drake defeated.

She was being selfish but, more than anything else, freedom was what she wanted.

And the desire was all the more painful, and poignant, for her knowing that it was impossible.

They would kill her. The authorities had killed her once, without any provocation at all, and she had no doubt that they would do so again—whether in the process of torturing information from her, or in the due process of enacting the law of the land and executing her as a criminal killer.

She was as good as dead, but she had one more duty to perform.

She must not betray her friends, no matter how much they tortured her.

She had to be strong.

The cell door opened, startling her.

Two armed Paladins rushed in as if storming a building and levelled their rifles at her. They were followed by a cruel-faced, dark-haired lieutenant clutching a nightstick.

He stood over her, repeatedly thwacking the nightstick into his palm.

"Ajia Snell," he said, smiling down at her without the slightest trace of humour in his expression, "you murdered a considerable number of my colleagues. And you didn't act alone."

She remained silent and switched her gaze to the floor.

The lieutenant went on. "You murdered Paladins near Dawley, Derbyshire, and then on the outskirts of Bradford you murdered a further eleven before fleeing with Bron LeRoy and the others."

She stared at her trainers, anticipating the first blow.

"We have a witness to the Derbyshire killings," he said, "and the method of murder in Bradford suggest the same perpetrator."

A witness? So had one of the Paladins survived? Was that how they had managed to trace the minibus from Derbyshire to Bradford?

"Where are the others? Bron LeRoy. Wayland Smith. Reed Fletcher. Daisy Hawthorn. Paul Klein"—he pronounced each name with evident distaste—"as well as other assorted... undesirables."

She looked up at him. "You bastards killed me once," she said. "Two coppers arrested me for mocking our Great Leader, tortured me so I'd confess. But they got a bit carried away, didn't they? And I died. So if you think you bastards can make me talk, you're wrong." She smiled up at him. "So why don't you just kill me now and have done?"

He stared at her, his face expressionless.

"Where is Bron LeRoy?"

"Fuck off—"

The blow was all the more painful for being unexpected. The

nightstick smacked against her right knee, and despite herself she cried out in pain and squirmed against the wall.

"I suggest you make this easy for yourself," he said. "Simply tell me where your friends are, or by God will you suffer."

"Fuck yourself!"

Lightning fast, he lashed her across the head. Her skull rang with the blow.

He smiled down at her. "You murdered more than thirty good men, Snell. Men doing their duty."

She tried to match the sneer in his voice. "You mean cowards crawling to the commands of your fascist leader."

He hit her across the temple again, stunning her.

"As I said, good men doing their duty..."

"Good men? Not good enough! You ought to train them better, you know? They were a bit on the slow side."

"So you admit you murdered them?"

"No, I executed the bastards before they could kill my friends. And you know what, I enjoyed executing every last one of the scum!"

She winced in anticipation of another blow.

It never came.

When she looked up, the lieutenant was smiling.

"Oh, I pity you, Ajia Snell," he said.

He marched from the cell, followed by the armed guards.

The door *whumphed* shut behind them.

SHE MUST HAVE fallen asleep.

She came awake suddenly at the sound of the cell door opening.

Four armed Paladins hauled her to her feet while one of their number shackled her ankles and wrists. She marched her from the cell at an awkward shuffle, escorted by the sadistic lieutenant. They loaded her into the back of a waiting armoured car identical to the one that had brought her here. She was locked into a cage guarded by two armed Paladins. The vehicle started up and drove off.

She closed her eyes and wondered where her friends were now, whether Mr LeRoy had recruited more eidolons and was right now heading south. The desire to be with them, among the people she had come to think of as family, was like an ache.

Perhaps an hour later the vehicle stopped and the doors swung open. The armed Paladins hauled her from the cage, and they were led by the lieutenant along a grey concrete corridor and into a vast chamber. In the centre of the chamber stood a white, corrugated shipping container.

The lieutenant crossed to the container and opened a door in its flank, then gestured for the guards to escort her inside. He favoured her with a mirthless smile as she shuffled past him.

Something about the interior of the container frightened her.

It was obvious that it had been specially repurposed. She passed down a short corridor towards an door like that of a bank vault. A Paladin swung it open to reveal what looked very much like a padded cell. The guard jabbed her in the ribs with the muzzle of his rifle. "Inside."

She stumbled into the cell and the Paladins followed her in. One attached her ankle shackles to a hook in the far corner, then retreated. The door sighed shut behind them as they left. The back of the door was, like the four walls, floor and ceiling, covered in large, diamond-shaped, quilted padding.

She sat down and snuggled into the corner. The cell aroused a primal fear of the unknown within her. But at least, she told herself, it was more comfortable than the last place. The padding was thick, like a mattress, and the room was warm.

Be strong, she told herself.

Don't show the bastards how frightened you are.

THE PADDED DOOR swung open. It couldn't have been more than ten minutes since her arrival.

Something was prodded inside.

Something...

A monster.

Ajia scrambled into a crouching position and pressed herself into the padded corner.

Beyond the thing, the lieutenant was staring at it with obvious distaste. He stepped forward and jabbed the monster with his nightstick. It lurched into the cell and landed on all fours. The doors swung shut.

The monster braced itself on its thin arms, for all the world like a sprinter about to launch itself at her. Ajia made a sound of revulsion in her throat and tried to squirm deeper into the padding.

The thing was small, perhaps no taller than three feet tall, an emaciated creature with stick-limbs and a huge bald, domed head. It wore a ragged loin-cloth and nothing else, and its huge eyes stared at her with inhuman intensity.

As if its appearance were not bad enough, it stank. Ajia had never inhaled the scent of a month-old corpse, but she suspected that it could be no worse than the putrescent stench that wafted from the being before her.

A zombie child—or an ancient man who had died and returned to life?

She recalled the monsters which had confronted her in Sherwood Forest, and what Fletcher had told her about them. That the Paladins had a cadre of these uglies, to use against their enemies.

This was one of them.

As she stared at the monster, she wondered if her fear was affecting her vision. The thing seemed to blur before her, lose its definition. She wondered if she were passing out, and fought to keep conscious. Who knew what depravities the creature might get up to if she were to pass out.

Not that it might desist if she were to remain conscious, she thought.

She found her voice. "What do you want?" She kept her breathing shallow, so as not to fill her lungs with its corpse-stench.

The thing had risen to its claw-like bare feet, hunched over, but still staring at her.

As she watched, it jerked spasmodically, its emaciated limbs twitching. It seemed hardly in control of its movements, a marionette controlled by a palsied puppet-master.

Its head rolled on its scrawny neck and its face—huge eyes, tiny hooked nose and slit mouth—contorted as if in pain.

And it blurred again, and Ajia knew that this time it was nothing to do with her vision.

The grey-blue skin of its arms and legs pulsed, as if maggots writhed beneath the surface of the monster's flesh. It fell to its knees, and its hands rose to its head in a gesture at once horrible and somehow familiar.

Then she had it: Edvard Munch's *The Scream*.

It gibbered. It emitted a strong of high-pitched gibberish, not one word recognisable to Ajia.

It looked as if, for all the world, it were fighting with some inner demon.

The monster jerked, and flung itself back against the far wall, where it slid down into a sitting position and stared across at her.

It appeared oddly calm now, and its gibbering had ceased.

Its breathing was slow. Measured. Even.

It spoke, and its voice was at odds with its earlier high-pitched outburst. For one thing, Ajia understood every word.

"Do not be afraid," it said in a deep-throated croak.

"Who...? What are you?" Her heartbeat thudded in her ears.

The monster replied, "The body I inhabit... it is known as a phouka."

"You 'inhabit'?" she echoed. "But... So who are you?"

"That does not matter. Indeed, it's better that you don't know, for now."

Ajia drew her knees up to her chest and hugged hers shins. "But... But you work for the Paladins?"

"The phouka does, yes. But I control it, now. As I said, do not be afraid, I am on your side."

"On my side?"

She was instantly suspicious. This was too good to be true. The Paladins were tricking her. They were using the phouka to elicit the information about the whereabouts of Mr LeRoy and the others.

"Just who the hell are you?" she asked.

The phouka hesitated, then said, "I am responsible for... for everything that has happened to you, to Mr LeRoy, Wayland Smith and all the others. Every eidolon now roaming this benighted country. All my doing, Ajia."

She shook her head. She wanted to believe it, but knew that it would be dangerous to do so. This was a ploy of the Paladins.

"So why are you here?"

"To help you escape," said the phouka, "to reach Mr LeRoy and the others, to communicate with him."

"Escape?" She didn't know whether to laugh or to cry. What sick game were they playing with her?

"Escape? In case you haven't noticed, we're locked in a fucking box surrounded by armed Paladins. How the fuck do you think we can escape?"

The phouka seemed unperturbed by her outburst. "You can escape, not I."

That treacherous spasm of hope again, fluttering within her chest.

"Escape how?"

"The phouka is a unique creature from Irish mythology," said the thing before her. "It can transform itself. Metamorphose. It is a shapeshifter."

"A shapeshifter?" She nodded, still very wary. "Okay. A shapeshifter. So how the hell will that help me get out of here?"

The phouka gestured, turning its long, taloned hand in the air. "Why, by changing its shape," it said.

She considered this. "I don't buy it, buddy. So the Paladins just threw you in here so you could help me escape? No, you work for them."

"They *think* I work for them," it said. "Indeed the phouka does, or did. But as I said, I have taken control of its form, to assist you. And I will do so."

Ajia stared.

The phouka was changing its appearance.

Its feet transformed first. From thin hideous, sinewy claws, they gained substance, changed colour. It was as if her vision was blurring, as if she couldn't trust the evidence of her eyes. The phouka's feet were no longer bare feet, but...

She blinked. They had changed into a pair of blue Nike trainers, and the ankles above them were no longer stair-rod thin but fleshy and shaped and clothed in white socks, and its legs now wore black jogging bottoms.

"I don't believe it."

She stared at the creature's head—or rather where its head has been. It was as if she were looking into a mirror, staring at a perfect reflection of herself, identical in every way.

Soon all that remained of the phouka of old was a lingering remnant of its foul body odour.

The creature, the semblance of herself in every detail, stared back at her with something like insouciance in its—her—expression.

But could she trust this being?

Or was it part of the Paladins' masterplan?

"So?" She shook her head. "I still don't see—"

"The Paladins will return, take you away from here, and let you go."

She sneered. "Just like that? And why the fuck would they let me go?"

"Because I, the controller of this body, as I mentioned earlier, formulated the plan. They will let you go because they will think that *you're* the phouka, mimicking Ajia Snell, and you will then lead them to what they want—Mr LeRoy, Wayland Smith, Reed Fletcher and all the others—with this."

The phouka did another remarkable thing. It reached a hand into its chest—Ajia watched, incredulous, as its slim brown fingers passed through the material of its T-shirt to a depth of inches—and produced a slim silver cylinder perhaps two inches long.

"And what the fuck," she said, "is that?"

The Phouka smiled with her face. "A tracking device. You will secrete this about your person, leave here and return to your people—leading the Paladins, or so they hope, to Mr LeRoy and the others."

"And you, the controller, set all this up? Persuaded them to use the phouka, then took it over?"

"Exactly," it said, smiling the smile she had seen so often in her bathroom mirror. "I said I would help them if they agreed to set me free."

There was, she thought, something not quite right about what it claimed.

Then she had it. The flaw. The lapse of logic that proved the phouka was working for the Paladins, despite everything it said.

She pointed across at the perfect simulacrum of herself and said, "But how did you persuade the Paladins that the phouka, having transformed itself into me, would know where the hell Mr LeRoy and the others were?"

She stared across at the phouka, triumphant.

The creature matched her smile. "Because I told them that as well as taking on your physical form, the phouka would have access to your memories. I told the Paladins that you would know where Mr LeRoy and the others were, or were going, and that I would have those memories and would lead them there."

Ajia was aware of her pulse again, as hope grew.

"And," she began tentatively, "when I get out of here—*if* I get out of her—I'll take the tracking device, lose it somewhere, then go on my own way and try to locate Mr LeRoy?"

The phouka inclined its head. "I would advise you to set the Paladins on a wild goose chase, leaving this"—it held the cylinder up before its face—"on some form of transport heading north. Then you will head south and locate your friends."

"Easier said than done, pal. I don't know where they are."

"I do, Ajia."

She blinked. "You do?"

"They are presently travelling down the M5 in a pantechnicon, followed by three other vehicles containing eidolons and assorted folkloric allies, towards the West Country. By nightfall they will have reached the village of Hewden, and a woodland on its outskirts, where they will make camp. You will rendezvous with them there, with this information. Listen carefully, and report this to Mr LeRoy in every detail."

Ajia leaned forward, holding her breath. "Go on."

"You will meet up with Dr Neve Winterton, who runs the Cry-Org Cryogenic Research Institute near Glastonbury."

She nodded. "Neve Winterton," she repeated. "But why does Mr

LeRoy need to meet this Winterton person—and for that matter, just who the hell are you?"

The phouka shook its head. "It is better if you remain in ignorance, Ajia, in case…"

"In case the Paladins capture me again and torture the facts out of me, right?"

"And now take this," said the phouka, "and hide it about your person." It passed her the cylinder and she slipped it into the pocket of her trainers.

Then she saw the cuffs on her wrists and ankles. "Just one problem here," she said. "How the hell do I get out of these things?"

Her mirror image smiled again, pushed itself from the wall, and crouched before her.

The phouka placed a finger on the locking mechanism of the cuffs shackling her wrists, and something thin and white—a length of bone?—extruded from the flesh of its fingertip and inserted itself into the keyhole. The phouka twisted its finger this way and that, and the manacles sprang apart.

Ajia rubbed her wrists as the creature used the gruesome osseous key to perform the same operation on the cuffs shackling her ankles. In seconds she was free.

She moved to the far wall against which the phouka had crouched, while the creature placed the manacles on its ankles and wrists and snapped them shut.

They sat against the walls, regarding each other.

"When the Paladins return," said the phouka, "they will take you from here and drop you, as per my instructions, at Manchester Piccadilly station. There you will 'lose' the tracker and board a train south. Do not worry that they will be following you. It will be the tracker they'll be concentrating on. And also," the creature added, "do not in any way evince any hostility or resentment towards your captors when they lead you away from here. And do not speak while in their company, as you will be unable to replicate the phouka's tone of voice, and so give yourself away."

Ajia nodded, still only half-believing that any of this was true.

Was she really about to be released by the Paladins, or was it merely part of some devious scheme she was too stupid to fathom?

"I told the Paladins that the transformation would take one hour," said the phouka. "I estimate that we have only ten minutes left to wait."

She looked across at the phouka. "And you?" she asked. "What will happen when the Paladins realise that you're not really me?"

The phouka smiled. "I can maintain the phouka in this guise for perhaps another three or four hours. Then I shall relinquish control. I will take great delight in watching their consternation when they realise their mistake."

"But will they take it out on the creature?"

The phouka shook its head. "It's too valuable an asset for them to harm it. Though they will be mystified as to how the mix-up happened."

Ajia smiled at the thought, then sat back against the wall and closed her eyes.

She wondered at Mr LeRoy's reaction when she walked, as large as life, into their woodland campsite near Bristol that evening.

Best not look too far ahead.

The cell door opened, startling her. She opened her eyes, her pulse loud in her ears.

Two armed Paladins entered the cell, one of them training his rifle on the phouka shackled in the far corner while the other covered Ajia. The lieutenant followed them in, glancing from Ajia to the phouka. He smiled down at the shackled creature, which he assumed to be her, Ajia, and sneered, "We'll attend to you later."

The phouka gave him a resentful stare, brilliant in its mimicry of her, then lowered its face to its raised knees.

The lieutenant nodded to the armed Paladins, indicating Ajia. "Get this thing out of here," he said.

One of the guards took Ajia by the upper arm and pulled her to he feet. Recalling the phouka's instructions, she rose without demur, sleepwalker-like, and followed the guards from the cell.

They marched her from the shipping container. The lieutenant crossed to where a tall, familiar figure was standing watching the operation, and saluted.

Ajia stared at the officer.

Major Wynne, the bastard who had shot Perry dead at Summer Land all those days ago.

Her first impulse was to shout her rage at him—but she recalled her saviour's instructions, quelled her rage, and kept her expression neutral.

She was escorted to a small room, still under armed guard, and there the lieutenant passed her a manila envelope. "For contingencies, as you'll be needing cash. I understand you've been briefed on what to do?"

Ajia took the envelope and nodded, keeping her expression blank.

"And you have the tracker?"

Ajia touched her chest.

"Very well," the lieutenant said, obviously uncomfortable in the presence of the shapeshifting creature in the guise of his erstwhile captive. "Good luck."

He nodded to the guards, who escorted her along the corridor and into the back of the armoured car. Once again she was locked in a cage and driven away at speed.

Even now, when it seemed that she was almost free, Ajia couldn't allow herself to believe it. What if whoever was inhabiting the phouka lost control, and the Paladins realised their mistake and contacted the driver?

She tried not to dwell on that awful possibility.

Her thoughts were brought up short when the armoured car came to a halt and the rear door swung open. A Paladin unlocked the cage and gestured for her to get out.

They were in the car park of a big railway station, milling with commuters. The sight of them—everyday, ordinary people going about their everyday, ordinary lives—made Ajia realise that perhaps she would soon, truly, be free.

"Right, you little phouka," the Paladin said, laughing at his joke. "On you way."

Keeping her expression neutral, Ajia strode from the vehicle and joined the flow of pedestrians moving towards the station entrance.

Even then, when she passed into the station and out of sight of her captors, she felt that her freedom was too good to be true. She turned and studied the crowd flowing in after her, but saw no Paladins and no one paying her any attention.

She clutched the tracker in her pocket and wondered at the best course of action.

She hurried through the station until she found an information display listing all the departing trains. A train for Glasgow was leaving the station in seven minutes. She took the escalators to the footbridge and hurried to platform fourteen.

Before boarding the train, she looked back along the length of the platform. No one appeared to be watching her. She slipped on to the last carriage and found an empty seat. She took the tracker from her pocket and stared at it, gave it a quick kiss and inserted it down the side of the cushion, then checked her handiwork. The slim silver cylinder was hidden from sight.

Two minutes before the train was due to depart, she alighted and made her way to the main concourse where she found an information display. A train for Bristol was due to leave from platform five in twenty minutes.

Ajia hurried to the ticket office, bought a single to Bristol Temple Meads, and boarded the train when it pulled into the station.

Only when she settled into a window seat and the train pulled away from the platform did she allow herself to believe that she had done it. She was free.

AT BRISTOL, AJIA found a newsagents and bought a map of the area, then picked up a train and bus timetable. At a café she bought a cup of tea, a sandwich and jam doughnut. She devoured the meal while poring over the spread map and timetables. She need to get her strength up. She had a lot of running to do in the next few hours.

She found the village of Hewden on the map, twenty miles south east of Bristol, but decided that it would be a waste of energy to run all the way. A local bus ran to Hewden, leaving Bristol in forty-five minutes.

She studied the map. There were two patches of woodland marked near the village, either of which might be where Mr LeRoy and his entourage were planning to camp for the night.

It was now just after six o'clock. She finished her coffee and made her way to the bus station.

Thirty minutes later she was riding in the almost empty single-decker, trundling slowly between the rural towns and villages in this idyllic part of the west country. It was the end of a bright summer's day, with sunlight turning the green land hazy. She watched the rolling farmland and occasional village pass slowly by, anticipating her reunion with Mr LeRoy and the others.

When the bus stopped at Hewden, she climbed down, consulted her map, then left the station. She walked from the village in the direction of the first patch of woodland. When she was sure that she was unobserved, she slipped into Puck mode and sprinted southeast.

She laughed into the headwind. The world slowed around her as she tore along the winding country lane. Only now, sprinting freely for the first time in what felt like days, did she feel truly liberated. She wondered about the phouka, and whether the Paladins had realised their mistake yet. She recalled the lieutenant, striking her with his nightstick, and relished the thought of the shit he would find himself in for allowing her escape on his watch.

She came to the woodland on the side of a hill overlooking a collection of honey-coloured cottages. It was small, scarcely more than a spinney, and it was obvious within a minute of searching that Mr LeRoy's convoy was not here.

She consulted her map again, found the second, larger woodland to the north of the village, then located it in reality—a haze of green occupying a hillside perhaps a mile away.

Ajia sprinted, almost bursting at the thought of meeting her friends... her family.

She slowed, pushed through a hawthorn hedge, then climbed the hill towards the woods. She found a lane winding into its interior. Her heart surged when she saw, in the ruts on either side of the tussocky central strip, the impression of fresh tyre tracks.

She sprinted up the hillside and stopped dead when she came to the clearing.

She fought back tears as she gazed at the idyllic woodland scene.

Two big removal trucks and three small vans were drawn up in the clearing, and perhaps a hundred people—humans, boggarts, goblins, elves and brownies, were gathered around a central fire.

She saw Mr LeRoy, seated like the king he was on a fallen tree trunk. He was deep in conversation with tall, rangy Smith and the smaller, lithe figure of Reed Fletcher. To one side Daisy Hawthorn was laughing at something a brownie was telling her.

As Ajia stared at the gathering, she realised she didn't recognise most of the faces: these were the people Mr LeRoy had dragooned since leaving Cumbria—fellow travellers in the fight against Drake and the Paladins.

Someone saw her as she stood very still on the margin of the clearing, and a silence swept over the gathering. Faces turned her way, the curious eyes of strangers wondering who she might be, and the incredulous gazes of those individuals who knew very well who she was.

Mr LeRoy exclaimed, and Fletcher hauled him to his feet accompanied him as he made his way, at first slowly but with increasing haste, to where she stood.

He stopped a couple of yards from her, tears streaming down his cheeks. "Ajia? Puck? Is it...? Can it be...? Is it really you?"

Daisy Hawthorn joined him, smiling as she looked at Ajia. She held out her arms.

Ajia hugged her, then Mr LeRoy, then Reed Fletcher, and Smith, and all the others, the brownies and elves and boggarts with whom she had shared the fight in Derbyshire.

"But we left you for dead!" Mr LeRoy cried. "We assumed the worst. And here you are! But how?"

He led her across the clearing, a buzz of conversation filling the air as those who didn't know Ajia were apprised of the miracle of her return. She sat on a log before the fire, and Fletcher thrust a bottle of beer into her hand. She raised it in a silent toast, and little by little—with much questioning and amazed interjections from the listeners—told the tale of her arrest by the Paladins and her eventual escape.

"And the phouka had an important message," she told Mr LeRoy at last. "We must rendezvous with someone called Dr Neve Winterton, at the Cry-Org Institute in Glastonbury."

Mr LeRoy nodded to himself at this. "That makes sense. Glastonbury... *Avalon*. And Neve Winterton, who is surely going to be the last eidolon recruit on this long and arduous journey. And then, my friends," he finished, staring round at the gathered faces, "and then let the last battle commence!"

THIRTY-TWO

HARDLY ABLE TO contain his euphoria, Major Wynne watched as the phouka, transformed into an incredible likeness of Ajia Snell, was escorted from the warehouse.

The tide was turning. His run of bad luck and ill-fortune, which had started with the defeat of his forces in Derbyshire and continued with Harriet's inexplicable snubbing of him, was coming to an end. Soon the phouka would lead him to LeRoy and his murderous renegades, and this time there would be no pussyfooting around. He would be merciless. He would isolate LeRoy's forces and bomb the holy fuck out of the bastards.

The notion brought a smile to his face.

But before that, there was the little matter of Ajia Snell to deal with.

He would be merciless with her, too.

She was responsible for the deaths of over thirty of his men, horribly murdered in the line of duty. Their deaths had proved two things: that she was both dangerous and desperate, which was always a lethal combination.

Fortunately, now, she was in no position to be dangerous, although she might be desperate. And despairing.

Wynne paused outside the container, anticipating the imminent encounter.

Manacled as she was, hand and foot, she would provide little opposition. Robbed of her only attribute, speed, she would be at his mercy.

Oh, how the little bitch would suffer.

A little softening up, to begin with. Verbal, at first. He would taunt her. Let he know who was in command. Remind her why she was here. Let her know that she would pay dearly for her crimes.

And after the words, which would put the fear of God into her, a little physical work-over.

He had a nightstick to hand, and he might employ that at first. But what he was really looking forward to was hitting her with his fists, beating her into puling, wailing submission.

And then...

And then the real fun would begin.

He was feeling more than a little deprived in that department of late, since Harriet's withdrawal of her favours.

But his lust would soon be assuaged.

"Lieutenant Noble."

His second-in-command crossed to him. "Sir?"

Wynne indicated the container. "I'm going in there to question the prisoner. I might be some time, and I do not want to be disturbed. Understood?"

Noble grinned. "Perfectly, sir."

"You might want to have a go yourself, when I've finished."

The lieutenant's grin intensified. "Sloppy seconds, sir?"

Wynne grimaced. "If you must put it like that, Lieutenant. Unlock the door."

Noble did so, and Wynne stepped into the container. When the outer door slammed shut behind him, he moved down the corridor and unlocked the cell door.

What a pathetic sight the girl presented.

Curled in a corner, shackled hand and foot, head in her hands, snivelling.

In his mind's eye he recalled her as gamine, lithe and pert-breasted.

But, over the course of her detention, she had lost any attractiveness she might have had.

When she looked up and stared defiantly at him, she seemed puffy-faced and almost... ugly. And her trim teenage body appeared to have lost some of its shape.

Wynne leaned against the wall across from her and let the silence stretch.

At last she looked away, submissive.

He smiled.

"I'll give you this, you're a fighter."

She flicked him a contemptuous glance but said nothing.

"And I like to see that in a woman. Or even a girl. A little spunk. But I think you've chosen the wrong enemy this time. Oh, you might have dealt my forces a minor blow here and there, but then it's led to this, hasn't it? Your arrest, and the imminent annihilation of Bron LeRoy and his terrorists." He paused, then went on, "I'd very much like to hear you say you regret your actions."

Her eyes stared at him blankly. "Go to hell," she croaked, sounding far from her old self.

He laughed and pushed himself from the wall.

"First, I would like an apology, for the deaths you've caused, for all the trouble you've put me and my men to."

She looked away, muttering something to herself.

"What was that? Did I hear a 'sorry'?"

She remained staring at the door.

Enraged, he stepped forward and swung his nightstick.

He caught her a hefty blow across the cheek, and was surprised by the effect it had, or rather the lack of effect. It was as if her face had absorbed the impact. She hardly flinched, and Wynne had the odd impression of the weapon actually sinking into the girl's flesh.

He hit her again over the head. He would knock her unconscious, he decided, and then take his pleasure.

He rained blows over her skull. She rode them with fortitude, her head moving minimally this way and that, taking the punishment and coming back for more, lifting her head between blows and staring at him mutely.

Panting with exertion, he ceased his attack. "Stand up."

She remained cowering on the floor.

"I said stand up!"

Reluctantly she dragged herself to her feet.

She faced him, staring straight ahead at a point over this right shoulder.

She appeared dazed. The nightstick had had its effect. Now for a little fisticuffs. He transferred his weapon to his left hand and, lightning fast with his right fist, he struck her in the midriff.

It was as if he'd hit a ball of dough. His hand seemed to sink into her belly.

He pulled it out with an effort.

What the hell?

She was smiling.

The smile infuriated him.

Snarling, he backhanded her across her smirking face.

Oh, sweet Jesus Christ...

He stared in horror at what he had done.

Where his backhander had impacted, her right cheek was sunken, indented with the impression of his knuckles. Her entire face appeared knocked out of true, warped and lop-sided. And she was still smiling.

"Why, you little cunt!"

He hit her again, first in the belly, and then in the face. His hand sank up to its wrist in her stomach, and he retrieved it with effort. The second blow...

He stood back, staring in horror at the result.

His fist had created a great crater in the middle of her face, a hollow where her nose should have been, but without the slightest sign of blood.

He reeled away, gagging as, before his very eyes, the girl began to change shape.

She shrank, lost her definition. She seemed to blur, become something indeterminate. No longer a girl, but neither anything else he recognised.

And then he realised, and groaned.

Before him, the thing that had been Ajia Snell—or a presentable likeness of her, anyway—was revealed in its true nature: the phouka.

How in hell's name…?

He stared in horror at the shrivelled homunculus before him, its stick-limbs, concave torso and swollen, domed head sickening him.

And its claws.

He felt a second of panic.

In its transformation, it had slipped its shackles.

And now it dived at him.

Only Wynne's superior physical strength and training in unarmed combat saved his life.

He fought savagely, fuelled with fear and rage. He expended on the phouka the anger he had saved for the girl. Somehow she had evaded him, turned the creature before him and fled. He laid into the phouka, smashing its frail frame with his nightstick and kicking it when it fell and attempted to climb to its feet.

It fought back, even when one of his kicks scythed through its midriff and sickeningly split it into two almost equal halves. A clawed hand reached out and raked his left leg, drawing blood, while the torso re-joined itself to its legs and it drew itself to its feet and dived at him, bearing a set of hideous fangs. Wynne smashed a fist into its mouth, shattering teeth and lacerating his own flesh.

The phouka reeled back against the wall, screaming in rage.

Wynne ran for the door. He hauled it open, dived through, and slammed it shut behind him. He collapsed against the wall, drawing deep breaths as the creature shrieked and rage and pounded ineffectual fists on the padded door.

He looked down at himself. He uniform was shredded, his knuckles dripping blood. Relieved that he had escaped with his life, he felt rage at what this meant.

Ajia Snell had escaped.

And, sooner or later, Drake would have to be informed.

He opened the outer door and staggered into the warehouse.

Lieutenant Noble looked aghast. "Sir?"

Wynne leaned against the container, breathing hard.

"Sir?" Noble repeated, approaching him. Something in the

lieutenant's incredulity at seeing his senior officer like this enraged Wynne.

"You!" he screamed. "YOU! LET! HER! ESCAPE!"

"Me, sir?"

"You, Noble! You went in there, didn't you? You let her out?"

Noble looked suddenly pale. "I… I let the… let the phouka out, sir. I mean, it looked like the girl. It wasn't shackled."

"You let the girl out. Ajia Snell!" He thumbed over his shoulder. "The fucking phouka is still in there, you cretin!"

Noble swore under his breath.

"Which means, Lieutenant, that Snell is still out there, somewhere."

"I'll alert—" Noble began.

"Stop!" Wynne said. "Drake needs telling, and you can be fucking assured that it's not me who's going to tell the bastard. Get through to him and…" He paused. "On second thoughts, contact the Minister of Defence and explain the situation to him."

That, at least, might buy Wynne a little thinking time.

As Lieutenant Noble crossed the warehouse and spoke falteringly into his mobile phone, Wynne slid down the corrugated wall of the container and closed his eyes.

ONE HOUR LATER Major Wynne, sticking plasters criss-crossing his injured hand, was roused from fantasies of what he would do with Ajia Snell when he caught her.

His mobile was ringing.

His stomach turned as he stared at the screen. "Drake here," the Prime Minister drawled.

"Sir," Wynne said.

Drake spoke slowly, calmly, and it put the willies up Major Wynne.

"Major Wynne," said Drake, "you have excelled yourself."

"Sir?"

"Let me get this straight, Major. Tell me if I go wrong. Now, I'm right in understanding that you had Ajia Snell in your custody?"

"That's right, sir."

"And am I also correct in understanding that—how to phrase

this?—you allowed her to escape?"

Wynne closed his eyes. "That's right, sir. I'm sorry. You see—"

Drake cut him off. "No excuses. You're relieved of duties, Wynne, with immediate effect. Report to Swindon, where there's a desk job awaiting you. Noble will be joining you. Oh, and there's one other thing."

"Sir?"

"When all this is over, Wynne, when the dust has settled and Snell and the others are dead and forgotten, I will personally supervise your court-martial."

Wynne's blood ran cold. "Court-martial, sir?"

"Not only for your incompetence in the line of duty, Wynne, but for the flagrant sexual harassment of my wife. I've seen the little attachment you sent her yesterday." He paused. "You sicken me, Wynne."

And before the major could reply, Drake cut the connection.

Wynne looked up, across the chamber, to where Lieutenant Noble stood, stunned, staring down at the screen of his mobile.

"That was the Defence Minister," Noble said in barely a whisper. "I... I've been demoted. And have you seen the latest?"

Wynne sighed. "The latest?"

Noble indicated his mobile. "Escalation of hostilities between Britain and Russia, sir. We're on nuclear alert."

"Christ."

"Apparently Drake's bolted to his castle near Glastonbury. Last stand, kind of thing." Noble fell silent.

Wynne climbed to his feet, staring at his second-in-command.

Or rather, his ex-second-in-command.

"How many Paladins do we have up here, Noble?"

The Lieutenant blinked. "How many? Ah, thirty, sir. And another twenty up in Cumbria."

"And," Wynne said, calculating, "how would you assess their mood in light of recent losses, Lieutenant? Losses incurred when we followed the orders of a... might I say a madman?"

Noble looked uncertain. "They're... You might say they're a bit pissed off, sir."

"'A bit pissed off'," Wynne smiled. "I'd say a lot pissed off myself, Noble. Now, how would you like to atone for your error, Lieutenant?"

"Atone, sir?"

"Drake's gone far enough. He's responsible for the decimation of the Paladins, and we're on the edge of nuclear Armageddon. We've got to stop him, don't you agree? Contact Captain Whiteley and Corporal Hall," he went on. "We're advancing on Glastonbury."

DEREK DRAKE WAS also advancing on Glastonbury.

Ensconced in the back of the limousine purring along the M4 towards the West Country, with the Holy Grail in its walnut carrying case on the seat to his left, Harriet to his right, and the Nuclear Briefcase laid flat on his lap, Drake felt supremely confident.

He was, after all, the latter-day manifestation of King Arthur. Emrys had told him so, and it made sense. Even his name, apparently, pointed to that truth. "Derek" was a shortening of Theoderic, which meant *gifted ruler*, while "Drake" had its roots in the word dragon. Who, therefore, was better suited than Derek Drake to be the re-embodiment of the monarch known as Arthur Pendragon?

The revelation that he was a latter-day King Arthur filled Drake with a sense of righteousness and entitlement so all-encompassing that even the bad news from Manchester—the blithering duo of Major Wynne and Lieutenant Noble had managed to let Ajia Snell wriggle from their grasp—could not dent his mood of optimism. He had immediately demoted the pair and contacted Major Worthington-Price at Swindon, promoting him to commander of the Paladins with immediate effect. Now that Snell was back on the loose, and her band of terrorists somewhere out there, Drake had experienced a moment of apprehension before ordering Worthington-Price to select thirty good men from the barracks at Swindon to accompany him down to Fairleigh Castle. An armoured car was at the van of the cavalcade, with three heavily armed Humvees bringing up the rear. With a squad of Paladins already in situ at the castle, he would be well protected.

Meanwhile, news on the Russian front, so to speak, was encouraging. Drake's pre-emptive release of the compromising footage had had the desired effect of wrong-footing Vasilyev. He'd not heard from the Russian Premier in two days. HMS *Nautilus* was ready and waiting in the Baltic, and Drake had despatched a SAS Commando unit, armed with mobile nuclear warheads, to the Estonian border with Russia. In the Channel, just west of the Dover Strait, Royal Navy battleships were shadowing the three encroaching Russian ships with orders to blow them from the water on Drake's command.

Everything was set for the ultimate showdown.

Beside him, Harriet squeezed his thigh. "Derek?"

"Mmm, my darling?"

"Did Emrys tell you?" she purred.

Drake smiled. "He did indeed."

Ahead, the tower of Fairleigh Castle hove into sight, rising above the massed greenery of the Somerset countryside with Glastonbury tor in the background.

Harriet snuggled closer and kissed him.

THIRTY-THREE

NEVE WINTERON WOULD never forget that crisp January day, six months ago, when her life changed for ever. Two momentous events occurred that morning. The first was her own death, and the second—perhaps even more unbelievable—was the death of her father and what had happened afterwards.

At seven that morning she had left her cottage, as was customary, to drive three miles to the village of Watermead on the outskirts of Glastonbury and the headquarters of Cry-Org Inc., the research institute she had set up five years previously.

Her work as head of the institute had not been going well; her research had stalled. Her father had counselled patience—a virtue of which she was always in short supply—and said that the path of science was notoriously tortuous, and that world-changing discoveries were never made overnight. These clichés and truisms had proved little comfort and done nothing to change Neve's dissatisfaction with her work.

For the past five years she had done some ground-breaking research into the freezing of subjects, but the difficulty, the insurmountable stumbling block, was not so much the actual freezing of corpses but the tricky process of resurrection—bringing those subjects back to life. She had managed to freeze hundreds of animals, but not one had survived the process of thawing.

As an impatient perfectionist, this drove Neve to distraction.

She blamed her preoccupation on the problem, that morning, for her inattention as she rounded a bend in the lane at speed.

She had seen the errant sheep, stationed moronically in the middle of the road, at the very last second. In swerving to avoid the animal she had skidded on the frosty road and lost control of the BMW.

A conveniently placed oak tree had impeded the car's progress, buckled its bonnet into the shape of a concertina, and driven a low branch down through the windscreen and into Neve's chest.

She had not the slightest doubt that she had died instantly.

And had regained consciousness, sometime later, to stare down in horrified fascination as a pair of hands—her own, she saw incredulously—pulled the javelin-like branch from the left side of her chest.

Where a hole the size of a saucer gaped, displaying a ladder of broken ribs, ripped flesh, and steadily pulsing blood.

Unbelievably, she felt no pain.

Unbelievably, as she stared, the blood ceased its pumping flow and her ribs—two curved sections, stark and white in the morning sunlight—came together like attracted magnets and knitted themselves whole within seconds. Then, subcutaneous tissue aggregated itself around the ribs, and purple musculature built up over the mound, and flesh on top of that. Within fifteen minutes, she calculated, the wound was healed and only the rip in her Burberry coat showed where the branch had impaled her.

Oh-kay, she thought. *I'm hallucinating. I've suffered concussion and this is the consequence.*

She raised a hand to her head. She felt neither a cut nor blood. Come to that, she felt no pain, not even a headache.

But I still must be hallucinating.

She checked her legs, but they seemed to have survived the crash intact.

Forcing the door open, she extricated herself from the wreckage and stared around.

She saw the cause of the accident, the sheep, lying in the middle of the lane.

Something made her approach the animal, kneel before it, and reach out. The sheep was still alive, breathing shallowly.

As her fingers touched the creature's off-white fleece, something very strange happened.

She felt something flow from the core of her being, down her outstretched arm and into the sheep. Something elemental and... cold. Freezing. And as she watched, open-mouthed, the animal froze within seconds.

Which was, she told herself, impossible.

Just as impossible as my pulling a branch from my chest and surviving.

She stared at the sheep, frozen solid with its legs projecting at right angles from its body like table-legs, and laughed hysterically.

She pulled the frozen sheep to the side of the lane, so that it wouldn't be hit by the next passing motorist, and made her way to the village of Stanton-on-the-Water where her father had his country retreat.

If anyone could talk sense into her, give a rational explanation for what had happened that morning, it was her father.

She came to the garden gate, took a deep breath to compose herself, and rehearsed what she would tell him.

Dad, I've just survived a car crash which killed me... Oh, and I just happened to have deep-frozen a sheep...

In the event, she was spared the necessity of trying to explain herself.

Monday was the day of her father's constituency surgery in Glastonbury, and he never left home before midday. He would probably be still in bed, knowing him, and as Neve had a key she let herself into the three-bedroom cottage and called out with a cheeriness she did not at all feel.

"Dad, it's only me!"

She found her father sprawled on his back on the sitting room floor, glassy-eyed and manifestly dead. From the colour of his face—a pale puce, his lips a shade darker—she suspected he had succumbed to the heart attack his GP had been warning him about for years. Edward Winterton had been a big man with a big appetite for everything in life, and that included food and drink. By the look of him, he had been dead for a good twenty-four hours.

Neve wept, bereft, and found herself reaching out.

It was not a conscious gesture, she told herself later, but an instinctive response. She reached out and touched his cheek—and was astounded to feel that same elemental force flowing from her and into the corpse of her father. As ridiculous and inexplicable as it seemed, she knew that she was doing the right thing.

Whatever that might be.

What she did next she knew also to be right, and just as instinctive. With much difficulty, as her father weighed thirteen stone, she dragged his dead weight from the sitting room to the garage, through the door which connected the two. A greater feat of strength was called for when lifting him into the boot of his Range Rover. But an hour later, sweating profusely, she had her father's frozen corpse safely stowed in the car and was driving from the cottage and down the same lane where, three hours earlier, she had met her own end.

And had come back to life.

She was often the first to arrive at the low-slung, ultra-modern headquarters of Cry-Org, and that morning had been no exception. Her plan was to drive into the garage next to the elevator entrance, fetch a gurney, and manoeuvre her father's body onto it. The institute was often in receipt of the carcasses of animals large and small, with a garage and adjacent lift to transport the corpses to the freezing labs in the basement.

Thirty minutes later she had her father's body locked securely in a mortuary drawer more suited to containing the corpses of farm animals.

Only a little later, sipping coffee in the staff canteen, did she question herself about the events of the day—and her motivations, perhaps subconscious, in doing what she had done.

The subsequent news of her father's mysterious disappearance had been a Nine Day Wonder, taken up with lip-smacking relish by the likes of the *Daily Mail* which thought up all manner of far-fetched scenarios—from kidnap by foreign powers to suicide and the pre-planned disposal of his own body—though none as unlikely as the truth. Derek Drake had even weighed in with a few insincere words—the bastard!—telling the world that a statesman like Edward Winterton was the backbone of our great nation and would be sorely missed... When in fact her father had been one of Drake's fiercest critics who considered Drake a crackpot Christian and a megalomaniac.

Somehow, over the course of the next few months, Neve had held her sanity together.

As if it were not sufficient that she had died and come back to life, and then flash-frozen a sheep and her father, what happened next drove her to the brink of hysteria.

Her work at Cry-Org underwent a significant step change.

She discovered, while monitoring an experiment to resurrect a frozen cow, that just as she had the ability to induce a cryogenic state in a subject, she could now bring it back to life without recourse to the complex cocktail of chemicals that she and her team had been experimenting with for years.

It was fortunate indeed that she had been alone when making this discovery; and in panic she had quickly reversed the process and refrozen the unfortunate creature.

She had left the institute that afternoon in a daze, and over the course of the next few days had experimented with a variety of animals, from mice to birds, freezing them and then bringing them back to life.

Her success rate was one hundred per cent.

Neve Winterton was a scientist, a rationalist, and her sudden and arbitrary—and wholly unscientific—ability did not sit easily with her world view.

But the upshot was obvious: if she could bring dead animals back to life, then what was to stop her from doing the same with her father?

The idea was so vast, and the consequences so great, that she had hesitated over making the next step.

Until now.

*   *   *

THE DREAMS HAD begun soon after the accident.

She was alone in a winter forest, a vast stretch of frozen woodland where she felt wholly at home. In the recurring dream she was one with the leafless trees, unified with the frozen lakes and glaciated waterfalls. And then on one occasion she had sensed intruders, invaders who always took the same form: dark, terrifying shapes which chased her through the forest. She had awoken in terror time after time, and rationalised the dark invaders as the Paladins that Derek Drake had formed as his own special protection force.

Lately those dreams had changed. She was alone within the icy woods, and the dark invaders did not appear. Instead, she was visited by a voice in her head, a soft, lilting, insistent male voice which urged her that *now* the time was right, that now she should act on her instincts and work her magic on her father.

She had awoken this morning with the urging still at the forefront of her mind, and she knew she would act on it.

Neve drove from her cottage, passed the bend where six months ago she had met her end, and proceeded to the headquarters of Cry-Org Inc.

It was early, and only one other colleague was at work—a technician busy at the far end of the laboratory. Neve sketched a brief wave and took the elevator to the basement.

She locked the vault door behind her and approached the mortuary drawer.

Now that the time had come to reanimate her father, she was nervous. She told herself that her apprehension was groundless. She had brought a dozen or more creatures back to life, so why might the process of resurrecting her father be any different?

Because he's my father, she told herself, *and if I screw up...*

Then she could always reverse the process and re-freeze him.

She took a breath, tapped the code into the locking mechanism, and slid out the heavy drawer.

She pulled back the nylon sheet which shrouded Edward Winterton's corpse and stared down at her father.

In her dream, she had objected that even if she reversed the process of freezing and attempted to bring her father back to life, then the heart attack which had killed him would keep him dead. But the voice in her head had said that this was not so, that miraculously upon awakening he would be cured of the thing which had killed him.

Impossible, she thought

But then so had been her own resurrection.

Neve reached out and touched her father's chest.

The method of resurrecting the dead was similar to freezing a corpse, with one great difference. When imbuing the freezing process, Neve experienced a force leaving her body and investing the subject with glacial stasis. When reanimating a body, the force that flowed from her was life-giving, a positive warmth like channelled sunlight.

She had often tried to analyse the process, to break it down scientifically and come to some methodical understanding of what she was doing. But to her consternation she could only couch her action in vague and maddening metaphor.

The main thing, she told herself, was that it worked.

Understanding, perhaps, would come later.

She pressed her flattened palm to her father's chest and felt a tingling heat pass down her arm.

Her father's stone-cold corpse responded. He grew warm, and a minute later, startling her, he took a breath. Beneath her tremulous fingertips, his chest began to rise and fall.

Neve felt hot tears trickle down her cheeks.

Edward Winterton opened her eyes and smiled at her. He sat up slowly, swung his legs off the shelf. Neve embraced him, weeping.

"How...?" she managed, shaking her head.

He smiled again, the warm, confiding smile she remembered so well, and placed a fingertip on her lips.

"I will explain everything in time," he said. "Everything—even who I am."

She stared at him.

His voice...

His voice was subtly different, not the oratorical baritone that had rang out across the floor of parliament. This voice was lighter, lilting, more sing-song.

It was the voice that had spoken to her in her dreams.

"Who...?" she echoed.

"Your father will be fine, in time. I am... I am merely utilising your father's body for the interim."

"Who are you?" Her voice shook. "What are you?" She shook her head. "My... my ability? My death and... all this... You're responsible!" Her fragmented speech perfectly matched her frantic thoughts.

He reached out and took her hand. "I am responsible, yes. I am using you, and others, to bring about change. Change for the better. You must trust me."

"What do you want?"

His reply filled her with tremulous hope, and fear.

"The defeat of Derek Drake," he said. "And you can help me, Neve. Or should I call you Jack Frost?"

THIRTY-FOUR

AJIA SAT BETWEEN Mr LeRoy and Reed Fletcher in the cab of the pantechnicon as they travelled south, and she felt as if she had never been parted from the people she considered her newfound family. Around the campfire yesterday evening she had recounted the events of her capture, her incarceration, and what the phouka had revealed to her. Mr LeRoy had found this last detail particularly interesting. "But he didn't say who was controlling it, and what his—or her—motivations might be? Intriguing."

Dawn light was laminating the horizon as they approached Glastonbury.

As well as the pantechnicons, there were three other vans in the convoy, and according to Mr LeRoy dozens of other folkloric creatures, as well as eidolons, were converging on Glastonbury. They were drawn, he surmised at one point, by the same force that had controlled the phouka and which was responsible for the initial awakening of the eidolons.

A little before nine o'clock, still ten miles from Glastonbury, Mr LeRoy passed Ajia the iPad on which he'd been monitoring the news.

She stared at the BBC clip of Prime Minister Drake, in a convoy of military vehicles, being driven through the gates of his summer retreat, Fairleigh Castle. She counted one armoured car and three Humvees, and calculated that they could be carrying no more than thirty personnel between them. It was impossible to make out, from the brief footage, if they constituted the entirety of the Paladin guard. More might be within the castle grounds. It would be best, she told Mr LeRoy and Reed Fletcher, to assume that their opposition would be greater than thirty.

"And our precise objective?" she asked, staring at Mr LeRoy.

Mr LeRoy considered the question. "Perhaps that should remain nebulous until I have consulted with Neve Winterton," he said. "I have little doubt that she holds the key to our little sortie."

"Who is she?" Ajia asked. "I'm guessing she's one of us."

"That she is. A cryogenicist who has become the eidolon of Jack Frost, impish avatar of ice and snow."

"Got it." Ajia peered down at the map spread out over her knees. "How far now?" she asked Fletcher.

He slowed down and glanced at the map. "A couple of miles. There it is." He stabbed at the paper with a blunt, dirtied forefinger, indicating a small village outside the town of Glastonbury. "And five miles further on is Fairleigh Castle."

They came to the village minutes later, and Fletcher followed signs that read: CRY-ORG 500 YARDS. He turned down a narrow lane and pulled up outside a long, low, ultra-modern building.

Mr LeRoy frowned across its manicured lawns, frowning.

At last he said, "She isn't there."

"You can sense that?" Ajia asked.

He nodded, reached out a hand, and held it over the map. "But she has been, and left not too long ago—and she wasn't alone. She was with someone. Someone important. An eidolon, maybe. I am still picking up their emanations."

"Where did they go?" Fletcher asked.

Mr LeRoy pointed to a symbol on the map. "Towards that," he said. "Fairleigh Castle."

Fletcher indicated a patch of woodland adjoining the castle grounds. "We head for the wood, take cover, and assess the situation then, okay?"

He slipped the truck into gear and set off.

Presently he manoeuvred the pantechnicon along the lane that fringed the woodland then eased it down an even narrower, unmetalled track into the heart of the wood itself. When he could go no further, he braked and Ajia jumped out. The other vehicles in the convoy drew up behind them, their passengers climbing out in ones and two and stretching tired limbs after the long journey.

They were not the only people to have chosen the forest as an ideal location for the pre-battle gathering. As Mr LeRoy led the way from the track to a clearing, Ajia was aware of shadows between the trees, and caught glimpses of fleeting figures keeping pace.

Only when they reached the clearing, and Mr LeRoy stood at its centre with Reed Fletcher, Smith, Dustin Wolfson and others, did the elusive figures deign to show themselves. Ajia stared with amazement as at first two or three, then ten and twenty brownies, boggarts, elves and goblins and all manner of other folkloric beings trooped from the greenery and approached Oberon, their leader.

He greeted them like the monarch he was, with the gravitas of a leader welcoming allies to the cause.

Daisy Hawthorn nudged Ajia and indicated the gathering. "It's a small army," she said in wonder.

"And we'll need every one of the critters if we're to bring down Drake," Paul Klein said.

Reed Fletcher took command and organised the troops. He pooled all the weapons at their disposal—a dozen assault rifles, a couple of submachine guns, three pistols and dozens of knives, and distributed them amongst the boggarts, goblins and elves who had shown an aptitude with the weapons in Derbyshire. Then he split the hundred and thirty-five combatants into approximate groups of ten, each with a designated leader and second-in-command. Each leader carried a mobile phone, and would keep in regular contact with Fletcher himself.

As in Derbyshire, Fletcher suggested that Ajia, after battle commenced, act as a loose cannon. She nodded her agreement, a kitchen knife clutched in one hand and a mobile in the other. The knife had a 20cm serrated blade and was designed for slicing bread or carving meat. It was a far cry from the little paring knife she had first learned to kill with and, for her purposes, a distinct improvement.

Fletcher drew a rough map in the soil, outlining the castle and the woodland with the point of a twig. "We approach from the east, in the cover of the trees," he said. "Ajia, once we're in position, you scout the lie of the land and report back on the position of the Paladins. When we have this information, we plan our next move."

"And if Neve Winterton, otherwise known as Jack Frost, is already at the castle?" Wayland Smith asked.

Mr LeRoy frowned. "In that eventuality," he said, "it would be impossible to communicate with her until we've dealt with the Paladins."

"I'll deal with the feckin' Paladins single handed, so I will," Dustin Wolfson said, smacking a huge fist into the palm of his left hand. "Just let me get at the shitehawks!"

Smiling, Fletcher gave a decisive nod, then looked around at the gathering. "All set, then? If everyone's ready, let's move it."

He led the way, with Ajia at his side along with Daisy Hawthorn, Smith and Paul Klein. Dustin Wolfson darted ahead, still muttering about the grievous injuries he would inflict on the enemy. Mr LeRoy followed, towering over a host of babbling brownies and boggarts. They kept off the worn pathways through the forest and moved with stealth through the undergrowth. Within minutes Ajia caught sight of the crennellated battlements of the castle's western tower. A grey stone wall, perhaps ten feet high, surrounded the grounds.

The Green Woman worked her magic, kneeling at the foot of the wall where a skein of ivy provided ground cover. As Ajia watched, Daisy reached out and the ivy writhed and spread, creeping at speed up the face of the wall. When it reached the top, Fletcher nodded to Ajia and she took off.

In Puck mode she sprinted at the wall, clung to the ivy and hauled herself up the growth. Clambering up the final yard, she slowed and peered over the wall into the grounds.

The three Humvees, along with Drake's limousine and a green Range Rover, were drawn up on the gravel drive before the castle's porticoed entrance. The armoured car was stationed at the barred gate, two hundred yards to the left of her position. She counted nearly thirty Paladins stationed around two sides of the castle in groups of twos and threes. No doubt there were more on the other side. As well as the Paladins, a dozen uniformed security personnel patrolled the gravelled pathways of the perimeter.

She clambered down and reported the situation to Fletcher. Beside him, Mr LeRoy sat cross-legged on the ground, bent over the map. He placed his palms over the symbol of the castle, his brow buckled in concentration.

He looked up. "Neve Winterton is in there," he said. "I can sense it."

"In the castle with Derek Drake?" Paul Klein said. "Why the ruddy hell would she be there?"

"More to the point, what do we do?" Smith asked.

"Do?" Wolfson said, his battered face looking incredulous. "I'll tell ye what we do, we go in there and hammer the shit out of the feckers, that's what we do!"

"Admirably put, Dustin," Reed Fletcher said. "We do what we came here to do. We attack the Paladins. We stop Derek Drake before he does any more damage, and if that means killing him, then so be it. Agreed?"

A chorus of assent greeted his question.

With a bodyguard of two armed boggarts, Daisy Hawthorn moved around the perimeter wall and threw up dense, accelerated growths of icy and other creepers which could be utilised by the invading hordes, positioned at intervals of twenty yards.

When these were in place, Fletcher ordered each group of ten to take up positions before the makeshift ladders, but halted the army before it set off.

"One thing. Ajia, did you see if the security personnel were armed?"

"They didn't appear to be."

He looked around at the gathering. "Then we don't kill them until they try to kill us, all right? If they do turn out to be armed, don't hesitate to defend yourselves. Otherwise, incapacitate them."

He hesitated. "Needless to say, no such mercy should be shown to the Paladins."

Smith stepped forward, clutching his hammer. "I'm coming with you," he said.

Fletcher stared at his old friend. "No, you're not, Smith. You're staying here with Mr LeRoy. If you join us over there"—Fletcher indicated beyond the wall—"you'd be dead in seconds."

"I can't just stand by."

"You can, and will."

"Reed's right," Ajia said. "You're needed here, with Mr LeRoy."

Smith relented and, reluctantly, agreed to remain on this side of the wall, out of harm's way, until such a time as Fletcher deemed that safe passage could be negotiated across the grounds and into the castle.

"And then," Mr LeRoy said, "I shall personally confront Derek Drake and Major Dominic Wynne. Oh, how I relish the thought."

Dustin Wolfson refused to take the submachine gun that Fletcher offered. "And what'll I be needing that for? I've got these, sure enough." He held up two balled fists the size of cauliflowers. "And I've got me rage, what's more. Oh, and this." He reached into his jacket pocket and pulled out a bottle of Bushmill's.

"Are you sure?"

"Sure I'm sure. Stop your worrying, fellah."

The centurions made their way around the perimeter and took up positions beneath the improvised ladders of ivy.

Five minutes later, on Reed Fletcher's order, the attack commenced.

Ajia slipped into Puck mode. She climbed up the ivy, jumped from the top of the wall, and landed in a flowerbed. She paused like a sprinter in the blocks and stared across the lawns at the castle. Her precipitate arrival had not been noted by the nearest group of three Paladins who stood a hundred yards away. Gripping the knife in her right hand, she took off towards them.

They had not expected an assault of any kind, still less from a slip of a thing armed only with a knife. She came to a sudden stop behind the first Paladin, reached up and drew her blade across his throat. The knife grated against something—and it certainly wasn't flesh and bone. His neck was protected by some kind of flexible Kevlar collar. He turned, crying out in surprise, and in doing so provided Ajia with a perfect target. She stabbed the knife into his face. The blade sliced through his eyeball and deep into his skull. She pulled it out, the serrated edge grating on bone. He fell to the ground, screaming. Ajia whirled, oriented herself, and ran at the second Paladin. As if in slow motion, he was raising his rifle and taking aim at where she had been. His expression of horrified surprise, along with his retarded movements, struck her as comical.

As she stepped towards him, she saw that he too wore a protective Kevlar collar—and she had time, before she slashed at his face, to wonder if the issuing of these was in direct response to the havoc she had wrought among their number in Derbyshire and Bradford. Well, it would make her job a little more difficult, but not impossible. The Paladin fell with the slow grace of a wilting ballerina, dropping his weapon, and in one flowing movement Ajia snatched it up and squeezed off a round at the third, advancing Paladin.

She took off, heading for a box hedge that flanked the driveway. From here, crouching, she turned and watched the advance of her army over the perimeter wall and across the immaculate lawns.

It was like a scene from a film. The oncoming tide of humanity and folkloric beings looked like a cut-price, rag-tag mob of desperate extras, crying out at the top of their voices and shaking their weapons above their heads as they advanced. She saw Reed Fletcher leading the way, his bow and arrows relegated in favour of an assault rifle, followed by a host of boggarts and elves wielding guns, axes, machetes and long knives. Wolfson was in the pack, and as Ajia watched she could have sworn that his image became a blur and that he was bounding along on all fours. Then he was lost to sight among the mêlée as the invaders came from all sides, swarming over the walls and flowing towards the castle in a terrifying phalanx of noise and motion.

Battle was joined. The Paladins sprinted across the lawn to meet the advancing horde. The long box hedge, where Ajia crouched, divided the opposing armies. She was in prime position to take advantage of the Paladins' advance. At speed, she ran to the end of the hedge and sprinted in a great loop around the back of the uniformed goons. She counted at least twenty Paladins as she came upon them from the rear. She fired judiciously, aiming at their unprotected legs, and one after the other they fell like bowling pins.

And then the invading army, led by Fletcher and a host of boggarts, burst through the hedge, yelling and screaming, and fell upon the writhing Paladins, hacking and chopping, beheading and sectioning, with gusto.

She was allowing herself to think that they might, just might, have a rout on their hands, when something alerted her. She turned in time to see an armoured car round the end of the castle and accelerate across the lawn towards her. Seeing the futility of attempting to ward it off with the assault rifle, she ran towards the castle's facade and concealed herself behind the statue of a naked Venus. From this vantage point she looked out across the lawn and attempted to work out her next line of attack.

She had been correct in her earlier circumspection about the number of Paladins at the castle. She had counted around thirty entering the grounds, but evidently there were more in situ. Now they showed themselves, perhaps fifty black uniformed goons sprinting from a building adjacent to the castle and fanning out across the lawn.

Ajia took aim and picked them off one by one, reluctant to betray her position by spraying the phalanx with a sustained bout of gunfire.

Three more armoured cars sped around the side of the castle and careered towards the enemy, firing as they went.

So far, she thought, it *had* been a rout.

But the tide was turning.

Boggarts, elves and brownies fell, blown apart by gunfire. She searched desperately for Fletcher in the chaos, but such was the confusion on the lawn—with Paladin footsoldiers mixing it with the invaders in hand to hand combat—that she found it impossible to make out individuals.

She contented herself with picking off the Paladins one by one.

* * *

DAISY HAWTHORN, ACCOMPANIED by a bodyguard of two loyal boggarts, Gregor and Oleg, dropped from the wall at the rear of the castle and was startled to encounter not the chaos of battle she anticipated but a scene of serene quietude. A meadow stretched towards the back of the castle for perhaps half a mile, with the line of a ha-ha diving it from sloping lawns. The panorama appeared idyllic, a typical English summer's day, with a couple of jersey cows steadily cropping the meadow and the song of a skylark filling the air.

Then the firing began. It came as a distant crackle, muffled by the bulk of the castle itself, and ceased as abruptly as it began.

Then it started up again, sustained this time, and Daisy felt sick as she imagined the consequences for her newfound friends.

She saw movement a mile away, on the far side of the castle grounds: four armoured cars disappearing from view as they made their way around a corner tower.

"This way!" Gregor cried, sprinting in a crouch towards the ha-ha.

Daisy took off after him, looking this way and that for the security guards Ajia had warned them about. The way ahead appeared clear.

They made the cover of the ha-ha and crouched, Daisy's heart thumping madly.

As they stared over the lip of the grassy ditch, a guard rushed from an annexe building abutting the castle, saw them and approached warily.

"Hey, you!" he began, drawing a pistol from inside his jacket.

Beside her, Oleg leapt up, aimed his gun and fired.

Daisy closed her eyes, but not fast enough.

The security guard disintegrated in a hail of bullets.

She saw movement to their right, and then to their left, and in panic she feared that the gunfire had alerted the Paladins. She laughed with relief when she saw knots of elves and boggarts swarm across the meadow and join her.

The diminutive Paul Klein slumped against the wall beside her, panting. He clutched a pistol in his right hand and a wicked-looking kitchen knife in his left.

"We... jumped right on top... of a couple of guards," he panted, drawing a breath between words. "And fuck what Reed said about leniency. The bastards were armed."

The boggart beside Klein grinned. "So we butchered 'em."

Daisy nodded, grimacing. It might not be pleasant, but what had to be done, had to be done.

"So, what now?" she said, looking around. Perhaps thirty assorted folkloric beings waited in the cover of the ha-ha.

Paul Klein took command, relishing his role. "We advance," he said, looking for support from the boggarts. "The main battle's on the far side of the castle, and the bastards have armoured cars and fuck-knows what else."

He passed Daisy his kitchen knife, and she took it reluctantly.

"Let's go!" he said.

The army swarmed up and over the ha-ha, and the Green Woman took a grip on her fear and followed.

REED FLETCHER SQUEEZED off a round into the head of an advancing Paladin and looked around for his next victim. He would, all things considered, have rather conducted the fight with his bow and arrow, but needs must. And he had to admit that though his weapon of choice might not have been this Glock killing machine, it was shockingly effective.

It was just a pity that the enemy was equipped with equally lethal firepower.

Already he calculated that he had lost a third of his men—he used the term 'men' loosely—and still the Paladins kept coming. Not only were there fifty or more footsoldiers, but they had numerous armoured cars and Humvees in their arsenal too.

And the machine guns mounted on the armoured cars were making mincemeat of the invading army.

"Behind ye, man!" The cry came from nearby, more of a bark than anything from a human throat.

Fletcher whirled in time to see a Paladin raising his rifle. Before he could bring his own gun to bear, something leapt at the soldier. He saw a whirl of flesh and fur, human and hound in a single bizarre entity, with a long, savage jaw, and great loping legs attached to a human torso. Wolfson hit the soldier and sank his teeth into the hapless man's throat, shaking his head viciously and tearing out the bloody gizzard. Then he dropped the soldier's corpse, turned on all fours and selected his next victim. He moved like the wind—almost as fast as Ajia, Fletcher thought—and was feeding on the Paladin before the man could react.

Elsewhere across the lawn, however, things were not going as well. For every Paladin who fell, Fletcher estimated that three invaders met their end.

He ducked into the cover of a rose arbour and looked across at the entrance of the castle. If he could make his way inside, find and capture Drake, then he might gain the leverage needed to force the Paladins to cease the slaughter.

But he saw, his heart sinking, that a force of Paladins had perhaps foreseen that very ploy. They had manoeuvred a banqueting table into the foyer of the castle and now it barricaded the entrance. And behind it were stationed six Paladins and a tripod-mounted belt-fed .50-calibre machine gun dealing death from its steaming muzzle.

Fifty feet to the right of the entrance, he saw Ajia jumping back and forth behind the wholly inadequate cover of a statue of Venus, firing into the mêlée on the lawn before her.

She was so intent on the battle that she didn't see what was going on to her right. Under the mullioned windows of the castle, a boggart and a Paladin were slogging it out. The soldier had lost his gun but had drawn a dagger and was slashing at the boggart who was armed with an axe. Fletcher found himself staring, hypnotised by the sight of two crazed killers fighting to the death, trading blows that hacked and sliced into flesh until it seemed impossible that living, breathing beings could survive such bloody depredations.

Then the Paladin delivered the coup de grâce, plunging his dagger into the stomach of the boggart and wrenching the blade upwards. Fletcher stared, horrified, as the little man's entrails spilled over the Paladin's knife-hand in a slick, steaming cataract.

Then the Paladin looked up, seeking his next victim.

He saw Ajia and crept along the facade of the castle towards her. And she was still firing at the Paladins on the lawn, oblivious to the approaching danger.

Fletcher yelled out a warning, his cry lost in the cacophony of the battle. He lofted his rifle to his shoulder and fired. The shot missed the Paladin but shattered the window above the soldier.

The Paladin ducked, and Fletcher saw with relief that Ajia had seen the movement. She vanished in an instant. One second she was behind the Venus, like its darker twin, and then she was gone. She appeared next as she barrelled into the Paladin, knocking him off his feet and rolling with him through a flowerbed.

But Ajia had met her match. As they rolled, the Paladin gained the upper hand, pinned her to the ground and raised his dagger.

Fletcher sprinted from the cover of the arbour, conscious that he might be mown down at any second, and launched himself across the flower bed. He hit the Paladin hard, almost knocking himself unconscious in the process. When he pushed himself to his knees and looked around, he saw Ajia poised to dive at the Paladin. She moved like a striking cobra, sliding the blade of her knife into the soldier's neck.

Panting over the spasming body, she nodded at him. "Owe you."

He dragged her along the façade to the statue and crouched.

"It's a fucking massacre!" he cried above the din of gunfire. "We need to…" He stopped.

"Need to…?"

"Gather our forces. Make a tactical retreat. There's a ha-ha behind the castle." He stared across the lawn to where groups of boggarts and elves had taken cover behind hedges, arbours and outbuildings. "Can you get the word to them? We've got to retreat."

He stopped again.

"What?" Ajia cried desperately.

He stared across the lawn towards the gates of the castle.

"Oh, sweet Jesus Christ on a broken bicycle," he said.

Ajia followed his gaze, and her heart sank.

*   *   *

MR LEROY PACED back and forth on the far side of the wall. "Oh, but this is unendurable!" he cried.

"Calm down," Smith said. "There's absolutely nothing we can do." He sat on a mossy log, his hammer gripped in his twitching hand.

"And that's the worst of it!" Mr LeRoy wailed. "The thought of my friends over there, dying for our cause…"

"They wanted it as much as you did," Smith said.

"Perhaps you could get through to Reed and ask him how it's going?"

The other man looked dubious. "I think he's got enough on his plate at the moment, Mr LeRoy."

"If only I could see how the battle is progressing."

Smith considered the ivy clinging to the perimeter wall like a vast green antimacassar. It would hardly take Mr LeRoy's weight, he was sure, even if the big man had the strength to climb it.

But further back in the forest was the rusted ladder that had belonged to an old water tower, which Smith had noticed earlier. He vanished into the undergrowth and emerged dragging the ladder in his wake.

"What on earth…?" Mr LeRoy began.

Without replying, Smith set to work, looking for all the world like a mad xylophonist tapping away on his instrument as he moved up and down the length of the ladder, striking it here and there with his hammer.

A minute later the ladder was repaired and reinforced. Now it would take even Mr LeRoy's considerable weight. Smith leaned it against the ivy and lodged its base in the earth. "Up you go. But be careful when you get to the top. You don't want to lose your head."

"Thank you, my boy."

Mr LeRoy placed his foot on the first rung and ascended gingerly. Smith gripped a handful of ivy, kicked his foot into the springy mass, and hauled himself up alongside his friend.

At the top, they peered over circumspectly.

Blood, body parts, entrails, and a mass of humanity—and others—fighting it out hand to hand and with guns… It was like a scene from Bosch, only worse. And it was obvious, as the pair stared down on the battle scene, that the Paladins had the upper hand.

"It's hopeless," Mr LeRoy sighed in despair.

As Paul Klein and Oleg the boggart led the charge around the castle tower, Daisy Hawthorn fell behind along with her bodyguard, Gregor.

It would be carnage on the front lawn, and she was armed with nothing more than a kitchen knife. What possible effect might she have on the outcome of the battle? She looked up, seeing an open window on the ground floor of the tower.

But if she could get into the castle, locate Derek Drake and perhaps, with Gregor's assistance, incapacitate the Prime Minister...?

She laid a hand on Gregor's muscled forearm, indicated the open window, and outlined her plan.

Gregor made a stirrup of his linked hands, and Daisy stepped into it and hauled herself up and through the window. The boggart followed, scrambling up the wall and tumbling into the room.

They were in what looked like a storeroom, stacked with shelves of laundry, folded towels and bedsheets. She crept across to the door, opened it a crack and peered out.

The corridor beyond was deserted.

Gregor joined her, poked his head through the opening, then said, "After me."

She followed him into the corridor, her heart thumping. At least Gregor was armed; and his presence was reassuring.

The two of them moved along the corridor, then turned right along another corridor where suits of armour stood sentinel on either side.

Just as they began to creep carefully along this next passageway, an armed Paladin careered around the far corner.

Gregor raised his weapon, but too late. The Paladin, hefting a pistol and ready to fire, shot Gregor in the head without a second's hesitation, then aimed at Daisy.

"Gregor!" She fell to her knees beside the boggart's twitching body.

She looked up. "You…!" she spat.

"Shut it, bitch. Stand up. Drop the knife and put your hands in the air. Or you'll join him."

Numbed, Daisy climbed to her feet and raised her arms above her head.

"That way," he said, indicating a nearby oak door. "It just so happens we've got a couple more of you troublemakers stowed right here. You can join them." He stepped back so that Daisy could pass, keeping his pistol trained on her head all the while.

She walked towards the door.

"Knock and open it an inch," the Paladin ordered.

She did so. The Paladin called out over Daisy's shoulder, "Another one, sir." And to Daisy, "In you go."

She pushed open the door and stepped into the room.

The first figure she saw was a tall, dark-haired Paladin armed with a snub-nosed machine gun.

Two other people occupied the room, a man and a young woman seated side by side on the floor opposite the Paladin.

Daisy stared. She didn't recognise the raven-haired woman, but the grey-haired old man…

Edward Winterton? The politician?

But she recalled reading news reports of Winterton's mysterious disappearance months ago.

The Paladin guarding the pair barked an order, "Over there. Against the wall, with the others."

The pretty young woman smiled at her, reassuringly, as Daisy stepped across the room and lowered herself against the wall.

"And don't make a single move or you're dead." The Paladin glanced at his colleague. "How's it going out there?"

"Almost over, Captain. The twats didn't stand a chance."

"I want the ringleaders rounded up. As for the rest, make sure there are no survivors."

"Very good, sir." The Paladin withdrew and closed the door behind him.

Daisy closed her eyes. Over the past few days she had come to know, and love, many of the brownies, elves and boggarts that constituted Mr LeRoy's army.

And they had gone into the battle with such confidence...

The girl reached out, slowly, found Daisy's hand and squeezed.

The Paladin seated himself in an armchair, keeping his machine gun trained on them. "So you must be, if I'm not mistaken, Daisy Hawthorn. I've heard a lot about you, and what you did in Derbyshire. And I'm not talking about what you grew in your nursery. You'll pay for your crimes, Hawthorn, when all the mess out there is cleared up."

"Go to hell."

"Ah. Fighting spirit. That's what I like to hear. Unlike the cowering silence from these two," he finished contemptuously.

Edward Winterton said, "I'd rather not waste words on scum like you, Captain. As I said earlier, I want to speak to Drake."

Behind the seated captain, the window was open a crack. Daisy saw a shoot of ivy, with a single leaf blowing in the summer breeze.

"And when I read of your disappearance," the Paladin said, "I thought I'd heard the last from you."

"I'm *so* sorry to disappoint," Winterton replied with faux chivalry.

Daisy, plunged into despair at Gregor's death and her capture, was too stunned to realistically think that she could do anything about her current situation.

But she could try.

She stared at the ivy shoot and willed it with all her might.

Nothing happened.

She concentrated harder as the captain and the politician traded barbed insults. The leaf fluttered. Or was it just the breeze from outside that provided its motive force? She felt a familiar power flow from her, cross the room, and invest the living plant with energy and locomotion.

There. That was more like it. She had lost focus, through fear. Now she had regained it.

The ivy shoot wound its way over the pitted stone embrasure, soon joined by others stalks and fronds. Under the Green Woman's subliminal prompting, they braided themselves, three separate strands weaving into one thicker, tenacious braid.

Little by little, it crept towards the chair in which the Paladin sat.

The pressure of the young woman's hand intensified.

Daisy sensed, from how Winterton was maintaining his badinage with the Paladin, that he had seen the eerie creep of the plant, too, and was buying time.

"What I'd like to know," said the Paladin, "is where you've been holed up for the past six months, and just what the hell your little game is, coming here and demanding to see the Prime Minister." He gesture to the front lawn and the battle still raging there.

"Perhaps, if you live long enough, you might find out."

Daisy felt herself trembling as she fought to maintain her hold over the ivy. Not only did she have to invest the plant with energy, which sapped her own strength, but she had to direct the shoot, too. She felt as if she might collapse with nervous exhaustion at any second.

The ivy crept, inch by slow inch, along the back of the armchair towards the Paladin's head.

Then down the back of the chair...

Towards the captain's shoulder...

Touching his right epaulette...

Hesitating...

Inching along, very slowly, towards his exposed neck.

The Paladin started, twitched, then exclaimed and made to brush the intruding vine from his shoulder.

The brief distraction was enough.

Edward Winterton leapt. For a big, burly man well past the first flush of youth, he moved with surprising alacrity. He dived at the captain, punched him in the face, then tore the machine gun from his grip.

All this took place in a second or two while Daisy looked on in shock. Then the young woman was on her feet, reaching out and touching the struggling Paladin on the shoulder.

Instantly he ceased moving and slumped. As Daisy stared, incredulous, the man grew deathly pale and his entire body seemed to stiffen.

The girl glanced at Daisy. "No, I don't begin to understand it, either." She nodded towards Edward Winterton, who had snatched up the Paladin's machine gun and was moving towards the door. "He said he'd explain everything, when all this is over."

Daisy pointed to the Paladin. "What on earth did you do to him?"

"He's frozen stiff," she said. "Neve Winterton, by the way."

"Daisy Hawthorn. Mr LeRoy refers to me as the Green Woman. And you are clearly the one he calls Jack Frost."

"Funny, that's the second time someone's used that name for me. I suppose it makes a kind of sense. Although perhaps, all things considered, it should be Jackie Frost instead. Who is Mr LeRoy?"

"You'll be meeting him soon enough, I'm sure."

They joined Edward Winterton at the door.

"What now?" Daisy asked.

"Now," the man said, opening the door an inch and peering out, "we find Derek Drake. He has his study on the top floor of the west tower. This way."

They crept from the room and along the corridor.

AJIA STARED AT the castle gate in horror.

"No!"

Until now she had refused to accept that they were fighting a lost cause, even if the odds were stacked against the invading army. But with the sudden arrival of half a dozen Humvees to relieve the Paladins within the castle grounds, perhaps defeat—or at least an ignominious retreat—was inevitable.

She turned to Fletcher "What do we do?"

He just stared at the thundering Humvees trundling through the gates. He appeared, for once, bereft of strategy.

"Reed?" she said.

He shook himself. "We retreat," he said, "before we're wiped out."

Ajia took in the sporadic battle still raging on the lawn. Groups of boggarts and elves had armed themselves with the weapons of their fallen enemy and had taken refuge behind the scant cover of box hedges, ornamental walls and outbuildings. From these vantage points they attempted to pick off the Paladins still standing—perhaps twenty-five soldiers in all—who likewise were making the best of meagre cover.

She saw movement to her right, at the far end of the castle's facade. A mob of boggarts rounded the corner, yelling like a Viking horde. Some brandished guns, but most were armed with knives and the occasional sword. They were, she thought as she watched their foolhardy advance on the rearguard of the Paladins, a pathetic sight.

But they had the element of surprise and managed to mow down half a dozen Paladins before the survivors turned and sprayed the advancing phalanx with gunfire. She watched boggart and elves fall as they ran, blown apart and reduced to so much steaming, bloody offal. Among their number was Paul Klein, and when he saw his compatriots to his right and left being torn apart, he vanished...

Or rather shrank.

Ajia stared at where he had been, then saw a mouse-like figure scurrying across the lawn. He reached the first Paladin, who was spraying the boggarts with bullets. Ajia stared, incredulous, as Wee Paul in an attack both suicidal and martially effective assumed his normal height between the legs of the Paladin with his sword up-thrust. The blade ripped into the soldier's nether regions, effectively splitting him in two. The cloven corpse slithered to the ground, dousing Wee Paul in a shower of blood, innards and excrement.

The little man screamed his rage and swung his sword at an advancing Paladin, beheading the soldier. He turned, looking for his next victim—but the closest Paladin was twenty feet away across the lawn, and he had seen Wee Paul's startling re-appearance and bloody despatch of his colleague. Raising his gun, he accounted for the midget with a minimum of bullets.

Wee Paul had made his final bow.

"No," Ajia cried.

Beside her, Fletcher indicated a boggart crouching fifty feet away behind an huge mock-Roman urn. The stunted man appeared to be commanding the fight back. "Samsor!" Fletcher yelled. "Retreat! Behind the castle!"

If the boggart heard him, he gave no sign, but poked his gun from his cover and accounted for another Paladin.

"Look!" Ajia cried.

The newly arrived Humvees were disgorging their personnel, Paladins in battle armour toting rifles.

"We don't stand a chance," she breathed.

Then, as she watched, something remarkable happened.

The relief force of Paladins turned their guns on their comrades and mowed them down where they stood. She saw one of the newly-arrived Paladins with a shoulder-mounted RPG launcher take aim at a Paladin armoured car: the weapon jolted, smoke issued from its muzzle, and the vehicle exploded in a ball of flame. Screaming personnel tumbled from the wreckage, blazing like human torches.

The defending Paladins, under attack, turned and began fighting back, and for ten minutes the bloodiest battle Ajia had ever seen raged without cessation or concession across the lawns before her.

"What the...?" Fletcher began.

"Mutiny," Ajia said.

She ducked as Humvees and armoured cars belonging to both sides exploded like powder kegs. Of the six newly-arrived Humvees, only one was still intact, and few of the original Paladins defending the castle remained standing. Only the soldiers barricaded in the entrance, manning the .50-calibre machine gun, were left fighting.

As she and Fletcher watched, hardly able to believe the miraculous turn of events, the last Humvee accelerated along the drive. It approached the castle at speed, zigzagging to avoid the .50-cal's shells. It reached the entrance, swerving at the very last second. The figure behind the wheel lobbed a grenade into the entrance and ducked as the blast blew shards of timber and lacerated flesh in every direction.

Then the driver leapt from the cab and sprinted into the castle.

And Ajia recognised the Paladin.

It was the very same one who had watched her being escorted from the warehouse and who, just days ago, had coldbloodedly murdered Mr LeRoy's lover, Perry.

Major Wynne.

She was aware of the knife in her hand, and her desire to use it.

Ten paces to her right, Wolfson was rolling on the ground with a Paladin, snarling his hatred. As she watched, Cuhullin the Hound gained the upper hand. With a ferocious yelp, he opened his huge jaws and bit into the soldier's skull, cracking it with a sickening crunch.

Fletcher called Wolfson to his side and the dog-man bounded over, bloody and sweating but elated.

"Find Mr LeRoy and Smith," Fletcher ordered. "Tell them the battle is almost won. Then bring them in when I give the word, okay?"

Grinning, Wolfson took off across the lawn.

Ajia looked at Fletcher, and he nodded.

Together they left the cover of the urn and sprinted towards the castle's shattered entrance.

THIRTY-FIVE

ONE HOUR EARLIER, Derek Drake had unlocked the door to his study on the top floor of the castle's west tower and strode into the room, smiling at the thought that he was coming home. He had always felt an affinity for the castle, but in the past could never work out quite why he felt so at ease here. Now, thanks to Emrys, he knew. This part of the world was his ancient stamping ground, after all. His ancestral birthright.

He crossed to the solid oak table, opened the Nuclear Briefcase and set it down, and next to it the walnut carrying case containing the Holy Grail.

He was all set for the showdown, and he was supremely confident.

Ajia Snell, Auberon LeRoy and his bunch of murderous misfits might still be at large, but Drake had sacked the incompetent Wynne and Noble and mobilised his remaining Paladins. They were in position around the castle now; Drake was impregnable. Also, reports from his ministers bolstered his confidence. In the Channel, three British warships were containing the Russian battleships. Meanwhile, the SAS squad was in position on the border of Estonia, and his admiral aboard the HMS *Nautilus* was ready and awaiting his command.

He had never felt more powerful.

His confidence communicated itself to Harriet. She pressed herself to him and murmured that he should make the most of the bedroom on the floor below.

The suggestion was tempting. Harriet had never looked more beautiful, or seductive—and there were few greater aphrodisiacs than the knowledge of the power one held over one's fellow man.

But he couldn't be distracted now. He had matters of state to settle. He held the future of his great nation, its very fate, in his hands.

At the far end of the table, the phone connected to Whitehall shrilled.

Drake snatched it up. "Yes?"

It was his Minister of Defence. "Word from the Channel, sir."

"Go on."

"The Russkie ships are blockaded ten miles off Dover. We're awaiting your orders."

"Hold tight," Drake said. "Prepare to give the order to attack."

"Very good, sir."

Next he got through to his man in Estonia. "What's the situation, Dennison?"

"Reports are coming in that a small force of Russian insurgents have crossed the border at Palo, killing a couple of Estonian guards."

"And the SAS team?"

"They have a chopper ready and waiting ten miles away, sir. What should I do?"

Drake considered his options. "I'm going to issue an order to strike the invaders forthwith, Dennison. Prepare a statement for Estonian consumption to the effect that Britain will not stand by impotently while the sovereign territory of a staunch ally and neighbour is illegally transgressed by hostile forces."

"Very good, sir."

On an encrypted landline, Drake reached his military command centre in London and issued the order for the SAS in Estonia to launch a commando attack on the Russian invaders.

Then he sat back and smiled to himself.

Harriet rubbed his shoulder, almost purring her contentment. "You make me proud, Derek."

He took her hand and kissed it. "You've seen nothing yet, my dear."

He glanced across at the red button in the centre of the open case. Harriet saw the direction of his glance. He could have sworn that she was swooning.

"You'll do it?" she asked.

"If needs must, Harriet, then yes. I'll give the command. Britain won't be pushed around by a tin-pot dictator."

And neither will I, he thought.

There was an element of bravado at work here, of course. Drake would not consign millions to a hideous, fiery death, at least not idly and not without a great deal of soul-searching and remorse. Yet he needed to believe he could in order for Vasilyev to believe he would; and believing it was halfway to accepting its necessity.

The look his wife was giving him now only stiffened his resolve. A man might do anything, dare anything, anything at all, just to have the woman he loved gaze at him that way.

A knock sounded at the door, and Major Jakeman appeared. "Sorry to interrupt, sir. But we've apprehended a couple of civilians in the grounds."

"Civilians? Who the hell are they?"

"Won't say, sir. But they want to see you."

"Tell them to go to hell. No, scrub that. Arrest them and find out what they want."

"Very good, sir." The door closed behind the retreating major.

Harriet moved to the far end of the table and caressed the open case, the gesture almost sexual. "You'll really give the command, Derek?"

He smiled. "You think I wouldn't? Someone needs to take a stand. The heads of state of Europe are a bunch of lily-livered pen-pushers. Vasilyev needs to be shown who's the—"

His words were interrupted, rudely, by the sudden chatter of gunfire

"What?"

He leapt up and rushed to the window. Harriet joined him, clutching his arm and squeaking with fright.

Three Paladins lay dead on the lawn directly beneath the tower. As Drake stared down, his pulse racing, a mob swarmed over the perimeter wall and surged across the lawn, some armed with guns, others wielding knifes and machetes.

To his relief, the Paladins were rapidly mobilised and battle was joined.

He got through to Major Jakeman. "What the hell's going on, Major?"

Above the rattle of gunfire, Jakeman shouted, "We think it's LeRoy's terrorist mob, sir. We'll soon have things under control."

"LeRoy?" Drake's heartrate quickened. "Report back to me as soon as you have."

He cut the connection and watched the invaders and his Paladins slaughter each other far below.

His mobile phone sounded. He strode to the far end of the study, a finger pressed to his left ear to block out the sound of the battle.

"*Dobriy den'*, Prime Minister," Vasilyev said.

"Ah, Premier Vasilyev," Drake said, smiling to himself. "Just the man I need to speak to. I'm so glad you saw fit to call."

"We have the little matter of what is occurring in the Channel to discuss, Prime Minister."

"You refer to the illegal incursion of Russian battleships into British territorial waters? What is there to discuss, Vasilyev? We have your boats blockaded. Furthermore, if you don't order their immediate retreat... Well, let's just say that things might turn a little nasty."

Drake sensed the Premier's unease. After a second, Vasilyev said, "You have gained—what is the phrase?—Dutch courage from your pre-empting of the video clip? Very clever of you, Prime Minister, I will give you that. Very clever indeed. But you will soon learn that I do not like to be threatened. Have you heard the news from Estonia, by any chance?"

Drake laughed. "Have you? I think you'll find that your little invasion force has been wiped out, Vasilyev."

There was a profound silence from the other end of the line, then the connection was cut.

Elated, Drake strode to the window and stared out. It was obvious, from his vantage point, that the Paladins were gaining the upper hand. It was a bloodbath down there, with LeRoy's ugly brutes being torn apart by the defence force's superior firepower and tactics.

Harriet ran a hand through his hair. "You don't know how it turns me on to hear you talk to him like that."

His phone shrilled again, and Drake took the call.

"Vasilyev. Somehow, I thought I'd be hearing from you."

"This means war, Drake!" Vasilyev spluttered.

"Oh, you're referring to your abortive invasion? War? I'm more than happy to discuss the notion, Premier. In fact, I'll go so far as to issue an ultimatum. Withdraw your battleships and issue a statement describing the incursion into Estonia as the act of a rogue colonel, and you might not suffer the consequences."

"The consequences?" Vasilyev echoed.

"I have nuclear weapons trained on Moscow and ready to launch when I give the word. It's up to you. Do as I say, and save Moscow."

"You're insane!" Vasilyev cried. "Or... or you're bluffing. I, too, have nuclear weapons, and the largest of them is trained on London."

Drake laughed. "Then call my bluff, Vasilyev, if you dare."

He replaced the receiver.

He moved to the window to see how the skirmish was progressing, just in time to witness the arrival of more Paladin in the form of six Humvees trundling through the perimeter gates. He smiled. Soon, LeRoy would be grovelling before him, begging for mercy. And Ajia Snell with him.

Then, as he stared down, the arriving Paladins opened fire of the castle's defenders.

His hand shaking, Drake got through to Jakeman. "Major, what the fucking hell—?"

The reply was hard to make out about the rattle of gunfire and explosion of grenades. "Under attack... Major Wynne, sir... Withdrawing into..." The line went dead.

Drake paced back and forth, Harriet watching him worriedly. He snatched up the land line and got through to his Defence Minister. "Any news?"

"The Russkies are holding fast in the Channel, sir. They're refusing to budge. And in Estonia…"

Drake's heart pounded. "Go on."

"Reports are coming in of a second Russian incursion further along the border. Orders, sir?"

"Sit tight. I'll get back to you."

Drake ceased his pacing and stared down at the table, at the Nuclear Briefcase open before him, its red button prominent and inviting. He had already taken the precaution of entering the launch codes. Now, literally at the touch of a button, he was able to unleash hell.

He switched his gaze to the walnut box containing the Holy Grail, opened it to reveal the chalice, then dropped to one knee. If ever he needed Emrys's sound advice…

"I bend the knee in supplication," he said.

The Grail did not respond.

Drake stared at the chalice, its jewelled inlay glinting in the sunlight.

"Emrys?"

The Grail remained obdurately silent.

"Emrys! Don't desert me in my hour of need, I beg you!" He licked his lips. "I bend the knee in supplication," he repeated.

The study door open and an voice—a very familiar voice—spoke to him, "It's no good, Derek. I no longer inhabit the Grail."

Drake struggled to his feet and whirled to face the newcomer.

And stared in disbelief.

Beside him, Harriet gave a gasp.

Edward Winterton stood just inside the doorway, incongruously armed with a submachine gun, and beside him was his daughter, Neve. A small, dumpy woman Drake vaguely recognised stood beside the young woman.

Drake felt himself trembling. The arrival of Winterton, seemingly from the dead, was enough of a shock—but even more shattering, and inexplicable, was the sound of his voice.

Rich, deep, and singsong...

Welsh.

"Emrys?" He shook his head. "No. No, it can't be."

The big, silver-haired man smiled. "Why not, Derek? If I could inhabit the form of the Grail, then what would be so difficult about taking over, albeit temporarily, the body of your *bête noir*, Edward Winterton?"

"Emrys, is it really you?" Harriet gasped.

Drake gestured, reaching out an arm as if in supplication. "But *why*, Emrys? Why take on his body?"

Winterton, or rather Emrys, gave a heartfelt sigh. "Because I am sorely disappointed in you, Derek. I have been for a long while. And the time has finally come to act."

"Disappointed?" Drake tried to laugh. His legs felt weak. "No. No, this is some kind of... of joke. A charade. You've... you've disabled the Grail somehow, Winterton. You're imitating Emrys. That's the only way this make sense."

Winterton's patrician features relaxed into a smile. "If that's the case, then how would I know that, on your last meeting with me, Emrys, I told you who you were? That you were the eidolon of King Arthur, and that you should come here, to Avalon?"

Beside Drake, Harriet gave a shrill laugh, "King Arthur?" she cried. "But Derek isn't King Arthur, you fool. He's Jesus Christ!"

Drake turned and stared at his wife. Was the woman stark, staring mad?

His voice faltering, he said to Emrys, "What do you want?"

"As I said, Derek, I'm disappointed."

"But why?" Drake reached out again. "I owe everything to you, Emrys. Everything. I trusted you."

"And I trusted you, Derek, but that trust proved to be misplaced." Winterton hesitated, then went on. "After the crash, when I found myself inhabiting the Grail, and in receipt of untold power. Power to bring forth the eidolons, to rouse the folkloric hordes to life for the good of all Britain. I had long since seen you as our great unifier, Derek, and so I invested you with the spirit of Arthur, that other great unifier. You would be the leader who would rally the citizens,

I thought, and bring pride back to our country. I was and always will be a patriot who believed in the ineluctable superiority of this nation and its people. But I never thought that we had the right to abuse that power."

"Abuse?" Drake echoed weakly.

"It started even before you were a politician, but the Summer of Terror," Winterton said, "your willing sacrifice of innocent victims so that you could blame the atrocity on Islamists and gain political advantage..."

"What is he talking about, Derek?" said Harriet. "Innocent victims?"

"Hardly surprising that you've never told her," said Winterton. "There are some deeds too appalling for a man to share even with his wife. Your husband, Mrs Drake, instigated the bombings himself. He colluded with the secret services, setting up the rash of so-called terrorist attacks that became known as the Summer of Terror. It was a textbook example of what the Americans have dubbed a false flag operation. And when Edward Winterton was informed about it through a whistleblower in the same secret services, he confronted your husband. In return, you, Derek, engineered the circumstances which caused Winterton's fatal heart attack."

"Derek? Is this true?"

His lack of response was all the answer she needed.

"The Summer of Terror." Winterton shook his head sorrowfully. "That was when my misgivings about you set in, Derek. But still I told myself it would be all right. The means justified the ends. In hindsight, after the helicopter crash, I perhaps should never have bestowed on you the power I did. I thought, however, that I could still keep you in check and temper your tendency towards excessive behaviour. I kept voicing my concerns over some of your more extreme policies. Remember?"

Drake nodded. Emrys, as the Grail, had started out stern and oppositional. Later he had become less forthright in his views, and Drake had assumed this to mean that Emrys had come round to his way of thinking and giving him his blessing. Obviously he had been mistaken about that.

"More and more I realised I had blundered terribly," Winterton continued. "It took me a while to admit it to myself. It took me longer still to admit that I had to do something about it. That I had to stop you."

"Stop me?" said Drake.

"The only way I could. Since you were unlikely to listen to reason, I resorted to indirect, practical action. I created the eidolons. Auberon LeRoy, Reed Fletcher, Ajia Snell and all the others."

Drake felt suddenly sick. "You," he gasped. "You brought them back to life. You empowered them."

"To curb *your* power, Derek. Your autocracy had become unrestrained, and someone needed to bring your reign to a close. It has been a slow plan to evolve. It has taken years to ripen, and there have been occasions when I feared it would never come to full fruition. Now we see that, at long last, it has."

"But you've been encouraging me all this time. Sanctioning what I do."

"You have needed little encouragement. What I have been doing, for the most part, is leaving you to pursue your agenda while quietly, covertly pursuing mine. Day after day you have been visiting me and I have been telling you only what you want to hear."

"You mean lying to me?"

"Merely maintaining the pretence of being your ally. Giving you as much support as you've needed and no more. I could not have you suspecting that there was anything amiss, so I have diligently played the part of the kind, ever amenable mentor."

"While all along..."

"All along plotting your overthrow," Winterton said with a confirming nod. "I used to think of myself as the Merlin to your Arthur, Derek. Perhaps I even *am* the eidolon of Merlin, who knows? He was Welsh and wise, after all, and so am I. Back in my City days people even used to call me a wizard, when it came to financial dealings at least. But whether I am Merlin or not, it seemed only right and proper that, as the one who built you up to be a new Arthur, I should also be the one to bring you down. You are my responsibility. When a dog catches rabies and poses a threat to the public, the onus is surely on the owner to eradicate the animal before it can do too much harm."

"Is that all I am to you?" Drake said, crestfallen. "A rabid dog?"

"More's the pity, because you were once such an obedient, reliable hound."

Harriet moved to Drake's side. "Don't listen to him, Derek," she hissed. "This man's not Emrys, any more than he's Edward Winterton. He's an impostor." She clutched his arm. "Derek, you're Christ. Can't you see that? You are the Messiah arisen!"

Drake stared at her, his heart almost breaking. "But he—*Emrys*—he told me who I was," he said, gesturing at Winterton. "I'm King Arthur. I have to be. And he told me to come down here for the endgame."

"The endgame," Winterton echoed. "Your downfall."

"No!" Drake barked, finding sudden strength. He moved to the table and held a hand over the Nuclear Briefcase. "Don't move, any of you, or I'll…"

"What will you do?" Winterton said, his Welsh tones like honey. "Sanction the deaths of millions of innocent people, merely because their leader has had the temerity to oppose you? Even you, Derek, aren't that mad." He licked his lips. "Move away from the table."

Drake's hand hovered closer to the bright red button.

"Think about what you're doing, Derek," Winterton warned. "Where will it end? Vasilyev will retaliate. Untold millions of your people—the people you claim to represent—will perish needlessly, as well as untold millions in Russia and other nations. This great country will be no more."

"And the alternative?" Drake asked.

Winterton nodded his leonine head. "The alternative? You will seek to form a coalition government with Labour and the Liberal Democrats, with yourself still acting as Prime Minister."

"Don't trust him!" Harriet cried. "You heard what he said." She pointed to the lawns. "He caused all that in order to bring you down, not to have you installed as a puppet leader."

Her words were punctuated by a deafening explosion that seemed to shake the very foundations of the castle—an explosion followed by a profound silence. Everyone in the room, with the exception of Winterton and Drake, cowered as if in expectation of further blasts.

"Step away from the table, Derek," Winterton warned.

Drake's sweating hand moved closer still to the nuclear button.

Then the door swung open and Major Dominic Wynne burst into the room.

AJIA SLIPPED INTO Puck mode and raced up the staircase in pursuit of Major Wynne.

She turned a corner on the stairs and stopped suddenly. Before her was the open door of what looked like a study, and through it she made out Wynne standing just inside the door, brandishing his rifle. Beyond him she made out a tall, portly man she recognised as the politician Edward Winterton, a dark-haired girl, and Daisy Hawthorn. The other occupants of the room were hidden from view.

"Over there! Move it, or everyone dies. You," Wynne said to Winterton. "Drop the gun or face the consequences."

With Wynne's rifle trained on him, Winterton lowered the machine gun to the rug.

"Drake," Wynne said, turning to the politician, "move away from the table."

"Since when have I started taking orders from you?" Drake snarled.

"You're finished," Wynne said. "In case you need telling, your days in power are over. This is a coup."

"Dominic?" This was Harriet Drake, stepping forward, smiling at the soldier, a hand outstretched as if to coax a recalcitrant animal. "What are you saying? We need to talk about this."

"Stand back!" Wynne barked.

"We need to talk, Dominic," Harriet wheedled. "Is this all about me?"

Drake stared from Harriet to Wynne. The Paladin looked incredulous. "You?" Wynne said. "Oh, it's about far more than you, Harriet. For all that we—"

Harriet stepped towards the major, smiling. "Now then, Dominic..."

"I said stand back, or I'll..."

"Dominic." She took another step towards him.

"I swear I'll..."

Harriet laughed, and it was the very last sound she made.

Wynne carried out his threat and squeezed the trigger of his rifle. Pieces of Harriet Drake's skull exploded across the room and her headless body slipped to the floor, severed arteries pulsing crimson jets of blood across the Persian rug.

"No!" Drake wept.

Winterton turned his head minimally and stared at Ajia.

And she heard a voice in her head. Winterton's voice.

Move, it said.

She took advantage of the confusion to sprint through the door and conceal herself behind the full-length curtains at the far end of the room, her heart pounding.

Major Wynne swung his gun on Derek Drake, who was staring down in disbelief at his wife's corpse. "Your turn, *sir*," he snarled, applying first pressure to the trigger.

Drake shook his head, his face a mask of despair, and brought his hand down on the nuclear button.

And Ajia ran.

She sprinted from behind the curtains and dived across the table, her sprawling leap taking the Nuclear Briefcase with her. Drake's hand slapped polished oak.

She hit the floor, clutching the briefcase to her chest, rolled and came upright.

She faced Derek Drake across the table, her heart pounding.

Startled, Wynne relaxed his trigger finger slightly but still kept the rifle trained on Drake.

"Bitch!" Drake spat at Ajia, something more horrible than hatred twisting his features. "Give me that!"

She snapped the briefcase shut, glaring at the man she detested. "Come and get it if you want it so much, you coward."

He stepped forward, reaching out. "Give. Me. The. Briefcase.

You. Insolent. Little. Cunt."

Ajia remained very still, her heart pounding. He would let him get within range, then she would sling the case at his head and hopefully brain the bastard.

"Enough!" Major Wynne cried.

Drake whirled, sneering. "Really, Dominic? You wouldn't dare. You don't have the—"

Wynne fired, shocking Ajia. A volley of bullets shattered Derek Drake's head.

She dived, and Drake's death became a slow-motion *grand guignol* which would replay in her memory for a long time: the bullets entering the back of his head and the skull exploding along with an ejecta of brain, blood and shrapnelled bone which splattered across the oaken tabletop.

Wynne spun round, looking for Ajia as she ran, and during that second of confusion Reed Fletcher appeared in the doorway.

"Put it down, Wynne!" he ordered.

The major pirouetted towards the door, bringing his rifle to bear on Fletcher.

Who shot Major Wynne through the forehead with a single bullet. The Paladin slumped bonelessly to the floor.

Behind Fletcher, Mr LeRoy stood with Smith and Dustin Wolfson.

Mr LeRoy stepped into the room and took in the scene before him. "We seem," he said, "to have arrived at the party a little late."

Ajia stared around at the bloody carnage, at the bleeding bodies and the living.

No more killing, she thought. *It's over. Please, let it be over*.

She moved across the room, slowly this time, and fell into Mr LeRoy's outstretched arms.

EPILOGUE

Boggarts and brownies, elves and all manner of other creatures—not to mention humans—moved around the dancefloor in drunken approximation of an Irish reel. Dustin Wolfson led the way, hopping and skipping with a brownie girl laughing gaily on his arm. Reed Fletcher cavorted with Daisy Hawthorn, and boggart partnered boggart as if in a contest to find the very worst practitioner of the Terpsichorean art.

Smith had asked Ajia if she would do him the honour of a dance. She had assented, blushing, before bowing out an hour later, thoroughly exhausted. She might have run the equivalent of ten marathons that summer, but an hour hopping about on the dancefloor had given her a raging thirst.

The party thrown by Mr LeRoy at Kensington Town Hall in celebration of his army's famous victory, one month ago, had been going on all day. As the sun fell over London, the festivities were set to continue well into the early hours.

Ajia found a seat on the raised stage, watching the dancers and enjoying a bottle of ice-cold Brew Dog.

To her right, occupying centre stage, Mr LeRoy sat in a huge armchair like a throne. A comely elf—the spitting image of his dead lover Perry—sat on his right knee, while a brownie girl perched on his left and fed him from a bunch of grapes.

On a large-screen TV next to the stage, tuned to BBC News, Edward Winterton addressed the nation. It was a repeat of the interview he had given that morning, explaining the current political crisis and suggesting a way forward.

"Following the failed coup that led to the death of Prime Minister Drake," he said gravely, "I have agreed to lead an all-party emergency government until such time, hopefully in three months or less, as elections can be held." And later in the interview he had gone on to itemise the many crimes with which Derek Drake had disgraced the office of Prime Minister, not least of which was his own unlawful arrest and six-month detention in the dungeons of Fairleigh Castle.

Neve Winterton plucked a bottle of beer from the cooler and joined Ajia on the stage. "Reed's been telling me all about you," she said, "and I must say, I was impressed with what you did that day in the castle."

Ajia felt her face heating up as the pretty women smiled at her. She shrugged. "Anything I did, then and before, was... what's the word? Impulsive, reflex action? We were chosen—you, me and all the others. Given gifts by Emrys Sage, and we used them. We looked at what was happening in the country, and used them for the best."

"So what you did, what we did, *that* was just impulse?" Neve shook her head. "I don't buy it. We knew what was right and what was wrong, we thought about the consequences, and we acted."

Ajia smiled. "Okay, right. But that day in the castle, with Drake's briefcase—"

"Saving the country, the world," Neve said, "from nuclear Armageddon."

Ajia pulled a face. "You know something? When you put it like that, I feel sick. I mean, what if I hadn't been fast enough? What if Drake had hit the button?"

"Then millions of people, in Britain and Russia and probably also the countries bordering both, would be dead."

"Don't. I can't even think about it."

She took a self-conscious mouthful of beer. "And you, bringing your father back to life…" She gestured with her bottle "If you'd not done that, if your father hadn't directed us all to the castle, then Drake might have got away with mass murder."

Neve laughed. "Don't thank me, Ajia. All that's down to who was controlling my father. Emrys Sage. He had it all planned. My father's resurrection, the convergence of the eidolons on Fairleigh Castle, Drake's end…"

Ajia looked at the TV screen. "Is Emrys still in control?"

"No, he's relinquished the power he had over my father. He's gone back to wherever it is he was, before that day at the castle. My father has only a dim memory of what happened, which is perhaps for the best."

"And what will you do now?" Ajia asked.

"Oh, carry on with my cryogenic research, most likely," Neve said. "Try to establish some scientific hypothesis to explain my ability. I have this power now, as Jack Frost or Jackie Frost or whoever. If I can only figure out how it works, and apply it in some practical fashion, then who knows? I might be able to help millions around the world." She took a swig of beer. "But enough of me. What are your plans?"

They were interrupted by Reed Fletcher and Daisy Hawthorn drunkenly staggering across the stage, hand in hand. "Ajia! Neve!" Fletcher called out. "More beer! I demand more beer!"

Ajia passed them two bottles, and dug two more from the cooler as Dustin Wolfson and his brownie admirer joined them. "Ah, the girl's a mind-reader and so she is." He raised his bottle. "To youse all and everyone!"

Ajia looked across the stage to where Smith and Mr LeRoy were in deep discussion. She wandered across to the pair, joined by the others, and Mr LeRoy beamed upon his friends.

"Wayland was asking me," he said, "about Drake's power and whence it came."

"Emrys Sage," Neve said.

Fletcher hiccuped. "Also known as the Holy Grail, so-called."

Mr LeRoy leaned to one side, and dug in the commodious pocket of his great coat. He pulled out a small onyx cup decorated with coruscating jewels.

He held it on his palm and raised it into the air before his face.

"The Holy Grail," he breathed.

The gathering stared at the cup, transfixed.

Mr LeRoy looked around the group, and everyone fell silent. "It falls to me to be its guardian," he said. "Within this innocent-seeming object resides the essence of the man responsible, in many ways, for what Britain has become. For what we have *all* become, and I don't just mean we eidolons gathered here."

Then, startling them all, a lilting Welsh voice emanated from the Grail and filled the stage.

"The responsibility, and yes, the guilt, for all that sits heavily with me," said Emrys Sage. "I meant well. I did what I did for the good of the country. To my great and everlasting regret, it turned out that I unleashed a demon. But never again. My interfering is at an end. From now on, the destiny of our great land is in your hands. The hands of its people."

The destiny of our great land, Ajia thought, and exchanged a knowing look with Mr LeRoy.

Later, Neve said, "You never did tell me what you're doing next, Ajia."

Ajia smiled. "You know, I've been waiting until after the party. I didn't want to miss it."

"And then?"

"I'm going to India in a couple of days, flying to Mumbai. And…" She felt her throat constrict with emotion. "And then I'll run like the wind, and search and search, until I find my mother."

They were startled by a cry from one of the balconies as a brownie pointed into the sky and called out, "Look! Oh, look at them!"

Ajia jumped from the stage and ran to the balcony. She joined the brownie and looked up to where she was pointing. The sun was setting across the darkened rooftops of the capital, and the air was filled with the sound of a hundred wings.

Ajia looked up into the sky, her heart soaring.

All across London, parakeets were coming home to roost.

ABOUT THE AUTHOR

JAMES LOVEGROVE IS the author of nearly 60 books, including the New York Times bestselling *Pantheon* series, the *Redlaw* novels and the *Dev Harmer Missions*. He has produced five Sherlock Holmes novels and a Conan Doyle/Lovecraft mashup trilogy, *The Cthulhu Casebooks*. He has also written tie-in novels for the TV show *Firefly*.

James has sold well over 50 short stories and published two collections, *Imagined Slights* and *Diversifications*. He has produced a dozen short books for readers with reading difficulties, and a four-volume fantasy saga for teenagers, *The Clouded World*, under the pseudonym Jay Amory.

James has been shortlisted for numerous awards, including the Arthur C. Clarke Award, the John W. Campbell Memorial Award, the Bram Stoker Award, the British Fantasy Society Award and the Manchester Book Award. His short story "Carry The Moon In My Pocket" won the 2011 Seiun Award in Japan for Best Translated Short Story. His work has been translated into fifteen languages, and his journalism has appeared in periodicals as diverse as *Literary Review*, *Interzone*, *BBC MindGames*, *All About History* and *Comic Heroes*.

He contributes a regular fiction-review column to the *Financial Times* and lives with his wife, two sons and tiny dog in Eastbourne.

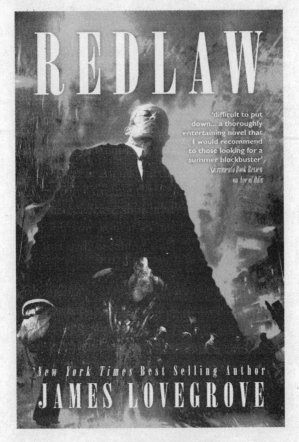

'difficult to put down... a thoroughly entertaining novel that I would recommend to those looking for a summer blockbuster'
Sacramento Book Review on Age of Odin

New York Times Best Selling Author
JAMES LOVEGROVE

POLICING THE DAMNED

They live among us, abhorred, marginalised, despised. They are vampires, known politely as the Sunless. The job of policing their community falls to the men and women of SHADE: the Sunless Housing and Disclosure Executive. Captain John Redlaw is London's most feared and respected SHADE officer, a living legend.

But when the vampires start rioting in their ghettos, and angry humans respond with violence of their own, even Redlaw may not be able to keep the peace. Especially when political forces are aligning to introduce a radical answer to the Sunless problem, one that will resolve the situation once and for all...

'Weston Ochse is the new voice of action science fiction'
New York Times bestselling author Jonathan Maberry

WESTON OCHSE

GRUNT LIFE

A TASK FORCE OMBRA NOVEL

Benjamin Carter Mason died last night. Maybe he threw himself off a bridge into Los Angeles Harbor, or maybe he burned to death in a house fire in San Pedro; it doesn't really matter. Today, Mason's starting a new life. He's back in boot camp, training for the only war left that matters a damn.

For years, their spies have been coming to Earth, learning our weaknesses. Our governments knew, but they did nothing—the prospect was too awful, the costs too high—and now, the horrifying and utterly inhuman Cray are laying waste to our cities. The human race is a heartbeat away from extinction.

That is, unless Mason, and the other men and women of Task Force OMBRA, can do anything about it.

This is a time for heroes. For killers. For Grunts.